Sinful Obsession

A Whitmore Elite Standalone

J.A. Owenby

Trigger Warning

Please click here to visit my website for trigger warnings or copy and paste https://authorjaowenby.com/about/sinful-obsession-trigger-warnings/

Download Your FREE BOOK!

SIGN UP FOR J.A. OWENBY'S NEWSLETTER and download your FREE book, Love & Sins. Stay up to date concerning exclusive bonus scenes, updates on upcoming releases, and more. https://authorjaowenby.com/newsletter/

Playlist

Whatever by Godsmack
Numb by Marshmello and Khalid
Blood on Your Hands by Veda and Adam Arcadia
The Hunted by The Rigs
Voodoo by Godsmack
We Are the Champions by Queen (sang by the football team)
Far, Far Too Long by Alexander Nate

Prologue

I grabbed her shoulders, piercing her with an intense stare. "Run, Lyndsay!"

"I can't leave you, Jacob. I won't." Tears streamed down her pale cheeks as she clung to my arms. She shook her head, her blue eyes wide with fear.

I gathered her in for a hug, and her petite body trembled against mine. "You have to. We'll both die if you don't go. Now." I rubbed her back, hoping it would give her the courage she needed to save herself —to save us.

The dogs barking in the distance were closing in on us fast. Our time was running out.

She threw her arms around my neck and sobbed into my shirt. "I love you. I'll bring help and come back for you, I swear."

"I love you, too." I tilted her chin and placed a kiss to her mouth. "Go." A lump lodged itself in my throat as she turned and ran for her fucking life. She had to make it. She had to come back for me. She was my only hope, especially now that I'd helped her escape. But if we made one mistake ... our lives would be over.

Fear scraped its sharp talons down my spine as I whirled around on the heel of my black boot and ran in the opposite direction. I tried to pick up my pace, stumbling over the ground that was thick with brush and sticks, only the pale half-moon to light my way.

The sound of dogs barking pricked my ears. They were close. Too close. "Fuck," I breathed into the frigid air. I slowed and listened, then realized the best way for me to ensure Lyndsay's escape was to stop the guards. Sweat beaded on my forehead as I ran in the direction from which the mutts were barking.

It wasn't long before I met the three guards. This time, the dogs weren't hunting for food. They were hunting Lyndsay and me.

"It's just me, Jacob." I held my hands in the air, surrendering. "I took a walk when I couldn't sleep and got lost."

"Where's Lyndsay?" one of them asked, jerking on the leash as his overgrown pup snarled and jumped toward me.

I backed away slowly, not wanting to be shredded to death. "I don't know. I had no idea she was outside, I swear."

"You two stay with Jacob. I'm going to search for the girl," the dark-haired man said, eyeing me suspiciously.

Shit! I had to stop him from going after her.

"I fucked her," I spat, with more venom than I thought possible. "She's no longer a virgin."

Gilmore, the lead guard, growled. "What the hell did you say, boy?"

The three stepped toward me, and I backed away with my hands still in the air. I had to keep stalling, even if it cost me my life. I would gladly give mine for Lyndsay's freedom.

"Lyndsay and I love each other, and there's no way I would let the elders fuck her. *She's mine.*"

One of the guards threw his head back, filling the air with his maniacal laughter.

"Boy, you're the one fucked now. You know the consequences for defiling a young girl."

My nostrils flared and my hands fisted. There was no way this would end well for me.

"I love her." My voice held steady, even though my legs were anything but.

Another guard gave his leash to the other, then approached me.

"We're taking you to the elders, and they can decide your punishment for disobeying the law," he snarled.

"You have to catch me first, you fat piece of shit." A rush of adrenaline flooded my system. Not once in my fifteen years had I ever considered talking back.

Instinct kicked in, and I hightailed it away from the guards and in the opposite direction Lyndsay had run.

"Little punk." Footsteps followed me as the cursing drew nearer.

At least I had speed on my side. One of the elders loved a game called football, so he taught the kids how to play every day there wasn't rain or snow. I'd fallen in love with the sport, and he worked with me one-on-one. I was the running zigzag king, and if I could see where the fuck I was going, I could outrun anyone here. But the one thing I'd counted on to keep Lyndsay and me safe that night had just turned into my enemy. It was so dark I struggled to see more than a few feet ahead, which slowed me down.

A strong hand grabbed my arm and jerked me back. I glowered at him over my shoulder, projecting an air of confidence that wasn't feasibly possible at the moment.

"Have it your way." The guard raised his club, a devious grin on his ugly mug.

I attempted to cover my head as I saw him swing, bracing for the impact. The thud knocked me forward, and I stumbled, stars dancing before my eyes. My vision clouded, then turned as black as the night while I collapsed onto the frozen ground.

Chapter One

Brie

"Are you nervous?" my mother asked, clutching one of my many packed boxes in her arms as she hurried up the sidewalk behind me.

I bumped the door open with my hip, then entered the small living room. At least it was an open floor plan, so it felt bigger. I set a laundry basket full of clean clothes on top of the kitchen counter and turned to Mom. "A little. At least I have the other team members from the cheerleading squad. This summer gave me a chance to meet and get to know a few of them. Having some friends here already helps. Gabby and I hit it off immediately. It was almost as if we'd known each other for years instead of a few months before classes started."

Mom sat down the box she was carrying, then blew a wisp of hair out of her eyes while she planted her hands on her slender hips. A smile lit up her face.

"Brie!" My five-year-old brother called as he rushed into the living room full speed ahead. He abruptly stopped and gave me his bottle of bubbles. "Can you play with me?"

His sweet expression was full of love and trust. Since Mom and Dad had Conner later in life, I'd had an opportunity to help take care of him and be a part of his everyday routine. I loved this little guy a ton, and I would miss him the most.

I reached down, grabbed him under his arms, and hauled him up, sitting him on top of the white kitchen counter. "As soon as we're done unloading, I'll take you outside, and we can play before you have to leave." I gently tapped the tip of his nose, adoring his dusting of freckles.

His lower lip formed a cute pout. "I don't want you to stay here. Come home, Brie." Tears welled in his eyes, and I wrapped him up in my arms.

"We will FaceTime every week. It will almost be like I'm still there with you."

"Promise?"

I kissed his forehead. "Buddy, I wouldn't miss it for the world." I glanced at Mom, her wistful expression tugging at my heartstrings.

"He's really going to miss you. We all are," Mom said softly.

"Son of a bitch!" Dad swore, as he stumbled through the doorway, the side of a large box bouncing off the door frame.

"Rodger, language." Mom shook her head, grinning while she grabbed one side of the heavy load and helped him. Once it was safe and sound on the black leather couch, Dad brushed off his hands.

"Sorry, bud. Don't say that word at school, okay?" Dad raised an eyebrow at my little brother, and I attempted to stifle my giggle.

Conner scrunched up his nose. "That was four words, Dad."

We broke into laughter, my heart singing. Shit, I was going to miss my family something awful. Unlike a lot of nineteen-year-olds, I was close to my parents. We traveled together, had movie nights, and shared our wins of the day every night at the dinner table. I cried on Mom's shoulder when my first major crush had rejected me, then laughed alongside her when, two years later, he had it so bad for me that he followed me around like a heartsick puppy.

"I'm so glad we hired movers to bring the furniture. Good grief, it's too hot to move today." Dad wiped the perspiration off his forehead with the back of his hand. His salt-and-pepper hair was slick with sweat, and his grey T-shirt was plastered against his body. Dad was in good shape for his fifty-six years, but moving had kicked all our asses.

My cell buzzed, and I reached into the back pocket of my jean shorts to fish it out. I grinned as Gabrielle McCallister's message popped up. Gabby, as her friends called her, had welcomed me to the squad, along with her friends, Leighton and Everlee.

Are you moved in yet?

I tapped out a response: *Almost! A few more boxes to bring in.*

Sweet. Get your cute little ass to my place so we can catch up on all the things since we last saw you.

I snorted, then replied. *It was only three days ago. LOL.*

Gabby's message vibrated my phone. *Whatevs. Just hurry up.*

I set my cell on the counter next to Conner.

"You look happy," Mom said.

"Yeah, the girls I mentioned I'd made friends with want me to hang with them after we're done unloading. Gabby and Everlee are on the team and are also roomies."

Dad's expression faltered. "I'm sure it would have been easier if you had roommates, but ..."

"I know. I'll be fine. I promise. The privacy and quiet will help me study since I have my own place."

"Also, when you're ready, there is a box in the bottom drawer of your dresser."

"Okay." Mom didn't need to say anything else. I knew what she was implying. Whatever Mom had put together for me would have to wait until ...

Mom grabbed me for a quick hug. "You know if you need us for anything, we're only a call away." She smoothed my long, wavy blonde hair.

"I know." The air around us crackled with anticipation. My parents had been bound and determined to set me up for success and found a cute little house for me close to the Whitmore University campus. And even though we wouldn't speak it out loud, we were all holding our breath to see if I would stay. Some demons I could never get rid of. They rode me piggyback, whispering dark thoughts into my ear while they clawed at my soul.

"Well, if you have plans, we'd better finish up." Dad slid his arm around my shoulders.

"And play bubbles," Conner reminded, poking me in the side with his finger.

I giggled, then turned to him. "Tickle monster!" His fit of laughter filled the space and lit up my heart. At the same time, I'd spent the last several years helping out my parents with his care, and I desperately wanted to see what life was like outside of my family. Here at school, I was only responsible for myself.

"Why don't we wait on the boxes and take care of your room?" Dad gave my arm a gentle squeeze.

"Okay." My pulse hammered against my wrist. I hated this part, but it was necessary, especially while living alone.

I followed Dad down the hall, then closed the door behind us. He walked over to the dresser as I glanced at the queen-size bed and frame that were already put together. The area was actually a decent size, so my matching nightstand and dresser fit beautifully and left plenty of space to walk. Thankfully, the rustic brown furniture helped offset the stark white walls.

The sound of a box opening pulled my attention back to the job at hand.

"Are you ready?" Dad's voice was peppered with worry.

I gulped as I stared at the leather strap of the handcuff. "Yeah," I whispered.

Chapter Two

Kane

"We gotta do something different this year, man. I'm getting bored of the same ol' pussy," Quinn stated. He leaned against the worn, brown leather couch and stretched his arm across the back.

The society members had grabbed a room on campus that the drama club normally used, but today it was empty. It ensured us some privacy while we dialed in the details of the secret society for the fall college term.

"What do you propose?" I asked, my gaze sweeping over my best friends, who were also some of my football teammates. I tugged on the hem of my Seattle Seahawks jersey, waiting to hear from them. "The society has run well with the guidelines in place."

Once the society's founder had moved on, he'd left it in my hands to do with as I wanted. Although I was stoked about it, I had to be careful after being approached to play for the Seattle Seahawks. I had to keep my nose clean if I didn't want to fuck up my entire future. At the same time, I wanted to make this year our best. Hell, as far as I was concerned, the society kept us out of bad situations since the guys weren't looking to get laid at parties where the girls were drunk off their asses and wouldn't remember what the hell had happened after. That spelled trouble all the way around.

"We have a shit ton of new applicants, so I don't know what the fuck Q is talking about." Sterling placed one ankle on the opposite knee, confusion embedded on his face. His sandy-blonde hair flopped into his eyes, and he brushed it aside.

I sifted through the top pieces of paper the guys had submitted, but it would take a while to vet the girls properly.

"First, are we keeping the current name? I say we honor the founder and continue to call it The Viper Secret Society." I rose and placed my palms against the large conference tabletop, eyeing each member.

Remington shot me a quizzical glance and propped his feet on the corner of the battered square table nestled against the wall.

I chuckled. "I'm open to other ideas, though." I ran my hand through my short brown hair, my brain running a mile a minute. At the end of last year, I had to find a new location for our activities, and I wasn't interested in a warehouse like the previous place. I couldn't believe my luck when I'd found a house twenty minutes away from campus, surrounded by woods. To my surprise, it had a nicely remodeled full basement and plenty of space to ensure we had all the kink rooms we wanted. Except mine.

"Who cares about the name as long as we get to use the new location soon." Quinn grabbed his crotch. "I'm ready for some action."

Laughter filled the air. Quinn could be a total asshole, but when you needed him, he was there.

Sterling grinned and massaged the back of his neck, his gaze flickering with mischief. "I'm in on the name for The Viper Secret Society. It's a salute to the guy that made it all happen."

"Let's vote." Before I could even ask who was in favor of keeping the name, all hands shot up. "Well, that was easier than I thought it would be."

Remington tipped his chin. "I've got an idea, Boss."

"What?" I asked, slightly annoyed with his nickname for me. He'd started calling me that when I landed the team quarterback position last year. It had been one hell of a move because I was noticed by the NFL, which had been my dream since I was fifteen and learned the National Football League existed.

Remington cracked his knuckles. "Let's update the website and ask the ladies what their kinks are. While I was at home with the parents for the summer, I overheard my sister and her best friend talking about threesomes and even rape fantasies."

My brow shot up with curiosity. "Like they were into it?"

"Like they had no idea it was a thing until another chick talked to them about how she wanted to be chased, pinned down, and have her brains fucked out. Guess they have fantasies and shit, too. I say we find out what the ladies want, dude. Their wish is my command." He bowed slightly, his grin full of playfulness.

"Hell, why not?" I asked. I had no problem with fucked-up kinks as long as the girls were willing to play. If our identity was ever found out, it could cause us to lose any chance of playing professionally. I could protect my team from most shitty situations, but accusations of rape ... not so much.

"I think it would be great. Just shows they're down with how the society plays," Sterling said.

Quinn barked out a laugh. "I'm happy to train the newbies."

We all chuckled at Q's offer.

"Remington, I like the idea. We'll handpick the girls based on their tastes. Let's update the website as quickly as possible. I think we can all agree we're ready to blow off some steam before our first game on Saturday." I laced my fingers behind my head, tired from a long practice earlier that day.

"On it." Remington rose from his seat, appearing more relaxed than when we'd first gathered.

"Everyone can meet at the new place tonight around eight. We can drink, look through the applications, and crash out there. I need to get some shit done before then, though. I'll meet you guys later." It would have made sense if I lived at the house the society would use since I bought it with my grandmother's inheritance, but my friends would also want to move in and live there since there was enough space, and I couldn't allow anyone to get too close to me.

The guys filed out of the room, and I followed. My mind drifted to what was next for me, and my cock twitched with anticipation.

I waved to them as we left the building, then I hurried across the grassy lawn toward the parking spot where my silver Jaguar was waiting for me.

Five minutes later, I pulled out of the college parking lot and headed north. My cock strained against my jeans, begging for a release. A release that I paid a lot of money to keep secret. The society was great, but a few times a month, I had to feed the beast inside me.

I blasted the stereo, feeling the stress slip away from my neck and shoulders as I listened to "Whatever" by Godsmack. It had been a hot fucking minute since I'd heard that group, but I loved their music. Adrenaline pumped through my veins as I drove closer to my destination. Finally, I turned into the gravel parking lot of a small, windowless grey building and headed to the back, where I could park my vehicle without being seen.

Popping open the glove box, I secured my phone, then closed it before I exited my car. The rocks crunched beneath my tennis shoes as I approached the entrance, where I pushed a white button in the middle of a small black box. I peered up at the camera, my heart in my throat. If this ever went south, my face would be all over the fucking footage. But I wasn't sure what else to do. If I didn't soothe the beast, I was afraid it would consume me, and with my future looking damn good, I couldn't chance it.

The lock clicked, then I pulled on the handle and let myself in. I took a breath as I hurried down a narrow hall. Stopping in front of another entrance, I gripped the doorknob tightly to turn it, then walked into the dimly lit room.

"Hello, Kane. It's nice to see you," a beautiful middle-aged woman with shoulder-length blonde hair and stunning blue eyes said as she approached. "I'll help you get ready, then leave you alone."

"Thanks, Madeline." I gave her a kiss on the cheek.

The room was the same one I used each time I visited. Dark, dingy, small. Exactly the way I needed it.

She watched as I stripped down to nothing, my cock growing harder with each anticipated second of what was about to happen.

"Let's do this." I turned my back to her and waited in silence as scuffles and soft voices reached my ears.

"It's ready for you," Madeline said, holding the small trap door open for me.

I nodded and closed the gap between us, then located the ladder and climbed into the hole. Panic clawed at me as Madeline lowered the door and I heard the lock click into place. Pitch-black surrounded me, and the smell of fresh dirt assaulted my senses.

"Hello?" I whispered.

Chapter Three

Brie

The rest of the afternoon, I spent time with Conner and my folks before we all said a teary goodbye. Placing my forehead against the living room wall, I shuddered with my last cry and sucked in a big breath. I reassured myself that moving halfway across the country was the right thing to do. It was a fresh start. Once I gave myself a pep talk, I hurried to my bathroom to shower before I met the girls. My heart catapulted to the floor, cracking open with the quiet. It was funny how silence could scream louder than a house full of people. The dark hole inside me threatened to swallow me whole, but I had to be strong. Maybe moving states would help fill the ever present dark hole I'd struggled with for so long.

When I was cleaned up, I locked up and made my way to my brown Lexus coupe. The color reminded me of root beer, but with tiny gold flecks that you couldn't see unless it caught the sunlight just right. Mom and Dad had covered the expenses of my rental, but they'd surprised me with a new car for graduation as well. I immediately fell in love with the tan and cream leather interior, seat warmers, and Bluetooth stereo system.

I climbed inside and turned on the engine. She purred to life, and I buckled up, ready to put my sadness on hold for a while. Ten minutes later, I parked in front of Gabby's home. Locking up the vehicle, I hurried to the covered entryway, but before I could knock, the door flew open.

"Hey, babe!" Gabby pulled me in for a big hug before ushering me inside.

"Bitch, it's about time." Everlee jumped off the grey leather sofa and hurried to me, her hazel eyes flashing with excitement.

"Hey." I laughed as Everlee grabbed my arm and dragged me through the living room and into the kitchen.

She waved her hand to the collection of alcohol on the dark, antique table that could easily seat six people.

My brows arched while my attention swept over the cider, beer, vodka, rum, and tequila.

Everlee flashed me a big smile. "What's your poison?"

"Holy shit. I've never seen this much alcohol outside of a supermarket before."

"Oh? You don't drink?" Everlee cocked her head and tapped her finger against her chin. "You don't even need to answer me. I can tell by the bewildered expression on your face that you don't. So, let's start with something light so you don't take a trip to hangover city that ends with you on the floor, worshipping the porcelain throne."

Gabby strolled in after us and grabbed a cider, her big emerald-green eyes filled with interest. She flipped her straight brown hair behind her shoulder, popped open the can, and handed it to me. "Right in time for fall and the upcoming Halloween season. I think you'll like the Bad Apple Cider. It's made here in Oregon."

I held the can close to my nose and took a sniff. "It smells good." Taking a small sip, I smacked my lips afterward. "Hmm, I think I like it."

I followed the girls back into the living room, where we all plopped down on the couch or matching recliners. Finally, taking a good look at the decor, I noted what I liked. My white-walled house felt bland, and I wanted to spruce it up. Other than the dark wood floors, grey furniture, and big flat-screen television that was mounted over the fireplace, the one thing they had in abundance was photos—pictures of them with other cheerleaders, with their families, and on summer vacations. My friends were beaming or laughing in all of them. My heart plummeted to my toes. I had plenty of pictures, but Gabby and Everlee seemed to have what I didn't—a sense of belonging. The friends I had back in Tennessee, I could count on one hand. For some reason, it was difficult for me to connect and feel like I fit in. It was as if I were standing on the outside of my life looking in, and I had no clue why. The feeling of belonging and safety that I craved, I only felt with my family.

Even though I was on the cheer team in Tennessee, I would rather have spent a Friday night at home with my nose in a good book than hang out at a party. My ex-boyfriend Marc had other ideas, though. We attended all the social events and were in the small town's spotlight since he was the high school running back and super popular. I learned to plaster a perma-smile on my face and fast. A part of me was relieved when we broke up before we started college across the country from each other.

This is a new start, and Marc took your secret with him.

Recalling that Gabby had asked about my new house, I glanced at the floor, then at the girls. "It's quiet." I ran the tip of my finger along the rim of the can. "But I'll adjust."

"You've made a big move from Tennessee," Gabby said. "Plus, this is your first year in Oregon, where the winter is dark and wet."

"Any tips on how to get used to all the rain?" I took another drink, then rested the can on my thigh.

"Alcohol and sex," Everlee blurted, giggling.

I snickered. "I'm down with that. The alcohol is new, but I left my ex-boyfriend back home, so the well is dry." I wiggled my brows.

Everlee laughed. "Girl, same. I need a man to dip his wick in my honeypot."

"There's a party this weekend, so you can peruse the inventory there. Or I can set you up with a hottie from the football team. There's a new player this year, but I know him from high school. His name is Mason."

"Oh, he's yummy," Everlee chimed in.

I gave a half shrug. "Will you girls stay close to me at the party if I say yes?"

"Of course! We all stick together. Then later, if we have a hookup, we split up," Gabby explained.

"Then why not? I have nothing to lose." I raised my drink to them. "To amazing friends and good boy toys."

The room filled with our cheers as we toasted.

Over the next few hours, I sipped my cider and chatted about the upcoming football season, classes, and guys. Once again, I was super grateful I'd met these girls before school started. For just a while, the loneliness was held at bay.

It was nearly ten when I arrived back at my new place. At least there were four other houses around mine, which helped the move not feel so daunting. I would have preferred a roomie, but I couldn't risk it.

Walking to the mailbox, I spotted a piece of mail on the sidewalk. I knelt and scooped up the black envelope.

"Hmm, no return address." I stared at the gold calligraphy, my brows knitting together. Only a first name appeared on the front, which meant I couldn't give it to her since I didn't know anyone named Sasha. I flipped it over, realizing the back of the envelope was unsealed.

I glanced around before deciding to knock on my neighbors' doors and check if anyone had dropped it. Even though it was late, lights were on at each house, so I figured I'd see what I could learn about the mystery letter.

After introducing myself at each of the four households and

asking if they knew a Sasha, I let myself into my home with the mail in hand, unsuccessful in my errand. I turned on the overhead lights before placing my keys on the kitchen counter.

"Alexa, play my favorite playlist from Spotify." I leaned against the wall and stared at the open flap, then decided that, since there wasn't a return or a recipient's address, I wasn't breaking the law by looking at the contents. I removed a white card, and my forehead creased while I read it.

You've been chosen to attend The Viper Secret Society initiation. Use this code to log in for additional information. Come alone and tell no one.

Confused, I flipped over the card, but it was blank. Overrun with curiosity, I hurried down the short, brown-carpeted hall to my room and grabbed my MacBook from my dresser. I plopped down on the unmade bed, powered up my computer, and typed in the website that was listed and waited for it to load. A large king cobra appeared on the screen with a red *enter* button on its body. Moving my cursor to its back, I clicked the red circle. I rubbed my arms, comforting myself. I fucking hated snakes.

The camera followed an animated person in a black cloak as they walked down the hall, then pushed open a door, the creak ringing through my speakers. Fixated on the screen, I entered the code.

The figure sat in a chair, and my attention was glued to the white skull mask with black around the eyes. It covered the head and neck, meeting the cloak.

"Hello, Sasha," a computer-generated voice said. "Thank you for replying. Please join me Thursday evening, September twenty-second, for a night you'll never forget. Pay attention to the rules."

I focused on the details scrolling across the bottom of the screen, grabbing my phone from my back pocket and plugging the address into my Google Maps app as soon as I saw it. *Twenty minutes away.* Once again, he impressed the importance of keeping the invitation and participation a secret. *Like, who would I tell?* Plus, I had no idea what the message was even referring to.

"I'll be expecting you, Sasha. But before you go, complete the questionaire. When you've finished, any trace of this video and website will disappear," the voice said.

I drummed my fingers against my thigh, watching the form load. A little shiver shot through me, making me wish I'd already changed out of my shorts and into my pajamas.

My mouth gaped, then I leaned closer to the screen while my attention scanned the questionnaire.

Holy. Fucking. Shit.

Chapter Four

Kane

It was tradition that a team member threw a massive party after the season's first football game. Quinn had volunteered to host the get-together that week, which was packed, and the music was thumping. Before the crowd arrived, the team had moved the pristine leather furniture out of the way and covered the couch and recliners with sheets in a lame attempt to protect them. Then we set up tables along the walls and multiple trashcans all over the fucking house. His father was cool with parties as long as the mansion didn't take any damage and was cleaned up afterward.

We'd kicked ass on the field earlier that day and had reason to celebrate.

I leaned against the living room wall, watching the crowd cheer for the guys playing a drinking game. A few girls were swinging around the white columns in the entryway, pretending they were stripper poles. Through the years, college parties had started to all look the same. Drunk people were grinding against each other and making out, and girls were dancing on top of any surface possible.

Since the society members didn't hook up with girls at a party, it was common for most of us to leave early unless it was one of our homes everyone was trashing. The evenings we left early, we returned to help clean up the mess, though.

I took a long pull from my beer as I mentally reviewed the plays in my mind where we'd fucked up, and the opposing team had intercepted the ball. I understood we had some work to do if we were ready for the playoffs. Oddly enough, running plays and possible scenarios in my head was how I relaxed.

Jagger Whitlock approached me, wearing a huge smile, and we bumped fists. "Hey, great game today," he yelled over the beats of "Numb" by Marshmello and Khalid. Jagger had returned to the team after taking a season off due to medical reasons, and he'd scored our opening points within the first minute. Even though he was a little hotheaded, in the year Jagger and Ariana had dated, she'd managed to tame him some, which had also made him better on the field. Jagger was a hell of a player, and I was glad to have him back.

"You, too. I'm excited about this year." My attention swept the crowd, spotting Ari and Teagan dancing. Teagan had hooked up with our running back, who had signed a pro ball contract, and she was back visiting Ari and the girls for the weekend.

Jagger took a drink of his beer, looking much more relaxed than earlier in the locker room.

"It feels good to be back. I hadn't realized how much I'd missed it until practices started. Not that I was looking forward to Coach busting my balls all the time, but the energy of the game is addictive." He ran his fingers through his dark hair, his blue eyes narrowing in Ari's direction.

I glanced over to where a few guys were trying to dance with the ladies. As hard as I tried, I couldn't stop from chuckling.

Jagger glowered. "I gotta remind these fuckers who Ari belongs to. I'll catch up with you later."

"No fighting, Jag. Not this year. You're too valuable to sit on the fucking bench." I pinned him with my stare. As the team captain and quarterback, it was my job to keep the guys under control the best I could.

Jagger tipped his head and gave me a tight smile before moving his way through the crowd toward his girlfriend.

Quinn sidled up to me and handed me a red Solo cup. "Drink up, man. We're celebrating, and we can sleep in tomorrow."

I took the drink, sniffed the brown liquid, and took a big gulp. The rum and Coke traveled down my throat, burning all the way to my stomach.

"Thanks, Q. I probably needed that. Why aren't you out there in the middle of the ladies?" I quirked my brow at my teammate.

"Would you believe me if I said I was saving my dick for the society?" He raised his cup to me before he took a gulp.

"Not really, but it would be smart. It would keep your ass out of trouble and maybe keep your dad off your back."

His steel-grey eyes flickered with interest. "We have some new cheerleaders this year that are superhot. Maybe I'll actually try to date someone."

I looked at him. "Seriously, dude?" Disbelief dripped from my words. Quinn had sworn he would never settle down since he liked different pussy every night.

"Look at them, man. They're fucking hot. I mean, I get all the sex I want in the society, but every once in a while, a conversation might be nice." He released a soft whistle. "*Who* is that?"

My attention bounced around the group, trying to figure out who the hell he was talking about.

"Who?" I yelled over the loudly playing song, "Turn the Lights Down Low," with Timmy Trumpet and R3HAB. People began to jump to the tune, making it even more challenging to see who Quinn had suddenly taken a considerable interest in.

"She's dancing with Mason Longbecker. He's new on the team, second string," Quinn explained.

Once the song had ended and everyone stopped bouncing around, I spotted Mason. My gaze traveled to the group that surrounded him then abruptly halted. An ugly, bitter feeling stabbed me over and over in my chest. My molars ground together, my pulse kicking up and pounding so hard my heart hurt. The alcohol had to have hit me harder than I realized because I was fucking imagining shit. But the second her smile slid into place and her bright blue eyes filled with excitement, I knew it was her. The one person that could ruin everything I'd worked so hard for.

"Dude, are you okay? You look like you've seen a ghost." Q nudged me in the side with his elbow.

"Yeah. What did you say the new cheerleader's name was?" I managed to hold my tone steady, even though anger was ripping through me faster than a fucking bull in a china shop.

"Her friends call her Brie, but her full name is Brianne Langston. She transferred here from a college in Tennessee, and her family is fucking loaded. Rumor has it that she has her own place close to campus. What I mean is that she doesn't have any roomies. I would definitely like to find out if that's truly the case." Quinn cupped his dick through his jeans, grinning.

Fury broke through my well-controlled façade, and I spun on him, backing him against the wall. "You fucking touch her, and I'll goddamn kill you," I growled, startling not only Quinn but myself.

Bewildered, Quinn raised his hands in surrender. "I didn't realize you knew her, Kane. If you mark her, then let us know, and she's all yours."

I resisted the urge to punch him in the face, my white-hot fury burning out of control. "Consider her marked, and let the rest of the guys know."

"Kane, you know it doesn't work like that, man."

I backed away and glared at my friend before I finally had the sense to get the hell out of there before I really lost my shit.

I elbowed my way through the crowd and into the kitchen, where empty blue and red Solo cups and liquor bottles littered the black granite countertops. Slipping out of the house through the back door, I sucked in a huge breath. The memories bombarded me, gouging my heart and tearing me to pieces. I shook my head, the darkness threatening to overtake me. I couldn't lose control. Not here.

I drained the last of my rum and Coke, then tossed the cup into the large trash can located on the back patio before I started jogging toward my car, which was parked halfway down the driveway. Hopefully, I wouldn't have to deal with some dumbass blocking me in. To my relief, I had plenty of room to move my vehicle.

I fished around for my key fob in my front pocket, then unlocked the doors and climbed in. Only one place could help me get my shit back together. I whipped the Jaguar around and peeled out of Quinn's driveway. Massaging the back of my neck, I drove north. It had only been a week since I'd visited Madeline, but she was the only person who knew my secret, and I needed help. I was fucking drowning and the most fucked-up thing about it ... there wasn't a drop of goddamn water anywhere.

Blasting my stereo, I forced my thoughts away from Brie and to football, running plays through my mind and focusing on the field. After a few minutes, it took the edge off, but I needed the goddamn fire inside me doused.

Half an hour later, I pulled into the gravel parking lot, the rocks crunching beneath my tires as I drove around to the back of the building. I was out of the Jaguar before I remembered to turn off the car. Once it was secure, I hurried to the entrance and pushed the button on the little box. The lock popped open, and I practically ran into the building and down the hall to my room.

Madeline's heels clicked against the floor. "Kane? Hon, are you all right?"

I hesitated before answering "No."

She approached me, cupping my cheeks in her warm hands. "This is twice in a week. What's eating at you? Talk to me."

"I can't," I whispered, my voice sounding foreign to my ears.

"Okay. Okay. I'll get you taken care of, but you need to give me a few minutes. I wasn't expecting you." She flung open the door, and I followed her in. "Sit down and collect yourself. You look awfully pale."

I sank onto a blue velvet chair, propped my elbows on my knee, and gripped the ends of my short hair. "Hurry. Please." Goddamn, I was fucked up. My leg bounced up and down as I lost myself in the memories. "Football," I whispered to myself. "A hammer counter run." Tears burned my eyes, and I slammed them closed while I quietly called off plays.

Madeline's sweet voice finally broke through the brutal torment. "It's ready, Kane."

I shot off the chair and quickly shed my clothes. The creak of the door in the floor as it opened started to calm my nerves. It was going to be okay. *I was going to be okay. Liar! You've never been all right. You're just a good fucking actor.*

Pushing away the obnoxious words, I walked to the hole in the floor and used the ladder to lower myself down. Madeline closed me in, and the sound of the lock rang through the small space. Complete darkness enveloped me, easing my mental pain.

"Hello?" a soft female voice asked.

"I need a minute." I spread my arms, placing my palms against the cold dirt walls. The hole was tiny, maybe 6x8, but probably not even that big. I inhaled, clearing my mind of anything except where I was. It was so dark that I couldn't see the other person with me, but they couldn't see me either, which was exactly what I wanted. Anonymity.

"On your fucking knees," I ordered, my cock responding immediately.

Small hands gripped my hips, then she ran her tongue along the tip of my dick. Threading my fingers through her hair, I allowed myself to take control of my past by reliving it in the present. But this time, I dictated the fucked-up, twisted narrative.

Chapter Five

Brie

"I'm going to head out early." I tucked my hair behind my ear, inhaling the fresh, crisp evening air. It felt good on my clammy, sweaty skin. I had danced so much with the girls and Mason that my boyfriend jeans and baby blue crop top clung to me from the sweat. At least my deodorant hadn't flipped me off and failed.

"Are you sure you don't want to crash at our place?" Gabby asked. "Everlee and Leighton are hooking up, so they won't be home until the morning."

"We're going to Gabby's, too!" Teagan bounced out the front door and joined us on the paved driveway in front of the house. She brushed strands of her dark hair from her face, her cheeks flushed from the heat of the crowded party.

"Yup," Ariana said, popping her *p* loudly and then giggling. "We have a designated driver, so if you want to join us at Gabby's, you should. We have all the dirt from the party tonight."

Jagger sidled up to her and slid his arm protectively around her waist. "I'll be there, too. I'm not sure who else will end up there, but I'm the designated driver."

A jab of envy pierced my heart, but more than that, something familiar flickered in the back of my brain with Jagger's movements. He reminded me of someone, but I was too tired to figure out who. Unease swirled inside the pit of my stomach, but I attempted to brush it off.

I'd had a few drinks over the last several hours, so I was fine to drive home. "As much as I would love to stay with you, I'll have to take a rain check," I said apologetically.

Gabby pushed her lower lip out in a pout, then smiled. "Okay, bitch, but I won't take no for an answer next time." She wobbled over to me and gave me a quick hug, clearly drunk.

"Promise." I gulped down my lie, hoping she wouldn't remember that I'd agreed to sleep at her place at some point. I wish I could, but it wasn't in the cards. A sharp pain stabbed my chest as I wondered if I would ever belong somewhere and if the gaping hole in my heart would heal.

"Text me tomorrow." She winked at me, then blew me a kiss. I caught it and laughed.

"Jagger, do you need help getting them to the car?" I asked.

His low chuckle warmed me, and I took a step backward, not understanding my reaction to him. I mean, he was hot as hell with his black hair and ice-blue eyes, but he was Ari's boyfriend and off-limits. What bothered me even more was that I wasn't attracted to him—not physically, at least. A distant thought danced in the back of my mind, but my exhausted brain couldn't grab hold of it.

"I've got it. Are you sure you're good to drive? I can drop you off. It's not a problem," Jagger assured me.

"I'm good. Thanks, though." I appreciated the fact that he cared enough about his girlfriend's friends to ensure they arrived home safely.

A silly smile coasted over Ari's face. "He's the best. I love him sooo much." She swayed slightly, then placed her hand on his chest and glanced up at Jagger as if he'd hung the stars in the sky all by himself.

My heart flip-flopped. I would never have what Ari and Jagger had. Hell, I couldn't even allow anyone to get close enough to share my secret with them. Only one person other than my parents and therapist knew. My new friends would judge and ask a million questions, and I wasn't sure how to answer them.

Feeling out of place, I took another step away from the group. "I'll talk to you guys later. Have a good one." Before anyone could try to twist my arm into staying, I whirled around and hurried toward my car.

Finally arriving at the house, I tossed my keys onto the kitchen counter and headed to my bedroom. Once I changed clothes and brushed my teeth, I checked to ensure the sliding glass door was secure and attempted to close the lame vertical blinds. Maybe I could replace them with ones where the slats didn't leave gaping holes to see through.

Leaning against the window, I stared into the little backyard, recalling playing bubbles with Conner a week ago. Mom and Dad had mentioned on our last call that he was having a tough time adjusting without me. Shit, he wasn't the only one. A deep yearning pulled at me. It was hard being so far away from home, and at times, I wondered if I would make it. I had to, though. I had to prove to myself that I could make it through anything and stand on my own two feet.

Raising my hands above my head, I stretched and yawned, the tattoo on my lower abdomen catching my attention. I traced the red roses that weaved around the blue and green eye. Frowning, I attempted to remember when I'd added the flowers, but apparently, I'd been so drunk with friends in Tennessee I'd blacked out and forgotten. Everlee thought I hadn't ever drunk alcohol, but she hadn't let me finish. I drank a lot in Tennessee and blacked out often, sending me into a full-on panic when I couldn't remember shit. I'd promised myself I would slow down when I moved to Oregon.

I sank onto the edge of the mattress, the evening's events playing through my mind. Mason had asked me out to a movie next weekend, and I'd agreed. He was sweet and cute, but I knew he wasn't my type. Plus, I'd just ended a long-term relationship and wasn't ready to lock myself into a commitment again. Before moving to Oregon, I'd promised myself that I would take my time and have fun. I wanted to have new experiences, meet new people, and make decisions that I wanted to make. Not ones that my therapist or parents had put into place.

I tugged on the pink tank top of my matching pajamas, loneliness blanketing me. At times, I'd felt my family had been controlling, but they'd always had my best interest at heart. The structure had been precisely what I needed over the last several years, but attending Whitmore University was something I was doing on my terms.

Stifling a yawn, I stared at the lamp on my nightstand that burned a soft white light. For whatever reason, I found it calming. I stood, then turned down the peach comforter and blankets before I crawled beneath them, snuggling deep into the bed. I glanced at my alarm clock. It was almost one in the morning, and I was ready to get some sleep.

"Dammit," I muttered, realizing I'd forgotten the last detail of my nightly routine. I scowled as I sat up and reached for the handcuff, wrapping the soft leather around my wrist and securing it. Anger pumped through my veins, the revelation that I might never be free flooding my system. I pulled on the long chain attached to my bedframe. Before Dad left, we checked to make sure that I could move around in the room some but not walk into the bathroom or reach the mirror on the other side of the room ... or anything else that might be dangerous. "I fucking hate you." I could hate it all I wanted, but this was my horrible reality.

I flopped back onto my pillow and burrowed under my covers again. Clearing my mind of the day's events and forcing myself to relax, I closed my eyes. "Not tonight," I whispered to myself. "Not tonight."

Twigs and leaves crunched beneath my feet as I fought to see through the darkness. Tears streamed down my face, strands of hair clinging to the moisture on my cheeks. Dogs barking in the distance propelled me faster, my breathing ragged with fear.

A large door suddenly stood in front of me. Safety. I was almost there! I pushed it open, my bare feet padding down a narrow hall instead of the forest floor. Where was I? I slowed, trying to recognize where I was. Voices reached my ears, and I tiptoed forward. I slapped my palm over my mouth, my attention landing on a naked young woman strapped to a table. My gut rolled, but I was rooted in place. The room shifted, then I gasped in horror. Turning to flee, a large hand grabbed my arm and jerked me backward.

"It's your turn, little girl," he said.

I bucked and kicked at him, but he was too strong and quickly overpowered me. A hard pressure tugged on my wrist, tethering me to something, but I wasn't sure what.

My knees landed with a thud on the floor, jarring me awake. Tears prickled my hazy stare while my legs quaked, and nausea bubbled in my belly. I hunted for the trashcan I kept by my nightstand and brought it closer just in case I puked. Sweat trickled down my spine as I frantically searched around, identifying my surroundings.

"I'm in my rental near Whitmore University. I see my nightstand, dresser, lamp, and favorite novels." I sucked in a deep breath, willing myself not to lose the contents of my dinner. Trembling, I pulled myself off the floor with my free arm, then situated myself on the edge of the mattress. I opened the drawer, located the key for my cuff, and set myself free. It was going to be a long night. I made my way to the en suite bathroom, and after washing my face, I returned to bed. This time, I turned on the television. No way was I going back to sleep and dealing with another night terror.

Chapter Six

Kane

When I left Madeline's, I felt a little better, but it hadn't brought enough relief. I drove around for another hour, my mind racing with a million possibilities. There was no way that the girl I saw at the party was the same one I knew years ago. The one I'd loved with every fiber of my being and had risked my life to save. The same one that had betrayed me.

I gripped the steering wheel of my car, the dark clouds rolling into my thoughts as I sifted through the memories. Whoever she was, she was stunning, but she couldn't be my Lyndsay. Lyndsay had disappeared five and a half years ago, right after I'd helped her escape.

I love you. I'll bring help and come back for you. I swear.

Slamming my fist onto the dashboard, I yelled, "You never came back for me!" With my pulse racing, I realized I should go to the society's new home. If I was going to lose my shit, then I had no business driving a car. Plus, I needed to find out more about who the new cheerleader was. I *had* to be wrong.

I'd been told Lyndsay had died, but apparently, I'd been lied to because either Lyndsay showed up at the party tonight or she had a doppelganger. My nostrils flared in disgust with yet another broken promise.

My anger and fear tumbled around inside me, stirring up the memories I'd attempted to lock away long ago. Until *now*. My head and heart played a brutal game of tug-of-war between the love I had for Lyndsay at one time and the hate I felt for her now. One thing I understood, I had to learn the truth and fast. If Lyndsay was alive, then she had the power to destroy me and everything I'd worked so hard to accomplish. "Fuck that. I won't let that happen. I'll ruin her before she has a chance to utter a single goddamn word about my past," I said aloud.

I massaged the back of my neck, trying to relieve the tension that twisted my muscles into a shit ton of knots. Before I drew any more conclusions, I had to dig into this girl first and then make a plan. It was imperative that I stay calm, and if the buried feelings erupted, I had to do everything I could to get in front of that explosion. It had the power to destroy me in its wake.

I drove up to the house used for the society, spotting the lights on in several rooms. The guys probably wondered what the hell had happened to me, but they would get over it.

My tennis shoes slapped the black asphalt of the driveway, then I climbed the steps to the entrance. I opened the door, my stress easing from my shoulders as my gaze swept the living area and kitchen. I inhaled slowly, reminding myself that these guys would do anything for me and vice versa. We were family. That's what was important.

"Dog! Where you been?" Sterling asked, never taking his attention away from the large-screen television mounted on the wall where he and Remington were playing Call of Duty on the Xbox.

Remington rocked back and forth on the black leather sofa as though he were dodging real bullets rather than the ones in the game. He was pretty animated when he played, and most of the time it was entertaining as hell, but I wasn't in the mood to watch.

I chuckled as I spotted the bags of chips and beer bottles all over the floor. It was good to see everyone settling in.

"I had some shit to take care of." I tucked my keys into the front pocket of my jeans as I made my way to the refrigerator, where I located a beer. Twisting off the lid, I took a long drink.

The guys cheered and trash-talked, all of them glued to the game except for Anderson, who strolled toward me. He ran his hand over his short blonde hair, his grey-blue eyes intense. "The stack of applicants is on the kitchen counter. I'm happy to weed through them if you want."

I quirked a brow at him. "You don't want to school the winner of the game?"

"Nah. I would rather get the society operating smoothly." He gave me a lopsided grin.

"So, no pussy all summer?" I slapped him on the back, then located the forms.

Anderson's face paled. "You know my parents are super religious. Dude, don't fuck around about it."

I pulled out a chair at the dining table, the legs scraping across the beige tile floor. I sank into it and popped my neck before I dove in. "That's a bitch you can't just be yourself around them. Don't you feel like you live a double life or some shit?" I suspected he did, but I wanted to know I wasn't the only one that struggled with that issue.

"I fucking hate it. It eats me up sometimes, but there's no need to discuss it. I'm ready to have a good year away from them."

I gave him a silent nod, turning my attention to the papers lying on the scuffed and worn brown tabletop. Cutting the stack in half, I slid some of them to Anderson. "You know what to look for."

Without another word, we began to read the answers the girls had provided on the website.

"This one's in. Damn, I like her already." I placed the questionnaire to the right of my stack. "Fantasies include rape, kidnapping, sucking off a guy while she's in a cage, foursome ..."

Anderson grinned. "Sounds like she's perfect."

My forehead creased as my attention landed on the next one. "Who the hell picked these girls? Shit, here's another one who likes spanking, anal sex, and flogging, and wants to be blindfolded and raped." I pointed to Anderson's pile. "What are yours like?"

Anderson began to read the next girl's preferences. "BDSM, praise kink, rape, but she wants to rape the guy and use hot wax." Anderson looked at me. "I think some gossip got around last year, man. They might not be giving specifics, but this batch of ladies is better than what we previously had, for damn sure. Holy shit."

Over the next hour, we picked out the best girls, and I was relieved that I could stop thinking about the cheerleader with Mason for a few minutes. But then I realized it still wasn't long enough. I rose from my seat and stretched, yawning.

"Did you see the chick with Mason at the party?" I grabbed my empty bottle and tossed it into the recycling bin.

"Who didn't?" Anderson stood and gathered us a few more beers from the refrigerator.

I took the drink from him. "What do you know about her?"

Anderson's lips curled up. "She's clearly gorgeous. This is her first year at Whitmore, but she's a sophomore. I hear she's from Tennessee. Wonder if she's got a Southern accent."

"What's her name?" Quinn had already told me, but I wanted to make sure.

"Brie Langston. She's in with Everlee, Gabby, Leighton, and Ari. Rich and popular."

Brie had Lyndsay's looks but not her name. I *had to* be wrong about her. "Quinn said she had a rental near campus. Can you find out where?"

Anderson glanced at me, his eyes flickering with curiosity. "Dude, I already know where."

I laced my fingers behind my head, waiting for him to tell me.

"126 West Gardenia Lane."

I swallowed over the tightness in my throat. "You sure that's the correct one?"

"Very. A few of us followed her home tonight. Ya know, made sure she arrived safely." He chuckled. "That sounded creepy as hell, but we wanted to know where she lived." He gave me a half shrug.

I ground my molars. "She's marked. Don't fucking touch her if you don't want to be shredded to pieces." My voice was low and calm, but I felt anything but.

Anderson raised his hands in surrender. "No one's intentionally stepping in your shit, man. But you need to let everyone know, then follow the rule you put into place and mark her."

Letting out a heavy, uneven breath, I nodded. I stomped into the living room, where the other guys were still playing the Xbox.

"Listen up, motherfuckers. Brie Langston is marked. She's off-limits. I find out anyone else has followed her home or even looked at her sideways, I'll make sure you regret it."

A heavy silence hung in the air as all eyes stared at me, bewildered.

"Understood?"

Ten different voices responded with a *yes*.

"Good." And with that, I spun around on my heel and headed out the door again. If I couldn't sleep, then I had something I needed to take care of on West Gardenia Lane, and it couldn't wait.

Not even ten minutes later, a burning urge to learn the truth exploded in my chest as I turned onto the road. It was nearly three-thirty in the morning, but I was used to staying awake all night. Even though it had been five and a half years since my life had changed, the demons of my past called to me in my dreams, forcing me into a spiral of insomnia at times. At least I'd faced it straight on. That's what I told myself anyway.

I turned off my car's headlights as I approached the dark home. As soon as Anderson had provided me with an address, I remembered Mom had said a college girl moved into the rental she and Dad owned. The blinds were closed, and the sage-green siding stood apart from the typical white of the neighbors' houses.

I turned off the car, then quietly slipped out and jogged up the street until I reached the residence. I snuck around the back to the sliding glass door that led to the master bedroom. The previous tenants had left some light damage, and I'd helped Mom replace the blinds before Brie moved in. I wasn't sure why Mom had insisted on the vertical ones that never fully closed, but now I was glad she had. Sucking in a breath, I flattened myself against the outer wall and cautiously peered through the window. I nearly barked out a laugh as the internet headline scrolled through my mind: *Star Football Player Arrested for Stalking and Voyeurism.*

My pulse pounded in my neck as I laid eyes on *her*—Brie Langston.

The soft light from the television cast an eerie glow over her face as she huddled beneath a peach comforter. My attention followed the curve of her perky nose, then travelled over her full lips and down her slender shoulders. Suddenly, she tossed the covers aside and climbed out of bed. She stretched, the hem of her pink tank top rising above the low waist of her matching pajama shorts. My world tilted, and I flattened my palm against the house, trying to hold on to reality. But reality had just become clear.

She tugged her shirt down, but not before I saw it. A tattoo, above her left hip bone, of an eye, but hers had roses around it.

My breath stuttered in my throat. This girl was *not* Brie Langston —the beautiful girl in front of me was Lyndsay Jennings. The love I'd once had for her solidified to stone before crumbling into dust. Seeing for myself that she was alive and happy ... I fucking hated her with every fiber of my being. Channeling the fury uncurling inside me, I stayed focused. If it was the last thing I accomplished, she was going down for what she had done.

Chapter Seven

Brie

I sank onto the leather couch in my living room, then pulled my computer onto my lap. Over the last few days, Gabby and Everlee had helped me pick out some art for my home's walls, along with bookends, a cute antique clock, and a new lamp. The purple, red, and gold splashes from the pictures brightened up the drab scenery outside. At least we still had sunny days. The girls had mentioned we only had a few weeks left before the rainy season settled in, and I wasn't sure I was ready.

I opened my MacBook in time for the incoming video call.

A dark-haired woman in her late thirties with round, black-rimmed glasses flickered into view. Her warm smile helped me relax. "Hi, Brie. How's your week going so far?" Alida, my psychiatrist, asked. Since Alida was originally from Oregon, then moved to Tennessee, she was licensed in two states which had worked in my favor.

I plastered a smile onto my face. "Good! My new friends helped me decorate, so the house has a warmer vibe to it."

"Good. You have a lot of big adjustments happening all at once. It can be a lot to cope with, so it's nice to hear you're spending time with your new friends." She tucked a strand of hair behind her ear, her warm hazel eyes seeking mine.

I pursed my lips. "Yeah. Some days are better than others. I'm not sure what I would do without the cheer squad. And I have a date this weekend, but I'm not sure I should go."

"Oh? Do you want to talk about it?"

I fidgeted in my seat, my shorts riding up and my bare thighs sticking to the leather. "His name is Mason, and I met him at a party after the football game. He's nice enough." My voice trailed off. I reached for my ponytail and twirled my blonde hair around my fingers, a nervous habit I seemed unable to break.

"But?"

"I'm not into him."

"Brie, you don't have to be into a guy you just met. There's nothing wrong with that. I know you talked yourself into dating Marc in Tennessee, and I would hate to see you do that again, but you're allowed to take your time and decide later."

"Yeah. I tried to like Marc, but I knew we would never end up married. He was decent in bed, at least." I gave a half shrug, then giggled as I felt the flush creep up my neck and feather my cheeks. My forehead creased as my thoughts returned to the party. "Something odd happened, though."

"With Mason?" Alida pushed her glasses up her nose.

I toyed with a loose string on the hem of my baggy navy T-shirt. "No. My friend's boyfriend. It was really strange. It was like I felt an unusual attraction to him, but it wasn't really. I know when I see a guy that I want to hook up with. It wasn't that at all. It was like he was familiar, but at the same time, I haven't ever met him." I tossed my hands up in the air. "Plus, I do not go after a guy that's in a relationship. That's a hard no for me."

"It sounds like you're clear on your boundaries, which is fantastic.

You've done a lot of work over the last few years. Can you tell me more about how it felt to see this guy?"

"His name is Jagger." I drummed my fingertips on the arm of the couch. "I can't tell why he seems familiar. I mean, haven't you ever had a déjà vu feeling when you met someone?"

"I have, but only once." Alida grew silent, allowing me to think, but I came up with a big nothing.

"It's okay. If you see him, maybe try to put a name to the feeling if it happens again."

"I'm sure I'll see him a lot. As I said, he's dating one of my friends. Jagger is also on the football team, so I'll watch him play at every game." Uncomfortable with my reaction to him, I was ready to change the subject. "I'm not sleeping, so that might be messing with me."

Concern flashed in her expression. "How many hours are you getting a night, Brie?"

"Maybe two. I'll doze off, then wake myself up." I rubbed my wrist where the cuff had dug into my skin last night.

"If I prescribe you something to help you sleep, will you take it? You can't keep up your grueling schedule of cheer, classes, and a social life if you're running on fumes all the time."

I massaged my temples, wincing from the throbbing headache that had suddenly appeared. I was not fond of medication, but I would try it. The few times I'd been prescribed an antidepressant, it had made me feel weird, and the side effects had sucked. Reminding myself that I didn't have to take it every night but only when I really needed it, I agreed.

By the end of my session, my phone buzzed with an alert that my prescription was ready for pickup.

Closing my laptop, I set it on the cushion next to me and stood. My stomach growled, and I glanced at the clock. If I picked up my medication and dinner, I could maybe crawl into bed early and watch some television. For once, I didn't have any plans, and I wanted to curl up and not have to pretend that everything was perfect in my life when it wasn't. It was exhausting.

I gathered my keys and purse, then headed out the door, locking it behind me. It wasn't dark yet, but the sky was filled with wisps of blue and orange streaks from the setting sun. My shoulders relaxed as I realized I could settle in for the evening soon. Most people saw me as an extrovert, and I was, to a degree, but I definitely recharged with alone time.

Once I had stuffed my face with the juicy hamburger and fries I picked up, I took my first sleeping pill. Securing the cuff around my wrist, I fluffed my pillow, then wiggled down into the bed. I pulled the comforter up to my chin as I started to watch season one of Bridgerton.

A few minutes later, my lids fluttered closed, and I forced them open again. It was good that I didn't have a class until eleven the following day. As a precaution, I'd set the alarm on both my phone and my clock, though. Since I wasn't familiar with how the pill would affect me, I had to ensure I woke up on time.

I jolted upright, the chain jingling beneath my bed as I moved. My breath hitched in my throat, and my heart slammed against my ribs as I attempted to clear the sleep from my vision.

"Who? Who are you?" I blinked rapidly at the person in the corner of my bedroom.

He rose, smoothing his black shirt with a masculine hand. His clothes were so dark that I might not have seen him if it weren't for the white skull mask that covered his head and neck. Without a word, he walked over to the side of my bed. All rational thoughts of screaming or uncuffing myself fled my brain as terror gripped me.

He pushed me back against the mattress and placed his other palm over my mouth. My breaths came in short, panicked bursts.

"Are you afraid, Brie Langston?"

I gave him a frantic nod, realizing his voice was disguised.

"Good. You should be." He planted a knee on the edge of the bed, then took out a dark piece of material from the pocket of his black slacks. He removed his hand, then shoved the cloth into my mouth. I clawed at his arm, desperate to escape him, but he quickly overpowered me. He flipped me over onto my stomach, grabbed my arms, and secured them behind my back.

"What's this?" He tugged on my cuffed wrist, then a deep chuckle filled my room.

I muttered against the rag, still squirming on the bed and trying to break free.

He smoothed my hair, then roughly he jerked my head back. I looked at him wild-eyed, tears spilling down my cheeks.

"I was raised to believe sex outside of marriage was a sin. One that earned beatings if my cock got hard. Now? I take what I want, when I want it."

I whimpered as he pushed my face into the pillow, then pulled my pajama shorts and panties down to my ankles.

"Such a sweet little ass, begging to be spanked. You've been a bad girl, Brie, cheering in that short little skirt and getting yourself tossed in the air for everyone to stare at your beautiful body. Tell me, the guy that catches you, does he slip a finger into your bodysuit and stroke your pussy?"

I trembled as his touch skimmed down my back, over my ass cheeks, and between my thighs. He straddled me, then nudged his knee between my legs, forcing them apart.

I begged him not to hurt me, but the gag muffled my pleas.

He grabbed my hips and forced me to my knees, my butt in the air. A loud slap against my skin made me lunge forward, nearly hitting my head on the wall.

"Tempting all those men, Brie," he tsked before he spanked me again.

My flesh burned with the repeated harsh contact. His weight shifted on my mattress, and I sucked in a sharp breath as he traced over my slit.

"So wet. Are you wet for me?"

Grunting against the material shoved in my mouth, I attempted to answer him. Not that he could tell. My eyes slammed closed as he rubbed my clit. He parted my ass cheeks, his sudden intake of breath audible in the otherwise quiet room. Easing a finger inside me, he continued to massage my bundle of nerves.

Oh, God! Fuck, what was I trying to say? But ... a soft moan escaped me as he continued, the pleasure pulsing through me, and I rocked against his hand, greedy for more. I had no idea who he was, but sex with a stranger in the middle of the night was hot as hell.

The sound of his zipper reached my ears, and although I should have been afraid, his touch was electrifying. Whoever this was, he knew what he was doing.

I peeked over my shoulder to see his thick, long cock in his palm. He firmly stroked it with one hand as he played with my sensitive flesh. Panting, I squirmed helplessly against him as my climax built, and a mind-blowing orgasm flooded my senses.

His moan followed mine, and I felt his hot liquid landing on my ass cheeks and between my thighs. He remained silent and still for a moment, then hopped off the mattress. I collapsed on my stomach while he untied my wrists. My cuffed arm fell to the side of the bed, and I shook it, encouraging the feeling to return.

He placed a palm on my back, then brought his masked mouth near my head.

"If anyone knew the truth about you, no one would ever love you."

I dug my nails into my bedsheet and lay still as I heard his footsteps retreating, then the sound of my sliding glass door opening and closing.

Removing the gag, I rolled over onto my back as the tears streamed down my cheeks.

The early morning sun peeked between the blinds, filling my bedroom with bright, golden light. I rubbed my eyes, then sat up. Still half-asleep, I reached into my nightstand, located the key, then unlocked the cuff from my wrist. Finally realizing my alarm clock was blaring, I slapped the off button, silencing the obnoxious sound. At least it had worked and gone off. I flopped back onto my mattress. *Damn, that sleeping pill had given me one hell of a dream.* I massaged my temples, trying to recall what I'd dreamt but couldn't remember. I climbed off the bed and stood, then my mouth hit the floor.

"What the actual fuck?" My attention traveled down my bare lower half. "Where are my pajama bottoms?" I glanced around, then stumbled backward. My panties and shorts were on the top of my dresser, folded. My mind scrambled to understand what had happened. Had I walked in my sleep, or was I teetering on the edge of sanity? Maybe moving across the country had been too soon.

I worried my bottom lip between my teeth as I recalled completing the questionnaire for the secret society, including the kind of fantasies I wanted to explore. Maybe that's what had happened, but how would someone have entered the house?

Terrified, I hurried to the sliding glass door and tugged on it, but it didn't budge. The lock was firmly in place. I covered my face with my hands as relief washed over me. It was all a dream, and that stupid sleeping pill had been the source of my fear. Irritated, I gathered some clean clothes and stomped to my bathroom. Still groggy from sleep, I turned on the shower, grabbed my toothbrush, and brushed my teeth. When I finished, I pulled off my pink pajama tank and tossed it on the floor. Something catching my attention as I twisted my head to where it landed. I straightened and froze as I stared at the little scorpion drawn in red lipstick on the upper corner of my mirror.

Chapter Eight

Kane

I woke the following morning in a foul mood. Lyndsay had fucked with my head so bad I'd only caught a few hours of sleep, which had royally screwed with me during practice.

Removing my helmet, I wiped the sweat from my temple with my hand as I began my trek toward the locker room. The new synthetic turf gave way beneath my cleats, and a part of me never wanted to walk off the field to face the rest of the world. But I had never been a coward, and I sure as hell wouldn't start now—especially because of *her*.

"Hey, man. Are you all right?" Jagger asked, joining me. "You seem off."

I glanced at him. "Shit day and it's barely even started." I shot him a wistful smile.

"Maybe you need to blow off some steam. We can invite a few people to my place if you want."

I hoped like hell that I'd hidden my shock. Jagger and I had known each other since high school, parted ways at the start of college, and now we were playing on the same team again. He hadn't ever been my favorite person, but it seemed like he'd grown up some.

"Thanks, but I've got plans." *At the society or in the hole.* It just depended on which direction my mood went.

"No worries. I'll catch up with you later." Jagger nodded, then jogged ahead of me.

As soon as he was gone, Quinn strolled up to me.

"What's up your ass?" Q smacked me on the back. "Your game is off—like it fell off the cliff to its death kind of off."

I shook my head, reminding myself of why I was friends with Quinn in the first place. He could occasionally be stupid as hell, but he always had my back, and he was loyal as fuck to the team and to the society. It helped me overlook the times when I wanted to punch his teeth clean out of his damn mouth—like at that very moment.

"Just got some shit going on. I'll get it handled," I assured him.

"Let me know what you need, dude. I do highly recommend that whatever is punching you in the balls gets straightened out before Saturday. It's a big game."

"I know," I growled at him. Like I didn't know how important every game was. Since I'd been approached by the NFL, the recruiters were crawling all over our team, which said a hell of a lot about our players and coach. I couldn't let them down. I had to get a fucking grip and stop giving Lyndsay headspace. She wasn't worth it. *Betrayers weren't worth it.*

Quinn and I walked the rest of the way to the locker room in silence. I swung open the door and the stench of sweat slapped me in the face.

"I need a shower. I'll see you later." I gave Quinn a quick wave before I reached my locker. My first class of the day wasn't for another hour, so I had time to think about my next steps to eliminate my problem. Quinn was right. I had to take care of it as quickly as possible. My brain spun out in a million different directions, from making Brie mine to what was best for my future. Even though she would always be Lyndsay to me, I realized I needed to refer to her as Brie, so I didn't fuck up around other people.

She wasn't worth me throwing my career in the shitter. I refused to leave my entire life at Whitmore, including the team and the society, which only meant one thing. She had to go. Under no circumstances was she welcome here.

The monster that had slept inside me for the last several years was stirring. One thing was for sure, though. *Lyndsay* had made me that monster.

I parked my car, grabbed my phone, and sent a quick message to a chick I knew who worked in the college's administrative office.

I need someone's schedule. Can you hook me up?

Katy's reply came through quickly. *What's in it for me?*

My deep chuckle filled the car. *What do you want?*

Katy had proven to be a good distraction on occasion, but I had the society and all the pussy I wanted there, or at Madeline's, so I didn't need Katy for sex. I needed her for the students' files she had access to. She didn't know that, though.

My screen was filled with an eggplant, a cat, and a water emoji. My cock stiffened, pressing against my jeans at the thought of her huge tits and being inside her. Hell, why not? It was worth fucking her to get what I wanted.

I sent her a thumbs-up and provided her with the name and what I needed.

Be there in ten.

I chuckled to myself. Katy could be bossy, but sometimes it was kind of hot. One thing I would say about her, she was a little daredevil. Honestly, she should be in the society, but I think she liked to feel special when I called in a favor.

Tossing my phone onto the passenger's seat, I started the engine, then shifted into reverse. I was slowly turning into less of a grumpy bastard as a plan began to simmer in my brain to make Brie pay. Once I got what I needed from Katy, I was on my way to ridding myself of my problems and moving forward with my life.

I located a parking spot, then hurried inside the admin building and headed toward the office where Katy worked. The bell jingled over the door as I entered. Katy glanced up, her dark brown eyes assessing me as though I was a bull up for auction.

"Hey. I have what you need." She stood, showing off her pink sweater that accentuated her huge tits and slender waist.

Her short skirt hit her mid-thigh, and my attention traveled down her long legs to her black ankle boots.

"Excellent. I appreciate it." I glanced around, finally realizing the office was empty. "Where is everyone?"

"Meetings." She handed me a manila envelope, a sly smile slipping across her pretty face. She tucked her brown hair behind her ear. "Come with me."

Glancing around nervously, I followed her into one of the empty offices. If we got caught, I would most likely get kicked off the football team, and my career would be over before it started. I'd already compromised myself at Madeline's, but at least she had security protocols in place. A desperate person makes desperate choices. I needed information on Brianne Langston, and this was the quickest way. Katy closed the door behind us, then lowered the window shade.

I tossed the envelope onto the chair, my dick begging to get free.

"Whose office are we in?" I asked, backing her up, my attention trained on her giant tits that I suddenly needed to come all over.

"An empty one." She placed her hand on my chest and pushed me back, then hopped up on the desk and parted her legs.

"Fuck, no panties."

"Stop talking, quarterback." She pointed to the floor.

I chuckled, then dropped to my knees, eyeing her pussy. Flipping the button on my jeans so I could relieve some pressure from my dick and focus better, I ran my tongue along the inside of her thigh. My nose nudged her clit right before I licked her sweet little slit.

"You ready to come?" I asked before I spread her apart, her scent nearly making me crazy.

"Oh, yeah," she panted.

I feasted on her, and slipped a finger inside as I sucked on her. She squirmed; her pants and gasps became more frequent with each passing second.

"That's it, Kane. Such a good boy."

I growled against her skin. I wasn't into the praise shit like she was, but I assumed I would need another favor from her at some point, so she could say whatever the hell she wanted.

Freeing my cock from my jeans, I stroked my long shaft.

"No touching."

I glanced up at her, slowly running my tongue over her bundle of nerves before I backed away.

"Do you want to come, or do you want me to leave you to finish yourself later?"

Horrified, she gasped. "You wouldn't."

"I would, and we both know it." I massaged her clit with my thumb, bringing her near orgasm before I stepped back. Sometimes it was nice to flip the tables on someone when they least expected it. "I need to see those huge tits."

She giggled, then pulled off her sweater and tossed it on the desk. Katy released the clasp of her bra, then slid the red straps off her shoulders, setting her breasts free. She cupped them, rolling the nipples between her fingers while I watched.

I returned to her soaking wet cunt, keeping my attention on her while she played with her titties. Sliding my hands beneath her ass cheeks, I tugged her closer, fucking her with my mouth. Katy grabbed the back of my head and rocked her hips against me, her juices drenching my lips and running down my chin with her climax. She whimpered as I continued, not allowing her to catch her breath right away.

Finally, I stood and gripped my dick. "Lie down."

Still breathless, she collapsed onto the desk again. I straddled her and positioned my shaft between her tits, then pushed them together and fucked them. She lifted her head and sucked the tip of my sensitive dick. *Fuck yeah.*

"Take it all in." I shifted, sliding in and out. "That's it."

Katy dug her nails into my ass cheeks, pulling me to her until I hit the back of her throat. I slammed my eyes closed, losing myself in the feeling of her hot little mouth. *Goddamn.* I thrust faster, heat traveling down my spine and my balls tightening.

I pulled out, grabbed my dick, and jerked off, my milky white come landing all over her tits. Staring down at her, I scrambled backward so fast I nearly fell off the damn desk. Her face flickered in and out of focus, and Lyndsay's briefly replaced Katy's. *What the actual fuck?*

"Kane?" She frowned. "What's wrong?" Katy sat up, removed a tissue from the blue-and-white box next to her, and began cleaning off her chest.

I massaged my neck, then placed my feet on the tile floor. "I'm fine. See ya later." I hurriedly tucked myself back into my jeans, then zipped and buttoned them. Practically running to the chair, I collected the envelope Katy had provided when I'd arrived. Apparently, I needed to take care of Lyndsay quicker than I realized. The bitch was getting into my head.

I hurried to the parking lot, climbed into my Jaguar, and opened the manila envelope as fast as possible. My attention swept over Brie's schedule. I had access to her house, but for some reason, just knowing where Brie was at any point during the day gave me peace. I checked the time on my phone. It was Tuesday, and my class was near hers, but I only had half an hour before they started.

I practically peeled out of the parking lot, then drove across campus to see if I could find Brie.

The late-morning sun peeked through the red, yellow, and orange tree leaves as I gathered the papers in the passenger's seat before I climbed out of my car, then locked it. Jogging across the lush, green grass, I slowed as I gained on the building where her class was held. I unrolled her schedule, which was still in my hand. It would give me something to pretend that I was looking at instead of stalking the one person I hated more than anything or anyone else in the world. Whoever said to take the higher road and forgive those who had wronged us was full of shit. They clearly hadn't lived through what I had. In this case, I would do anything to break Brie and force her to leave.

I leaned against a tree, checking my watch every few seconds. Sucking in a deep breath, I started to recite football plays quietly to myself. It was my go-to when my thoughts were too fucked up. That and visiting Madeline's. My pulse settled down as I continued until familiar female voices reached my ears. Everlee, Ariana, Gabby, and Brie were laughing as they made their way to the door of the building.

My gaze swept over Brie's gorgeous face, her beautiful features sending me into a rush of dark memories, including the ones of us swearing our undying love for each other. I pursed my lips, forcing myself to stay present. She was stunning, and her laugh echoed through the area, but that wasn't the girl I used to know. Fresh hate slithered down my spine, and my fingers fisted. How? How had she left me behind, then rebuilt her life as though I never existed? She broke her promise and lied to get her way and my support. Never again would I let some chick use me like that. Never.

The paper in my hand crinkled, and I realized I had a death grip on her schedule. Before I forced her to leave, she had some questions to answer. The little bitch owed me.

My thoughts whirled around, deciding what to do next. By the time I finished with Brie Langston, she would be so emotionally wrecked she would have no other choice than to go home to Mommy and Daddy in Tennessee.

Chapter Nine

Brie

I was struggling and possibly going insane. As hard as I tried to focus on my philosophy class, it wasn't working. Thankfully, Gabby sat next to me, so whatever I missed Professor Simmons saying, I could ask Gabby for her notes later.

Even though I pretended that I was fine, the sleeping pill had apparently royally fucked with me. I'd spent all of my waking hours looking at the facts of what had happened last night—the doors were locked, I woke half-naked, and the medication had me questioning reality. On top of that, the prescription had given me a hell of a hangover. Not only was my brain cloudy, but I was also pretty sure I'd lost any grasp on what was real and what wasn't. I was officially losing my mind, and it scared the shit out of me.

Although I was awake, I felt as though I were still muddling through a dream world. Hopefully, I could make it through cheer practice without killing myself or, worse, someone else.

I stared at the blank sheet of paper, attempting to make sense of my evening. I remembered bits and pieces of a dream, but nothing concrete. What had fucked with me the most was the scorpion on my mirror. I must have done it. Even though I didn't wear lipstick every day, I probably owned that color, and it was buried in the bathroom drawer. When I got home, I would have to double-check to see if it was the one used. *Of course, it was, dumbass. No one was in your house last night. You're always making shit up, thinking it's real when it's not.*

Panic clawed my chest, and my leg bounced up and down as images of a hospital flickered through my mind. I sucked in a breath. It must have been part of the dream I was trying to remember.

Gabby leaned over and whispered, "Hey, are you okay? You don't look like you're feeling so hot."

I swallowed hard, attempting to force myself to feel better. "I think I'm sick." Jesus, she had no idea how fucked up I really was. I was barely keeping a grasp on reality, but it hadn't been the first time I'd struggled with it. With a shaky hand, I retrieved my backpack off the floor and shoved my belongings into it.

"I need to go. I'll see you at practice." I stood, then shuffled past Gabby and a few others in the row. I glanced over my shoulder to see Gabby's face filled with worry. I bolted into the hall and out the building's door, my tennis shoes smacking against the cement steps as I fled. Fuck. I couldn't do it. I was losing my shit, and I'd only been at school for a fucking week and a half. I should have known I couldn't make it without my family. The only reason I'd made it this long without losing my mind was due to years of therapy and my family's love and support. Tears welled in my eyes as I sucked in a breath of fresh air.

"Brie!"

Fuck! Gabby had followed me. I slowed and bent over, placing one palm on a knee while I held my backpack in my other hand.

"Girl, you are not okay. Casper has more color in his face than you do. Let me take you home." Gabby took my bag from me and touched the small of my back. "Brie, it's okay. I'll take you to your place, then, if you're not feeling better later, I'll have Everlee help me bring your car over."

I nodded, slowly straightening. "I took a damn sleeping pill last night, and it's making me sick. I feel like I'm walking around in a hazy dream."

"Is it a prescription or over the counter?" She slid her arm around my waist, apparently afraid I might topple over at any given moment.

"Prescription."

"Then call your doctor when you get to your place. I'll stay with you for a bit. My sister had a script for a while, and it royally fucked with her. She walked in her sleep and would wake up on the other side of the house. That shit's dangerous."

"She did?" A flicker of hope welled inside me. Maybe I wasn't losing my sanity after all.

"Yeah, it was bad. I think she tried to push through the side effects, but after two weeks, she told the doctor no more. You just never know how it will affect someone."

Gabby led me across the grassy patch of lawn and to the parking lot.

"That actually helps. I mean, I'm sorry your sister went through that, but at least I'm not crazy. I was starting to wonder for a minute."

We reached her BMW, and she waved a hand in front of the handle, making the locks pop up. She opened the door for me, and I crumpled into the soft red-and-black leather seat. Gabby tossed my bag in the back seat, then hurried to the other side, climbed in, and started the engine.

"Are you cold or hot?"

"Cold." I rubbed my arms, warding off the chill, while Gabby adjusted the temperature and vents.

"Buckle up, babe." She nodded to the seat belt that I'd forgotten.

I belted up, then leaned against the headrest and closed my eyes. A tall figure in black flickered across my thoughts, and my eyelids popped open again. As soon as I got my bearings, I needed to call Alida, but first, I needed to sleep off the medication. I just had to set my alarm for cheer practice so I wouldn't get booted off the team.

As if she read my mind, Gabby said, "If you miss practice today, I'll vouch for you so it's not counted as a strike."

"Really?" I asked, hope and gratitude in my voice.

"Hell, yes, bitch. You look like shit." Gabby flashed me a silly grin. "You're still a sexy beast, though." She winked at me, attempting to lighten the mood.

She had no idea how much I needed her humor.

Trusting Gabby to talk to our coach, I didn't bother to set my alarm when I tumbled into my bed. Gabby hung out for a bit, then locked the door behind her when she had to leave, assuring me she'd check in after practice.

Three hours later, I sat up and rubbed the sleep from my hazy gaze. I stared at the wrist cuff on the floor, and my shoulders slumped. I hadn't bothered with it for my nap because I hadn't expected to actually sleep. At least I felt better, though. It seemed like sleeping meds were similar to hangovers; I had to sleep them off. I stood, making sure my jeans and sweater were where they were supposed to be—on my body.

Since my brain was much clearer, my thoughts returned to the events of the prior evening. Remembering that my shorts and panties had been folded on top of the dresser, I gathered the cuff and stretched the chain to see if it would reach my dresser. It did. Then I walked toward my bathroom. I studied the length of the restraint and the distance to my mirror where the scorpion was drawn in the corner. It wouldn't reach. My toes met the edge of the en suite, and that was it.

I dropped the cuff, and fear flickered in my chest. Closing the rest of the gap, I opened the small cabinet drawer where I kept my makeup. I rummaged through the mess until I spotted a red lipstick, then removed the lid. In seconds I'd written *fuck off* on my mirror near the deadly bastard. Fearing the worst, I took a few steps back and turned on every light available. My legs trembled beneath me, and my tummy flip-flopped. The shade wasn't a match.

After a frantic scramble for my other lip colors, I tested each of them. Blinking several times, I stared at the samples across my mirror. None were a fit.

I could feel what I'd just witnessed making my stomach churn as if I were on a rickety boat lost at sea. Sweat beaded on my forehead, and I wiped it off with the back of my hand, my breathing ragged as reality seeped into my bones. Someone had been in my house last night.

As quickly as possible, I cleaned the mirror, all but the *fuck off* because it made me feel a bit better. My heart sank to my toes as I realized I had nothing to tell the police, so it was pointless to call them. They would brush it off as a side effect of the pill. Plus, the slider was still locked this morning, and so was the front door. The only thing that had happened was there was a scorpion painted on my mirror in red lipstick.

"Get it together, Brie. Maybe the sleeping pill hit you before you even knew it, and you were walking around drunk before you used the wrist cuff. Maybe the lipstick was left from the previous renter, and you found it, decided to get creative."

I rechecked every entrance. Finding each one still locked, I realized I should call Alida. Maybe she could help me sort it out. An idea nudged me in the side, and I hurried into the kitchen. Spotting the large trashcan, I flipped open the lid, my eyes widening when I saw the contents.

"Son of a bitch." I reached for the L'Oréal black tube, then removed the lid. The lipstick had been used. Running down the hall, I rushed into my bathroom and scribbled on the mirror. It was a match. *Oh. My. God.* I hadn't lost my mind. Well, at least not in this instance.

My thoughts whirled from processing the events, and I tossed the lipstick in the trash. It was definitely time to call Alida. She would be the key for me to understand what had happened.

Locating my cell on my nightstand, I pulled up her number in my contacts, then held it to my ear. To my surprise, she answered on the second ring.

"Hello?"

"Alida? It's Brie. I'm surprised I didn't have to leave a message for you." I walked to the living room, then sank onto the couch. Grabbing the throw pillow, I hugged it tightly to my stomach.

"You just caught me before I left for the day," she responded, sounding tired. I couldn't imagine how exhausting her work was.

"I can call tomorrow and let you get home." I closed my eyes, mentally pleading that she had a few minutes.

"Brie, in three years, you've never used this emergency line before. Talk. I'm here for you." I imagined her attentive, kind eyes looking at me.

"I think the sleeping pill did a hell of a number on me last night."

"What happened?"

I rattled off the events to the best of my knowledge. The dream was still hazy, but I'd finally remembered a man in a mask.

"Brie, I'm sorry you had that experience, and I'm glad you called. Did the pharmacist review the possible side effects with you?" Her voice was even and calm, and I felt a little better just hearing her talk.

I slapped my palm against my forehead. "They asked if it was new, and I said no. I don't know why other than I was distracted." I could practically hear her frown through the phone.

"Okay, so there should be a pamphlet that came with the prescription. You always need to read those for new meds, Brie. Promise me that you will, moving forward."

"I promise," I muttered, pissed at myself for not taking a few minutes to look it over.

"Okay, so sleeping medication can be tricky, and everything you described to me fits in with the side effects—sleepwalking, dreams you can't remember, brain fog, or feeling hungover the next day. It's pretty normal."

"It is?" Relief washed over me like the bucket of water thrown over the star player of a football game.

"It is. There's nothing wrong with you. With that information, let's back you down to one-fourth of a tablet, and try it for a week. However, if you have any more issues, please call. Don't wait until the next session."

"I will. I called today."

"You did. Are you feeling better now that we've talked?" Papers rustled in the background, the sound filling the line, then silence.

"Yeah. Thank you, Alida. I don't know what I would do without you."

"I appreciate your kind words. Try and get some sleep tonight, okay?"

"I will."

After our goodbyes, I hung up the phone and tossed it on the floor before I flung myself onto the couch. Fuck, that had scared the shit out of me. Hopefully, the lipstick had been left by the previous renter, and I hadn't gone dumpster diving in the neighborhood. It wouldn't have been the first time I'd unlocked the cuff in my sleep, but it was rare. I rubbed my temples, ready to relax and find some food.

My phone vibrated with a text, and I scooped it off the floor and read the message from Gabby.

Hey, babe. You need me to stop by and bring you some dinner? Coach was cool.

My fingers flew over the keyboard as I responded.

Yes, I'm starving and feeling so much better. I slept for almost three hours. Get your cute ass over here.

My cell buzzed with another message, and a huge grin eased across my face as I stared at the picture of my family decorating the front yard of our house for Halloween—skeletons, a coffin, spider-webs in the trees, Frankenstein, and anything else Dad could talk

Mom into. I'd been so busy with school that I hadn't realized how much I'd missed them until they texted me.

I typed out my reply.

Miss and love you!

Little dots floated at the bottom of the screen.

Love you, too. We'll send more pics when we're done.

Loneliness settled on my shoulders. It would be good to hang out with Gabby. I was so afraid of getting close to people that I often pushed them away early on. That needed to change. Gabby had been an amazing friend so far, and I was closer to her than the other girls on the squad. Maybe, just maybe, it was time I opened up and shared my secret with her. Only a few people knew, but my gut told me I could trust Gabby.

There was only one way to find out.

Chapter Ten

Kane

I pulled into my parents' driveway and parked. I was so preoccupied with how I was going to force Brie to leave Whitmore that I nearly forgot I had dinner plans with my family.

Collecting my phone, I climbed out of the car and locked up. Although the house was in one of the wealthiest areas in the state of Oregon, I hadn't always lived here, so locking doors was second nature to me.

I tucked my light-blue button-down shirt into my jeans as I strolled up the walkway and approached the entrance. Before I could ring the bell, the door flew open, and my thirteen-year-old sister flung herself at me.

"Kane!" Her big brown eyes were filled with excitement.

I laughed as I wrapped her in a tight hug. As far as sisters went, I was pretty sure she was the best out there.

"Hey, Alexandria. I've missed you, too."

She released me and took a few steps back, her gaze narrowing. "It's been, like, a month." She placed a hand on her hip, jutting it out.

"Football *cannot* come before your family. Well, at least me, anyway." She spun on her heel, flipped her long strawberry-blonde hair behind her shoulder, and strutted away, giggling.

I closed the door, then reset the alarm system. "I see Dad all the time."

Alexandria looked at me and rolled her eyes. "That doesn't count."

I lunged toward her, wiggling my fingers. "Are you giving me attitude, little sis?"

She screamed as I chased her through the foyer and into the living room, our laughter echoing through the house. Once I caught her, I tickled her mercilessly until she collapsed on the floor, tears from her uncontrollable giggles flowing down her cheeks.

"There you are," Mom said, joining us. She smoothed her navy slacks, her lips curling up in a wide smile. She never had a hair out of place and was always a picture of perfection and class. I wondered if I would eventually marry someone like her one day.

"Hey." I approached and gave her a big hug.

"Are you hungry?" She patted my arm. "We're eating in the formal dining room tonight. And we have painters coming tomorrow, so all the furniture is covered in protective cloths."

I glanced around, finally realizing that the wingback chairs and couch in this area were also covered. The mansion was gorgeous, with marble floors and counters, triple crown molding, and all the luxurious features a multi-million-dollar home should have. It was amazing how much Mom and Dad could make it feel like a home, not a museum.

"Are you leaving the columns white?" I walked over to them and ran my fingers down the side, recalling the first time I'd laid eyes on them. To everyone else, they were beautiful décor, but to me, they represented a field goal—a small one, but still. I'd broken several expensive vases and paintings while practicing throwing a football right down the middle of these columns. Mom did everything she could to get me to stop, but it was just too much temptation, so she moved all the breakables. Once Dad got me outside and noticed I had a talent for football, the real training started, and I finally felt like I belonged somewhere. Even then, it was a hard road to heal the damage.

Dark memories flickered in my mind, and I shoved those nasty bastards back behind the door where they belonged. I turned my attention to Mom again.

"Yes, but we're finally having them repainted since you've moved out." Mom laughed and squeezed my bicep.

"Son." Dad's voice boomed down the hall. "Glad you could join us."

"Me, too. I know it's been a while since we were able to catch up off the field."

Dad flashed me a big grin as he strolled toward us. "Hell of a team we have this year, but let's chat over dinner." He motioned for us all to follow him as he led the way to the formal area.

Once we took our seats and dished up, I stared at my plate. "I have no idea why I don't visit more often. The food smells amazing." I speared a large bite of pot roast and shoved it into my mouth.

"I told Bella to make your favorite since you were joining us," Mom said.

"It's my favorite, too," Alexandria said, a little whine in her voice.

Dad's dark brow rose slightly, his way of telling her to knock it off.

"Do you think we'll make it to playoffs?" I asked Dad around a bite of fresh bread that I'd slathered in butter.

"I do, but don't let it go to your head." He chuckled.

"Yes sir, Coach." I gave him a salute and an ornery grin. "I'm a little surprised we still keep that secret."

"Me, too, especially since some of the other boys know that the coach is your father." Mom nibbled on her dinner, then dabbed the corner of her mouth with a white linen napkin.

"The few guys that know can keep their mouths shut. Hell, I

trust them with my life." They had no clue how much I trusted Quinn and Sterling, in fact.

"Language," Alexandria said in a singsong voice.

I rolled my eyes at my sister. "I haven't lived here since attending Whitmore, so it's been pretty easy to keep that fact quiet." In no way was I ashamed of my dad, but I didn't have time to get razzed about special favors from the coach or his friendships with some big players in the NFL. I wanted to make it clear to myself and everyone around me that I'd worked my ass off to get where I was.

"Not to mention you're adopted," my sister gushed.

"Alexandria, that's quite enough. You know we don't separate our family into categories. Kane is as much our son as you are our daughter." Mom's blue eyes flashed with irritation.

"Sorry." Alexandria slumped in her chair. "I didn't mean anything by it, Kane. I just meant that it was probably easier to keep it a secret. I wouldn't want to be treated differently because my dad was the coach, either."

"It's all right, kid. I get it." I winked at her, letting her know I wasn't mad.

"I hear the housing market is doing really well. Do you think you'll sell your place if you sign on with the NFL?" Dad took a sip of his red wine, then placed the goblet back on the table.

"Honestly, I was considering renting it out in order to keep it."

Dad shook his head. "You always have a home here, son. You're also diligent about taking care of yourself, but accidents on the field happen. I think it's wise for you to have a backup plan in place. But if you play your cards right with your career, you'll have more than enough money to own several houses and live comfortably the rest of your life."

"That's what I was thinking, so a bit of income on the side from the beginning makes sense." My family had no idea I'd used my inheritance to buy another house for the society. I was twenty, so it was my business what I did, especially since I supported myself. However, I had a full ride to the university, which allowed me to spend my funds on other things. As long as my grades were good and I played ball, every penny needed for school was taken care of. After Mom and Dad had adopted me at fifteen, I felt that I owed them. They had saved my life, and I'd put them through hell until Dad discovered my love of football, then he spent every evening and weekend teaching me what I didn't know. He was also my introduction to the NFL. During football season, we watched the games and studied them instead of running plays. Because of him, I was an excellent quarterback, and I owed Mom and Dad everything. The least I could do was pay for my education.

"Speaking of houses, I need to stop by and check on the new tenant. The one on Gardenia Lane." Mom folded her napkin and placed it on the table.

"I can do it, Mom. It's only a few miles away, so it's not a problem. Who did you rent it to?" I ensured my mask was in place, not letting it slip that I already knew who was there.

"A young lady named Brie. Her parents took care of the rent for six months up front. They're very lovely people from what I gathered. It was clear that they're a bit worried about her at a new campus so far away from home." Mom glanced at Alexandria. "I would only hope that someone would be kind enough to check on our daughter if she were states away."

I contemplated how much I should say but decided it was best to keep my mouth shut. "Yeah, I know what starting over is like. I'm happy to look in on her and ensure she doesn't need anything."

"Do you still have a key, hon?" Mom asked.

"Yeah. I guess I forgot to give it back after we painted and cleaned the place up from the last renters. I'll stop by tomorrow."

"That would be great. Make sure she has my phone number in case she needs anything, or if the house does. I gave it to her parents and asked them to pass it to Brie, but just double-check for me, please." Mom offered me a sweet smile.

"I will." What no one knew was that I'd already visited Brie last night, talking to her softly before I left my calling card of a scorpion on the corner of her mirror. When the society first started, each of us chose a deadly insect or animal as our identity to anyone outside of the organization. We were the elite of Whitmore University, and everyone on campus knew it. But when it was time to wear the skull mask, it was a simple reminder of who ruled.

My dick woke up with the memory of how beautiful she looked while asleep. I used to watch her sleep years ago, too. It was in those moments that I fell in love with her. My heart galloped with the thoughts of our first kiss. Back then, I thought she was special, the one I would marry, but then everything abruptly changed.

My brain reminded the beating organ in my chest that she was the enemy, but my cock had a mind of its own. Plus, I suspected Brie had one hell of a dream because she began to moan softly in her sleep while I was there. I shifted in my chair, reining in the vivid replay of last night's visit.

Although I hadn't touched her while I was there, I'd whispered in her ear while she slept, messing with her mind.

My body remembered our times together before she betrayed me and when she'd been sweet and innocent. We were each other's first, so it was awkward for a while, but we'd figured it out.

Clearly, Brie wasn't that girl anymore, and if I were smart, I would mourn the person I used to know and get the fuck on with my life. It would be simpler if I could forget about her, but there was no way because she had to pay for what happened. I had to get rid of her.

Over the next several hours, Mom, Dad, and Alexandria chatted about school, work, and everything except football. Dad and I had agreed that we could discuss it briefly, but family dinners weren't about sports.

For just a little while, I was able to forget about the girl pretending to be someone she wasn't, but as soon as I left and returned to my car, the burning desire to destroy her rushed in with a vengeance. I couldn't lose my family or the potential NFL contract. I'd given up everything before, and it had almost cost me my life.

Never again. Betrayal was a bitch, and I was about to return the favor.

Mom and Dad probably knew and just hadn't ever mentioned it, but there was a back way to enter the property they were renting to Brie. I'd discovered it one day on my way to drop off paint for the house a few years ago and had basically forgotten about it ... until now.

I parked the car, then closed the door softly and locked it manually. I'd swapped my light-blue button-down for a black hoodie, then grabbed my mask I used in the society from my trunk.

The alley that led to the backyard was dark, but I'd counted on the cover of the night to hide me. My throat suddenly grew dry, and I swallowed hard when images of my past slammed into me, making it difficult to breathe. The last time I'd depended on the darkness to protect me, it had failed ... horribly.

Jogging through the alley, I hopped over the six-and-a-half-foot tall white picket fence, then crouched in Brie's backyard. It was after midnight, but I wasn't sure if she would be asleep or not. I quickly moved until I pressed my body against the back wall of the house, where the sliding glass door to her master was located. The television was on, but Brie was sprawled out on her back in the middle of the bed, her eyes closed and her lips slightly parted. *Perfect.*

Cautiously, I made my way to the front entrance, then used the key to let myself in. I pulled on the white skull mask with the voice disguiser and adjusted it. If she woke up, I couldn't risk her seeing who I was. Sliding on my leather gloves, I realized that it would be seriously fucked-up if she discovered that I was also connected to the society. That fact, coupled with a long list of reasons why she had to leave Whitmore, scrolled through my mind as I made my way down the hall. I paused at her doorway, my gaze landing on her perky breasts. Her nipples pushed against the white material of the sleep shirt, and I fought the urge to touch them. The cream-colored bedsheet had been tossed to the side, revealing her toned legs in her pajama shorts. I might hate her for what she did, but Jesus, she was beautiful. My breath snagged in my throat, and my cock begged to be inside her.

Spotting a chair in front of the slider, I frowned. It hadn't been there last night. Not that it meant anything, but it was just strange. Was this her lame attempt to keep me out?

Brie released a soft moan as I sank into the chair, watching her sleep. I gripped the arms of my seat, my eyes narrowing on the handcuff fastened around one of her wrists. What the fuck was that all about? I spotted the prescription bottle on her nightstand and grinned. It had been another stroke of luck that I'd been in Walgreens when she was picking up her order. The pharmacist had no clue what it meant to talk in a discreet voice, so I heard what the medicine was for—a sleeping pill.

Brie rolled her head from one side to the other, her hand landing on her lower belly. My cock and emotions played a brutal game of tug of war. I studied her—her curvy hips, flat stomach, and toned thighs. The first time we'd had sex wasn't long before she ran for her life. I had thought I was in love, but I'd been so wrong. People in love didn't lie and manipulate the person they swore their future to.

Anger simmered beneath my skin, gaining momentum like an avalanche. My brain skipped down a memory lane of our stolen moments together before my world had been ripped apart. My heart slammed against my ribs, my fury roiling to a full boil. I rose from the seat, then strolled over to the bed. I suspected she'd taken another sleeping pill, but it didn't matter. I would make sure she was awake for this.

I crawled onto the mattress and settled next to her, my fingertips skimming her cheek and down to her collarbone. I wrapped my fingers around her pretty little neck, then applied pressure slowly until her blue eyes popped open, and she clawed at my gloved hand.

"Hello, Brie. I have a message for you." She stiffened, her face turning red.

I loosened my hold just enough for her to breathe. "You don't belong here. Go back to Tennessee as fast as your perky ass can pack, and don't ever return. If you're not gone by the end of the week, I will fucking ruin you. Those pretty little lips of yours will be begging and pleading for mercy, and I'll laugh as I destroy you."

She attempted to nod. I held her for another moment, then released her and climbed off the bed. I took my time walking down the hall, grinning beneath my mask. Goddamn, it felt good to scare the shit out of her. Brie had been terrified, and I would be back to my car in the alley before she stopped shaking and could locate the key to remove the handcuff. If she were smart, she would be gone by this weekend.

Chapter Eleven

Brie

Life had been hell, but at least it was a bye week for the football team. I had stayed at Gabby and Everlee's house, afraid to stay alone at mine. I'd barely slept, debating if I should give in to the threat and leave or hold my ground. That wasn't the only thing bugging me. I didn't know many people here, so who in the hell wanted me gone? The intruder was definitely a guy from the masculine build, but who would threaten me like that? I'd almost driven myself nuts speculating who he was, but I was coming up with a big, fat blank.

At least it had provided me with a good reason to explain my lack of sleep, which was true, but that situation was also because I couldn't handcuff my wrist to the bed while sharing a room with someone. Hell, I hadn't even told Gabby the real reason why I needed to stay at her place at first. I'd finally told her I'd seen a prowler and was scared to stay by myself.

Worse than that, I'd only taken a fourth of the sleeping pill that night the masked intruder threatened me, and I remembered every word that monster had said. *Leave by this weekend or I will ruin you.* A part of me debated whether to pack up, but the other was fucking pissed and didn't want to give in. I'd lost everything, and I was bound and determined to build a future here while I finished college. I'd even considered waiting for him next time ... with a loaded pistol in my lap. As tempting as it sounded, going to court and possibly prison for murder wasn't on my bucket list. After a lot of back and forth, I finally made up my mind.

"Are you sure you want to go back to your place?" Gabby asked, concern in her expression.

"Yeah. I'm sure I made a big deal out of nothing. I'm not used to all the shadows at night. It would probably help if I turned off the television before I went to sleep." I shifted on the couch and looked at the floor. My palms slickened with sweat, and I wiped them on my skinny jeans. No matter how much I wanted to tell her that a masked man had threatened me, I couldn't. Although lying to her felt like shit, I had to be careful. I didn't want to risk putting her in danger. I glanced over, realizing that while I might be keeping that secret, there was one I felt safe sharing, and I urged myself forward.

"Can I tell you something super personal?"

Gabby twirled her brown hair around her finger, then pinned me with an intense stare. "Girl, yes. Anything."

"Okay, but you can't tell anyone. Like ever. Please." I hated sounding desperate, but I was terrified of trusting anyone other than my family with this information. My leg bounced as I searched for the words. "I have night terrors," I whispered, looking away from her. "I've had them for years, and ... and I have to handcuff myself to the bed, so I don't hurt myself while I'm sleeping."

Gabby's eyes widened, then filled with compassion. "Brie, that's awful that you have to live like that." Understanding slipped over her expression. "That's why you hadn't wanted to sleep here until you got spooked?"

I nodded, willing my leg to be still even though my nerves were full-on yelling for me to move. "When I was in high school, one night

I ..." The walls I'd built around me shivered with fear. "I have no idea how it happened, but my parents said they heard a window shatter and ran into my room. I woke up, hanging onto the ledge of my window on the outside of the house. I was screaming my head off and crying hysterically."

"Holy shit. That's intense." Silence filled the space between us. "But Brie, it's nothing to be ashamed of. Your real friends would understand. If the handcuff keeps you safe, then fucking bring it over, and you and I will just share my bed. If you have a night terror, I'll beat you with my pillow until you wake up. It's that simple."

Tears welled in my eyes while I absorbed her words. No judgment, no shaming, just Gabby accepting me and my fucked-up baggage. I wiped away the moisture before I looked at her.

"I've been seeing a psychiatrist for a few years to see if we can find out where the terrors are coming from. One of the options that my parents and psychiatrist came up with was for me to cuff myself to the bed so I wouldn't jump out of any more windows."

Gabby leaned over and took my hand in hers. "Does it work?"

I nodded. "The chain isn't that long, and Dad helped me set it up at my new place. It won't reach the sliding glass door or the bathroom. The mirror was a concern," I explained.

"If you're safe, that's all that's important. Really, don't ever feel like we can't talk about it. Besties have an automatic safe zone for these things. You, Teagan, Ari, Everlee, and Leighton are my bitch pack, and nothing will come between us."

"Really?" I whispered, tears flowing down my cheeks now. "You have no idea how much that means to me. Even though I was popular in high school, no one knew my secret ... except Marc, my ex-boyfriend. That mistake nearly destroyed me and cost me a year and a half of being forced to stay in a relationship I didn't want anything to do with. The fucking asshole blackmailed me." There was the other part of my confession.

"What the actual fuck? What a goddamn bastard!" Gabby dropped my hand and hopped off the couch. She paced the room, her bare feet smacking the hardwood floors as her fingers curled into a fist. "Oh, I wish the son of a bitch had come to Whitmore with you. By the time you and I were done with him, he would never mess with a girl again. Piece of shit," she spat.

Wide-eyed, I watched her pace. I hadn't ever seen her react so strongly. A giggle slipped from my lips. "You might be a little scary, Gabby. But ... I like it."

Gabby slowed, then sat down again. "We all have secrets or things that we're embarrassed to admit. Anyone who uses it against us is lower ..." She pursed her mouth into a thin line. "I'm so mad at that douche canoe I can't even find the right words."

I giggled. "I think you found plenty of words. Lucky for him, he's across the country, and I haven't heard from him since I moved to Oregon." I'd felt so relieved leaving him behind, I didn't want to give him too much headspace when I had more important things to deal with—like how I was going to stay here without attracting more unwanted attention from the masked stranger. A shudder worked its way up my spine. "I should go. I have some studying to do." I stood and grabbed my duffel bag stuffed with my dirty clothes from the week.

"If you need to come back, don't even bother to call. Just show up." Gabby hopped out of her seat, then pulled me in for a big hug. "But I have something for you."

Curious, I watched as she hurried to her backpack near the set of stairs that led to the bedrooms. She rifled around for a moment, then returned and held out a small black canister. "Mace."

"Thank you." I grinned. "It helps knowing you're only a few minutes away, too." I quickly hugged her, then strode to the door.

Gabby followed, then watched me as I walked down the driveway and to my car. Once I was inside, she gave me a little wave and disappeared back into the home.

Before I left, I turned on Spotify, and "Blood on Your Hands" by Veda and Adam Arcadia flowed through my speakers. I grimaced at the lyrics. "Mm, not right now." I quickly changed the song. To my dismay, "The Hunted" by The Rigs played next. Apparently, I had dark taste in music, but this wasn't the time to listen to it. Turning off the music, I opted to focus on the drive. Soft raindrops landed on my windshield, and my anxiety kicked up the closer I got to the house. At least I had some mace now. The only problem was the night terrors. What if I accidentally sprayed myself while asleep?

Every mile that went by, my heart rate spiked with my nervousness. I wasn't as brave as I told myself I was. If I were honest, I was fucking terrified, but I wouldn't allow someone else to dictate to me.

By the time I arrived at my place, I was struggling to breathe. Forcing myself to get control, I stood at the front door, squared my shoulders, then marched inside like I was fucking Wonder Woman. Rage exploded inside my chest. *How dare that motherfucker come into my home and threaten me?* Whoever he was, he had another thing coming if he thought he could bully me. Marching right to my bedroom, I placed the keys and mace on my nightstand, then tossed my bag into the middle of the bed.

Chills peppered my arms, and I rubbed them as I realized I needed to check the place for anyone hiding and waiting for me. "Fuck. What are you doing?" Looking around to make sure I was safe should have been the first thing I'd done, but at least now I was more pissed than scared. That was progress.

I collected the little black canister of courage and ensured that I aimed the mace away from my face.

Five minutes later, I flopped onto my bed. All the doors and windows were locked, and the closets were empty of any lurking assholes wearing a mask and waiting to try and force me to leave Oregon. The mirror was also free of any lipstick other than the *fuck off* message I'd left.

"Shit," I muttered, climbing off the mattress. I'd forgotten to check the backyard. My fingers tightened on the mace as I peeked outside. Seeing no one, I opened the slider in my room. The sun had already set, and the rain clouds made it darker than normal. I stepped out onto the little cement patio, realizing there was nothing to be afraid of, I breathed in the fresh air. No monsters were in sight. A flash of light caught my eye, and my curiosity got the most of me as I walked across the yard. A dog barked in the distance, and I glanced over my shoulder at my bedroom. Even though I was feeling a lot better, my nerves apparently were still wound tight.

Crouching down to see what had caught my attention, I frowned as I picked up a little metal box with an eye on it. I traced the strange image, intrigued. Footsteps sounded, but before I could turn to see where they were coming from, a gag was shoved into my mouth, and a bag was pulled over my head from behind me, causing me to drop my mace.

I kicked and screamed, fighting the unknown figure, but I was quickly overpowered. My hands were forcefully secured behind me, then I was lifted off the ground. Some kind of ropes were wrapped around my ankles, leaving me completely helpless. I couldn't tell how many people were carrying me off, but I could hear several sets of footsteps. Panic clawed at my chest, then I landed with a thud, and a click reached my ears. I struggled to breathe through the coarse material covering my face as tears streamed down my cheeks. I should have fucking listened and left school. The fucker wasn't playing with me. I wasn't positive, but I was pretty sure that I'd been kidnapped and tossed into the trunk of a car.

I closed my eyes, trying to remain calm, but the moment I did, flashes of dark figures clouded my mind. *What in the hell is happening?*

Chapter Twelve

Kane

"It's initiation night, guys!" I hollered to everyone in the living room. "Head downstairs, and let the games begin."

Since I bought the place, I'd added the finishing touches and renovations for the new society location that included a meeting area, camera system, toys for every kink we had, and soundproofing in the ten rooms. But one special space had been built for initiation, and I couldn't fucking wait to use it.

The guys followed, eager to see the place as well. I released a chuckle as everyone's footsteps pounded down the stairs, sounding like a stampede. Once we reached a silver door, I pressed my thumb to the keypad, and the lock popped open.

"Damn. We're stepping it up this year, huh?" Sterling said over my shoulder.

"Our safety and security are the main priorities. We all have way too much to lose if shit goes south." I pushed the entrance open, the cool air rushing into the stairwell. I strolled into a hallway and passed multiple rooms on my right and left. "Every space offers all the fuckery we want." I cracked a grin. "Also, each one has a keypad that reads your thumbprint. You're all set up."

"Oh, that's why you had us roll our thumbs on that little machine," Anderson said.

I nodded.

"Can we see the new renovations?" he continued, excitement in his voice.

"Go for it. It will be a good opportunity to test the keypads, too." I waited in the hallway as the group dispersed.

They excitedly checked out the new spaces, then joined me again a few minutes later. I strolled over to an additional door at the end of the hall and unlocked it with my print. "This is the office and meeting area." The light automatically turned on as we entered. I moved out of the way, allowing the guys to join me. When we were all inside, I opened the closet and distributed the dark hooded robes.

"The brotherhood of The Viper Society." I slipped mine on, leaving the hood down. "Our skull masks with the voice disguisers are over there." I nodded to the large table in the corner, near a few couches and plenty of chairs for the eleven of us to sit comfortably. They all finished slipping on their robes, then I led them to the area where we would hold our first official initiation of the girls that had been selected for the semester. My cock throbbed, thinking about all the pussy that awaited us.

Walking silently, I strolled into the large room dimly lit by strategically placed torches and located at the opposite end of the house. Eleven girls with hoods over their heads kneeled in the middle of the grey concrete floor with their arms bound behind them. I stood in front of the first one, then everyone else lined up in front of a female as well.

"Welcome to The Viper Society. Initiation will begin." I folded my hands behind me and walked to the end of the line, my cock eager to fuck. "Ready."

One of the brothers hurried behind the row of girls, then removed the first girl's hood. I tipped her chin up and looked into her eyes, rimmed red from her tears. I brushed her dark hair from her cheek.

"Your gag will be removed. Do you vow your body to the men in the society and to no one else?"

Her gaze widened with understanding, a hungry look flashing across her expression. She swallowed, her tongue wetting her lips before she spoke.

"Yes," she answered breathlessly.

I ran my thumb down her cheek, recalling the information that I'd reviewed on her before she landed here. "Stand."

She got her feet beneath her, then stood. I reached for the buttons on her top and flicked them open one by one, exposing the swell of her breasts in her white bra. My attention traveled down the creamy skin of her flat stomach to the waist of her short skirt.

"Remove her panties," I said to one of the brothers.

He did as I asked and pocketed the article of clothing. He pulled the hood over her face again, then we continued to the next girl. As the leader, I had first choice of which girl would be selected to serve me that night, but I wasn't sure who it would be yet. The second I looked at her, though, I would know.

Ten girls had started their initiation, but I was waiting to see the last before I made my decision. Her hood was removed, and fearful blue eyes stared at my mask. Startled, I took a step back. *What the fuck?*

I blinked, attempting to understand. It was hot as hell in the damned mask, and sweat had blurred my vision more than once during the ceremony. But there was no way I was mistaken. Brie Langston knelt before me, ready to be initiated.

Snatching the hood, I jerked it over her head again, then grabbed her arm and jerked her off the floor. I ignored her whimper as I walked her down the hall, my heart pounding in my ears with every pissed-off step I took. I quickly unlocked the first room and shoved her inside ... alone.

"What's wrong?" A voice came from behind me as I closed Brie in.

I motioned for whichever member it was to follow, and I walked to the office. Practically shoving him inside, I slammed the door shut after us, then ripped off my mask. He did the same.

"God dammit. Who the hell brought her here?"

Sterling shot me a confused look, then grabbed the stack of applications on my desk. He shuffled through a few of them, then shoved it at me.

"Sasha Duncan."

My gaze narrowed as I stared at the paper and the picture of Sasha—dark hair and brown eyes. "How the hell did this get past me? That girl is not Sasha."

"All I know is that the guys went to each address listed on the forms and brought back the girls." A defeated look flashed across Sterling's expression. "Shit. Someone got the wrong chick by accident, didn't they?"

"Jesus Christ. We go to great lengths not to fucking kidnap the wrong person!" I slammed my hand against the wall, ignoring the zip of pain that shot through my arm. "That isn't Sasha Duncan. That's Brie Langston," I roared.

"Holy shit. The girl you want to mark?"

Sterling took a few steps away from me. My guess was that a murderous look was on my face. "No one can touch her."

"Dude, I know you're fucking pissed right now, but you're aware of the rules. You have to fuck her to mark her. Otherwise, she's fair game."

My chest tightened with his words. Shit, I was the dumbass that had put that rule into place at the beginning of the school year since a guy would claim someone to cockblock another member, then change his mind. I shoved my hand through my short hair, the weight of reality nearly choking me.

"Leave the fucking bag over her face and her wrists bound. Put her back in the initiation room—alone." My hands fisted. "Then find out who fucked up. I'll deal with them later."

"Sure thing, boss." Sterling practically ran out.

Most of the time, I was able to keep my temper, but this fuckup was due to someone thinking with their cock instead of their head, and that shit would get us in trouble and fast.

I stared at the clock on the wall, pacing the office as I figured out what the hell I was going to do with Brie. She was supposed to have left campus this weekend, but she was clearly still here and posing a challenge. For some stupid reason, I thought that one threat would be enough. I'd promised her consequences if she didn't leave, and this was a perfect opportunity to not only fuck with her body, but also her mind. When I was finished with her, she would be begging me to let her move back to Tennessee. Once she was out of my space, I wouldn't worry about her blowing my career for me.

Over the next ten minutes, I realized that fate had just knocked on my door and delivered me the perfect gift.

Chapter Thirteen

Kane

When I returned to the initiation room, it was empty except for one person. Recognizing her blue shirt, I approached Brie, who knelt in the middle of the floor. The bag was still over her head, and I ripped it off, staring at her. I wanted her to see everything that was about to happen.

Gripping her arm, I jerked her up. She whimpered around the gag in her mouth, and my dick screamed to be let out so it could fuck her in every hole possible. But first ...

"You're not Sasha. You're Brie Langston. You're not supposed to be here."

She glanced at me, bewildered, but Brie knew that she'd completed the questionnaire under someone else's name. Brie was much calmer than when her hood had first been removed. None of the girls had known they were being kidnapped for us that evening, but every damn one of them had kidnapping on their list. How could we not help their wishes come true? What they didn't realize was that they would serve us, not just fulfill some sexual fantasy.

A large raised cement slab stood in the corner, and torches now lit the area, casting shadows over the altar. I untied Brie's hands, scooped her into my arms, and placed her on the cold platform. I hopped up, pinned her down, then spread her arms and restrained them above her head. Once I'd secured her ankles as well, I jumped down. Focusing on her, I tore open her blue shirt, and the little white buttons popped off and bounced on the concrete floor. Reaching into the pocket of my slacks, I removed a pocketknife. Her eyes widened, and she began to shake as I moved it to her chest. I trailed the tip between her breasts, then, with a quick slice, I cut off her bra. The lilac lace shifted away from her tits, exposing her nipples to the cold air.

"You've been a very bad girl, Brie. Do you know what happens to naughty girls?" My cock pressed against my pants, begging to be inside her. I was going to have to free it soon, but for now, I wanted to feel the pain. Not only did it fuel my fury toward Brie, but sometimes I craved it with sex.

She muttered against the gag in her mouth, and I laughed as I removed my black cloak. Never in my wildest dreams would I have imagined that the girl who left me for dead years ago would be spread out and ready for me.

I forcefully unbuttoned her jeans and jerked them down her legs, along with her matching lilac G-string. I untied each leg in order to remove the last of her clothing, then secured her again. I sucked in a breath as I stared at her naked. It had been one thing to watch her sleep and imagine what she looked like beneath her clothes, but this— her. *Don't forget she destroyed you, asshole.*

I stepped away, then collected a candle and lit the wick in a torch.

Staring down at her, completely vulnerable and under my power, I watched as the shadows danced across her face. Brie was a perfect example of beauty only being skin deep. Inside, she was manipulative and a liar. Anger jolted through me as dark and jagged memories ripped through my chest. I ground my molars, then dripped the first bit of wax onto her stomach. White drops cooled against her flesh, and she sucked in a breath, pulling on the restraints.

I chanted phrases that hadn't left my lips in years as I continued the wax play. My heart raced, my breathing erratic and labored as memories roared to life from when I was younger.

Brie's nostrils flared as she squirmed. I watched her carefully for any recollection of my words in her gaze as I continued. When I reached her pussy, I spread her apart and dipped my fingers in her juices. She was soaked. Little Brie had grown up into a girl that liked pain and fear. It fucking turned her on. My brow rose with the revelation. If that's what she wanted, then I would happily deliver.

I slapped her core, suddenly needing to turn her over my lap and spank her. Carefully, I set the candle down and blew it out, then removed the gag from her mouth and freed her from the restraints. I hauled her off the altar by her bicep, then practically dragged her behind me as I looked for the chairs that were tucked into the corner. I sat down and glared at her. Not that she could see through my mask, but I was well aware of how much I hated her.

"Bend over my lap."

She stared at my crotch, her lips parting slightly before she obeyed. My hand slapped her ass cheek, forcing a cry from her. Her body rocked against my legs as I continued, leaving red welts across her creamy flesh.

"Do you know why you're being disciplined?"

"No," she whispered.

I parted her thighs and ran my finger over her soaking wet slit. "You're lying." Anger clung to my words.

"I'm not." She sucked in a sharp breath as I eased two fingers inside of her greedy little cunt. She writhed on my lap as I brought her close to release, then stopped and spanked her again. Her cries nearly made me come, but I forced myself to wait.

"How many guys have fucked you?" My throat was tight while I waited for her response. The memories of us together when we were young bombarded my senses, the agony of the loss threatening to jerk my heart out of my body and stomp all over it until it was no longer recognizable.

"Three."

Rubbing her clit, I frowned. For some reason, I'd expected more. "Who?" I ordered. "What are their names?"

I withdrew my touch, bringing her back from the edge of orgasm again.

"Marc, Felix, and Davis."

"There's another," I said, harshly.

"No one else. I swear." Her voice trembled.

My chin shook with a rush of emotion, anger and the reminder of the betrayal hitting me all at once. "Once a liar always a liar." I dumped her off my lap and onto the floor. "On your knees."

She looked up at me, raw lust in her blue eyes, and the hunger for more, but she wouldn't get it. Not tonight.

I opened my slacks and freed my throbbing cock. With several firm strokes, I shuddered while I shot my come all over her face and hair. I realized I was supposed to fuck someone to mark them, but I couldn't. Brie Langston had to suffer, and by her expression, she wanted me to ravish her body, but I would happily deny her.

I tucked myself back into my slacks, then gripped her chin, hard. "If anyone knew the truth about who you really are, no one would ever love you."

Brie blanched, the color draining from her cheeks as she trembled. Furious, I stormed away, my black dress shoes slapping against the concrete floor. There was somewhere else I had to be—Madeline's. It was the only way to purge myself and soothe the beast before I lost my shit and did something stupid.

Chapter Fourteen

Brie

I lay face down on my pillow, sprawled out in the middle of my bed as the cheery fucking morning sunshine spilled through the blinds and into my room. My ass hurt like crazy from the spanking the evening before, but a part of me loved it. I thrived on the pain.

I rolled over, twisting the sheet around my legs, and I laughed. Who knew that I would have been so turned on by being tied down? The candle play had been insanely hot, and I didn't just mean the temperature.

Staring at the ceiling, my forehead creased in confusion, then the hole in my heart burned with an uncontrollable grief. What had he meant by saying those cruel words that no one could ever love me? It might be how I felt, but I hadn't ever shared that with anyone—not even Alida.

My emotional pain flipped to pissed off, and in less than sixty seconds, I was in bitch mode. *What. The. Actual. Hell?* Whoever was behind the skull mask had humiliated me by jacking off on my face and hair. Someone had a huge pair of balls to pull that shit. From the questionnaire I'd completed as Sasha, it was supposed to be all fun and kinks. I was cool with most of it, but not what he'd said to me. Maybe expecting to meet Sasha had sent him into an uncontrollable asshole fit, and I caught the brunt of it.

"You did use someone else's invitation," I whispered to myself. I wondered if I would be invited to return since I'd rattled him. What was even stranger than that entire experience ... why would he give a shit about how many partners I'd had? The society was an exclusive invitation-only sex club, but we were all adults, so most of us would have had more than one partner.

I shook my head. A part of me wondered if last night had even happened, but I was well aware that it had, otherwise my butt wouldn't be sore. Massaging my temple, a nervous giggle escaped me. What in the hell had that dude been chanting? It sounded like he was speaking Latin, but whatever it was had been some weird shit.

Kicking off the blankets, I sat up on the edge of the bed and frowned. I hadn't used the wrist cuff last night, and as far as I knew, I hadn't had any horrible dreams. After I'd been tossed into the trunk of a car and returned home, I'd taken a fourth of one sleeping pill, and in minutes, I was out. My brain seemed pretty clear, too. Maybe I'd found the right dosage of the medication. I stood, then stretched my arms toward the ceiling.

I showered and started laundry, then grabbed my cell to message Gabby. Humming to myself, I strolled to the living room where I collected the dirty coffee cup I'd left on the corner table a few days ago, then my heart lodged itself into my throat. My entire body began to shake uncontrollably as I sank to the floor, attempting to make sense of what I was seeing.

Red letters were painted all over the white walls of the living and dining room. I gasped as I began to read them aloud. *"Stop pretending you're not a fucking lying bitch. Leave or the world will know what you really are."*

Chapter Fifteen

Kane

My phone vibrated against the nightstand, waking me. Grabbing it and squinting at the screen, I frowned, then looked at the time. It was nearly eleven in the morning.

I answered Mom's call. "Hey." My voice cracked, still heavy with sleep.

"Honey, I suspect you have plans today, but I need your help." She couldn't disguise the urgency in her tone.

"Of course. What's going on?" I pulled myself up to a sitting position, yawning. It had been one hell of an evening, and I hadn't crawled into bed until around four a.m.

"Someone broke into the house on Gardenia Lane. We need to paint the walls, change all the locks, and have an alarm system put in. Brie is beside herself. The poor thing was crying so hard she could barely talk."

I froze. *Shit!* I hadn't expected her to go running to my mom, but it seemed my obsession with Brie was clouding my judgment. "Oh, yeah. I just remembered that I'm supposed to help Anderson's family move some furniture today, so I can't go with you."

"I'm sorry, Kane, but you'll have to cancel. I really need you to go with me. Your father has an important engagement, or he would take care of it. So, get your rear end out of bed, shower so you don't reek of alcohol and shenanigans, and I'll pick you up in an hour." Mom didn't even bother to say goodbye. She simply hung up, which meant I'd really pissed her off.

I groaned and threw the phone on my mattress. "Fuck my life!" How in the hell was I going to get out of this one? Mom had clearly seen through my lame-ass excuse. Under no circumstances could Brie see my face. I wasn't worried about what had happened so far—I was always covered—but if she did see me, she would know who I am. Massaging the back of my neck, my brain scrambled for a legit excuse to try and get out of helping Mom. Dammit. In my opinion, I'd already given her a solid reason, though, and she pulled the parent card on me. Mom didn't do it often, but when she did, there was no use arguing with her.

I sat up, my bare feet landing on the walnut wood floors. My gaze swept the room, then landed on my navy-blue baseball hat. Maybe it would help if I wore it low on my forehead, then Brie couldn't see me very well.

While I showered, I recalled the evening before. Brie hadn't ever seen my face at the society, but that was the least of my worries. I could almost imagine the shock registering over her pretty features and her cherry-red lips forming an O.

Seeing tears in her eyes last night when I came all over her cheeks and hair made me hard just thinking about it. I used the soap to lather up, then wrapped my fingers around my shaft. With each stroke, my mind drifted to her well-rounded tits and ass. But her mouth. Jesus, I bet that mouth was like a goddamn hoover. My lips parted as I imagined entering her sweet, wet pussy and banging her so hard we were breathless. I moaned with my release, but the name that left my tongue wasn't Brie—it was Lyndsay.

I pounded on the shower wall, then leaned my forehead against it as the pain and rage swirled inside of me. The memories of her laugh, the softness of her hands on my body, her wide-eyed innocence that she'd shared with me ... What had happened to make that girl disappear and the new one take her place?

Disgusted, I reminded myself that girl was gone, and she'd left me to fucking rot. I slammed my eyes closed, a lump of anguish lodging in my throat.

"Fake Statue of Liberty, Hail Mary ... Hidden Ball Play." Water streamed down my face as I continued to call out football plays, seeing each of them unfold in my mind.

When my thoughts quieted, I took a deep breath and tried to figure out how in the hell I was going to manage the situation with Brie and my mom.

Once again, when I thought the universe had dealt me a sweet hand, it turned into a fucking shitshow. At first, Brie landing in my parents' rental was exactly what I needed. I hadn't expected it to bite me on the goddamn ass, though. Not to mention, I had to clean up my own fucking mess and swap out the locks. That wasn't the problem. I would have a new key, but an alarm system was a big issue all on its own. If my parents wanted to add cameras, there was no way I would be able to stay off the radar, which meant I had to change my plan.

Once I showered and dressed, I grabbed my baseball hat and phone, then hurried down the stairs and into the kitchen. When I bought the place, I had a designer come in and help with the kitchen remodel. The rest of the place needed new floors and paint, but it was in great shape. The two-thousand-square-foot house had offered enough space for a gym, three bedrooms, two baths, and now had a top-of-the-line kitchen and outside patio. It was my heaven. Too bad the devil was knocking, ruining my solitude.

I had just enough time to make some eggs and a large cup of coffee before Mom arrived. My short hair had dried, for the most part, so I slipped on the hat before I met her at the door, then locked it behind me.

"I certainly hope you've had an attitude adjustment." Mom crossed her arms over her chest, pinning me with a don't-mess-with-me look.

I drew her in for a big hug, then placed a noisy kiss on her cheek. "I'm sorry, Mom. I was asleep and not thinking clearly. I didn't mean to be a jerk. You know I'll do anything for you." I meant every word I just said. I would do anything for her, but the situation was about to kick me in the ass if I didn't play my cards right.

The tension eased from her small frame, and I released her. Tears welled in her blue eyes. "Apology accepted. This is so serious, honey. Poor Brie is a wreck, and the idea that someone can break in and cause damage to someone else's home unnerves me. If anything happened to her, and I had to call her family ..." Mom looked away, pursing her lips.

"Hey, we'll get it fixed. Try not to stress. Let's get over there so you can talk to Brie while I work on the locks. What time will the security company arrive?" I slid my arm around Mom's shoulders as we walked to her Mercedes. I opened the driver's door for her, then hurried to the passenger's side and climbed in.

"They'll be there at two. I paid extra for a Sunday installation, but keeping Brie safe is my main priority at the moment."

"That's what makes you an amazing person. You really want to do right by people." I squeezed her hand as she shifted the car into drive, then headed toward the rental.

"Thank you, honey. Your dad loaded the trunk with the new locks, tools, paint, and everything else you'll need for the job."

"Okay."

Mom focused on the back road from my place to the rental, and my thoughts returned to what my fate would most likely look like in a few minutes. Although Mom and Dad knew about my past, they didn't know a lot of details. All the secrets that I preferred to stay buried were about to climb out of the grave and haunt me all over again. Panic spiraled through me. *What if I lose everything?* Would the NFL no longer be interested once they found out who I was and where I came from? If that happened, I could kiss my career goodbye. No team would want me after that, and my dream would go down in a blaze. What if the guys voted me out of the society, then gave me the cold shoulder on and off the football field? These people and things were my life—my home—and I would defend it at all costs.

My heart skipped a beat as Mom pulled into the driveway. Before I could say a word, she turned off the engine, then jumped out and made a beeline for the entrance. The door opened a crack, then far enough to let Mom in. I couldn't see Brie, but for now, I would count my blessings.

Pulling the hat down lower, I hoped like hell it was enough to disguise my face. Once I unloaded the items from the trunk, I made my way to the house. Out of courtesy, I knocked before I let myself in. Well, it wasn't out of courtesy for Brie, but my mom would rip me a new one if I were rude.

Mom and Brie were at the kitchen table when I entered, and Brie barely glanced up. She and Mom were in a deep conversation, which worked for me. Mom held her hand while big tears streamed down Brie's cheeks. It made me happy as hell to see her so wrecked.

I took a step back and admired my handiwork on the walls. When I painted last night, the place had been quiet and peaceful. Brie was sound asleep in her bed, and I closed her bedroom door so the paint fumes wouldn't wake her. Plus, I opened the kitchen window for some ventilation. It hadn't taken long to leave my message, along with my signature scorpion.

"Honey, are you sure you don't want to call your parents? If you were my daughter, I would want to know. And I'm happy to refund the rent money if you need to go home to Tennessee," Mom said.

I set the items down on the kitchen counter, holding my breath that Brie would agree to leave.

"No. I think with an alarm system and new locks, I'll be fine. I know I'm rattled, but I've never been one to run. Besides, if whoever comes back, I'll be waiting." Her voice shook with the threat.

Bring it on, little girl. I will always win.

"Okay, but I think you should at least tell your parents what happened." Mom patted Brie's arm.

I forced back a scream that threatened to erupt. Mom had no idea who Brie really was—what she'd done.

Mom leaned over and hugged Brie. Rolling my eyes, I was grateful that the bill of the hat covered my disgust with how Mom was coddling her.

"They'll want me to come home, and when I say no, they'll worry themselves to death. I can't do that," Brie said in a hushed voice. "Thank you very much for helping me with the paint and locks. I can clean up, too."

I turned my back to them, busying myself with opening the package for the front door bolt and doorknob that Mom had purchased.

"I'll start with the slider in the master," I muttered, staring at the floor as I strode from the kitchen and walked past them.

"Kane, take off that awful hat and say hello to Brie. I think you left your manners somewhere, and I highly recommend that you find them quickly."

Fuck. I just got told off by my mom in front of a chick. Not just any girl, but the one I hated with every damn cell in my body.

"I need the hat so I don't get paint in my hair," I replied.

"Take it off, then put it back on," Mom said, her tone clipped.

I'd definitely pushed her too hard. My teeth clenched as I prepared for my entire world to implode. I removed the baseball hat, then raked a hand through my dark hair. My gaze traveled from the carpeted floor to Mom, then slowly to Brie.

Time stopped as we stared at each other, speechless for a moment.

Brie frowned, then shook her head, confusion morphing her features as a dusting of pink feathered her cheeks. *Bingo.* Her mouth opened and closed as if she were searching for what to say, then thought better of it. "You're our quarterback, right? Kane Cooper?" She cleared her throat. "Sorry, I've heard your name, but I've only seen you with your helmet on or at a distance. It took me a moment to realize it was you." She fidgeted in her chair. My presence was making her uncomfortable, exactly like I thought it would. "I didn't know your parents owned the rental."

What the hell? Was she trying to trick me into thinking she didn't recognize me? That fake bullshit would be right up her alley.

Hopefully, she would have the decency to keep her mouth shut about how she knew me in front of Mom. "Not many people do. I like to keep my personal life ... private." My words didn't seem to bother her, and she was apparently damn good at hiding her facial expressions. She probably didn't want our past to come to light in front of my mom either. At least we had that in common.

"Thank you for helping today. I'll change clothes and help you paint. It will give me something to do other than stress." She stood, then smoothed her little pink robe. "I didn't realize you would be here, or I would have changed."

With that, she hung her head and hurried past me.

What the hell had just happened? Maybe she was a better actress than I'd thought or—

"That wasn't so hard, was it?" Mom shot me a disappointed look. "Whatever is happening with you, son, get your crap together. Your Dad and I will do anything we can to help, but being rude isn't a part of our family's values, and you know it." Worry flickered through her features.

"I can't explain it now, but it'll make sense later." With that, I spun on my heel and marched out of the front door. Since Brie was so insistent on helping me, I would start with the locks first. And maybe, I could figure out what the fuck had just happened because when I stared straight into Brie's eyes ...

My brows knitted together. Now that the house was off-limits for me to fuck with her, it looked like she would be called back to the society a hell of a lot sooner than I'd anticipated.

Chapter Sixteen

Brie

It had been a long-ass day between painting and cleaning, but at least I'd had company while the alarm system had been installed. After realizing someone had been inside the house while I slept, I wasn't too keen on having strangers around. The installation guy knew where all the cameras were and, most likely, how to work around the system if he ever wanted to break in, so I definitely felt safer with Kane and his mom there with me, even if Kane didn't appear to be my biggest fan.

I was stunned that Kane's parents owned the place I was living in. Pondering, I wondered if I could find an excuse for him to return and fix some things. Regardless of his attitude, that man was breathtakingly hot. I'd caught myself watching him as he painted and changed the locks. His jeans clung to the curve of his ass and long legs. Even though he seemed upset that he was there, I hadn't cared. I was good with the eye candy all damn day, and it was nice to have a distraction.

Kane had also remained quiet, which was odd after all the

wonderful things Gabby and the girls had said about him. Apparently, he was fun and outgoing, but that's not who I saw earlier. He'd been broody and sullen. I'd tried to start a conversation with him several times, but it had quickly fallen flat. For his mom's sake, I'd attempted to be polite, but I suspected it would be more fun to bang my forehead against a brick wall than convince him to talk to me.

The red paint on my walls returned front and center in my thoughts. It had to be a previous renter messing with me, or maybe it was someone very skilled at breaking in without a trace. Regardless, it was over, and I could breathe again.

Once Kane, his mom, and the alarm installer had left, I realized I hadn't checked my mailbox in a few days. To my surprise, a black envelope with my name and no postage was mixed in with the junk mail. I had no idea how long it had been there, but I suspected someone had left it while Kane and his mom were with me.

I stared at the glow of the car's dashboard that evening, watching as the clock changed to nine. I inhaled deeply, attempting to rid myself of the tension knotted in my neck and shoulders. At least I'd left the house with confidence that no one would enter without me knowing about it.

The invitation had mentioned parking at the back of the home, then entering there. I still wasn't sure why I'd received an invite after what I'd pulled, but I was about to find out. Maybe whoever ran the society decided I was a threat and had chosen to keep me close.

After I climbed out of my car and locked up, I shoved my phone and key fob into my purse. I clung to the strap of my Gucci handbag as I walked to the back entrance, my legs wobbling with each step I took. Before I could knock, the door opened, and I was greeted by someone dressed in dark clothes and wearing a white skull mask with black around the eyes.

"Good evening, Brie." Masculine hands waved me inside, then

the click of the lock behind me echoed through the hall. The person gripped my bicep and silently led me down the ominous corridor, stopping at a door on the left. He placed his thumb on a keypad, popping the lock open, and he motioned for me to enter the room.

I nervously smoothed my emerald-green silk blouse and black skirt. The instructions mentioned not to wear a bra or panties, and I was a little chilly.

The person disappeared, leaving me alone. "Voodoo" by Godsmack played through the speakers, and I glanced around. Unlike the room before, this one was small and held a couch, table, and a few chairs. Candles scented the space with cinnamon and vanilla, their flames casting an eerie glow on the walls.

A throat cleared as a side entrance opened, and someone strolled in.

"Nice of you to join me." Again, black slacks, black shirt, and a white skull mask with a voice disguiser. He shoved a hand in his pocket and walked closer to me.

"Are you the same guy from last night?" My nerves betrayed me, and my legs shook with my question.

I gripped my purse tightly, unsure of what to expect. Last night had been wild and weird, and I hoped like hell he wouldn't spank me again. At least not too soon. My tender flesh hadn't had an opportunity to recover.

He circled, then stood in front of me. Tilting my chin up with his fingers, he stared down at me. My pulse pounded so hard that my ears briefly rang.

"Do you know what happens to girls like you?"

My brows creased in confusion. "I don't understand what you mean," I whispered.

A deep chuckle rippled throughout the space. "Betrayers. Deceivers. People who don't think twice before they destroy others. People. Like. You."

I shook my head, not following him. "I haven't betrayed anyone."

"Silence!" He placed his hands on my shoulders and pushed me to my knees. "Your deceitful and disgusting choices ripped lives apart, Brie Langston. Now, you'll pay. You serve me and no one else. When I call, you run here. No other man is allowed to touch what's mine."

Was this all a part of the society's game? I was totally cool with the role-play.

"Only you." My eyes locked onto the big bulge in his slacks. I bit my bottom lip, my gaze skating over his erection before swooping back to his mask.

Whoever he was, he loved to dominate, but I was good with that. My core clenched, begging to be fucked hard.

"Get on the table and spread your legs like a good girl." He stepped away, then sat down.

I rose from the floor, then climbed onto the table slowly. My skirt was short, and I knew I was giving him a peek. Settling on the hard surface, I did as he asked and waited for his next command.

"Touch yourself." He leaned back in his seat.

Oh, God, why was this so insanely hot? I spread myself apart, then ran my finger around my clit. I trained my attention on him as I continued, a soft little moan escaping me as I quivered beneath my touch.

Silently, he stood, then reached behind the chair and produced a vibrator.

"On your hands and knees." He approached me as I shifted to all fours. "I asked you last night, and I'll ask you again, who has fucked this cunt?"

Even with his voice disguised, I caught the anger in his tone.

He shoved the toy inside me, and I lurched forward. The vibrator turned on, sending delicious tingles of pleasure through me.

"Only the names I gave you last night." I moaned as he thrust it inside my slick walls.

He picked up the pace, my body quivering as he continued. To my surprise, he pulled it out, then tugged my legs out from beneath me. I hit the table with a thud, pain shooting through my breasts with the impact.

He flipped me over onto my back as though I weighed nothing, then pushed my knees up to my chest, exposing me fully before he shoved the toy inside me again.

"This pussy is mine, little girl."

Panting, I replied, "Only yours." Hell, if he kept this up, I would happily do anything he wanted me to. My core clenched the vibrator, and my back arched off the table.

"Unless I tell you otherwise." He pulled out the toy again.

The door opened, and another guy walked in wearing the same dark clothes and mask.

"Fuck her."

It was quickly becoming clear who was in charge. "Wait, what?" I scrambled backward, but the second masked figure grabbed my ankles and tugged me to the table's edge. I was down for a threesome, but a warning would have been nice.

The leader returned to his seat, then sat down. The other unbuttoned and unzipped his slacks, freeing his thick cock. In seconds, he removed a condom, ripped open the wrapper, then rolled it on.

"Take her from behind," he said from his seat.

I looked over at the guy in the chair before the other one roughly flipped me over, then his hands groped my hips. A moan escaped me as he shoved his cock inside my slick walls. I peeked over at the leader watching as his buddy fucked me. Apparently, that's what he was into. Fine. As long as I had some fun, too.

The sound of our bodies slapping together, and the scent of our arousal filled the room. I looked over again, staring at him as his friend rubbed my clit while he pounded into me. Holy shit, this was off-the-charts hot. I wondered what else he was into. Group sex? Did he want to watch his friend eat me or fuck me in the ass? Damn, all of it sounded good.

"Oh, God." An orgasm uncurled in the pit of my stomach, and my cry of pleasure rang in my ears.

With a few more pushes and pulls, the guy fucking me shuddered and grunted, then stilled. He pulled out, then hopped off the table.

I collapsed as the sound of the door opening and closing reached me. Glancing over my shoulder, I realized the other person had left.

"Is that what you like? Watching?" I asked who I had determined was the leader of the society. But I was still trying to figure him out.

He stood, then pointed to the floor in front of him. "On your knees."

I picked up my thoroughly fucked body and did as he asked. I peered up, curious about who was beneath the mask.

He quickly undid his slacks, then wrapped his fingers around his thick shaft.

"Open."

Oh, hell yes.

He shoved his dick between my lips until he hit the back of my throat. Pulling my hair, he held me in place as he fucked my mouth, choking me every time he slid all the way in.

"You seem to like sucking my cock, Brie. But just remember the reason I'm fucking your mouth and not that pussy is because you don't deserve to get fucked by me. I'll use you, then toss you away like the trash you are."

What was happening? Why did he think he could emotionally rip me to pieces, then throw me to the side as though I were a dirty whore? Was I only good enough to be fucked by his friend? Tears welled in my eyes as his come filled my mouth, and he forced me to swallow.

He finished, tucked himself back into his pants, then left the room without another word. I crumpled onto the floor, his words spearing through my heart. No matter how hard I tried to get my life together, there was always a black hole inside my soul. And for the first time, someone else had seen me for what I truly was. Dark and broken.

Chapter Seventeen

Kane

I'd given Brie one last chance to be honest with me and tell me who else she'd slept with, but again, she'd lied. Even though I'd told Quinn to fuck Brie in front of me, it had taken everything inside me not to beat the hell out of him, but I refused to give her what she wanted. When she'd looked up at me while I was fucking her with the vibrator, the look on her face said it all. She needed me inside her. I'd given her what she'd wanted before, but not again. I would deny her over and over until her self-confidence was shredded, and I mentally destroyed her, just like she had done to me.

I had driven straight home after leaving the society, my need for revenge almost consuming me. It was nothing a fifth of tequila couldn't fix, though. Between Brie's presence at the rental house today, then nearly driving myself mad wanting to fuck her, I needed to blow off some steam.

To my surprise, Q was waiting for me on my porch when I pulled into the driveway.

"Hey," I said as I approached and moved to unlock the front door.

"What in the hell is going on with you, man?" Quinn shoved his hand into his jeans pocket and followed me inside. "You're all over the place with Brie. First, you say she's marked, then you have me fuck her in front of you. It's obvious that you can't make up your mind about her. She's making you crazy."

As I slipped off my shoes, I answered him with my silence, then made my way to the kitchen. Quinn pulled up a chair to the round dining table while I opened the cabinet and placed two glasses on the black granite counter. Locating the bottle of tequila, I poured us a double shot, then brought them to the table and sat down across from him.

Wide-eyed, he took one. "If you're into the tequila, something has you torn the hell up."

He had no fucking clue how messed up I'd been since I had laid eyes on Brie this term.

I drained every last drop, the alcohol burning the back of my throat. Shuddering, I stared at him. "It's complicated."

He slammed his shot, then set the glass down. "Then uncomplicate it, and tell me what the fuck is going on. Do you or don't you want Brie?"

I leaned back in my chair. "Both."

Quinn grimaced. "That shit won't fly with me right now. I've never seen you as hot and cold as you have been. Your temper flares up, then you're all cool again. You look like you're not sleeping much, and your game has been off. What gives, Kane? You've got too much riding on another good year. Is the pressure too intense?"

"Nah. It's not that." I got up and grabbed the bottle of alcohol, then refilled our glasses.

We drank the additional shots, and I took a deep breath. "Not one word of this to anyone, motherfucker." I gave Quinn a pointed look.

Quinn raised his hands in surrender. "You've told me shit before, and I've always kept my trap shut."

That was true. Quinn had been a loyal friend.

The alcohol eased my thoughts, and I drummed my fingers against my thigh. I chuckled as I realized I hadn't changed out of my clothes and into something more comfortable yet.

"I know Brie." There, I said it.

Quinn's brows shot up to his hairline. "Seriously? Why the hell didn't you just say so in the first place?"

"Because it's complicated, and I don't want anyone to know. She's from my past, and she knows shit about me."

"Like what kind of shit, Kane?" Quinn's tone grew serious.

I rubbed my slightly stubbled jawline, buying myself a moment. "Like the kind of shit that could make me lose my football career, family, and most likely, my friends."

Quinn let out a low whistle. "That's intense, dude."

"It is. But ... I've tried to get her to tell me the truth, but she keeps denying it. She hasn't changed. She's lying through her teeth to save her own ass." I grabbed the bottle, refilled our glasses, then downed the tequila. With each drink, I was finally able to relax.

"How long ago was it?"

"Five and a half years. It's been almost six years since I saw her until she bopped right onto campus all gorgeous and happy as if nothing had ever happened. She fucked me over, then went on to live a great life."

"I'm not trying to fuck with you, man, but are you sure she remembers you? I mean, hell, we've all changed in the looks department. Some of us for the better ..." He gave me a wistful glance. "Some not." He cracked a grin, then laughed.

"I don't look that much different. I mean, I'm taller and more filled out." I gave him a half shrug.

Quinn jumped up, nearly sending his chair flying behind him. "Show me a picture. I bet you look a lot different."

I shook my head, realizing that this wasn't up for negotiation. This motherfucker would push me until I gave him what he wanted. "Fine."

"Good. I'll be back after I take a piss, and don't give me some lame photo that no one can see you in. I want to see all the sexy you were ..." He paused, then counted on his fingers. "At fifteen." He threw his head back and laughed, clearly shit-faced.

But so was I. I grabbed my phone from my back pocket and searched for some old photos of when I first landed in foster care with Mom and Dad. Staring at the screen, I realized I wasn't smiling in the picture at all. I was a terrified, scrawny kid with sandy blonde hair. Over the years, my hair had turned brown, and I'd grown about five more inches. I sure as hell wasn't scrawny anymore, either.

Shit, maybe I had changed more than I thought I had. I'd worked so hard to block out those years. I enlarged the image, attempting to clear my vision as I really looked at fifteen-year-old me. It was right before my facial reconstructive surgery to fix my broken jaw and nose. I gulped over the ball of emotions that had lodged itself in my throat as I spotted the tiny scars on my upper and lower lip. How had I managed not to remember? Apparently, working my ass off to block out the pain had worked.

"All right, let me see."

I quickly minimized the image, still trapped in the wake of the aftermath of the dark memories, then handed the phone to Quinn.

"Bitch, you look nothing like this." Quinn held up the cell for me to see.

"You're right." A heavy weight settled on my shoulders. If I didn't recognize that kid anymore, maybe Brie hadn't, either. It was time that I found out, though. I had to shut the door on the ghosts in my life once and for all. Even if it cost me everything.

Chapter Eighteen

Kane

I was about to fucking lose my mind. Each moment I talked myself out of finally confronting Brie face-to-face, my stomach churned, and I wondered if I would be able to keep my lunch down.

Coach blew the whistle on the late-afternoon practice, and I removed my helmet as Quinn, Sterling, Jagger, and Anderson hurried over to me.

"Guess who's back?" Quinn offered me a fist bump.

The other guys punched me in the arm for dialing in my shit on the field again. Maybe my decision to talk to Brie had cleared my thoughts enough to stay focused in practice.

"Man, your throws were like fucking butter," Sterling said, drawing his hand back and tossing an imaginary ball into the air.

"It felt damn good. Hopefully, I'm on point Saturday." I removed my helmet and wiped the sweat off my forehead with my gloved palm.

"You will be. Whatever was fucking with you seems to be taken care of," Jagger added, grinning at us. "Playoffs, here we come."

"Isn't this your last year?" Quinn asked Jagger. "You're a senior, right?"

"Nah. I've got one more season ahead of me. After the accident, I took a light class load when I returned." Jagger's eyes held a faraway expression.

"Sweet!" I slapped Jagger on the back. "Not about your accident, but that you're with us for another year. I think we've got the best team the university has seen in a long-ass time."

Sterling broke out into "We Are the Champions" by Queen, and we all joined in, some loudly singing off-key.

I laughed as we headed toward the locker room, then I remembered that I might be kissing all of this goodbye. My throat tightened with fear. I was playing Russian roulette with my future, and it fucking sucked. Football wasn't something I did. It ran through my veins and saved me when I needed it the most. I couldn't sit on the sidelines, watching my life pass me by. Not fucking again.

Quinn elbowed me in the side. "You good, man?"

"Yeah," I muttered. "I need to meet up with someone, so after I shower, I'm out of here."

"No bitches tonight at the society, huh?" Quinn asked.

"Who knows? It depends on how it all plays out," I said, reaching the locker room and pulling open the door. At least some of the guys had already hit the showers, so the place didn't smell as bad.

"Catch up with me later, then." Quinn jogged in the opposite direction and gave me a small wave.

It was too bad that I couldn't wash away the past like I could the sweat and grime that coated my body.

There was a strong possibility that I was turning into a stalker, and Brie was my prey. After I'd checked her class schedule, I sat in my car, watching the cheer squad practice outside of one of the college buildings. I suspected the grass provided a softer landing than the track around the football field. What I hadn't really paid attention to was the fact that Brie was a flyer. I'm sure I probably noticed at some point, but it hadn't registered in my brain. Plus, when they practiced, I was normally on the field.

Watching her get thrown in the air, then get caught by some dude, wasn't sitting right with me. His hands were all over her ass. Jealousy reared its ugly head, and I shifted in my seat, uncomfortable with the sudden change in my emotions. I'd been clear when I told her she couldn't fuck anyone else unless I demanded it, but even watching Quinn make her come had pissed me off to no end.

I cracked my neck, wondering what the hell was wrong with me because the little shit who was palming her ass to hold her steady was pissing me off, too. It was probably the only action the guy got, and I should give him a break. I massaged my shoulders. They were tight as hell with the stress of finally confronting her, once and for all.

Half an hour later, Brie's practice was over, and she headed to her Lexus. I'd planned on following her home at a distance, then knocking on her door. It would be best if our conversation didn't go down in public.

I kept my eyes trained on her as a tall, blonde-haired guy approached her. He pulled her in for a big hug, but her arms remained at her sides. Curious, I climbed out of my Jaguar. I was parked about five cars away from her, with a good view, and I could hear what they were saying.

"What are you doing here?" she asked, attempting to take a step back.

"What do you mean, baby? I'm here to see you. Haven't you missed me?" the douchebag asked.

No. She hasn't.

"You should leave." Brie attempted to pull her arm away, but his fingers dug into her bicep.

"Don't be like that, Brie. You know what I can do to you."

"Marc, stop. I don't want you here. Go home. Live your life and leave mine alone." She stomped on his foot, then jerked her arm away. Brie marched off toward her car, frustrated.

I snickered. At least she held her ground.

Marc jogged after her, then slid his arm around her waist. The son of a bitch wasn't taking no for an answer very well. Brie elbowed him in the side, almost doubling Marc over. The moment she reached her car, he slammed her against the driver's door. He sneered at her, then tucked a strand of hair behind her ear. He whispered something, and the color drained from her face. Marc placed a forceful kiss on her mouth, and I fucking came unglued. Brie attempted to shove him away, but he'd pinned her with his body, and she couldn't move.

My nostrils flared. It was one thing for me to screw with her, but this guy needed to back the fuck up. Before I realized what was happening, my feet carried me across the parking lot to where Marc and Brie were. Somewhere inside me, a switch flipped, and everything that Brie had done to me faded momentarily into the background.

"Is there a problem, Brie?" I asked, my tone carrying a warning.

"Who are you?" Marc turned to me. He straightened his shoulders, and I could almost see the peacock feathers fanning out. His light brown eyes were trained on me, assessing the situation. Marc was short and stocky, but he wasn't a match for me, but only one of us knew that.

"A friend. Who are you?" I resisted the urge to punch him in his fucking nose.

"Her boyfriend, so you need to step off, motherfucker." He quirked a confrontational brow at me.

"Not from what I can see. Brie?" I looked around Marc at her. "Is he with you?"

"No. Marc isn't anyone that I want to talk to." She'd taken advantage of me showing up and moved away from the car and us.

Good girl. "You heard her, *Marc.*" My fist clenched and

unclenched. I was itching to hit this asshole, but I had to protect my hands at the same time.

Marc closed the gap between us, then poked me in the chest. "I'm here now, so you need to step off. Brie and I have been together for a few years. Much longer than she's known you."

I slapped his hand away. "Is that so?" I leaned down, a shit-eating grin slipping into place. "If she's yours, why did she fuck someone else Sunday afternoon?" I whispered, glancing at Brie, but she hadn't heard me. Marc's fist flew toward my face, and I jerked back in time. Catching him entirely off guard, I grabbed his wrist, stopping his throw mid-air. "I would highly recommend that you leave. This is your only warning," I growled, before shoving him backward. *Brie is mine.* Startled by the intrusive thought, I pushed it out of my head. I had to stay focused.

Marc's cheeks turned bright red as he stumbled, nearly landing on his ass. As I had expected, he came at me again, but this time, I let loose. Jagger would have been proud as I landed two hits to Marc's gut. As he doubled over, my fist connected with his jaw. Before the fight had even started, I'd finished it. He was now moaning like a little bitch on the ground.

"Shit. Kane, are you okay?" Brie ran over to me, taking my hand in hers and inspecting it. "You should get some ice on that right away." She glanced up, our eyes connecting. "We should probably talk," she said softly. "Why don't you come over? Give me an hour."

There it was. I figured she'd finally put together who I was by her expression. The shit was about to get real.

"Get in your car, and I'll stay here to make sure Marc doesn't follow you home." Wasn't I the nice guy? Little did she know that I'd been following her and had been in her house while she was asleep.

"Thank you." She hurried to her Lexus, climbed in, and locked the doors.

Good girl. At least she had enough sense to make sure he didn't climb in the damn car with her.

As she pulled away, my gaze landed on Marc again. "Where are you from?" I kept my distance in case he wanted to grab my ankle and jerk my leg out from underneath me.

"Tennessee. Brie and I went to high school together. Man, you don't want her. She's a fucking mental mess." He rolled over to his hands and knees, slowly picking himself up off the ground.

"Why is that?" My curiosity was getting the better of me now. Maybe he would unknowingly offer up a bit of information about her.

Marc flashed me a cocky grin. "She's a great fuck. It's the only reason I keep her around."

Careful. I'm about to put you in the hospital for saying that shit about her. I had to get ahold of myself, and quickly. Brie was the enemy. *Tell your heart that.*

"So, you came all the way from Tennessee to fuck her? You're a desperate little shit." I chuckled, thoroughly enjoying myself. "Why are you really here?"

Marc held his side, attempting to straighten. He grimaced, then briefly stared at his feet before he charged at me.

His head hit my stomach full force, knocking me down. The air whooshed from my lungs as my back landed on the asphalt. Marc straddled me, then threw a punch into my face. Red and black dots began to fill my vision, and I rapidly blinked as I managed to block his next hit. I bucked my hips off the ground, throwing Marc off-balance. It was all I needed to regain the advantage, but he'd fucked up. Memories of being held down and beaten bombarded my thoughts as I began to slip away from reality.

"Where is she, boy?" Elder Jasper said, kicking me in the side with his booted foot. "I know that you helped Lyndsay escape. Where is she?"

I curled into a ball and covered my head with my arms as the hits kept coming. Squeezing my eyes closed, I did my best to focus on football plays, but it was no use. The pain was too intense.

A strong hand jerked me backward, reality flickering in and out. I scrambled to stand, my breathing ragged.

"Son! Son!" Coach yelled at me.

Footsteps reached my ears before Jagger stood in front of me. He slapped my cheek a few times, then I realized he was saying something.

"Kane. Goddammit, Kane!"

I jerked away from him, the limp body on the ground coming into view.

"Get him out of here," Coach ordered.

Jagger grabbed my arm and began to run across the parking lot. "Get in," he said as we reached his truck.

What's happening?

The roar of the engine pulled my thoughts from my rage-induced fog.

"Where are we going?" I glanced over my shoulder, watching Dad talk on his cell phone.

"Coach had to call 9-1-1. You almost killed him, Kane." Jagger shot me a what-the-fuck look. "We're going to my place. I'll get you cleaned up, then give you a fucking alibi. Not sure what I'll say yet, but ..." His lips thinned, confusion washing over his face. "Jesus, Kane. I would expect that shit from me, but you?"

I stared out the window, trying to piece together what had just happened. One minute, Marc charged at me, and the next, I was back *there*. Swallowing over the stench of my past, I glanced at my knuckles. They were slick with Marc's blood. What the hell had I done?

The gut-wrenching truth stabbed me in the chest over and over. Little sweat beads formed on the nape of my neck, and my pulse throbbed wildly. There was no way that I could hide from it any longer. I thought the hate would protect me, but I was so wrong. I would never stop loving Brie.

Chapter Nineteen

Kane

Still in a daze, I followed Jagger into his house. I suspected that Ari had helped spruce up the place. There were a few pieces of artwork along with a coffee table, a matching brown leather recliner, and a couch that complemented the dark wood floors.

"Holy shit," Ari said, walking out of the kitchen and into the living room. She set her drink down and hurried over to us. "What in the hell happened?" Ari gave us a bewildered look.

"Babe, can you get some ice packs for his eye and lip while he washes his hands?" Jagger placed a kiss on her forehead.

"Of course. Kane, you can clean up at the sink in the kitchen." Ari motioned for me to join her. "Your eye is swelling. Who did you fuck up?" She gave me a weary smile.

I turned on the faucet and held my hands beneath the warm water, my mind reeling from the events from not even an hour ago. "Some fucker named Marc." I glanced over my shoulder at Ari.

"Why?" She placed an ice pack and towel on the counter.

"He was messing with Brie."

Ari's blue eyes widened. "You're into Brie? Or ... ?"

I appreciated how she kept the question open for another possibility.

"I don't like how he forced himself on her," I muttered. *Because what you've done is better.*

"Hmm." She folded her arms over her chest, studying me. "Does she know how you feel?"

Irritation coursed through me. "I'll talk to her when I'm ready."

"I'm not going to say anything, Kane. I swear. I like her a lot, so if some guy is giving her a bad time, I want to make sure she's okay." Ari grabbed a hand towel and gave it to me.

"Fuck." I patted my knuckles dry, surveying the damage. I flexed my fingers. They were sore, but nothing was broken. "I was supposed to stop by Brie's place to check on her."

Jagger strolled in, carrying a first aid kit with him. "That's a no, man. We have to come up with a plan."

Ari's brows knitted together. "I'll go see her while you two figure things out. I'll let her know you're with Jagger."

"Thanks, babe." Jagger pressed a kiss to her mouth, then Ari gave me a little wave as she left.

"I wasn't sure if we needed this." Jagger held up the first aid kit. "Looks like your hands are busted up and bruised, but nothing too bad. Hell, I've done worse." He walked to the fridge. "Beer or something stronger? I'll take you home if you want to drink."

"Shit, my car is still at school."

"Ari and I can pick it up, or I'll take you to get it in the morning. Either way, it's all good."

"Something stronger, then." I leaned against the counter, watching as he made a rum and Coke. When he was finished, he picked up our glasses and walked into the living room. Joining him, I sat down on the couch, my body aching from Marc slamming me onto the parking lot, but I'd been through worse. Much worse.

"Spill, dude. As I said, that's shit I would do. Not you." Jagger settled into the recliner, staring at me expectantly.

I gulped down my drink as though it would squelch the fire burning inside of me.

"I've told Quinn a little bit, but ..." I stared at the floor, then at Jagger. "Listen, you and I haven't ever been close. When I was interested in Ari, you made it clear we weren't friends, so how do I know I can trust you?"

Jagger's eyes flashed with respect. "I've got your back on the field, and I've got your back now. You need me as a witness. Marc will probably press charges unless we can get in front of the situation."

I blew out a sigh and shoved my fingers through my hair. "What I tell you, though, not a fucking word to anyone, especially your girlfriend." If I planned to share even a hint of what the hell was going on, I had to make sure he kept his mouth shut. Oddly enough, I trusted him.

"It won't be the first secret I've kept from her." Jagger took a drink, then rested the glass on his jeaned thigh. "My uncle is in an MC, and there's plenty of shit I can't discuss with her."

I nodded. He understood. "All right. Then I'll trust you, especially if you're going to lie for me."

Jagger gave a half shrug. "As I said, I've got your back on and off the field."

After another long gulp, I set the glass on the coffee table. "From what I can tell, Marc is here from Tennessee and said he was Brie's boyfriend. Brie didn't agree, though."

"How the hell did you end up jumping in?" Jagger asked.

"He hugged her, but she didn't hug him back, so I wanted to keep an eye on the situation for a minute. Marc grabbed her arm and practically dragged her across the parking lot to her car, then pinned her against it. He kissed her, and she tried to shove him off. That's when I jumped in. I told Marc he needed to leave Brie alone. He objected and thought it was a good idea to throw the first punch. He didn't get the last." I smirked, feeling a a bit cocky about putting the little shit in his place.

Jagger's phone rang, and he removed it from his back pocket. He stared at the screen, then at me. "It's Coach."

He answered, staring at me. I would say one thing about Jagger. He was intimidating as hell sometimes.

"Hey, Coach." He paused. "Yeah, he's with me. We're working on what to say, and I'll back him up. Don't worry about that. We're not going to lose him on the field."

Jagger frowned. "No shit?"

I scooted to the edge of the couch, my stomach in knots from the suspense.

"Well, from what Kane has said, he was getting rough with Brianne Langston. She's new to Whitmore and a cheerleader. It looked like self-defense if you ask me. Kane said he asked Marc to back off, and I saw Marc take a swing at him." Jagger listened for a minute then. "Yeah, I saw the entire thing."

I swallowed, grateful that Jagger had just lied for me. A part of me wondered if we would end up as decent friends after all this crap was handled.

"You bet. See you tomorrow." Jagger disconnected the call, then placed his phone on the coffee table.

"Marc is in the hospital. You did a fucking number on him, man. His face is busted, and the cops will be here shortly to take our statements, so we need to dial in the last part. Tell me what happened so we get our stories straight."

I massaged the back of my neck, the tension returning almost as quickly as it had left. "I told Brie to go home and that I would stay with Marc and make sure that he didn't follow her. At that point, he was on the ground. I'd landed a few punches to his gut, then his jaw. I don't think I really did any damage until after Brie left. Once she was gone, he charged me. His head rammed into my stomach, and I went down. He hopped on, got his shots in, then I got him off me. It only took me a second to flip the tables and pin him down, but I don't remember much after that."

Jagger placed his ankle on the opposite knee, wearing a serious expression. "Okay, I'll corroborate all of that. As I said to Coach, sounds like self-defense to me, and that's the angle we're using. If there's a problem and Marc presses charges, then I'll talk to my uncle in the MC, and see if he can take care of shit. But I don't think it will come to that. I just like backup plans." Jagger grinned at me.

"You and me both."

The doorbell rang. "Showtime, Kane." Jagger stood, then crossed the room to answer the door.

"Showtime," I muttered. At least my busted eye and lip would support the self-defense plan. Marc did take the first swing, which would also help what we were about to tell the cops. Even though Jagger said he had my back, I wondered why. We weren't close friends. Hell, we were barely friends at all. I just hoped like hell if he called in a return favor, it wasn't some crazy shit. Guess only time would tell.

Once the police questioned Jagger and me, I had Jagger take me back to my car. I'd only had one drink, so I was good to drive. I was more worried about seeing through a swollen eye.

My pulse quickened as I walked up the sidewalk to Brie's place. I wiped my sweaty palms on my jeans, mentally scolding myself for being nervous. She couldn't have any idea that she was under my skin, or she would flip shit on me. Maybe she would even stoop to blackmail when she found out how much I fucked up her ex-boyfriend.

Before I reached the front of the house, the door opened, and Brie stood in front of me with a concerned expression.

"Kane?"

"Yeah, hey." *Great opener, motherfucker.* Her long, blonde hair was wet, and she tugged on her oversized Whitmore University hoodie that hung off her frame and nearly hid the black bootie shorts she was wearing. The lingering scent of her watermelon bodywash tickled my senses.

My dick sprang to life, remembering her cries as Quinn fucked her. Her sweet little pussy clenched around the vibrator ...

"Marc did that?" She reached toward my face, then caught herself and stepped back, motioning for me to come in.

I almost felt bad for her. Brie had just invited the same man she feared into her home, the same man she wanted to screw behind the skull mask, and the same man who had saved her from her ex. I was twisted and fucked up on so many levels. But one thing had become crystal clear. As much as I hated Brie, I still loved her, which had my head and heart messed up more than anything else.

"Yeah. I should tell you what happened after you left." I closed the door behind me, then flipped the bolt and lock. "Have you had any more problems?"

"Um, no. It's been quiet since the alarm system was installed. I will say that I'm sleeping better." She flipped her hair behind her shoulder. "Do you want a beer or ..." She giggled. "No, actually just a soda. I don't drink much, so I don't have any beer." Her cheeks turned a pretty shade of pink before she walked away and into the small kitchen.

"Sure," I said, reminding myself why I was there. But the fact that we were alone, and she hadn't called me Jacob, told me that Quinn was right. The lighting was good in the house, and I wasn't wearing a hat to hide my identity, and Brie still hadn't recognized me.

"Have a seat. I know we need to talk, so we might as well get comfortable." She opened the fridge, produced two cans, then settled in at the opposite end of the couch. "What happened? It looks like he got you good." Her gaze traveled to my hands. "Oh, God. Did you break anything?" She leaned over and gently held my fingers, examining them.

A jolt of electricity shot through me with her touch. "No. It looks worse than it is." Over the next several minutes, I explained what had happened and that Marc was in the hospital.

"I'm so sorry I got you messed up in all of this." Tears welled in her eyes. "Marc is my problem, not yours."

Marc's words floated through my mind. "Brie, he said something ... he said that you were mentally fucked up. What did he mean?"

Brie jumped off the couch. She folded her arms across her chest and began pacing. "He said that?" Her voice cracked with her question.

I nodded, waiting for her to explain.

"He knows secrets about me that not many people do." She chewed on her thumbnail.

Here we go. I wanted to yell at her to tell me what had happened, why she never came back for me, but I reeled in my anger. Brie was finally about to confess her sins, and I wanted to hear every word of it. With her following words, I found myself speechless. It wasn't even close to what I had thought she would say.

Chapter Twenty

Brie

I stared at Kane, wondering if I could trust him. There was only one way to tell. I could feed him information about me a little at a time to see how he would react. If he helped me with Marc, maybe I could count on him. Maybe not, but my gut told me it would be worth a shot.

He stilled and looked at me. *God, he's hot.* His T-shirt stretched across his muscular chest perfectly, clinging to every dip and valley of his sculpted shoulders. The scent of his spicy, woodsy cologne sent my hormones into overdrive. Kane Cooper was insta-wet kind of gorgeous. *Focus, girl. Focus. This is not the time.* "He blackmailed me until I moved here. Those kinds of secrets."

"What the actual fuck? Apparently, the bastard deserved to get his ass beat even more than I had realized." Kane rubbed his clean-shaven jawline.

"It's a long and complicated story. He needs to leave. I refuse to be controlled like that again." I tapped my nails against the soda can, distressed.

"What does he have on you, Brie?" he asked softly. "I can handle him. I just need to understand why I need to."

"As I said, it's not your problem." If he knew I had to cuff myself at night, he'd think I was a head case, too. I hated to admit it, but Marc was right. I was a fucked-up mess. Alida and my family had no clue about why I had such horrible night terrors. "Plus, you could turn around and blackmail me, too." My jaw clenched before a nervous giggle slipped out. "Then I might have to kill you both."

Kane's face drained of color. "You already did." He stood, and his shoulders stiffened with tension. "I wanted to tell you what went down. I have to get home and study."

I gaped at him as I watched him walk out of the front door without another word. What the actual hell had just happened? We were being civil, then he stormed out of the house. More than that, what had he meant I'd killed him already? Kane was clearly alive. I might have some issues, but I could tell reality apart from fantasy.

I locked up and armed the alarm system, relieved that I had it since Marc was still in town.

"Dammit. I was supposed to tell him ..." I released a string of swear words, frustration and anger ripping through me. The entire day had been a complete shit show. First, the crap with Marc, then Arianna stopped by to check on me. She had no idea how much I appreciated her, but it had completely taken me by surprise. Hell, I'd just worked up my nerve to talk to Kane.

"Fuck you, Marc. I refuse to be controlled again." I groaned and balled my fists. It was only nine in the evening, but I had to focus on something other than what had unfolded earlier. It was eleven in Tennessee, so I couldn't call my parents to say hi either. My coursework was all caught up, which left television.

My stomach flip-flopped as my thoughts returned to Kane. Somehow, I had to make things up to him. I began considering how to fix the mess I'd helped make while I cuffed myself to the bed, then turned on Bridgerton.

After several attempts to pay attention to the show, I uncuffed myself, then messaged Gabby.

Sup?

Almost immediately, the little grey dots bounced up and down.

I'm bored. There's not even any good porn on. LOL.

I snickered. She should try the society. It was way better than porn. My fingers flew across the keyboard, smiling.

Do you want to come over? Bring your bag in case you want to crash here.

Seconds later, she replied.

Hell yeah. See you in twenty, bitch.

I hopped out of bed, hoping I had enough snacks and soda. After a quick perusal, I texted her again.

I have no alcohol. Can you buy some, and I'll pay you back?

A huge grin eased across my face as I read her response.

We have plenty here. I'll bring some ciders and rum. Got Coke?

I stared in my fridge, then updated her.

Yup, and Dr. Pepper, chips, salsa, ... oh, we can make nachos!

I feel like you're planning for the munchies, not drinking. LOL.

Whatevs. Get your cute little ass over here. I laughed, throwing her words back at her.

"Why haven't I indulged more? It takes off the edge." I took a sip of the drink that Gabby had so expertly made.

"I have no idea. As you could tell from all the liquor at the house, we girls drink. But, when everyone's boyfriend or date is over, then it's just a party. You should join us sometime. You can crash in my room." She folded her legs beneath her, then rubbed a palm on her thigh. Her navy sweater looked warm and comfy. I made a mental note to go shopping for warmer clothes other than the few sweaters I owned. My wardrobe was made for Tennessee winters, not Oregon's.

"It would be fun." I tucked my leg beneath me, shifting on the couch. "Are you seeing anyone? I've not asked before." I frowned, wondering if I was nosy or a bad friend.

Gabby sighed. "No. Ari and Teagan are in serious relationships, but I've not found my person. You?"

I snorted. "Girl, I haven't told you about the shit that's going down. If this is my life, I'll never date!"

Gabby's mouth dropped open. "You're holding out on me? That's completely unacceptable." She waved her hand in the air, emphasizing her point. "Spill. The. Deets. Now." She gave me a pointed look.

I took another drink, enjoying the fact that my body was finally relaxing after such a stressful day. "Marc, my ex, is in town."

"What?" Gabby jerked her arm, her rum and Coke splashing over the rim and onto her navy yoga pants.

I hopped up, collected a hand towel from the kitchen, and gave it to her.

"It gets better." Settling back in on the couch, I continued. "After cheer practice, I was walking to my car when I spotted him standing by it. I swear to God that my stomach did a hundred backflips. Like, I felt sick the moment I saw him."

Gabby's lips pursed. I wasn't sure if she was intent on listening or trying not to talk until I shared more.

"Anyway, at first, he was being sweet, which was a red flag right there. He told me how much he'd missed me, and how for the last six weeks he hadn't been able to stop thinking about me, he loves me, blah, blah, blah."

Gabby covered her mouth and giggled. "You're clearly into him, Brie. Maybe you should reconsider."

I laughed, appreciating her sarcasm. "I told Marc that I hadn't thought about him at all and that he needed to go back to Tennessee and move on."

"Oh, boy," Gabby said.

"Exactly." I ran my finger around the rim of my glass, deep in thought. "It made him mad, then he started getting a little rough. He grabbed my arm, demanding that we get back together."

"Oh girl, no, he didn't. He's already on my shit list for black-mailing you." Gabby's forehead creased.

"Well, apparently, he's on someone else's now, too. When Marc got forceful with me, he slammed me against my car and pinned me against the door. I tried to get him to calm down and explained that if he wanted me in his life again this was the wrong way to go about it." I rolled my eyes. "Like I'd ever give him the time of day, but ..." I took a long drink and wiped my mouth with the back of my hand. "Gabby, he's here to try to transfer to Whitmore. I never considered he would be a problem when I moved to Whitmore, so I told him where I was going." I slapped a palm against my forehead, realizing my stupid mistake.

"No. Fucking. Way." Gabby set her drink down on the end table before she shot up, pacing. "We have to stop him, Brie. You're just starting to settle in and make friends."

"I know. This was my fresh start. But I don't think we actually need to do anything." I tilted my head, watching her expression as I shared the next part. "Kane Cooper stepped in."

"Oh, hell. That's saucy." She collected her drink and plopped down on the couch again, her attention trained on me like a hawk's on its prey.

"Kane left here about an hour and a half ago."

"Kane Cooper was here? Jesus, he's so fucking hot." Gabby fanned herself, pretending to swoon like the Southern girls used to do during the *Gone with the Wind* days.

"Agreed, but it wasn't a hookup; he wanted to let me know that Marc is in the hospital."

Gabby's eyes nearly bugged out of her head.

"While I was still there, Marc threw a punch at Kane, but Kane dropped him to the ground like Marc was a fucking rag doll. Kane told me to get into my car and go home, that he would stay with Marc and make sure he didn't follow me."

Gabby placed her hand on her heart. "Brie, that's so sweet."

We giggled, feeling the full effects of the alcohol.

"I appreciated his help. I mean, I would have been very willing to fuck him properly ... I mean thank him properly." I wiggled my brows, breaking into a fit of laughter.

"If you do, I need all of the deets." Gabby motioned for me to continue. "But go on. You were telling me how Marc landed in the hospital."

"Oh. Yeah. So, Marc got up and charged Kane. I'm not sure how it all went down, but by the bruises on Kane's face, Marc got in some good shots."

Brie grimaced. "Damn."

"Right? Kane must have gotten the upper hand again because he beat the shit out of Marc. That's how he ended up in the hospital."

Gabby released a low whistle. "Just so I get this all straight ... Kane came over to tell you that?"

"Yup. I mean, he didn't have to." I squirmed in my seat. "I'd asked him to come over so we could talk, but he was a no-show. Then, Ari showed up. She explained that Jagger had taken Kane to their place so they could work out their story and Kane could get cleaned up."

"Wow, Jagger's helping. I tell you what, Jagger has always been seriously hot but also hot-tempered. I think Ari has tamed her bad boy enough for him not to be such an asshole."

"I'll take your word for it since I've only met him once." I worried my lower lip with my teeth. "I wonder if Marc will leave. I'm afraid Kane might kill him if he stays. He has his entire future ahead of him. I would hate to be the reason that he lost his football career."

"Brie. That won't happen, and even if it did, Kane's a grown man. He makes his own decisions. If Marc was getting rough with you ... well, I love that Kane stepped in. I will say that he's a bit of a mystery, but so far, he seems like a really good guy."

My gaze narrowed on her. "What do you mean a mystery?"

"He transferred last year, and it was his first year at Whitmore, so all the girls wanted to get to know him, including me." She raised a finger in the air, grinning. "But he's really private about his time before he showed up here. I mean, he talks about football and a bit about his family, but very little. No one has been able to find out much about him."

A beat of silence filled the room. "Sometimes you have to protect your future by burying the past," I whispered.

"Are you talking about Kane or you?" Gabby propped up her elbow on the back of the couch, then rested her head against her fist.

"All I'm saying is that it sounds like he has some bad shit he'd like to leave behind him. I respect that."

A memory of a night terror flickered through my brain. Screams filled my mind, and I clutched my chest.

"Brie, are you okay?" Gabby leaned over and placed her palm on my leg. "You're pale and breathing hard. Talk to me."

I looked up at my friend. "I don't know." I shook my head, attempting to clear my head. "I think I just remembered part of a bad dream." I swallowed hard, my throat suddenly dry and scratchy. "Someone was running, and there were screams." Tears welled in my eyes. "I sound crazy."

"No. You don't. But I have a sneaking suspicion Kane isn't the only one who wants to keep their past buried." She squeezed my hand.

Gabby had no idea how right she was.

Chapter Twenty-One

Kane

I pressed the accelerator of my Jaguar, the speedometer nearly reaching ninety miles an hour as I drove like a bat out of hell, leaving the university in my rearview mirror.

How the fuck had I let my guard down with Brie? I'd been weak while I'd watched Marc mess with her. One minute, I admitted I still loved her, the next, I wanted to fuck her over and laugh as she begged and pleaded for mercy. I'd grown soft and lost sight of the fact that she could ruin my entire life.

The second Brie said I would be able to blackmail her, then she would have to kill both Marc and me, I'd fucking come unglued. Images of that asshole getting rough with her came roaring back. I white-knuckled the steering wheel, willing myself not to turn around and visit the motherfucker in the hospital and finish him off. At the same time, I couldn't get his words out of my head. What in the hell had he meant that she had issues? Maybe Brie hadn't escaped our past as much as I thought.

Jesus, I was fucked up. This girl had flipped me inside out, mentally and emotionally, and I had to get a grip on my life again.

I turned into the gravel parking lot, desperately needing to clear my thoughts. Visiting Madeline's had become much more frequent since Brie had arrived at Whitmore University.

I locked the car, then hurried inside the building, welcoming the acceptance I felt while here. I nearly barked out a laugh. Here I was, visiting a discreet sex club because I had a kink that would send most people running, yet it was safe for me.

"Hi, hon," Madeline said, approaching me in the hall.

"You look gorgeous this evening." I kissed her on the forehead. "Special plans?" Raking my gaze over the fitted black blouse that amplified her full breasts, I wondered if she ever dated or just dedicated her time to the business.

She patted my cheek. "Such a charmer, Kane."

I chuckled as she slipped her arm through mine and led me down the rest of the hall to my room. "Are you sure you want to do this? You've never requested it before."

"Yeah. I'm sure."

Madeline showed me in. Ready to get started, I removed my clothes while Madeline opened the trap door in the floor. I hurried down the ladder and into the pit, then Madeline followed me. I moved my hands behind me, then she slipped on the handcuffs.

"I don't know how you do this, Kane. This hole barely fits two people. It's claustrophobic as hell."

"I know."

Madeline climbed out and disappeared.

I sat down, the cold dirt chilling my bare ass. The cold was nothing, though. I lay down and closed my eyes. Although I was aware that I had been with several different girls at Madeline's, I never saw them. I didn't want to. They had also signed a nondisclosure form, swearing they would never reveal my identity. In fact, Madeline had confided in me that she never used her client's real ages or names. All our files were encrypted on her computer, as well.

Whispers caught my attention, but I kept my eyes closed. Feeling another presence next to me, the creak of the door and the sound of the lock reached my ears, sending my pulse into overdrive.

A warm palm landed on my chest, and I shifted, the handcuffs biting into my wrists.

Chapter Twenty-Two

Kane

"Do you think it will work?" Jagger asked.

The sound of lockers slamming and showers running in the background helped drown out our conversation with the other guys. I sat on the bench next to him. It was funny how Jagger and I had become friends after he'd covered for me with the police.

"The cops aren't charging me with anything, so I figure I'll give it a shot. I have nothing to lose at this point." I slipped on my tennis shoes, then stood.

"As soon as Marc sees you, he'll probably shit his pants and sing like a little fucking birdie. I should go with you, though. Make sure you don't go off the rails again." Jagger pulled on his burgundy Whitmore University T-shirt.

I shoved my hand in my jeans pocket. "I hadn't thought about that. I just want some answers about Brie."

Jagger slapped me on the back. "That's what you have me for, to help you think through shit before you fuck up your entire life." He gave me a lopsided grin. "What time is he getting released from the hospital?"

I pulled my phone out of my backpack and glanced at the clock. "In an hour. He has no idea I'm going to be his ride." I chuckled.

"Actually, you're going to stay out of sight until he's in my truck. No one needs to see you there. I'll let Marc know that the university feels horrible about what happened, and they wanted to send someone to apologize and give him a ride."

I smirked at him. "I feel like you have a lot of experience doing shit like this."

Jagger laughed. "Welcome to my dark side, motherfucker."

Honestly, I was afraid to ask Jagger to elaborate, but at least he was helping me out for the time being.

"Where are we taking him anyway? If he's been staying at a hotel, then we can't talk to him there. If he starts screaming or some shit, it will cause trouble." Jagger pinned me with his questioning gaze.

I wasn't sure it was the most brilliant idea I'd ever had, but downstairs in one of the rooms at the society house would be perfect. No one would be there until later that evening. The one concerning thing, though? Jagger would have questions, and I needed to think of a story before we got there.

"I've got a place."

"Excellent. Let me call Ari and let her know I'll be out for a while, and I'll see her later tonight."

"She's got you on a leash?" I grinned at him as I scooped my backpack off the locker room floor and slung it over one shoulder.

"Asshole, please. It's not a leash. I love and respect her enough to tell her when I'm going to be late so she's not freaked the hell out that I'm dead in a ditch somewhere. Has nothing to do with being controlled. Some dudes would do well to learn the difference."

I stared at him, speechless. Never in a million years would I have guessed that Jagger would be cool about communicating in his relationship. It's clear to the entire world that he's jealous and possessive, but it sounded like he treated her right.

Brie's beautiful face flashed through my thoughts. Maybe at one time, we could have had what Jagger and Ari did. Chances are it wouldn't have worked, given our pasts, but even that opportunity had sailed. *You still love her.* Refusing to give that inner voice any attention, I slapped my hand over its mouth and gave it a swift kick in the ass.

"Meet me in twenty at my truck. I'm parked up the hill." Jagger fished out his phone, then walked to the door.

Although I'd agreed that Marc didn't need to see me when Jagger picked him up from the hospital, I watched shit go down right around the corner from the entrance.

"Hey, Marc." Jagger tipped his head at the female nurse who had wheeled Marc out.

"Are you his ride?" she asked.

"I am. Hopefully, he can get into the truck okay," Jagger replied.

"I'm fine." Marc stood from the chair, shooting Jagger a dirty look.

"Excellent. The university sent me to pick you up."

Marc's eyes narrowed. "Good. They should be kissing my ass after I was nearly beaten to death on their property."

Jagger offered him a tight-lipped smile. "Let's go. I have other shit to do than babysit."

Nice one, Jagger. I chuckled as Marc struggled to get into the truck on his own, but part of it was that Jagger's rig was jacked up and taller than the average by several feet.

Jagger pulled away from the pickup zone, then circled around. I jogged down the parking lot away from the line of cars waiting to load their patients in case Marc started screaming for help when I climbed into the backseat.

The truck stopped, then I jumped in. "Hello, Marc. Glad to see you're up and around." I smirked, then belted myself in as Jagger took off.

Fear wrenched Marc's facial features. "What the fuck? What are you doing here, you lunatic?"

"Don't get your panties twisted. We just want to talk ... somewhere quiet." Jagger's evil grin slipped into place, and for a moment, I was scared for Marc.

"You can't do this! Let me out!" Marc attempted to unlock his door, but Jagger was quicker and hit the button. In minutes, we were flying down the highway at seventy miles an hour. Unless Marc had a death wish, he wouldn't try that shit again.

"Take the Morrison exit," I said to Jagger. I hadn't told him where we were going, so I played backseat driver while I came up with a cover story. Something whispered to me that I could tell Jagger all about the society, and he would never say a word. I sure as hell got tired of keeping secrets, but my secrets weren't what this was all about. It was Brie's.

Other than giving Jagger directions, I kept my mouth shut and listened to Marc whimper and beg us not to kill him. How in the hell Brie had put up with this asshole was beyond me. I was ready to chuck him out of the vehicle, and it had only been fifteen minutes.

After what felt like an eternity, we reached the society's house, and Jagger parked in the back. I hopped out, then waited for Marc to hobble out, as well.

"Where are we?" Jagger asked under his breath.

"A friend's place. I keep an eye on it when he's out of town." Not the truth, but not a lie.

I pressed my thumb to the keypad, then the door popped open. Ushering Marc and Jagger inside, I followed, then secured the entrance.

The hall was dark, with only built-in lights near the floor to lead the way. I had already decided what room we would use to talk to Marc, and I nearly barked out a laugh as I unlocked it, then strolled in.

Jagger's eyes widened as the lights automatically turned on. "Holy shit. Some friend, dude."

Marc visibly trembled as he looked around at the torture rack, whips hanging from the wall, and a chair with arm and ankle straps to secure someone.

"Sit." I pointed to the seat.

"I don't know what you want from me, but this is fucked up." Marc sat on the edge of the chair, the color draining from his cheeks.

I folded my arms in front of my chest. "I want to know why you're here, then I want information."

Jagger remained by the door, his fingers clenching and unclenching. He glowered at Marc. "Answer him, or you'll be strapped down to that rack."

Marc gawked at him. "Nope, that's not necessary. I'll talk. I was looking to transfer to Whitmore. The last six weeks without Brie have been hell. I want her back."

A low growl rumbled in my throat. "She's not yours to have." I paced in front of him. "If she's so mental, then why do you want her?"

Marc held up his hand, and I finally saw all the bruises on his arm. They matched the black and blue on his face. He looked like a fucked-up Cabbage Patch doll.

"Don't worry. After this, I don't want to attend Whitmore."

"Good. Because if we see you on campus ever again, getting your ass beat will be nothing. You stay away from Brie. Don't text her, don't call her, don't look at her. Are we clear?" My tone was sharp and unfriendly.

Marc nodded in agreement.

I stepped up, our noses nearly touching. "Say it out loud, motherfucker."

"I'll never text, call, touch, or see Brie again. I swear."

I straightened, hoping like hell he wasn't lying. "Excellent. Now, what's up with her?"

Whatever he was using to blackmail her with, I wanted to know. It could come in handy.

"She sees a psychiatrist for night terrors. They're so bad she jumped out of a second-story window. Her parents found her screaming and crying, hanging on to the ledge of the house. She has them all the time, but to keep her safe, she handcuffs herself to the bed."

I caught myself before I frowned. I'd seen the handcuff when I'd watched her sleep. Night terrors could be some serious shit. It sounded like whatever was haunting her dreams had nearly killed her, and I wanted to know what had her all fucked up.

"What are the night terrors about?"

Marc shrugged. "She doesn't know. Sometimes she can remember bits and pieces, but most of the time, she can't. Brie has a shit ton of anxiety, although most people don't know that about her. I was shocked she wanted to move from Tennessee to attend a college in Oregon. Only her parents, her psychiatrist, and I know about the nightmares, but she's been terrified at the thought of leaving home."

"That's what you were blackmailing her with?" My hand clenched, ready to slam my fist into the asshole's face again.

"She's scared someone will find out. It will ruin any chances of her having a normal life experience. We're from a small town, and that information would travel faster than a wildfire with sixty-mile winds behind it."

"So, what's wrong with you? I mean, blackmailing a girl to be with you is sketch. You got a tiny dick or some shit?" Jagger asked.

Marc glared at him. "You think you're so funny."

"Answer him," I demanded.

"In middle school, I was an outcast. I was bullied and picked on, and I swore it would never happen again. When I learned Brie's secret, I realized it was the perfect plan. She was the most popular girl at not only our school but at several in the area. Every guy wanted her, and every girl wanted to be her. So did I. She helped me reset my image and be someone." Marc gave us a half shrug, as if blackmail was something he did all the time.

My hands itched to beat the shit out of him again.

"Wait, how did you find out about her night terrors?" Jagger asked, crossing his arms over his chest and rocking on his heels.

"I was sitting behind her mom at a restaurant when she talked to one of her friends about Brie. She wasn't sure how to help her."

Jesus Christ—spying, too? Internally, I cringed. Before they'd learned about my passion for football, my parents had been in that same spot, struggling to deal with me.

"But there's more," Marc said.

"Go on." I resisted tapping my toe against the floor.

"She was kinky as hell in bed," he said in a lowered voice.

I took a step closer, giving him a murderous look and raising my fist.

"Wait."

I backed up. "Talk fast, asshole."

"She's into threesomes, anal, and role-playing. Sometimes, she wanted me to tie her up, get rough, and pretend I was raping her ... but she called me Jacob when she came."

My blood froze in my veins as my entire world flipped on its side, and acid burned its way up my throat with his words. *She remembers.*

Chapter Twenty-Three

Brie

At almost eleven that night, I closed my chemistry book and tossed it onto the couch. Standing, I stretched, my over-sized grey sweatshirt rising and exposing my belly. My brain hurt after reading a chapter, then working on the assignment I had to turn in tomorrow. Between cheerleading and a social life, I was cramming in shit the evening before it was due.

The doorbell rang, and I frowned. I wasn't expecting anyone. Grabbing my phone from the coffee table, I opened the app to see who it was. Unfortunately, I couldn't tell who it was since they were staring at the ground and wearing a hat. *The same hat Kane wore the other day.* No way in hell would I answer until I knew for sure. I pressed the talk button on the app.

"Who is it?"

He looked up and removed his hat.

"It's Kane."

Odd. Why wouldn't he show his face to begin with? It was almost as if he wanted to scare me. Irritated, I stomped to the door and flung it open.

"You scared me. I couldn't tell who it was." I blocked him from coming inside. I didn't appreciate him showing up unannounced.

"I was making sure the cameras and system worked. Plus, I had to know if you would answer and just let anyone inside." He stood still, waiting.

I shuddered. Kane looked like a dangerous predator, ready to shred me to pieces.

"What do you want?" I wasn't sure who this Kane was at the moment, but he wasn't the guy I'd met when his mom was here.

"Like you said before, we need to talk." He easily pushed past me and into the house.

"You can't just come in, Kane. What is the matter with you?" I closed the door behind me, but I didn't lock it.

He stalked closer, never taking his furious gaze off me. "Cut the shit. Why are you at Whitmore?"

My heart raced, and my palms grew clammy, but I refused to let him know he was getting to me. I slipped past him into the open space of the living room. "To attend school and cheer. They have one of the best cheer squads in the country."

Kane shook his head. "Not good enough."

Who the hell does he think he is? "I don't need it to be good enough for you." I narrowed my eyes at him, growing angrier by the second. "You need to leave."

"I'll leave, but first you have to admit that you know who I am."

Exasperated, I threw my hands in the air. "You're Kane Cooper, the football god."

He closed the gap between us and slipped his arm around my waist, pulling me against his muscular body. I gasped from the proximity, heat stirring in my lower belly.

Kane leaned down and whispered, "Jacob."

Goose bumps danced over my skin, and I shivered against him. "I don't understand."

Kane grabbed my hair, forcing my head back.

"Stop lying!" he roared. "Marc told me how you liked to call him Jacob. You know who I am." He pushed me down, and I landed with a thud on my ass and scrambled away.

Tears welled in my eyes, and my chin trembled. "I don't know why I needed to call him Jacob."

Kane knelt next to me, then wrapped his fingers around my throat. I clawed at his arm, desperate to breathe. "Do you know what they did to me after I helped you escape?"

I wanted to reply, but I couldn't talk since his hand was cutting off my air.

"They threw me into a dark hole with no light for weeks. When I wouldn't break, they raped me over and over, but I still protected you. Protected what I thought was an *us*." He released me, and I gasped for air.

"Look at me!" Kane gripped my hair again, forcing me to look at him. "Do you see these little scars on my top and lower lip? Do you know what that is?"

Trembling, I stared at his mouth. The faint scars were barely visible, but they were there. "No," I croaked.

"When I wouldn't tell them where you were, they sewed my goddamn mouth shut."

A small cry escaped me as tears spilled down my cheeks. "I'm so sorry, Kane. I'm so sorry that happened to you."

"I was raped, beaten, and tortured, but I never told them the plan. Every day that I lived in the hole, I held on to two things. You and football. It was the only reason I stayed sane. But ..." His jaw clenched, fire burning in his gaze. "You never came back. You promised you would, and I waited ... and clung to the fact that you loved me. I couldn't even digest the thought of you betraying me. But I was wrong, and you left me there after I helped you escape. Goddammit, you left me to die!"

I sucked in a sharp breath. "Kane." My voice shook with his name. "I'm so sorry they did that to you. If I were in your shoes, I would hate me, too." I reached up and touched his cheek, hoping to break through the intense trauma and bring him back to reality.

Kane jerked away from my touch and gripped my wrist. "Your real name isn't Brie Langston. It's Lyndsay Jennings, so don't play like you have no fucking idea who we are and where we came from."

I stared at him, everything he said shattering my heart into a million pieces. "Let me explain," I pleaded.

"What is there to explain? It's simple. You fucked me over, and now you're back to make my life hell."

It slowly dawned on me that no matter what I said, he wouldn't be able to listen to the truth. I had to wait until he calmed down so he could hear past his anger and pain.

Kane glowered at me. "You have no fucking idea what you did to me. I've spent the last several years hating you, then you stroll back into my life, pretending that nothing ever happened between us." Kane's chest heaved, and he released me.

I watched him pace, agony twisting his expression as he started to calm down a little. Chewing on his last words, I debated what to say without throwing him into another violent tailspin.

He finally turned to me again.

"Kane, does anyone else know what happened to you?"

"My parents know a little about my past. No one else, though. I've had to hide it to protect my future." Kane never took his eyes off me. "You have to leave Whitmore. I have too much at stake. I can't risk people learning the truth, and I don't trust that you won't fuck me over again." Kane grabbed my shoulders and glared down at me. "Leave. Go home to Tennessee."

"No." Spittle flew from my mouth all over his face, my compassion for what he'd lived through flying out the damned window. "I have never backed down from a threat, and I sure as hell won't now. Get the fuck out of my house."

"This isn't over, little girl." He released and shoved me.

I stumbled backward but caught myself before I hit the floor again.

Kane stormed out the front door, slamming it so hard the windows rattled. I locked it behind him and set the alarm. Sinking to the floor, I rubbed my chest where my heart hurled itself against my ribs. Fear, adrenaline, and shock coursed through me while I tried to process what the fuck had just happened. Kane's expression was filled with hatred. But after what he'd lived through, I would hate someone, too. How had we ended up at Whitmore together? He was terrified that I would share our past and ruin him, but I wouldn't ever do that. Kane didn't realize he was missing some important information.

My stomach churned as I recalled what he'd said, how he'd been raped and tortured. How was he still in one piece? I sucked in a big breath, trying to steady myself. My heart ached for what Kane had shared. I wish he'd let me make things right, but I doubted he would.

I wiped my tears, then remembered what Mom had given me when I moved here.

Still shaking, I scrambled off the floor and ran down the hall to my bedroom. Mom had given me a box for when I was ready to look at the contents. All she'd said was that it contained things from my past. Refusing to look at it, I hid it so it wouldn't be in my line of sight every day.

I opened the drawer, my attention landing on the metal lockbox. Mom hadn't told me what was inside, but the look on her face had said it all. It wasn't anything good.

My phone chirped with an incoming text. The box would have to wait. I closed the drawer before I headed to the living room. I picked the cell up off the couch, then stared at the screen.

I require your presence tonight. Same place. You have twenty minutes. Don't be late, or you'll be punished.

I gawked at the message. Getting laid and having some kinky fun was what I needed after that bullshit with Kane. In record time, I slipped on my tennis shoes, grabbed my purse, and ran to my car.

Chapter Twenty-Four

Brie

The dimly lit room appeared empty when I arrived at the society. Once again, I'd been escorted down the hall by a person wearing a cloak with a hood.

"I see you dressed for the occasion," a disguised voice said from the corner.

I jumped, not realizing he was already there. "If I had changed my yoga shorts into something warmer, I wouldn't have been on time. You told me not to be late." Even though I appeared calm, I had no idea what to expect, and I was still reeling from Kane's visit.

A tall figure dressed in black and wearing a mask walked toward me. "Kneel."

My heart skipped a beat as I did as he said. I glanced up at him, waiting.

"We're going to play a game. For every lie you tell me, you have to remove a piece of your clothing."

"What if I don't tell you any lies?"

"Everyone lies, Brie Langston. Especially you. Shall we begin?"

I nodded, not clear where this was going. As long as I had my brains fucked out again, I didn't care.

"Where are you from?" He circled me, his black dress shoes scuffing against the wood floors.

"Tennessee."

"Why are you in Oregon?" he asked.

I gulped. There were multiple reasons, but I was willing to admit at least one of the major ones.

"To escape my ex-boyfriend." There, I'd said it. The biggest reason I'd fled Tennessee was to escape Marc, but the bastard had shown up after I'd been a dumbass and told him what university I was going to attend. A shudder traveled through me as I wondered if I would ever be free from him.

He stopped in front of me, and I was at eye level with the bulge in his slacks. I wanted to rip them open and free his cock. My G-string was drenched with the thought of sucking him dry.

"Why?" He reached out, smoothed my hair, then tipped my chin and roughly gripped it.

As crazy as it seemed, this was probably the safest place to share my secrets. Maybe I would even earn an orgasm.

"He was blackmailing me to be his girlfriend."

His loud chuckle sent chills up my spine, and I shivered. "Rather pathetic, isn't it?"

"You have no idea," I muttered.

He lowered, my face only inches from his mask. "It's also rather poetic."

A flicker of something on his shirt caught my attention, and I stared at it. I tried to determine what it was, but he straightened before I had the chance.

"Poetic?" I was confused about how anyone would think black-mailing someone was poetic.

"That's what I said." He paced in front of me. "Did you like my friend fucking you last time you were here?"

My nipples strained against the fabric of my bra, and my core throbbed with longing. "Yes. A lot."

"And you liked me watching?"

Oh, God, this was getting hot. "Yeah." I licked my lower lip, mentally pleading for him to rip my clothes off and touch me.

"How many guys have you been with at once?"

"One." *Two.*

"You just lied to me. Stand!"

How the fuck did he know? I rose slowly.

He walked behind me, then pulled my yoga shorts down, revealing my baby blue G-string.

I stepped out of them. His fingers slipped between my thighs, rubbing my sensitive flesh through the satin material, and I softly moaned.

"If you're a good girl, I might let you come." He moved his hand, then tugged my sweatshirt off.

I wanted to remind him he was supposed to ask me another question, but I didn't think he would appreciate it much since he was the one making up the rules.

He slid my bra straps off my shoulders, then released the front clasp with a flick of his finger. He tossed it on the floor next to my shorts.

"Get on the table."

Frowning, I turned around. I hadn't seen a table when I'd walked in, but it had been dark. A dim light flickered on, illuminating a large table and several items on it.

I climbed up, watching his every move.

He strolled over and picked up the nipple clamps that I'd spotted.

I sucked in a sharp breath as he placed them on my hard nipples.

"Does that hurt?" He ran his knuckles down my cheek.

"Yeah."

"Good. I want you to feel the pain. Lie down and spread your legs."

I flattened against the cold surface, the nipple clamps pulling as I moved.

Yelping with his rough touch, I realized he'd attached a clit clamp. He walked to the top of the table and grabbed my arms, moving them above my head. He tied them tightly, stretching them until I winced, then fastened the ties to a large hook mounted on the wall. I was helpless and at his command. Quivering with anticipation, he lifted a blindfold, then slipped it over my eyes.

"I own your body, Brie Langston. You are at my beck and call, and I will do anything I want to you."

Chapter Twenty-Five

Kane

I stared at her sprawled out on the table, blindfolded. When I'd left her house earlier, I hadn't planned on fucking her, but my dick had other ideas. While I'd wrapped my fingers around her neck, all I could think about was sinking my cock into her wet pussy. Hate sex never looked so damn good.

I threw a fist at her, checking to see if she flinched or if the blindfold was working. I grinned beneath my mask, then lifted it enough to reveal my mouth. Crawling up on the table, I positioned myself between her legs. Her scent made my dick twitch, and even though I planned on fucking her until she was raw, I would have to finish after she left.

Licking the inside of her leg, I nipped at her flesh as I moved closer to her center. I spread her apart, her moans of pleasure filling the room. I reached up and pulled on her nipple clamps. She squirmed beneath me as I flicked my tongue along her slit. The memories of the first time I tasted her flooded my senses. *Jesus.* As much as I hated her, I couldn't seem to walk away. Brie Langston was my sinful obsession.

I dug my fingers into her hips, holding her still as I admitted that she was my poison from the first moment I'd seen her on campus. She was as agonizing as she was mesmerizing, and I was stupid if I thought I could give her up again.

Releasing the clit clamp, I sucked her bundle of nerves until she pulled on the ropes attached to the wall and screamed with pleasure. Before she returned to earth from her climax, I removed a condom from my front pocket and rolled it on. I forcefully shoved into her, then stopped, overcome with a rush of emotions—fear, anger, regret, and relief that I'd told her what had happened after she'd left me.

I slammed my eyes closed, plagued with my past ... with her. I had almost lost my life because of Brie, yet here I was. Picking up my pace, I thrust into her over and over, her tight pussy clenching my shaft. Sweat beaded on my forehead, but I didn't slow down. She was my flame, constantly calling me to her, but Brie had the power to burn and destroy me. It would always be a risk to be around her.

Brie bucked her hips, her slick walls spasming as she released again. As soon as she finished, I pulled out, then jumped off the table, tossing the condom into the trashcan in the corner. I tucked myself into my slacks and zipped up before I untied her hands. Instead of heading home, I hurried to my office. Eventually, Brie would figure out she could remove her blindfold and leave.

It was after one in the morning by the time I arrived at the house, exhausted after a crazy day. My heart and head had played tug-of-war the entire day—pack Brie up and drive her to Tennessee myself to ensure she left ... or. There wasn't another option. I couldn't allow myself to love her as if nothing had happened between us. It was stupid and reckless, but the moment I was inside her again, all the good memories came rushing back, overshadowing the dark ones.

I slammed my palm against the steering wheel as I parked the car. "Get your head out of your ass and on your career!" Angry with myself for allowing her to get under my skin, I climbed out of the vehicle, then locked it. Shit, I'd been so busy with all things Brie, I'd forgotten to leave lights on inside or outside of the house. I berated myself as I stomped up the porch steps, peering through the darkness.

Fumbling around, I pressed my thumb against the keypad and opened the front door. A sudden cold draft raised the hairs on the back of my neck, sending a shiver down my spine.

I felt around on the wall for the light switch, but before I could locate it, something hard as hell hit my jaw, and my neck snapped to the left. I stumbled backward, completely caught off guard.

"What the fuck?"

A punch to my gut forced the air out of my lungs, and before I regained my footing, someone slammed into me, knocking me to the hardwood floor.

"Did you think I wouldn't figure it out, you son of a bitch?"

The punches came fast and furious, and I covered my face with my hands, trying to shield the hits.

"You fucking snuck into my home when I was asleep and painted my walls! You're a piece of shit, Kane Cooper!"

Brie? Gaining my wits, I rolled over, easily throwing her off and onto the floor. She kicked at my head, then scrambled away.

"Goddammit, stop!" I grabbed her ankles and pulled her toward me, pinning her down with my body.

"Get off me, asshole!" She pounded her fists into my chest.

Jesus, she was hot when she was worked up. I wedged myself between her legs, my erection pressing into her as she fought me.

"Give up, Brie."

"Never," she spat, her face twisted with fury. "Do you know I thought I was losing my mind? And all along, it was you screwing with me. Why? Did it make you feel like a man? Is that what gets you off? Dominating and scaring the shit out of women? You disgust me!"

Realizing she wasn't going to stop hitting me, I grabbed her wrists and pinned them above her head.

Her chest heaved with her ragged breaths.

"You're in the society, too. After you fucked me tonight, I put it all together."

"Then why didn't you talk to me about it instead of breaking into my place?" I seethed.

"Oh, that's rich coming from you! I could say the same. Why are you obsessed with me?" She squirmed, and I adjusted my hips, pressing my erection into her center. I loved her fight. I also wanted to rip off her clothes again and fuck her on my living room floor.

Brie stilled, finally realizing she was wasting her energy fighting me.

"Are you finished?" My tone bordered on rude. "How did you get into my house?"

Even though it was dark, I could see her smirk. "It seems like you secure the society's facility better than you do your home. Maybe you should install an alarm system. I *love* mine," she bit out.

"You owe me some answers, and I want them tonight. So, get the hell off me, then you have a lot of explaining to do." Her nostrils flared with her words.

I glared at her, wondering if I could trust her not to hit me again.

"Don't try anything, Brie. It won't go well for you." I shifted my weight, then stood. Holding my palm out to help her off the floor, I kept my attention trained on her. She was petite, but she packed a hell of a punch.

Brie slapped my hand away and got up, her gaze narrowing in a vindictive stare. I stepped back and searched for the light switch. Once I located it, the room brightened immediately, and I shielded my eyes.

Brie took advantage of the moment and rammed into me with her shoulder, knocking me against the wall. "You better not ever fuck with me again. I'm itching to do some damage to you."

I looked down at her and nearly smiled. With a quick move, I shot off the wall, kneeled slightly, then threw her over my shoulder. Her fists pounded against my back as I closed and secured the front door.

"Stop!" I slapped her ass, hard.

She yelped, then covered her butt as I walked toward the kitchen.

"If you want to talk, then don't hit me again, or you won't get what you want. You will get one hell of a spanking, though." For good measure, I smacked her ass again.

"Dammit. That hurts!" She stilled, hopefully giving in.

"Brie, you owe me, so let's make a deal. I'll tell you what you want to know, but you have to do the same. Answer my questions truthfully, or I'll tie you up in my bedroom." *Shit. That sounded really good. Then I could fuck her all night. Focus, asshole.*

Brie snorted. "You would like that, wouldn't you?"

"And you wouldn't?" I set her down in the kitchen, then pointed to a chair. "Sit."

Brie folded her hands over her chest, then sank into the seat.

"How did you know where I lived? It's not common knowledge." I leaned against the counter, assessing her anger level. It appeared that she'd settled down some, at least. Guess she wanted to hear what I had to say.

"I got your address from a girl on the cheer team. Apparently, her father had done some work on the house when you first bought it." She offered me a tight-lipped smile, still simmering. "Do you have anything to drink?"

"Seriously? Now you're all chill and want to just shoot the shit?" I laughed, realizing the hypocrisy of my comment.

"Something like that."

"Then, by all means." I bowed at the waist, then straightened and walked to the fridge.

"What do you want to drink? Beer? Soda? Water?"

"Water would be great." She placed her hand on her throat, and I wondered if she could still feel my fingers wrapped around her neck.

Gathering a Heineken, I twisted off the cap, then collected a water for her. I settled in at the table and gave her the drink. Fixated on her, I watched as she opened the bottle and chugged half of it. She wiped the back of her mouth, then replaced the lid. "Thanks."

"So." I laced my fingers behind my head and stretched my legs out in front of me, pretending that I didn't give a fuck that she was there when I did. She'd had some time to think about my visit earlier. "What do you want?"

She glanced away, then back to me, the anger slipping from her expression. Sometimes the opportunity of learning what you've been searching for trumped the fury. "Why didn't you get off tonight?"

I was pretty sure all the color drained from my face. No way would I answer her. I had to redirect the conversation.

"Just because I was blindfolded and tied up doesn't mean that I didn't notice." Her blue eyes remained on me. "How long have you been the leader of the society?"

I shook my head. "You're un-fucking-believable." I leaned forward and propped my arm on the table. "You show up after five and a half years, all happy and free from your past, then you have the goddamn balls to think you know my life?"

"Because my life is all fucking roses and sunshine." She glowered at me and rubbed her hand along her bare thigh.

I slapped my palm on the table, making her flinch. "That's right. You have bad dreams. Poor thing." Hatred dripped from my words.

She paused, her nostrils flaring. "I didn't expect this conversation to go well, but I wanted to let you know that I'd figured it out."

"What's that, Sherlock?"

"You ... you have a key to my house. It was you that painted my walls and left your little calling card of a scorpion. I almost missed it while I was with you at the society. But the little scorpion is stitched in red thread right beneath your collar. Not sure whose bright idea that was, but it's what gave you away."

She pressed her lips together, leveling me with her blue-eyed gaze. "All this time, I thought some crazy person was terrorizing me, or that I was finally losing my mind. But it was you. I'm not clear on something, though. Were the threats part of the society, or was it your vendetta to make me pay for hurting you?" Brie huffed, and anger briefly twisted her expression, but she didn't come at me again.

My heart stopped beating for a minute while I stared at her. "I want you gone."

"Why? I have just as much right to be here as you do."

I rubbed my forehead, wishing this would all disappear. Maybe it would be best to tell her the truth. It was probably what she'd been waiting for, exactly like I had.

"If my past comes to light, I could lose my friends and my career. I was approached by the NFL, and I can't blow this shot. I've worked my ass off for it. I want to move forward and leave it all behind. I deserve to be happy, just like you are."

Flashes of anger, confusion, then empathy ghosted over her face. "Were you really tortured and beaten?" This time, her expression corroborated the sincerity and compassion of her words.

I looked away, feeling incredibly uncomfortable that my emotions were hanging on my sleeve. "Yeah."

She swallowed hard, her eyes tearing up. A complete contrast from when I'd arrived home and she greeted me with her fists. "I would be angry, too."

"I can't afford for my past to see the light of day. It could ruin my career and everything I've worked so hard to build." I took a drink of my beer. "You're the only one that knows most of what happened, which makes you the enemy."

She gave me an awkward smile. "I've been in your shoes before, and I won't tell anyone, Kane. My actions have hurt you enough. I don't want to do any more damage." Brie leaned back in her chair, which was a good sign that her cold heart was thawing, and she had other feelings besides anger.

I rolled my eyes. "If you signed an NDA and a contract, then I might believe you. At this point, you ditched me once, so it's hard for me to trust you."

She squeezed the plastic water bottle, the crinkling cutting through the momentary silence. "I doubt an apology will be enough for you to move on, but I'm so sorry." She shook her head as if she were struggling to find her words. "I ... I ..."

My jaw tensed, and I found myself wanting to shake her. A lame apology meant nothing to me. "Sorry isn't good enough. I want to know what happened when you left. You've clearly changed your name and built a life. Did it ever fucking cross your mind what they might do to me for helping you leave?" My pitch rose with my desperation and anger. "Did you regret leaving me or think about me at all?"

She pursed her lips together, and the following words out of her mouth reached into my chest and ripped out my goddamn heart.

"No," she said quietly.

Chapter Twenty-Six

Brie

Kane's expression twisted with agony as if I'd stabbed him in the stomach, turned the knife, then left him to bleed out on his kitchen floor. I wanted to feel bad. I wanted to feel *something*, but I couldn't give him what he wanted. Not now, at least.

"Then why would you ..." He slammed his eyes closed, and I suddenly found myself wanting to kiss away the pain and make it all better.

As hard as I'd tried not to admit it, there was a pull to Kane I didn't understand. Once I'd calmed down, my emotions flip-flopped from being seriously pissed to wanting to heal his pain when I realized how much he was hurting. "Kane. What happened ... I never meant for it to play out like that."

Kane shot out of his seat, sending the chair flying backward and clattering to the floor. "Get. Out!" He pointed to the front door. Rage rippled through him, and his face glowed with fury.

I stood, then walked over to him, an eerie calm cloaking me. The toes of our shoes met, and my heart jackhammered against my chest as I struggled to speak the next words. I had to—for him and for me. This man was in so much agony, it was fucking killing me. I had to make it right. I had to try, at least.

"I will leave, but first ..." I placed my palms against his warm cheeks. "I never thought about you, Kane. I wish I had. I wish things had been different for you. For both of us." I ran the pad of my thumb across his jawline, trying to soothe his battered soul.

"Why?" he choked out. "We loved each other."

Tears welled in my eyes.

"Kane ... I have amnesia."

From his expression, my words had slammed into him like a freight train, and my chest tightened so much it physically hurt.

His cheeks turned red. "You're fucking with me. Can't you just tell the truth and stop lying and accept responsibility for what you did?"

"I'm not lying to you, Kane. I wouldn't lie to you about something so serious. I don't have any recollection of my life before I was almost sixteen. My now-parents found me unconscious on the side of the road when I was fourteen. Mom and Dad said I was diagnosed with amnesia almost immediately. On top of a knot on my head, they said the time before they found me and the year after were so traumatic that I shut down. Doctors told them I blocked it all out in order to survive."

He stepped away, disbelief flashed across his face, then shock. "Nothing?" he whispered.

I dropped my hands. Somehow, I had to fix this. I'd hurt him, and he was right. I needed to take responsibility and try to correct it. Plus, for some reason, there was something so recognizable about Kane. A pull to him that I couldn't break away from. "I'm so sorry I hurt you. What happened to you should never happen to a human being. For as long as I live, I'll take your secrets to my grave—both the ones from your past and present. It's the least I can do. I can tell you that I do feel something for you, Kane. Something familiar, but I'm not sure what it is. But I'll say this. I've seen glimpses of the man I think you really are, the guy I've heard about from others on campus who know you. I don't think you're a vicious asshole like you want me to believe. I think I nearly destroyed you, and I had no idea."

A heavy, suffocating weight crushed me. *Why couldn't I remember? What happened?* I backed away, my stomach dropping to my toes.

Scrubbing a hand down his face, Kane took a seat at the table. "Nothing? You don't remember sneaking off after curfew and making out when we were ten? We were each other's first kiss, first love, first ... *You* were my everything, Brie."

I tried to breathe past the agony that filled the room, but I couldn't. It pummeled my heart into the ground, leaving me gasping.

I wiped the moisture from my cheeks. "I don't remember. If I had, I would have come back for you, Kane." I sniffled, taking a moment to try and compose myself. "To hear that you were tortured after I left is fucking killing me. I don't know how to help."

Kane's emotions were trapped inside his tense stare as he looked at me. After several awkward beats of silence, his face crumpled, appearing defeated.

"I told myself you would be back. I would wake up in complete darkness, never knowing if it was day or night, but I rehearsed football plays over and over in my mind. The rest of the time, I thought about you. The plans we had together to see the world outside of the walls that had held us in captivity our entire life."

I folded my arms over my chest, pretending that I could hold myself together and not break into a million pieces. Scrambling to remember what he was describing, I wanted to scream with frustration and horror at what I'd done to him.

"I know it's hard to digest. When the doctors first told me, I didn't want to believe it. I've been working with a psychiatrist for the last several years. She suspects that my night terrors are memories of what I lived through, and my brain is protecting me. But Kane ..." I knelt before him, taking his hand in mine. "Please, you have to believe me. I would have come back for you." Tears streamed down my cheeks. "I would have protected you the way you did me."

He looked down at me, uncertainty clouded his expression. "How do you know? If you can't remember, how can you say that?"

I swallowed over the churning in my stomach. "I might not know who I was, but I know who I am now. I'm not the kind of person that breaks her word on purpose. I would have never left you, Kane. Especially if we were ..."

"In love," he finished for me. Kane reached out and touched my face, his fingertips tracing my cheek. "I loved you so much. I gave up everything to get you out and to keep you safe." He gulped, his Adam's apple bobbing in his throat.

"Thank you. From what you're telling me, you're the only reason I got away." My forehead creased. "What did I escape from?" I peered up at him, desperate for answers that were hovering right beyond my grasp.

He smoothed my hair, his eyes never leaving mine. "It's best that you don't remember, Brie."

I stood, stepping back from him as my heart sank to my toes. Until now, I hadn't had anyone to help me find the missing pieces of my past. I'd nearly destroyed the one man that could, and he despised me.

"Kane, you're the only person that knows what we went through. What memories I've lost. Please, tell me who I am. There's a hole inside me with only flashes of visions and flickers of thoughts. Sometimes I think I'm going to lose my mind. I need to know. I need to remember." I turned away from him, embarrassed that my fear and desperation drove me to beg.

Kane quickly leaned forward. "Brie, I can't imagine what you're going through, so I won't blow sunshine up your ass and pretend to. But you have to believe me. You're better off not knowing."

I sank my teeth into my lower lip, willing myself not to break down completely. Once I composed myself, I slowly pivoted my attention to him. "Will you at least tell me where we were?"

His mouth slammed closed, and the muscles on either side of his jaw pulsed. "Brie ... we were just kids. What happened there, we didn't know any better since we'd been born into it."

"Born into what?" *Please tell me.* Raw agony clawed up my throat as my brain tormented me with unanswered questions. Silence filled the room as I mentally pleaded with him for even a speck of the truth. Maybe it would jar my memories loose, and I could finally feel whole again. The ugly truth sank deep into my bones. The only man that knew my truth hated me.

Chapter Twenty-Seven

Kane

I stared at her beautiful face, warring with myself about whether I should tell her or not. What if I said the wrong thing, and it shoved her over the edge? I had no idea what to say and what not to say.

"Brie, are you still seeing your psychiatrist?"

"Yeah. I talk to her tomorrow. Her name is Alida. If it weren't for her, I would have killed myself by now. I owe her and my family everything."

She had no clue how well I understood the darkness that threatened to consume and destroy from the inside out. But I couldn't focus on that at the moment. The game had drastically changed, but I needed some time before I could forgive her. With a few words, Brie had turned my life upside down again, leaving me scrambling for pieces to our messy, fucked-up puzzle.

But now, Brie was in front of me in my kitchen. Never in a million years did I expect to see her again, much less have a conversation that finally explained why she never came back for me. I could no longer deny that I still loved her. If I were truthful, I hadn't ever stopped. Maybe Brie wouldn't have quit loving me either if she still had her memories.

I ran my thumb along her lower lip, thinking about fucking her at the society. I'd told myself it was just sex, but I knew I was a goner the second I was with her again. But now, I understood why she hadn't recognized me. I needed answers even more, and so did she.

Relief spread through me. Amnesia. She hadn't forgotten me like I thought. Somewhere inside her brain and heart, I was safely tucked away.

"If Alida will talk to both of us, then maybe we can decide what I can share with you." I wanted to pull her into my lap. Hold her the way I had five and a half years ago, and kiss her until we were breathless, but I had to process this shit and keep my hormones out of it.

"I'll call her in the morning. If you want to attend the session, I'm sure it will be okay. Plus, it might help if you two are connected. She probably wants to know what I lived through, and you're the only one with answers."

Brie was right. I was the missing piece to her past. "If Alida feels like it will help you, then I'll tell you."

Shocking the shit out of me, Brie threw her arms around my neck, hugging me tightly. "Thank you." Her voice carried so many emotions it unnerved me. She sounded so fragile, but she obviously wasn't, at least not physically. The girl had beaten the crap out of me. Granted, she'd caught me off guard, but still. She was a little spitfire, and I liked it way too much.

"You're welcome." I wrapped her in my arms, wanting to protect her. Somehow, I had to keep myself in check. Brie had the power to destroy me once and for all, and I couldn't allow myself to become vulnerable again. *Too damn late.* I closed my eyes, telling the voice to shut up as I allowed myself to feel her body against mine. It had been a lifetime since she'd hugged me. I released her and walked across the room, needing to take a breath before I did something stupid, like carry her up to my bed. "Let me know what time. I have football practice in the morning but not in the afternoon. Coach wants us to be rested for the game Saturday."

Brie gave me a shy grin, then strolled over and punched me in the arm. "You better win. I'll be cheering for you on the sidelines."

Damn, her smile is beautiful.

"I'll let you get some sleep, and I'll text you in the morning." Her brows knitted together. "I'll need your number. Hang on."

I watched as she walked away from me, her toned legs and the curve of her ass making me forget that, after all these years, we were about to exchange numbers. How swiftly the tides had turned.

Brie joined me in the kitchen again with her purse. She rifled through her handbag and removed her cell, then gave it to me. "Here."

I opened her contacts and added my information. Brie only had messages from the Red Scorpion, but those were from burner phones. "I'll be in practice from six until eight tomorrow morning, so give me some time to respond." Placing the phone in her hand, a spark of heat traveled through my arm and straight to my cock.

"Okay." She looked up at me, hunger in her beautiful blue eyes. "I'm sorry I broke into your house and hit you." The corner of her mouth twitched, and she faked a cough in order to hide her smile.

"Yeah. About that ..." I rubbed my neck, trying to ease the tension. "If I'd known about the amnesia, I wouldn't have ever painted shit on your mirror and walls."

Brie glowered at me. "And the lipstick in my trashcan?"

"I bought it on my way over that night." Why the hell did I feel like a little kid getting in trouble? I was a grown-ass man.

"Are we agreeing to call a truce? No more breaking into each other's homes and pulling shit?" She tapped her toe against the white tile floors.

I was genuinely relieved to hear her ask that. It took a lot of energy to detest someone. "Yeah. We're good."

"At least we got one thing cleared up through all of this. I hate what led us to this point, though." Brie pushed up on her tiptoes and planted a kiss on my cheek. "Get some sleep, and I'll talk to you tomorrow."

I stood rooted in place and watched as she let herself out. Leaning against the counter, I groaned as my shoulders sagged. I hadn't been completely honest with Brie. Even if Alida did say I could tell her what happened, I was worried that it would send Brie over the edge, then I would fall right along after her. I'd worked for five and a half years to keep the monsters at bay. Now I was inviting them to join us for fucking dinner and dessert.

Chapter Twenty-Eight

Brie

Cheer practice had been absolute shit that afternoon, and my balance was off, causing problems for the rest of the squad.

"What the hell, Brie?" Crawford yelled as he stumbled backward before finally putting me down safely on the ground. I wasn't sure what would be worse, landing on my ass in the gym or on the grass, but I wasn't interested in finding out.

I placed my palm against my forehead, feeling like crap for nearly hurting us. "I'm sorry, Crawford. Are you okay?"

He glared at me before he nodded. "Maybe you should work with Tim. We don't seem to be syncing well today, and one of us is going to get injured."

Coach Wilson joined us with her hands on her slender waist. "Brie, what's wrong?"

I stared at my feet. I couldn't tell her I'd run into my first boyfriend, who had sacrificed himself to protect me, and I didn't remember any of it. It sounded absurd when I even thought about it, much less spoke it out loud.

I leaned closer to the coach and said, "I have really bad cramps." It was the best lie I could come up with that was plausible.

"Go home and take care of it. There are only twenty minutes left in practice anyway. I'll see you tomorrow." She patted me on the back before she sent me away. I hadn't expected her to let me go, but I was grateful. Maybe after Kane, Alida, and I talked, it would help. Unfortunately, I had no idea what Alida would say, and her support would make or break my only chance to learn about my past. That couldn't happen. Plus, it really wasn't her decision to make. It was mine.

I scooped up my backpack off the ground, where we'd all piled our belongings before practice. We would have to move inside soon due to the rainy season but practicing outside after being cooped up in classes all day was nice.

Taking a deep breath and trying to calm my anxiety, I walked to my car. Kane would meet me at the house in an hour to talk with Alida. My palms grew sweaty, and I wiped them on my shorts and laughed as I climbed into my Lexus. My clammy hands had nothing to do with Alida. That was Kane's fault. Even though he'd harassed me, we'd fucked, and it had been hot as hell. Then, after we talked last night, I realized there was a lot more to him, and somewhere inside myself, I felt like I knew him—recognized his heart. As crazy as it sounded, I felt safe with Kane. Only time would tell if I was right to feel that way.

The doorbell rang, and I pulled my dark-green sweater over my head, then stepped into my boyfriend jeans before I hurried down the hall. Remembering that I had the alarm set, I used the app on my phone to make sure it was Kane before I disabled it.

I opened the door. "Hey, glad you remembered where the house was." I giggled.

"Like I could forget." Kane flashed me a smile, and I nearly melted on the floor.

Motioning for him to come inside, I unashamedly checked him out. His jeans hung on his hips, hugging his muscular legs and ass. His black sweatshirt displayed his broad shoulders, showcasing his biceps. I wondered if I could cancel with Alida and just drool over Kane. *Focus.* "I have sodas and water, so just grab what you want. Alida and I have my sessions on Zoom, so I figured it would be easier if we sat at the table." I felt like I was rambling, but the closer it got to the appointment, the more I was terrified the session would go south. It couldn't. I was so damn close to finding out where I'd come from. At this point, I was desperate enough to kidnap Kane until he told me the truth. It certainly was tempting. My mind drifted to what he would look like naked and sprawled out across my bed, handcuffed. *Oh, shit, I bet he's yummy.*

"How are you doing with all of this?" Kane asked, pulling me away from mentally having my way with him.

I chewed on the inside of my cheek. "I don't know how to answer that. One minute, I'm hopeful, and the next, I'm terrified, then my heart breaks all over again. For what I did to you and for what happened to me." Gripping the back of the kitchen chair, I steadied myself. I couldn't burst into tears in front of him.

"I get it. I think I've been riding the same roller coaster you have." He sat down and ran his hand over his dark hair. Kane seemed calm, but I suspected he was eager to get on with the session. It was an awkward situation, to say the least.

"Maybe we can get off soon." My cheeks flamed red as I realized what I'd said. "Um, I meant the roller coaster."

Kane chuckled, his gaze roaming over my body. His tongue darted across his lower lip, and I resisted the urge to crawl onto his lap and rip off his clothes. Ever since I found out he was the guy under the mask in the society, and the guy from my forgotten past, I wanted more of him. A lot more.

The alarm on my phone chimed, bringing me back to reality. I joined him at the table, then powered up my laptop. "Are you ready?"

"Yeah. Are you?"

My hand trembled as I opened the program we needed for the call. I'd hoped Kane hadn't seen me shaking, but he had. "Apparently not." My stomach churned, and I pushed down my fear, wishing that Kane was still able to distract me from my cruel reality.

Alida appeared on the screen, and I scooted the laptop back for Kane to be able to see her.

"Hey, Brie."

"Hey. Thanks for allowing Kane to join us." I motioned to him on my left. "Alida, this is Kane ... Kane, this is Alida." *Progress, the introductions were out of the way.*

"Nice to meet you, Alida," Kane said.

Fidgeting, I mentally frowned. The fact that Kane had manners just soaked my panties. I chided myself, but when I was stressed, my hormones ran full throttle. I pushed aside my desire for him, reminding myself of why he was here.

"You, too. Glad you could join us. It sounds like you and Brie knew each other before the Langstons met her." Alida's hazel eyes appeared brighter with her teal shirt.

Excellent way to articulate that.

Kane shifted in his seat, glancing at me before he responded. "Yeah, but she didn't learn that until last night."

"She mentioned that to me when she called this morning," Alida said.

All except for the part where I broke into his house through the window and punched him multiple times. I bet next time he'll check the locks before he leaves.

"Kane, Brie said you know about her night terrors." Alida slid her glasses up higher on her nose.

He nodded. I assumed he was waiting to see what direction Alida was taking the conversation before he said much. I was curious about where she was going with the session, too.

"Over the last several years of working with her, I'm pretty sure they're parts of her past that are trying to reemerge. With her amnesia, we really don't have anything to go on."

Kane glanced at me, then back to Alida. "What about when she was found?"

Alida offered me a supportive smile. "Brie, do you feel safe talking about that today?"

"Yeah. I would actually like to get to the important stuff. Don't worry about me. I'm fine. I'm ready to learn what happened so I can move on. I need closure." I tucked my hands beneath my legs, trying to control them from shaking. If Alida noticed, she would stop the session.

"Okay, why don't you tell him? I think it will help if you take control of the narrative," Alida said.

"Sure. From what my parents have shared, they were driving home from visiting relatives in Montana. It was at night, so they almost didn't see me. It was Mom who saw my hand poking out of the jacket. She said I was wearing all black, so she wasn't sure what she actually saw at first. Mom talked Dad into turning around, but he made her stay in the car until he could figure out what was going on. Mom said as soon as she saw the horror in his expression, she jumped out to help. They gently rolled me over. I wore a dress, had cuts and bruises all over my face, and I was barely breathing. Dad called 9-1-1, and they stayed with me until the ambulance showed up. Mom found some blankets in the trunk and covered me up while they waited. Later, she learned that she saved my life. I had hypothermia." I paused for a moment. "I don't remember any of it. I don't remember the week I stayed in the hospital, the doctors running tests on me, or being diagnosed with amnesia. I don't remember the cops talking to me, asking about my parents, family, or where I was from. This is all secondhand information from my parents. Dad said they searched databases across the country, looking for clues to where I'd come from." I looked at Kane, finding comfort in his dark-brown eyes. "We still don't know. Nothing ever turned up, and I haven't ever remembered."

Silence filled the room. "It was so cold that night, Brie. We were supposed to escape together, but they noticed we were gone. The dogs were barking in the background, and I realized they were close to us. I told you to leave." Kane closed his eyes, pain etching into his features. "I knew that if I didn't distract them, neither of us would have made it out. You promised you would bring help but never came back."

Kane stood, then disappeared down the hall.

"He needs a minute," I explained to Alida. "He remembers everything, and from the little he's shared, it was really bad for him."

"Brie, are you sure that you want to know all of this? In the end, what are you hoping to find? Peace? If so, I'm not sure that reliving the trauma will help you move forward. You've come so far and built a new life. You're healing, and I would hate to see you go backward."

"Sorry," Kane said, rejoining us.

"Take your time, Kane. There's no set schedule to get through this," Alida said.

"Yes, there is," I blurted. I reached over and placed my hand on Kane's. "The important thing is that he feels okay about sharing the past. You shared your concerns, but just to be clear, it's my decision—mine and Kane's choice, right?"

Alida winced, then tried to cover her slip. "Yes, you're in control of your life, Brie. I do have concerns, though. I would suggest that we have some sessions with Kane so I can support you with processing whatever he has to share. You're my client, and although I want Kane to be okay, my priority is your safety and mental health."

"So, you don't think I should tell her?" Kane's tone was low.

"I'm not saying that, but maybe don't tell her everything. Maybe just enough to help her finally have some answers so that we can address the night terrors and help her move forward. Over the years, we've also found some great tools for her to manage her anxiety and depression. She's doing really well."

Kane took a deep breath. "Brie, I'm sorry. I need some more time. It's not just about you. Opening up about the past again affects me as well. I've worked my ass off to keep the monster at bay, and you're asking me to open it and dance with the devil."

"Kane," I whispered, tears pricking my eyes. "Please, don't do this."

"Brie, try to hear what he's telling you. Whatever happened has the power to hurt both of you. Kane has made progress by leaving it behind. Do you really want him to relive it?"

"If he doesn't, then I'll hurt for the rest of my life. I'm missing years, and we all know my night terrors are what I lived through. How am I supposed to confront it if he won't tell me what happened?" My hands clenched into fists, anger surging through me with such force I couldn't sit still. I glared at Kane. "If you're not going to help me, then leave."

"Brie ..." Regret flashed in his gaze.

"Leave. Now." I pointed at the door. "Get out."

Kane stood, his shoulders sagging. "Nice to meet you, Alida." He glanced at me one more time before he walked out of my house, taking my hope with him.

Chapter Twenty-Nine

Kane

"Fuck!" I yelled as soon as I was inside my car. None of that had played out like I'd hoped it would. A part of me knew it was dangerous territory to tell her no, but I couldn't talk about what had happened to us. My throat had tightened up, and I was more stressed than playing for the football championship. She didn't understand that it would destroy not only her but me, too. How, in good conscience, could I do that?

Feeling like shit, I pulled away from her house. I had to clear my mind. Learning that she had amnesia had been eating at me since I'd found out about the diagnosis. The more I thought about it, the more I was able to shift from hating her to realizing coming back for me had all been out of her control.

With a left turn, I drove toward Madeline's. Brie had her way of dealing with the past in her nightmares, which was probably healthier than how I dealt with it.

Punching the accelerator, I sifted through everything I'd learned about Brie in the last few days, then allowed my mind to wander to when we were kids. The first time we'd snuck out after curfew, we'd met behind the barn and decided to kiss each other. She was so sweet and innocent. Neither of us had any idea why our bodies were changing or why we suddenly felt differently about each other. No one talked to us about puberty or sex. Not in the way most people would.

My heart rate climbed as the ugly memories quickly replaced the good ones of Brie and assaulted my senses. I checked around for any cops, then sped up. I couldn't get to Madeline's fast enough. Maybe Brie was searching for some sanity, but even if she knew the truth, finding peace would slip through her fingers, eluding her. I was living proof.

Minutes later, I turned into the parking lot, then zipped around to the back of the building. I jumped out of the car and locked it. I hadn't let Madeline know I was on my way, so I figured the setup would take a while. Plus, I had no idea if she had one of my regulars available.

Pushing the little white button on the black box, I waited impatiently. A buzzer sounded, then I entered the building. The familiarity of the dimly lit hallway calmed my nerves. Once I went through my ritual, my head would clear, and I could figure out what to do about Brie. *Brie. The girl I loved, the girl I hated, the girl who had amnesia.*

I walked down the hall, my footfalls echoing through the corridor. Images of Brie filled my thoughts, my chest aching from the expression on her face when I told her I couldn't talk to her about the past.

"Kane?" Madeline said, leaving one of the rooms. She smoothed her pink blouse as she approached.

"Hey, I'm sorry I didn't call. I'm happy to wait. I'll grab a drink."

Madeline put her hands on her hips. "You're not on the schedule to visit again this soon. Why are you here?"

I shifted my weight from one foot to the other. "It's my thing. You know that."

Her blonde brow raised, staring a hole right through me. "Whatever you're running from, it's clearly catching up to you. Hon, this isn't a kink you can have fun with. It's destroying you from the inside out. I highly recommend that you let the beast out, then slay that bitch. You have your entire life ahead of you. Don't keep doing this to yourself, Kane."

I froze, her words ringing in my ears. "I don't know if I can." My voice cracked, giving away how fucked up I felt.

"You can, baby. You just have to want it bad enough." She arched a brow. "Who is she?"

I chuckled, rubbing my jaw. "Is it that obvious?"

"What are you so afraid of that keeps you coming back? That pit in the ground can't do anything except swallow you whole."

"I feel like *she's* swallowing me whole. As hard as I'm trying, I'm disappearing into my past again, and ... it's ugly, Madeline." I looked away, surprised that I was having a deep conversation with her, but she'd always been kind to me. She never judged me, no matter how fucked-up my preferences were.

"Then let it be ugly. Get it out, Kane. It's going to destroy everything you've worked so hard for. Spank that beast on the ass until it calls you Daddy."

I barked out a laugh, appreciating Madeline's sense of humor during a tense time.

"With all of that, take a minute and think about it. Where do you really want to be? In a dark, dank pit underground? Or with the young lady that holds your heart in her hand?"

My stomach clenched as I admitted the truth. "With her."

"Then get your ass out of my club. You don't need to get laid here tonight." She flashed me a broad smile, then patted my cheek. "I don't want to see you here, asking for one of my girls, for a long, long time, but if you need to talk, I'll be here."

To my surprise, I leaned down and gave her a big hug. Sometimes, you just needed someone to call you on your shit.

A few hours had passed since Brie had ordered me to leave. Hopefully, she had time to calm down. Maybe Alida had been able to sort through what she was feeling.

I jogged up the sidewalk to her house and rang the doorbell. Glancing around, I spotted her car. She was home unless someone had picked her up. Impatient, I pushed the bell again and thrust a hand into my football jacket's pocket. She could see who I was through her phone app, but I wasn't sure she wanted to speak to me.

The sound of the locks flipping open reached my ears, and I waited with my heart in my throat.

"Fuck off, Kane."

She moved to close the door, but I shoved my foot through the opening.

"Brie, let me in, please. Let me explain."

Brie stood there for a few moments, giving me a murderous look before she stepped out of the way. At least she had let me in. There may be a chance she would listen.

"I can't imagine how hard that was for you to hear some details, then I had to leave." I closed and locked the door behind me. No way was I leaving until we were on better terms. I'd spent too many years being angry at her, and I was over it. It had been a huge waste of energy.

"No, you really can't." She folded her arms across her chest.

"Then tell me." I strolled into her living room as though I belonged there.

"You're a piece of fucking work. You turn on me in front of Alida, backing out on your word. Just last night, you said you would tell me."

"That's not what I said, and you know it. I said that if Alida was supportive, then I would tell you some things." Exasperated, I scrubbed my face with my hands, wishing she could understand.

"You lied to me. I even opened up and told you about my amnesia and how I was found. A part of me trusted you to do the right thing." Her pitch climbed the more she talked. "But nope. Kane Cooper is a selfish, little prick who doesn't care about anyone but himself! I hate you!"

Anger roiled to a boil in my gut, and I closed the gap between us, looking down at her. "Careful what you say, little girl. You don't have all the facts, and your mouth is about to get you in trouble."

Brie shoved at my chest. "Then let it. Maybe no one has ever called you on your shit. Oh, Kane Cooper is so perfect. He's got a killer body, is sweet to the ladies, and is amazing on the field. I see exactly who you are. You're a fucking fake."

My anger crackled through the room like an electrical storm, consuming me. Black dots danced before my vision, and I realized I was about to cross a line with her. I might be an asshole, but I wouldn't hit her. I stepped back, but Brie kept charging at me. Her cheeks flushed, burning bright red as she threw insult after insult in my direction.

I reached over and grabbed her wrists, holding them tightly. "Brie, knock it off. I'm not playing with you."

"Or what?" Fire blazed in her eyes.

I had to decide what to do, or this could end badly. Without thinking it through, I tossed her over my shoulder, then headed to her bedroom.

"What are you doing?" she screeched. She kicked and banged her fists on my back, knocking me off-balance and sending us both tumbling to the floor at the beginning of the hallway.

She crawled on top of me, seething. Brie was pissed, but she was also sexy as hell. She ground her hips against me, and my dick gave her a salute.

I dug my fingers into her hips, then rolled over, forcing her onto her back. I leaned forward, pinning her shoulders down with my hands. "Stop. You need to listen. I came here to talk."

"I'm not going to fall for that again." She tugged against my hold, fighting to get free.

Moving her leg with mine, I settled between her legs and pressed my erection against her. She sucked in a breath, her lips parting and her eyes softening.

"Get off me," she panted, her breasts moving with her ragged breathing.

"No." I released her shoulders, hoping she was beginning to calm down.

She wiggled underneath me. The longer she fought me, the more I wanted her. Brie rolled to her stomach with a quick flip, then crawled out from beneath me, clawing her way toward the living room.

I stretched out and grabbed her ankles, stopping her from moving forward. Brie reached the couch and attempted to pull herself up. Scrambling off the floor, I managed to get on my knees and pinned her against the furniture. I gripped the back of her hair, then wrapped my free hand around her neck.

"Is this what you want? You want me to take what's mine?" I growled.

Her whimper was her only response.

"You can hate and fight me all you want, but I *will* win. Plus, it's not true. You're just pissed."

"Oh, I'm clear on the fact that I hate you." She gritted her teeth.

I slid my fingertips down her neck, between her breasts, and to the waistband of her running shorts. "It seems you need a reminder of who owns you." I slipped my hand into her waistband, then gently touched her pussy. "Who does this belong to?"

A beat of silence hung in the air, and I tightened my hold on her hair.

"You."

I spread her apart, then thrust my finger into her slick cunt. She gasped as I played with her.

"Did Marc make you come?"

"Yeah, and he was much better in bed than you are," she bit out.

I chuckled against her ear, knowing she was bullshitting me in order to piss me off.

"Is that so?" Picking up the pace, I finger-fucked her until her core pulsed around me. "Sounds like someone wants to be punished."

Brie dug her fingernails into the couch, and her lips parted. She was about to come, but I hadn't given her permission. Pulling out of her, I smiled when a little whine escaped her.

"You come when I say you can. Is that understood?" I jerked down her shorts. As much as I wanted to spank her for her earlier behavior, I needed to be inside her more. With well-practiced fingers, I unbuttoned my jeans and freed my shaft. I located the condom in my back pocket and rolled it on.

Brie glanced over her shoulder, and I lined up the tip of my cock along her soaking-wet entrance. I shoved into her, losing my breath as her slick walls pulsed around me.

"Oh, God," she whimpered, grinding her sweet little ass against my dick.

"Do you like it when I fuck you, Brie?"

"Yes. Harder, Kane. Jesus, fuck me harder."

The sound of her begging sent shivers down my spine. I slid my hand around the front of her body and massaged her bundle of nerves while I picked up my pace.

"Oh, shit," she gasped.

"Not yet." I held her hips and eased out, then sat on the edge of the couch. I pulled her off the floor and over my lap, then my palm landed on her ass.

She cried out, but I spanked her again. After a few more slaps, I rubbed her tender, pink skin. I was painfully hard and needed some relief. Spreading her butt cheeks, I ran my fingers along her slit, slickening them with her juices.

"Such a tight little asshole. Has anyone fucked you there before?"

"Yeah."

I slid a finger into her puckered hole, her moans of pleasure filling the room. "That's it, Brie. You're mine now. Every inch of you belongs to me. Tell me you understand, then I'll give you permission to come."

"I understand. Kane, please let me."

Instead, I pulled out from her, the disappointment evident in her sigh.

"Get up."

After she was off my lap, I stood and led her to the kitchen table. I gripped the back of her neck and forced her to bend over, then moved her legs apart. Lining up my dick at her entrance, I slid inside. Then I rubbed her clit, coating my touch in her pleasure before I finger-fucked her ass again.

Her hands balled into fists as I fucked her. She was close.

"Are you ready to come all over my cock?"

"God, yes!"

I pumped into her, watching her tight hole clench.

"Be a good girl, and tell me who you serve, then you can come."

"You ... Kane Cooper," she panted.

Her screams of pleasure filled the house as her walls spasmed around my shaft. Her body tensed and shuddered, then she fell limp.

I pulled out of her and removed the condom. "Turn around and get on your knees."

She practically slithered off the table, still recovering from her explosive orgasm.

"Bow."

Her brows rose, but she knelt before me, her head nearly touching the floor. I stroked my dick a few times, watching her. "Look at me."

She straightened, her eyes connecting with mine.

"Open."

Her ruby-red lips parted, and I eased myself between them. "You're so beautiful." I smoothed her hair while I fucked her face.

To my surprise, Brie reached up and tugged my jeans and briefs down to my thighs. She cupped my balls, massaging them while she sucked me.

"Oh, yeah. I'm going to fill up that pretty little mouth with my come. Be a good girl and swallow every last drop. If you do, then I'll lick your pussy and make you scream my name."

She must have liked that idea because her suction tightened, and her head bobbed up and down as she picked up her pace. I grabbed the back of her neck, holding her in place while I released, my body jerking with the intensity. I allowed myself to revel in the feeling before I pulled out and helped her stand. I moved backward, then guided her until she lay on the table again.

Her blue eyes watched my every move as I sank to my knees, then spread her apart. I flicked my tongue over her little nub and licked the juices that coated the inside of her thighs. Brie's back arched off the hard surface, her fingers gripping the short strands of my hair as she writhed beneath me. Gripping her waist, I moved her to the edge, then shoved my tongue inside her.

"Kane," she gasped.

God damn, I loved hearing my name on her lips.

I licked along her sweet slit to her clit, sucking until she was breathless. Her hips bucked against me as she groaned with her release. Panting, she finally relaxed.

I stood and hovered over her. "Good girl." I smoothed her hair from her cheek.

"Was that hate sex?" She squeezed my bicep, staring at me.

"Do you really hate me?" I suspected I already knew the answer, but she needed to say it.

She reached up and traced my jaw with her fingertips. "No. I was angry. It wasn't hate sex for me. Have you been so close to having something you need, yet not been able to grab ahold of it? Kane, there's a huge, gaping void inside me."

I searched her beautiful face before I answered. "Yeah, with you. The day I saw you on campus, laughing and smiling with your friends ..."

"You thought I was happy?"

"It seemed as though you'd not only left me behind but had

rebuilt a life, even when you knew what you'd done." I placed my hands on her knees, realizing my dick was still out.

"I am happier, but I'm not complete. It's taken me years to even get to this point."

"That's what Alida said. It's one reason I didn't say anything, Brie. If you're doing better, then knowing that I had the power to destroy it all just fucked me up. Not to mention my own messed-up memories."

"Should we compromise and decide what's right for both of us? I know I'm asking a lot from you, but maybe we can find some way to get through this ... together."

I swallowed the lump of emotions threatening to overtake me. "Let's try. I'll share a little at a time, but if I see signs that you're not doing well, then that's it. If the night terrors worsen, Brie ..." I shook my head. "I can't go down that slippery slope."

Her blue eyes widened. "I don't want you to. I'm so torn. I don't want you to hurt, but I'm desperate for answers." She paused, then her brows furrowed. "You're planning to stick around to find out?"

I looked at her, silence filling the gap between us as Madeline's words repeated in my mind. "Yeah. If that's okay with you."

A silly smile eased across her face. "I would like that." She nibbled on her lower lip, thinking. "I think we fought and made up."

"Guess so."

She gently tugged on the collar of my black T-shirt. Her gaze landed on my mouth before she pressed her lips to mine.

I'd fucked a lot of girls in and out of the society, but I never kissed them. But Brie ... she tasted like a piece of heaven. *My* heaven.

I slid my tongue inside her mouth, kissing her with so much intensity her breath caught, and her heart hammered against my chest.

Brie pulled away, peeking at me beneath her long eyelashes, her cheeks still flushed from her orgasm. "Shower with me."

"How could I refuse that offer?"

Chapter Thirty

Brie

I was scaring myself. I'd flown off the handle in minutes, then had hate sex with Kane. It had been the best sex I'd had in my entire life. Hell, I wasn't even sure how it had happened. He'd pissed me off, then I was on him ... then he was on me.

I sucked on my lip as the shower water streamed down his chest and abs. My focus took a slow, sensual hike up and down his muscular body. It was the first time I'd seen him fully naked, and he did not disappoint.

His intense gaze swept over me, then paused on my hip and tattoo. "When did you get it?" He pointed to the eye and roses.

"I don't remember."

He faced the opposite direction, and my attention traveled across his broad shoulders, down his back, and over the curve of his sculpted ass as I started thinking about the off-the-charts sex we'd had so far. Then I saw it. Confused, I reached out to trace the tattoo on his lower back directly above his right ass cheek.

"Kane?" I asked. "I don't understand. That's the same tattoo, except yours doesn't have roses."

He turned slowly, sadness etched in his expression. "I noticed yours when I was here one night."

That information should have pissed me off, but I already knew he'd been in my house. It was old news, and I had no energy left to get mad at him again.

"Why do we both have the eye?"

Kane frowned. "Hand me your shampoo, and I'll wash your hair while I try to explain."

Anguish flickered across his features, but I did as he asked.

I needed answers any way I could get them, and I hoped we had come to an understanding after our fight. It seemed as though I was about to find out.

"Brie, it's an all-seeing eye. They're not really tattoos."

"What are they?" I tried to relax as he massaged my scalp, the suds streaming down my shoulders.

"Brands. We're branded."

Turning to look at him, I swiped at the soap on my forehead. "What? I don't understand."

Kane reached up and pulled the shower nozzle out of the holder. "Let me rinse your hair."

Irritated that he was stalling, I turned back around.

"They branded us in case we ever escaped. While we were there, a few people got out and changed their looks, but the green and blue colors of the brands are difficult to cover up unless you have surgery."

I placed my hand on my tattoo. "So, it's for recognition? Like how they tag wildlife?" Tilting my head back, I let Kane rinse my long strands. When he finished, I picked up the body wash and looked at him. "My turn." I grabbed the washcloth and loaded it with the watermelon-scented green liquid. I stifled a giggle since nothing about our conversation was funny, but badass Kane was about to smell like fruit.

"I suspect that you added the flowers after you left." Sadness clung to his words.

"Probably, but I don't remember. It's so fucking frustrating." I ran the washcloth over his pecs and down his abs. I smiled as his dick sprang to life. "As much as I would love to help you with that, I'm hoping we can talk for a while first?"

"I know. What can I say? He likes you." A lopsided grin eased across his face.

I giggled, then took my time washing his gorgeous body. I tried to ignore the tug in my chest but realized I could no longer deny that I felt something for him other than physical attraction. I could even pinpoint when I started to fall for him. It was the day Marc showed up, threatening me, and Kane stepped in. Kane's strength and power rolled off him as he protected me, and my feelings toward him changed. It was funny how I considered myself a strong, independent woman, but there was still something about a guy stepping in and defending me that made my insides turn to mush.

"Kane? Who are *they*?" I asked.

His shoulders visibly tightened. "I would prefer not to be naked in the shower when I tell you."

"Are you afraid that I'll hit you again?" I smirked. "Honestly, I'm not sure what happened. I normally don't attack people. I don't think I've ever been that angry before."

"I deserved it. I was a fucking prick to you, all because I thought you'd left me to die."

The conversation was getting intense, and I had nowhere to go if I needed some breathing room. "Let's finish up, then I'll make us something to eat."

A heavy silence hovered over us for the rest of our shower. One that threatened to rip my heart out. The few things Kane had already talked about gutted me, and thinking that I was responsible for what he'd lived through shredded me. Maybe I could make his life better, but he had to tell me the truth in order for me to try.

Half an hour later, we were dressed again. Kane cleaned the

kitchen table with Clorox wipes before we sat down to eat the grilled cheese sandwiches I'd prepared. It was a good thing Kane wasn't a picky eater because I wasn't the best cook.

"Where were we?" I took a bite of my food, glancing at him.

"You were asking who branded us." He wolfed down the sandwich, then went for the second one I'd made for him.

"And?"

"Since you started to rebuild your life, have you ever heard of the Light of David?"

I paused mid-chew, racking my brain to see if the name sounded familiar, but I came up empty.

"No, I haven't. What's the Light of David?"

Kane set his half-eaten grilled cheese on the paper plate and drank some of his water. He wiped his mouth, and I had the feeling he was stalling.

"Kane?" My heart pounded against my ribs while I waited for him to continue.

"Are you sure you want to know? Once I tell you, I can't undo it. I can't protect you from the pain of the truth." His hands fell to his lap, his gaze full of fear.

"I love that you want to protect me again, but I can't heal unless I know. Hopefully, it will shake up my brain, and I can finally be free from the amnesia. I would rather have bad memories than none at all. Whether my past was fun or agonizing, it made me who I am today. A fighter. Strong. Kane, I'm ready." I reached over, pulled one of his hands from his lap, and squeezed it. "For whatever reason, I feel better that you're with me when I find out."

Kane glanced at me, his chest visibly moving with his breaths. It killed me that this was so difficult for him, but there was no other choice but to drag him through hell with me.

"Brie ..."

Chapter Thirty-One

Brie

My heart pounded so hard I heard it in my ears as I held my breath, waiting for him to tell me.

"Brie, we were born into a cult." The color drained from his cheeks, and he pulled his hands away.

Nothing had prepared me for the undiluted wave of foreboding as my world tilted on its side, and my brain scrambled to make sense of what had just spilled out of his mouth. "What? Like a satanic one?" Kane had shattered every idea of who I thought I was—educated, caring, and an overall decent human being. I blinked at him a few times, trying to clear my head. Maybe I hadn't heard him correctly, but I knew that I had.

"No. The cult we were in had screwed-up religious beliefs." His tone bordered on curt, but I reminded myself that talking about this was difficult for him.

"Like what?"

Kane leaned back in his chair and stared at his lap. "For instance, we weren't allowed to touch anyone of the opposite sex unless an elder was around. A few times a month, one female would be tied down and everyone would take their turns fucking her."

I slammed my eyes closed. "Gang rape?" I'd learned enough about crime from watching television after Mom and Dad took me home with them.

"Basically, yeah. When a guy turned fifteen, they were a part of the rituals. When a girl reached puberty, they were also included. Any girl that was a virgin ... there was an entire ritual around her."

I reached for my water and gulped some down, my thoughts reeling from what he'd already told me, but I still had a ton of questions. "How old were you when you helped me run?" I held my breath, afraid to hear the answer.

"Fifteen."

"Did you? Did they make you have sex?" My tummy flip-flopped faster than a fish out of water.

Kane pursed his lips together. "I'll tell you this last part, then we take a break."

"Okay."

"The night we tried to escape, you were going to be the girl tied down and raped, and since I was the youngest, I would have been the last guy to be with you. What they didn't know was that you weren't a virgin. If they had found out, they would've killed you. It's why we ran."

Tears streamed down my cheeks. "You saved me," I whispered.

"I loved you. We had already been together, and you were my everything. Brie, you made life tolerable in the compound. If they had killed you, it would have been my fault." Kane wiped the moisture from his eyes.

"You got me out, though." My lip trembled as sorrow sucked me in like a whirlpool in the middle of the sea. Kane had sacrificed everything ... for me. He loved me enough to risk his life. I stared at the sandwich growing cold on my plate, realizing that our trauma connected us in a strange climate of trust and vulnerability.

"Are you okay?" Kane leaned forward.

I ignored his question. "How did you get out? If I left you behind, what happened? Did you try to escape again?"

Kane released a heavy, tormented sigh. "The FBI came in one night when everyone was asleep. Some of the leaders were shot, but most of the women and children were rescued. A girl by the name of Tabitha let them know where I was. In a way, she was the one that saved me."

"What do you mean? Were you in a jail or something?" My pulse skipped a beat as I waited for his answer.

He wet his lower lip before he answered. "Worse."

"What could be worse than everything you told me?"

"I'm sorry, Brie. I'll answer more questions later, but not right now."

I slumped in my chair. "I understand. But there are a million questions swirling around in my brain."

"I can only imagine, but for now, let's get out of here. You might want to swap out your shorts for jeans and grab a jacket."

My eyes narrowed at him. "Where are you taking me?" Shoving all the darkness out of my head, I focused on the man that had sacrificed himself for me. He'd shown me love in its purest form, unselfish and fearless. How could I not fall for Kane now that I felt a connection and knew who he really was?

"It's a surprise, but a good one." He stood, then collected our paper plates and tossed them in the trash.

"Let me change. I'll be right back." I hurried down the hall. At least I had already showered, but I suspected Kane wasn't too comfortable since he'd only put his jeans back on. I'd laughed when he'd shoved his boxer briefs in his jacket pocket.

Ten minutes later, Kane pulled away from my house.

"I like your Jag." I ran my fingertips over the supple, black leather seats. "Did you want one, or was it a gift?"

Kane kept his attention on the road in front of him. "It was a graduation present, but it was also a congratulatory gift for receiving a football scholarship."

"I'm not surprised you got a scholarship. You're incredible on the field." I offered him a smile, still sifting through what he'd told me earlier. Instead of asking more questions, I made myself focus on our conversation.

"You watch me?"

"Why would you be shocked? I mean, as soon as I started Whitmore, the cheerleaders filled me in on the football players to stay away from, and the good guys, too."

Kane chuckled. "Which category do I fall in?"

I smirked at him. "Who said they even talked about you? Maybe I watch you because you're the quarterback and have the ball a lot."

Kane's smile faltered. "Oh."

My giggle filled the car. "I'm messing with you. You were the first one they dished about. Apparently, you're deliciously hot and sweet, or some shit like that." I bit my lip, stifling my snicker.

"I'm not always the nice guy. It's just who people see when they don't know me well. Pretty sure Anderson, Quinn, and a few others could tell you the same. Especially lately." He eyed me.

"Why is that?"

Kane gripped the steering wheel until his knuckles turned white. "I've not been myself since you showed up."

My heart cracked open, knowing that, once again, I'd caused him so much pain. "I wish I could go back and undo it all. Take away the hurt. I'm so sorry, Kane. I hope someday you can forgive me."

Kane looked at me, confusion written all over his face. "Brie, it's a lot to process, but when you told me you had amnesia, and Alida confirmed it, there was nothing to forgive. It's up to me to work through it."

Even though I knew he was right, it didn't stop the burning sensation in my chest. There was one thing I could do to help him. It would mean I might never have answers to my past, but I was willing to take that chance—for him.

"Kane, I can leave." Tears stung my eyes the moment I looked at him. "I'll call my parents and move back to Tennessee. Being here is only making the situation worse for you, and I can't do that to you anymore. My presence is like pouring salt in a wound, not allowing it to heal."

Kane's biceps strained his shirtsleeves as he rubbed the back of his neck with his free hand, staring straight ahead into the darkness as he drove.

I held my breath, but I knew I would be packing tomorrow as soon as I suggested it. It was the right thing to do. Everything inside me screamed and kicked like a rebellious little child, though. I didn't want to be away from him, but I was the one thing causing his agony. It was my turn to save him, no matter the cost.

"No."

My ears were clearly playing tricks on me. "What?"

"You're not leaving. I know I wanted you to in the beginning, but that was before I learned the truth. You're staying."

I released the breath I was holding. "So, you get to decide if I come or go? Not sure that's how this works."

Kane turned onto a gravel road, and the full moon peeked through the leafless trees, lighting the way.

"I will always be the one to decide when you come." He grinned at me.

Laughing, I gently smacked his shoulder. "You know what I mean. In the society and in the bedroom, you can be bossy, but not when it concerns life decisions. Those are mine."

Kane didn't acknowledge my comment about the society, but I knew it was him. Once I'd put it together, I also recognized his hands. I suppose wearing gloves during kinky times would be kind of weird.

The car slowed to a stop, then Kane turned off the engine.

"Where are we?" I asked, unbuckling my seat belt and opening the door.

Kane climbed out of the Jag, then waited for me. He took my hand and led me through the trees and to an open field.

"Let's get something clear. You're not leaving." He reached up and smoothed my hair. "I just found you again, and I'm not sure I can let you go."

I looked at him, our gazes connecting. "Are you sure? After everything I've put you through, how can you want me around?"

He cupped my chin. "Because sometimes, it's worth the hell. You're worth the sacrifice, Brie. Let's give us another chance. I want to be with you again."

I placed my palm against his chest, his heart pounding beneath my touch. "For you, it's again. For me, it's the first time. But somewhere inside, there's a pull toward you I can't deny. It's not just the sex, Kane. You feel familiar and safe, and I'm quickly falling for you. Sometimes I wonder if you're in my good dreams, or if it's your voice I hear calling my name in my nightmares. I don't remember much, but there's always someone with me. I'm terrified I'll hurt you again, though."

Kane pulled me tighter against him, his hand running the length of my back. "Let me love you again, Brie. Let me in. Don't fight what feels right."

How could I argue with him? He'd saved me once, and I suspected he would save me this time too.

I pushed up on my tiptoes and gently pressed my lips to his. Butterflies scattered in my tummy, and I wrapped my arms around his neck. "So, what are we doing?" I grinned and gripped the collar of his jacket.

"It's simple. You're mine. I'm yours. Any motherfucker that touches you ..." Playing it cool, Kane shrugged, refusing to meet my eyes. "I'll put him in the hospital. If they need a reference, I'm sure Marc will be happy to provide one."

It was wrong to laugh, but I couldn't help it. "Marc is a piece of shit and had it coming." I kissed Kane again, loving how his mouth felt against mine. Maybe my brain didn't remember who he was, but it seemed like my heart did.

"He did. But I will deal with him later. Tonight, it's about us. I wanted to share something with you. Not many people know that I hide out here, so promise me this stays between us."

"Promise. And umm, isn't that a given with the kind of conversations we've already had? I mean, the cult, plus you're in the society." I stepped back and jogged away, grinning. "I know it's you, Kane. Why not admit it?"

He took a long step forward, then lunged for me. My scream echoed through the open field while I took off in a sprint, giggling my ass off. The sound of his laughter behind me made my heart leap with joy.

Kane caught up, wrapped his arm around my waist, and lifted me off the ground. "I'll admit nothing." He set me down, then tickled me until I begged him to stop.

Catching my breath, I looked at him. His smile was brighter than the moon, and my chest squeezed. I loved seeing him happy and wanted more of those moments with him.

Images flickered through my mind—men beating women and children crying. Doubling over, I placed my palms on my thighs to steady myself, gasping for air.

"Brie? What is it? What's wrong?" Kane knelt on the ground before me. "Look at me."

I peeked up at him, trembling. "I'm okay. Sometimes I have flashes, but not enough to reveal anything."

Kane stood and pulled me against him. "You're safe, babe. I've got you, and this time, I'm never letting you go."

Chapter Thirty-Two

Kane

Brie's body shook with tears as she grabbed my shirt, clinging to me. As much as I had tried, I hadn't been able to protect her. I'd failed, yet she was in my arms again, trusting me. Brie was right. This was my second chance, and she might never remember what we lived through, but I was convinced that wasn't necessary for us to have a good life together.

I rubbed her back as her cries subsided. "I know today has been a lot. We fought, fucked, then I told you part of our past. It's a lot to take in. One of the reasons I brought you here was to share some good memories, too."

Brie peered up at me, her tears clinging to her long eyelashes. It was crazy how one look at her could bring me to my knees. Even when we were young, I knew I loved her. She'd always been my anchor, the light in the darkness. Once I'd had a few days to process the amnesia, I realized that if we were going to be with each other, it was up to me to create new memories for both of us.

"I'm sorry. I'm ruining your surprise." She sniffled and wiped her cheeks.

"No, you're not."

She pulled away, appearing embarrassed that she'd broken down in front of me. Unfortunately, it probably wouldn't be the last time. We had a difficult road ahead of us, but she was worth every bit of the agony.

"What did you want to show me?" She peeked up at the sky. The moon was so bright the stars had disappeared in the background.

I took her hand, then led her across the field. "After the FBI found us, I had a difficult time adjusting. You don't remember, but one of the elders taught us how to play football. Once he realized that I was a natural, he spent a lot of time teaching me one-on-one. When shit would go down at the compound, I would recite football plays over and over or … think about you." I squeezed her hand. "Anyway, I was angry and gave my parents hell. One of my favorite things to do was throw the football between the white columns in the foyer of the house."

"You didn't." Brie gasped in horror.

I nodded. "Yup. Broke a lot of expensive vases, too. Mom was furious with me. The next day, Dad brought me here." I slowed as we approached the other side of the field, then glanced down.

"Oh, my God. A lake?" Brie released my hand, moving closer to the edge. A light breeze blew her hair behind her shoulders, and I wrapped my arm around her.

"It became a place that I could come to and release all the bundled-up rage. Even more than that, Dad drilled down and really taught me to play ball. I had the basics and understood some plays, but that was it. You and I didn't grow up with television or internet, so I didn't even know the National Football League existed."

"That would seem so strange unless we didn't even realize there was such a thing as Google. Were you excited to learn about the NFL?"

"It turned my life around. I finally had something to focus on, work my ass off for, and rebuild what had been stolen from me. Once Dad realized I was talented, he worked with me. He talked to the coach at my high school and convinced him to let me try out for the football team. I was the new kid, angry at the world, but I wanted to play."

"I'm guessing you nailed the tryout."

I smiled, recalling how excited I was. "The coach nearly pissed himself he was so eager to have me. It was that year I started making friends, settled in at home, and tried to become a good person."

"Kane, you are a good person. Why do you keep saying that you aren't?"

I stared at the lake below us and how the moonlight bounced off the water, calming me. "I've done some fucked-up shit. Still do. The cult ingrained it in us. We were bad—sinners. Do you remember a few weeks ago when I snuck into your bedroom and told you I'd been beaten for my dick getting hard?"

Brie frowned. "I ... with the sleep medication, I couldn't really distinguish what was real or a dream. I didn't realize it had actually happened. When I found Sasha's invitation and filled out the online questionnaire, I checked the fantasies I wanted to try. Someone breaking into my house and threatening me was one of them."

A chilly wind blew off the water, and she shivered against me. I rubbed her arms, attempting to warm her. "Guess I fulfilled your fantasy, or part of it, anyway. I didn't play out all of it."

"Yes, you did. Earlier in my living room."

I could see the corner of her mouth curl up in a smile.

"Guess you know my fantasies. Kind of puts me at a disadvantage. I think the Scorpion has some work to do."

I threw my head back and laughed. "You're not going to let that go, are you?"

Brie faced me. "Not until you admit it."

"You know I can't do that. It's called a *secret* society for a reason."

Brie's expression grew serious. "How many other girls do you screw?"

I nearly choked on her question. If I answered, it would confirm that I was in the society. If I didn't, it would hurt her. We'd made too much progress to go backward, but I wasn't sure I could give her the answer she was looking for.

"Brie, my sex life is a bit complicated."

"It's not a difficult question to answer." Her jaw clenched, one of her tics when she was irritated. "I don't care about anyone in the past, but moving forward, are you able to commit to just me physically? If not, then I need to know upfront. As you already know, I'm okay with multiple partners. Whoever the other guy I was with was damned good, but if you're a man whore, then I'm not going to wait around for you to show up at my door for a good fuck."

Shit. Shit. Shit. She's pissed and goading me. Step lightly, dude. We'd had a committed relationship conversation minutes ago. Now, I was scrambling backward. At least that's what she thought, but that wasn't true.

"Brie, when I told you I was yours, I meant it. I'm not going to fuck anyone else now that we're together, but there are some things you need to know about me if you intend to stick around. The cult messed me up in a lot of ways."

"I can accept that. I wanted to know if you would still be a part of the society. Since I found someone else's invitation, I know there are more girls than just me. As I said, if you want to be with other women, then just tell me."

Her words said one thing, but the tears in her eyes said another.

"Since the game is away tomorrow, I won't be able to explain any more until Monday after classes and practice. Can you trust me until then? Can we enjoy each other for a few days?"

Confusion and fear clouded Brie's expression. "You're afraid after I learn whatever this is that I'll not want to be with you?"

Panic spiraled through me. I couldn't lose her twice. "Yeah. It's why I haven't had a serious relationship since you were fourteen and I was fifteen."

Brie inhaled, pausing before she spoke again. "If you're taking a chance on telling me, then I'll take a chance that it won't scare me off. Focus on winning the game tomorrow, and then maybe we can celebrate together afterward." She placed her cold hands on my cheeks, then kissed me.

I knew she meant well, but I couldn't help but think that, once again, our time with each other was limited.

Chapter Thirty-Three

Brie

As hard as I tried, I couldn't sleep after Kane dropped me off at home. My body was tired, but my brain refused to stop spinning on that stupid merry-go-round. I'd learned more about my past through Kane's pain in a few short days, and it fucked me up.

I sat on the edge of my bed and unlocked my wrist cuff. Even though Kane hadn't said anything about it, I realized that since he'd been in my house while I was sleeping, he had most likely spotted the chain.

Glancing at the clock, I stretched and yawned. The game was only a few hours away, so I'd at least been able to lay in bed a little longer.

Heading for the shower, I attempted to make sense of what I'd learned about my past. I was born and raised in a cult. A fucking cult. I'd heard about them in general on *Dateline* with Mom and Dad, but not enough to really understand alot about it. Kane had mentioned it was a religious one, which meant I could probably ask Google to help me learn more. Maybe that would take some pressure off Kane, too. I felt calmer after realizing I had a major piece to the puzzle and could research independently.

"Holy shit, it's cold," Everlee said, jumping in place on the sidelines at the football game.

"Where's your jacket?" Gabby asked.

"I'll just turn into a black-and-burgundy popsicle if I wear it, then take it off for cheers." Everlee blew into her cupped hands.

"I'm sure the guys wouldn't mind seeing us snuggle up to each other," I laughed.

"Then they'll lose the game because they'll be thinking about the wrong balls," Gabby said, giggling.

"Looks like it's time to start. Before you know it, we'll be into the game and forget how cold it is." I flashed them a smile, my pulse kicking up as Kane was introduced. Shaking my pom-poms, I cheered loudly for him along with the other cheerleaders.

"Girl, what am I missing here?" Gabby asked, flashing me a devious grin.

My forehead creased. Gabby must have caught me staring at Kane for too long. "I have no idea what you're talking about." I wondered if I could play it off. I didn't think we were ready to announce we were together. At least, not until after Monday. *If I stay with him after his big reveal.* Surely, Kane was underestimating me. I shoved the worry aside, then focused on the game.

"Apparently, we need to have a little chitchat, Brie Langston." Gabby eyed me. "You're not getting off that easily ... oh, or are you?" She wiggled her brows at me.

I tried to hide my smirk, but my facial muscles betrayed me.

"Oh, hell. Mm, girl, you're fired for not sharing the juicy details with me." Gabby stared at me with her hand on her hip, missing the cue for our next cheer.

"Shit." She jumped into the routine, plastering a broad smile on her face, all while shooting me playful dirty looks.

After the cheer was over, she closed the gap between us. "Dish, babe."

"There's nothing to say ... yet. I'll know more next week." That was the truth. I hadn't lied, but I wasn't going to share with Gabby that I'd slept with him a few times, either. Not here, while the game was happening.

"That's a really odd thing to say, but okay. Make no mistake, I *will* find out what's going on." She nudged my side and quirked a brow at me.

"I'll tell you later, just not here."

The announcer began to speak, breaking up our conversation.

"Whitmore University is honored to have one of the best teams in its history on the field tonight," the first announcer, Chuck, said.

"That's right, Chuck. Not only is the defense tight, but the visiting team has had a great year as well."

I listened as the men chatted back and forth while the visitors had the ball. From what I could tell, the coach was talking to Kane.

"Interception!" Chuck yelled.

I cringed with the volume of his excitement.

Our offense jogged onto the field and settled into position.

"Ladies, the scenery is amazing from here." Everlee chewed on her thumbnail as her attention swept over the guys bending over at the forty-yard line.

I didn't blame her one bit. It was all about the tight end.

"What do you girls think about Sterling? Or Quinn? Hell, just give me a buffet line, and I'll sample them all." Everlee slapped her leg as if she'd told the year's best joke.

I barked out a laugh, then held my breath as Kane sent the football flying through the air in a long pass.

"Shit, shit, shit! Catch that ball, number eighty-nine!" I raised my pom-poms to my face and peeked over the top, watching the play unfold.

The crowd cheered and jumped to their feet as Quinn scored the first points.

"And a beautiful play to kick off the game!" Jim said, excitedly.

"Jim, hold on. While the touchdown happened, our star quarterback got sacked and is on the ground. We have a penalty flag for unnecessary roughness. My question? Is Kane Cooper hurt and out of the game?"

"What?" I ran to the edge of the field, trying to see what was happening, but the coaches and players were crowded around him, blocking my view.

The girls were hot on my heels, concern written all over their expressions. Gabby wrapped her arm around my shoulder. "He's tough, Brie. He'll be okay."

"Remember when one of the quarterbacks a few years ago got tackled too hard? It broke his collarbone," Everlee said, worry hanging onto her words.

"Are you serious?" My pitch rose with each syllable. I wasn't hiding my feelings for Kane very well.

"Wrong thing to say, Everlee." Gabby frowned at her.

"I'm sorry. It was the first thing that popped into my head." Everlee took my hand in hers. "Gabby's right. He's tough. Shit happens on the field all the time, and they get up and play."

I held my breath, my heart hammering while we waited to see if he was okay. Clapping from the stands filled the stadium as Kane was escorted off the field and to the sidelines.

"I ... I need to know if he's okay. What if he has a concussion or a broken bone? What if it's his arm?" Adrenaline pulsed through my veins. The only thing that mattered to me was Kane.

I hurried over to my coach. "Coach, are you able to learn if the quarterback has injuries?" I folded my arms over my chest, hoping she could help me.

"We're not allowed over there with the players. You know the rules. I'm sorry."

That wasn't acceptable. I had to learn what happened, and the announcers weren't saying anything. The other team had the ball, which gave Kane a few minutes, but …

"Okay. Thanks." I hurried back to the cheer squad and grabbed my friends.

"I need your jacket, Everlee. I mean, please. Then I need you all to block Coach's view."

Everlee jogged to the stands and collected her jacket for me. "Here."

"I have to talk to Kane." I slipped on the coat. "Please help me."

Gabby shot Everlee a look. "Then we need another girl to help block Coach's view. Hang on." Gabby hurried over to the end of the cheer line, then brought over Leighton.

"Hey, Brie. Gabby said you need to sneak over to Kane. I'm in. I'll help. I need to know if he's okay, and they aren't saying a fucking word."

I wasn't quick enough to hide my surprise at what she said. Had Leighton and Kane hooked up?

"I didn't realize you two were a thing." *Dammit, Brie. Shut up and check on him.*

"I've not said anything to anyone." Leighton offered a tightlipped smile.

Heat traveled up my neck and to my cheeks. *What the actual fuck?*

"Go check on him for us," Gabby said, taking my arm and moving me forward.

I wasn't sure I wanted to know if he was all right. In fact, if he and Leighton were getting together, I hoped his dick would fall off. Huffing, I did my best to stay concealed and made my way to the team.

"Excuse me. Is Kane okay? Is he hurt badly?"

"Ask him yourself. Hang on." The tall, slender player stepped through his teammates. "Hey, QB, some hot-as-hell chick wants to know if you're okay."

I pursed my lips together, not appreciating how he'd referred to me. The players parted, then Kane met me at the sideline.

"Hey, Brie. I'm okay."

"Are you sure? No broken bones? Will you be able to continue playing?" I controlled my anger at him. If he was hurt, I couldn't publicly beat him for being with Leighton and me at the same time.

He closed the gap between us, tilted my chin, and pinned me with an intense gaze. "I'm fine. I promise. But I need something for good luck."

My brows raised, then the entire world disappeared around me as he laid a searing kiss on my lips, completely ignoring that we were in public.

"Thank you for checking on me. If your coach gives you shit, I'll try to back her down." He kissed me again, then stepped away. "I've gotta go. I'll see you after the game?"

Breathless and giddy, I nodded yes. Kane Cooper had just kissed me in front of his teammates and the cheerleaders. He wouldn't have done that if he and Leighton were an item.

Forgetting that I was hiding from my coach, I jogged to my friends.

"He's clearly okay," Leighton snapped.

"Leighton, I had no idea he was going to kiss me."

"You sure? Looked like you two are together." She stomped off in the other direction. As much as I wanted to comfort her because she was my friend, I had no clue what to say. I had been as shocked as she was.

I touched my lips, smiling to myself.

Gabby and Everlee stared at me. "Is Kane okay?" Gabby finally asked.

"Yeah, he's going back into the game." Then, it dawned on me that Gabby, Everlee, and Leighton had been best friends for years, and I was the new girl. "Are you two upset with me, too? I had no idea Kane would kiss me like that."

"Girl, no. If we were upset over every time a guy we liked kissed another girl, we wouldn't have any friends left. Leighton was just hoping. At the beginning of the year, she kissed Kane, and he kissed her back, but that was it. He never called her or made an attempt to date her," Gabby explained.

A wave of calm settled over me. Kane hadn't lied, but I was embarrassed to admit that I went from zero to bitch in ten seconds. Dating Marc for the last few years, I'd never dealt with jealousy. I wasn't sure it was a good look on me. "Oh. Okay. I wouldn't hurt her on purpose."

"Girl, Leighton will be fine. We need to focus on the important things right now." Everlee pulled on the sleeve of her jacket I was still wearing.

"I'm sorry. You're freezing and need your coat. Thanks for letting me borrow it." I started to remove it.

"Brie! I wasn't talking about that. When did you and Kane become a thing? That's what matters." She clapped her hands.

"What she said," Gabby laughed.

I sighed happily. "Yesterday, but there are a few things we need to talk about before we tell everyone. It's why I didn't say anything, yet."

"By that kiss, well both kisses actually, I would say he was marking his territory for the world to see. So, you'd better hop on that train, girl. Not sure there's anything else for you two to figure out," Gabby said.

The announcer broke through our conversation, and we lined up as our guys jogged onto the field again. Kane looked in my direction, then focused on the play.

While we watched the rest of the game, I wondered if Kane had kissed me because the other football player had called me hot or if he was already comfortable with letting the world know about us. The only way to find out was to ask. Maybe he wasn't the only one that had a bit of a jealous streak. At least I'd learned something new about myself. Don't fuck with my man.

"Hey, beautiful." Kane wrapped me in his strong arms outside the visitors' locker room.

"I'm glad you're okay." I pushed up on my tiptoes, kissing him.

"Better than that. We kicked their ass." He smiled at me.

"Another win for Whitmore." I placed my hand on his chest, not minding that he was sweaty from the game. "I have a question."

"Shoot."

"Why did you kiss me in front of the team and ... well, everyone on that side of the football field? Were you jealous because a guy called me hot?"

Kane's brown eyes softened. "Did I embarrass you?"

"No. Not at all. You caught me off guard. I thought we were waiting until after Monday to let the world know." I glanced away, slightly embarrassed that I'd asked him. Maybe I should have left it alone.

Kane placed his palm against my cheek. "If I did, that wasn't my intention. I'll try to slow down for you. It's just ... Brie, I've been in love with you since I was eleven."

I gawked at him. "Really? "I mean, you talked to me about when we were fourteen and fifteen, but I didn't realize it was before then. Plus, you've hated me for many years in between." I smiled, letting him know that what I'd said wasn't a jab. I was attempting to lighten the conversation.

Kane leaned down, kissing me gently. "Hate is love wrapped up in an ugly package."

I sighed against his mouth. "You still didn't answer my question."

"Both. I did it because that asshole said you were hot, and I wanted to make sure there wasn't a misunderstanding. If he'd touched you ..." Kane's teeth clenched.

I shook my head. "He didn't. I wouldn't have let him anyway."

"I also kissed you because I want the world to know that the love of my life is back. You belong with me."

"But you said you're worried about Monday."

"I am, but if I show you how much you mean to me, then maybe it will stack the odds in my favor." He cupped the back of my neck. "Are we good?" His eyebrows tugged low, shadowing his brown eyes.

How could I resist him as he looked at me with so much love in his gaze? "We're good."

"Excellent. We're celebrating tonight ... all night. Your pick, my place or yours?"

I licked my lips and pushed away my nerves. I hadn't ever spent the night with a guy before, and not to mention, I would need to handcuff myself to the bedframe. But if Kane already knew my past, and his, he shouldn't have difficulty adjusting. He would most likely ask me to stay open-minded and nonjudgmental on Monday, so it was time that I made peace with my wrist cuff.

"Mine."

"Excellent. I'll meet you there in a few hours." He kissed my forehead before he walked to the locker room.

I watched as he strolled away, the muscles in his legs and ass flexing in his tight football pants. I sank my teeth into my lower lip, wondering if he would fuck me while wearing his uniform. I stifled my laugh, then walked back to the girls, who were waiting for me to join them for the ride home. I couldn't wait to see Kane later, but I would also need to tell my girls as much as possible. They were my friends, and I didn't want to hide my present like I had my past.

A spark of tingles traveled through me. For the first time, I was dating someone and had friends. Kane and Gabby even knew my secrets, and neither of them had turned their back on me. Life was looking up, and I was elated. Little did I know that what was lurking around the corner would change everything.

Chapter Thirty-Four

Kane

I paced my living room floor, reminding myself to breathe. After I spent the weekend with Brie at her house, I was scared shitless she would walk away when she understood how fucked up I was.

I ground my molars together, then recited football plays out loud. After five minutes, I gave up. My go-to when I was stressed wasn't helping. Nothing would make me feel better until Brie learned my secret.

I'd worked hard, giving Brie everything she could have possibly asked for while at her place. The plan was for her to fall helplessly in love with me, then she couldn't leave after Monday. I'd admitted that I was attempting to stack the deck in my favor, but even then, I understood that nothing could prepare her. Not for this.

After I'd asked Brie if she could wait until Monday, I'd called Madeline with an idea. I was stunned when she agreed to help. It was a good thing because I kept wanting to call off the plan, but I knew if Brie wanted to be with me, she would have to accept everything—the good and the bad. Hell, Brie had been vulnerable with me when she cuffed herself to the bed Saturday night. As hard as she tried to hide her embarrassment, Brie's insecurity was written all over her beautiful face. When she rolled over, turning away from me, I wrapped my arm around her and pulled her close. No way would I allow her night terrors to get in our way.

"We're here," I said to Brie as I drove into the parking lot of Madeline's club.

"From the way the building looks, I can't tell where we are." Brie leaned forward in her seat, peering through the darkness.

"You'll see." I discreetly wiped my sweaty palm on my shirt while she climbed out of the Jaguar. Nervous didn't even begin to cover my feelings, but I'd dealt with crazy shit before. This was nothing. *Just keep lying to yourself, asshole.*

I locked the car, then took Brie's hand and approached the entrance. Pushing the little white button on the black box, I waited for the locks to pop open.

"Ready?" I glanced at Brie.

"Yeah." She nodded.

I led her down the corridor to Madeline's office, my pulse pounding in my ears. The one stipulation that Madeline had was to meet Brie and have her sign a nondisclosure form. Also, Madeline insisted on remaining in the room with us. Brie had agreed to it all, but I could tell it was freaking her out a little. She probably thought I was an ax murderer who taxidermized my victims or some shit. At least I wasn't that fucked up, but close.

Reaching the office door, I knocked. Brie bounced on her tiptoes, her nerves showing.

"It's not too late to back out, Brie. I don't want to cause you any more—"

"I'm not backing out. Yes, I'm nervous as hell, but I want to do this. I need to for both of us."

She grabbed my shirt and pulled me down, kissing me. I wondered if she would want to touch me after she learned what I was hiding.

The door swung open, and Madeline met us with a big smile. "Hi, hon." She patted my cheek, then focused on Brie. "My goodness, you're a beautiful one, aren't you?" Madeline looked up at me. "Well done, Mr. Cooper."

"I certainly think so. Brie, this is Madeline."

Brie stuck her hand out to shake Madeline's. "Nice to meet you."

"Let's hope so, honey. After we're finished here, you might not feel the same."

I cringed. Why had Madeline said that? Whether Brie would admit it or not, she was one heartbeat away from bolting. I placed my palm on her back, attempting to soothe her overworked nerves.

"Well, let's get this started." Madeline stepped aside, allowing us in. "Take a seat."

Over the few years I'd known Madeline, I had never seen her office. It was pretty boring, with an old oak desk in the middle of the floor and a few black velvet chairs in front of it. At least it was well lit. The rest of the club was dim.

"Have a seat, Brie. Let's get started with the nondisclosure form. I'll help you through it."

Brie and I sat down, then Madeline reviewed what seemed to be a boilerplate form. Without hesitation, Brie signed and dated it.

"Okay, kids. I'll be in the adjoining room to this one. I'll be keeping an eye on things while you two figure this out, but you won't see me. It might feel like you're getting some privacy. This is for you, Kane. It has what you asked for." She placed a small recorder on the worn desk, then squeezed my shoulder before she left.

I stared at the small device. Sweat dotted my upper lip, and my deodorant threatened to fail me. Why had I thought this was a good idea?

"Let's get this over with before I fall on the floor from a heart attack. I don't think you're far behind me, which won't work well for your career." Brie's voice was low, haunted.

I nodded. "What do they say? Rip off the Band-Aid and get the pain over with?"

"Something like that." Brie gripped the arms of her chair, waiting.

I leaned over and pushed the play button, then adjusted the volume. The audio began to play, and I relived the moments in my head, watching Brie from the corner of my eye. As much as it might gut me, I had to see her genuine reaction.

"Jacob?" A female voice asked.

"Yeah."

"Are you afraid?"

"Always," I whispered.

"You know what you have to do to be let out, right?"

"I'll never tell you where Lyndsay is because I don't know." I gritted my teeth, reality and my past colliding in that fucking hole.

Beads of perspiration dotted my upper lip and forehead as I watched Brie, listening to not only what I did at Madeline's but a replay of my past. My gut churned as I forced myself not to pace the room.

She moved her hand down my stomach, then grabbed my limp cock. "I can make you feel better while you're here, Jacob. I can help you forget the pain and loneliness for a little while."

"Don't touch me." I jerked away from her, my dick lengthening in her palm. "The elders sent you."

"They did. They want you to get me pregnant."

I hissed. "I'm fifteen. I don't want a fucking kid."

"It's not your choice."

Her mouth sucked on the tip of my cock, sending delicious chills through me. "Don't you want to fuck me? I bet you'll feel so good inside my wet cunt." She shoved me to the back of her throat, sucking and stroking me. Her movements were almost silent, but not quite.

"You like it when I suck your big cock. But first, you'll serve me."

Her knees landed on each side of my head, and she gripped my short hair. "Have you ever eaten pussy before, Jacob?"

The tiny hairs on the back of my neck stood on end, and goose bumps grazed my arms as Brie looked at me, horrified. My heart folded in on itself as she continued to listen to the horror of my role-playing session with one of Madeline's girls.

"No." I turned away, and she jerked my head.

A sudden tightness in my chest made it difficult to breathe. Hearing the audio for the first time, I realized how reliving the days in the hole had nearly ruined me.

"I'm about to teach you."

Before I could object, she lowered over my face, gaining complete control over me.

I flicked my tongue over her pussy lips.

"That's it, Jacob. Nice and slow." She tilted my head back as she rubbed her sensitive flesh over my mouth.

I sucked and licked until her juices were dripping down her thighs and my chin. Her body trembled as she moaned softly. "So nice." She quivered and dug her nails into my scalp as she came. "Such a good boy. If you fuck me really good, I'll see if they'll let you out of the hole. Just put your baby inside me."

She grabbed my dick and ran it over her slick flesh. Holding me in place, she slid down and shoved me inside her. I bucked, overwhelmed by the feeling of her riding me.

"You're so thick and long." She bounced up and down, leaned over, and placed her palms on my chest.

"Come inside me, Jacob."

"No." I gritted out. "I won't."

"It's no use fighting it. I've already talked to the elders. If you don't impregnate me this time, then they have other plans for you." She rocked against me, digging her fingernails into my shoulders. "The elders said that Sheila and I could give you a show."

"What?" I had no idea what she was talking about.

"You'll be tied to a chair, naked, while you watch Sheila and I touch each other."

I sucked in air.

"You like that idea? Would you like to see her lick my pussy?"

"Oh, God," I moaned.

Heat zipped up and down my spine as my balls tightened.

"Maybe if you're good, you could join us. I would love to watch her suck your big cock while I sit on your face."

"No." I panted, unable to hold back any longer; my body jerked as I shot my come inside her.

"Yes." She rode me harder until she screamed my name.

Breathless, I slammed my eyes closed as she crawled off me.

"Roll over," she ordered.

The click of the cuffs opening filled the speaker. A soft knock, then the door shut again ...

I leaned over and pushed stop on the recording, bracing myself against the huge wave of emotion threatening to suffocate me. There was no way that Brie would be okay with what she'd heard.

"You're Jacob?" Brie asked, confused.

I stood still and pressed my fingers to my temples for a moment. "It was my name while we were in the cult. Mine was Jacob, and yours was Lyndsay. When the social worker and police questioned me after the compound was raided, they asked my name. I never wanted to be Jacob again, so I changed it to Kane."

Brie looked at me as though she were seeing me for the first time, without the façade or lies I hid behind.

"Who was that girl with you on the recording?"

"She's one of Madeline's girls. I have no idea who she is because I never see them. They haven't ever seen my face either. What you heard is part of what I lived through. It was true to life. When I first met Madeline, I told her I needed some role-play in order to feel ... satisfied."

Brie winced, and I realized I'd said the wrong thing. "Satisfied is the wrong word, Brie. I love every minute of being with you. It's getting off during sex that's the problem. I've been able to hide it, though, by finishing with a blow job or rubbing one out."

Each flicker of her emotions sliced and diced me. How had I thought this was a good idea? It was too much for anyone to handle. But I'd gone this far, and I would explain what she heard and answer her questions. At this point, I had nothing to lose because I was pretty sure I'd already lost Brie all over again.

"Where did this take place?" She stared at me with unwavering intensity.

I swallowed down my fear. Brie deserved the whole truth. At least it might help her answer some of the questions about her past.

Standing, I held my hand out to her. "I'll show you."

Madeline met us in the hall, then led us to the room I considered mine. Again, she left us, but I knew she was close by.

Wordlessly, I walked to the rug and rolled it back, revealing the trap door on the floor. The sound of the locks popping open broke the silence, then I lifted it. "Come on. I'll leave this open."

I watched as Brie lowered herself down the ladder and into the pit. Once she was there, I joined her. Frozen in place, I listened to my pulse roar in my ears. Every time I climbed into the hole, I realized there was no escaping the pain regardless of where I was.

Brie's entire body violently shook. "Th-they kept you in a hole?" She covered her mouth as her cries broke free. "Kane. Oh, God." She sank to her knees. "I'm so sorry."

"Hey, babe. It's not your fault. If I had to make the same choice again, I would. You got out, and that's all that mattered."

"It's not okay. Nothing about this is okay."

"Can I hold you?" I was afraid to touch her. What if it sparked memories of her own?

Brie reached for me, and I wrapped her in my arms. At least she was here for the moment, and that might be all I have left once she processed everything.

"How can you come back to this over and over?" Her voice sounded as broken as my heart.

"Sometimes it's healing since I have control over how it plays out. Other times, it's self-punishment if I fucked up a game or some shit."

Brie looked at me while the tears streamed down her cheeks. "I'm afraid to ask, but I need to hear the rest. What else did they do to you?"

I placed a kiss against her forehead, grateful that I was able to hold her while I talked. It helped me as much as it did her.

"Rape was the kindest thing that happened to me after you left. For whatever reason, I hadn't gotten any of the women pregnant, so the rapes stopped, but it had fucked me up in the head. Now, I can only come from a blow job, jerking off, or if I fuck someone while trapped in a hole underground. I've always faked it otherwise. A fact I've hidden from everyone."

Brie's mouth dropped, then she slammed it closed. "That's why you didn't get off that night at the society."

My head hung in shame. "You're the only person I've told. Now Madeline knows, but she's not my concern. You are." I wondered if Brie would still choose me after what she'd just learned, but I couldn't handle thinking about it yet.

"You said they sewed your mouth shut?" She ran her fingertip over my upper lip.

"Yeah. Because I wouldn't tell them where you were or where you were going. They assumed we had a meeting place since everything came to light once you had made it out. I told them we were in love, and you weren't a virgin anymore. I thought maybe they wouldn't look for you if they knew. My plan to protect you backfired."

"I was never worth what you went through. No one is." She hiccupped through her tears.

I tipped up her chin. "That's where you're wrong. I would move heaven and earth to protect you. I'm not sure you feel the same about me now that you know my secret."

Brie stood. "Kane, I know I have feelings for you, but this is a lot to digest. I need some time to deal with what you went through because of me."

An arrow of grief pierced my sternum, but I had to give her what she needed. "I understand."

Emotionally and physically exhausted from sharing my secret, I helped Brie out of the hole, then followed her. Closing the trap door, I swore I would do everything possible to get past the trauma if she stayed with me. Not even the pit was worth losing the love of my life. I would find another way.

Chapter Thirty-Five

Brie

I thought I could do it. Kane had been so supportive when I pulled out the handcuff, but his secret was on an entirely different level.

Kane dropped me off at home and hugged me goodnight. The moment I closed the door and set the alarm, I crumpled to the floor, distraught over what I'd learned. I was confused about how Kane found peace reliving his trauma, but he was as chained to his past as I was.

I walked to my bedroom, undressed, and located my pajamas. Staring at the wrist cuff, I gasped for air as I sat on the edge of the bed and massaged my temples. My vision flickered in and out, and my heart threatened to leap from my chest.

The scent of fresh dirt slammed into me, and I sucked in a sharp breath. "I'm okay. I'm safe. I'm not in the pit with Kane." I pinched myself, demanding that I remain in the present. Grabbing the half-full bottle of water on my nightstand, I opened then drained it. "See. I'm good. Kane's trauma is over. He's safe, too."

I placed my bare feet on the floor and wiggled my toes in the carpet, anything to help me stay calm. Staring at the bathroom door, I focused on the doorknob and placed my hand on my heart. "I love fall. I love the way the air smells as summer changes to autumn. I love the way the leaves rustle in the wind, changing to yellow, orange, and deep red. I love pumpkin lattes and the rain pattering against my window. I love Mom's homemade chili and my favorite light-pink sweater ..." I took a breath, allowing myself to focus on the things that made me happy. Alida had taught me several techniques, and this had been one of my favorites.

Feeling calmer, I reached for the remote and turned on the television. Giving myself permission to mentally check out until I felt as though I was more grounded, I started the next episode of Bridgerton. I doubted I would sleep, but I fastened the cuff and crawled under my blankets. The scent of Kane's cologne lingered on the pillow he'd used over the weekend. Tears burned my eyes as I planted my face in it, feeling safer with a piece of him still with me. Who was I fooling? Even though I needed some time, I couldn't walk away from him. I wasn't sure when it had happened, but I'd fallen head over heels in love with him. The time I needed to process wasn't about not wanting to be with him, but about whether I would be enough. With both of us having lived a horrifying past, could I be that person to love and support him no matter what and still show up for myself? The need to know where we were from was strong enough to drive me into darkness, but I was desperate to patch the hole inside and feel like I belonged.

I rubbed my temple, attempting to relieve some stress. Thank God I would talk to Alida the next day. The poor lady was about to get an earful.

"Strip."

I stared at my mother, horrified. "I'm sorry! Please don't do this, Mom!"

"You broke the law, Lyndsay. Your punishment has been decided by the elders. Now, strip."

My legs trembled so hard I wasn't sure if I would be able to stand much longer. My cries shook my shoulders as I removed my white floor-length gown, leaving me only in my white panties.

"On your knees," a male voice said as he approached me, his hands behind his back.

My palms covered my budding breasts, but my mother pulled them away and grabbed my hair. "Kneel."

"Mom, please don't. Please!"

Her facial expression never changed as she forced me to my knees.

"Do you understand that you have sinned, Lyndsay?"

"No! I don't understand what I did wrong."

Mother jerked my head back, then the man slapped me. The sting of his palm jarred me into silence.

"You're telling me that you didn't know not to touch a young man?"

Shocked, I glanced up at the older man in front of me. "Bobby and I were playing hide-and-seek." My voice wobbled as I attempted to explain.

Without another word, the man moved his arms, revealing what was in his hands—a whip.

"Repeat after me."

My tears fell to the floor as I sucked in a breath.

"God, hear my pleas of forgiveness for the corruption in my heart. Forgive me for touching the forbidden, wanting it for myself instead of what you have commanded. I am a daughter of David, following in his light and footsteps. As his chosen, I am no longer an individual, but a member of his family. I will save myself for the elders."

His brown shoes caught my eye as he moved. Then, I heard the whip before the leather straps connected with my back, and my screams filled the room, begging him to stop.

It felt like an eternity later when the beating stopped, but I was nearly unconscious.

"Two days in the hole. She has to be dealt with before it's too late."

Oh, God! Not the hole. I was lifted off the floor, trying to focus on my surroundings, but my eyes were blurry from crying. The cold air stirred around me as I was put down again. Curling into a ball, the creak of a door reached my ears ... then total darkness.

"Brie! Brie!"

My eyes flew open, and a scream tore from my throat.

"Baby, it's Kane. Listen to my voice. I'm here. You're here. You're safe."

Reality flickered in and out as I finally realized I was standing in my room, the chain stretched as far as it would go. Bruises began to bloom from where I'd struggled against the restraint.

"Kane? I don't understand. Why are you here?"

"Take a deep breath. As soon as you're calm, I'll look at your wrist."

I glanced down, frowning while panic ripped through me.

"What happened?"

"You had a night terror, but I'm here now. It's okay."

I stared at him, trying to recall what I had dreamed. My chest heaved, and I closed my eyes.

"Kane, for the first time, I remember ... I saw my mother, then a man with dark hair and brown shoes." I opened my eyes again, my heart jackhammering against my chest. "I was beaten, then thrown in a hole, Kane. That wasn't a night terror, was it?" My legs gave way, and I dropped to the floor. "It was a memory."

"I was afraid taking you to Madeline's would be too much. I'm sorry, baby. I'm so sorry."

"You knew? You knew I'd been beaten and locked away, didn't you?"

Anguish ghosted over Kane's face. "I did. I also understood that taking you to Madeline's might trigger some of the memories." Kane wiped away the tears from my cheeks. "It's one of the ways they punished us. When you called me to come over … I don't think I've ever sped faster in my life." Kane backed away, and I watched as he located a clean washcloth in my bathroom. After it was wet with warm water, he returned.

"Where's the key for the wrist cuff?"

I nodded at my nightstand. "Wait, I called you?"

Kane unlocked the cuff, then gently cleaned the gash on my wrist.

"Yeah. Your voice was different, though. I've done some research on night terrors, and they said the differences are often subtle and hard to identify if someone is in the middle of one. But the moment you said my name, it didn't sound like you. It was haunted."

I massaged my forehead with my free hand. "Thank you for coming. I don't remember calling you. I guess even in my sleep, I know who my heart belongs to."

Kane hesitated, his brown eyes full of worry. "Are you sure?"

I reached for him. "That was never the question, baby. I just have to make sure that I'm enough for you. I'm fucked up, and if I'm struggling, I don't know how to show up and give you what you need."

Kane gently kissed me. "Babe, don't. Show up for you first, and that will help me heal as well. We have to be patient and learn how to adjust as we start the next chapters of our lives … together."

"I don't understand how, after everything you lived through, you still love me."

Kane stroked my cheek with the pad of his thumb. "Loving you has been the easiest thing I've ever done."

Kane's mouth crashed onto mine. His kiss was so intense I forgot to breathe. I allowed him to consume me and lost myself in the safety of his touch.

"Let's get your wrist bandaged, then try to sleep."

Panic surged in my chest. "Are you leaving?" I stood as he led me to the bathroom.

"You couldn't get me to leave even if you tried."

"Good."

Chapter Thirty-Six

Brie

The following week flew by, even though I had two appointments with Alida and spent a few nights alone. I hated that Kane wasn't next to me while I slept. He seemed to keep my night terrors at bay. As much as I despised them, I wanted to see what else I might remember. I knew he was only a phone call away, and I promised to let him know if I needed him. To my disappointment and relief, I hadn't had any more nightmares.

The rainy season had settled over Oregon, and I hurried from my car to the mailbox. Pulling out a small pile of mail, I made a mad dash to my door and unlocked it. I shivered as I turned off the alarm, then flipped the locks into place.

It was cold in the house, and I went straight to the thermostat and increased the temperature. I needed to call Mom and ask her how the electric bills had been. Even though they had the money to cover my expenses, they'd also given me a good life the last few years, and I didn't want to abuse that privilege.

The corner of a black envelope caught my eye, and I pulled it out of the other stack. My name was carefully written in gold calligraphy on the front. I flipped it open, removed the white card, and smiled as I read the message.

Meet me in the red room at nine—no panties or bra. Don't be late, or you will be punished.

The Red Scorpion.

I jumped around, squealing as if I'd just won the lottery. After my flashback, and Kane sharing his secret, I was afraid the society fun would be over, but he still wanted to play. Hurrying to the shower, I mentally sorted through my closet. I had a hot date tonight at the society, and I did not want to disappoint.

"Good evening, Brie," the masked and cloaked figure said as I was led down the hallway of the society.

"Hi." I snickered to myself, not knowing what else to say. *Maybe, hi, I'm here to get fucked ten ways to heaven?*

He opened a door for me, and I gasped as I entered and left my escort in the hall. The soft click of the lock told me I was alone. The invite wasn't kidding when it said red room. The walls were painted a deep, dark red, and mirrors were on the ceiling and one of the walls. A chair with restraints, a BDSM bondage barrel, and rows of whips, toys ... I froze. A camera's light blinked in one of the ceiling corners. Holy shit. I hadn't ever made a sex tape before. I wondered if it would be used that night. My pussy throbbed with the idea. I was game for anything.

The door opened again, and I spun around, my attention landing on a different masked figure dressed in black. His hands were behind his back. He wasn't very tall, and his shoulders were broad.

Shit. Where was Kane? Why had I assumed the invitation was from him?

"Glad you could make it," he said, his voice disguised.

"Where's Kane? I won't be with anyone except him."

A soft laugh rippled through the air. "He's ... occupied."

"I'm sorry, what? What do you mean occupied?" My fear simmered to anger, and I clutched my purse, ready to run if necessary. Unfortunately, I had heels on and a form-fitting black dress. I wasn't sure how quickly I could make it out of here. And when I did, I would break every door down until I found Kane. I would beat him first, then the bitch sucking his dick.

I backed away, trying to calculate the best way to get out. If I was close enough to some of the toys, I could hit him with one, giving myself the few seconds that I needed.

"Why don't you let me look at you? Kane won't be with you tonight, but I'm here." He walked toward me. *This is a joke, right? Another society fantasy.*

I wasn't far from the wall of paddles and whips. Maybe I could reach something to bash him in the head with. "Let me leave, and I won't say a word to anyone."

My breath caught in my throat, fear whispering in my ear that whoever was beneath the mask didn't care about anything except for raping me. Maybe it was part of the fantasy I requested on the questionnaire, but something in my gut told me it wasn't.

"Who are you going to tell? Your daddy? The cops? I would love to see the description you gave them. Not to mention, the details of why you were here in the first place. The gorgeous, sweet Brie Langston has some dirty little secrets." He took a few steps toward me, and I reached for anything I could use as a weapon.

He lunged at me, slamming my back against the wall, forcing the air to whoosh from my lungs. I kicked and screamed, fighting the best I could. Unfortunately, he was too strong and easily pinned me as he unzipped his pants.

"Help!" I shrieked.

"No one can hear you. The rooms are soundproofed, so good luck."

With a powerful move, he spun me around, then pushed my face against the wall.

I shifted, trying to stomp on his foot with my high heel, but he caught on to what I was attempting to do.

He grabbed my hair, jerking my head back. "Just be still. It will be over in a few minutes." His dark chuckle ghosted over me, and chills of terror skated across my skin.

Chapter Thirty-Seven

Brie

Suddenly, Kane stormed in. The masked person spun around just in time to meet Kane's fist.

"You fucker. Don't you ever pull that shit again. I will kill you." Kane glanced at me. "Are you okay?" he asked in a low tone, the muscle clenching in his jaw.

Stunned and speechless, I nodded.

Kane grabbed the guy by his black shirt, then jerked him into the hall, closing the door behind him.

Relieved, I sank onto the chair, collecting myself. Since Kane had charged in here like a pissed-off bull, I knew the guy in the mask had lied to me. Kane was dressed in jeans and a sweatshirt when he barged in—no mask and no black shirt or slacks.

A little while later, Kane joined me.

"I'm so sorry, babe. That won't ever happen again. He'll be dealt with." His tone dripped with authority, and I rubbed my hands over the goose bumps that dotted my arms.

I loved this part of Kane, protective and jealous. My brow shot up. "So, you are the leader." That probably wasn't what I should have focused on, but I had.

Kane gave me a half shrug. "Lucky for you, huh?" He gathered me in his strong arms and pulled me to his chest. "I'm glad he didn't hurt you."

"He didn't. He messed with me, though. He implied you were with another girl." My nostrils flared at the mere thought of Kane with someone else. I understood he'd been with other women, but we were together and had even discussed we were exclusive.

Kane kissed the top of my head. "I wasn't even here. I'd stopped off at my parents' and was running late. I was on my way here to take care of you and some business afterward. I swear I haven't touched another girl."

I peered up at him. "I believe you. You haven't just showered, and you don't reek of sex or some other girl's perfume. Lucky you." I batted my eyes at him. "Did you at least send the invitation?"

"Yeah. That part was me." He placed his finger beneath my chin and tilted it. "You promise me he didn't rape you?"

"I would tell you, Kane. I swear."

"Okay." He dipped his head, planting a soft line of kisses down my jaw and neck.

A soft moan escaped me as I gripped his biceps. "I saw the camera." I pointed to the ceiling.

His chuckle sent delicious chills down my spine. "Do you like that idea?" He slid his hand down my back, cupping my ass in his palm.

"Depends."

"On?" He gently tugged my dress up, revealing my bare pussy.

"If you'll be on the video with me or off to the side?"

Kane knelt, then lifted one leg over his shoulder. I leaned against the wall, hoping I wouldn't fall over. His tongue ran over my swollen lips, and I moaned as he spread me apart.

He glanced at me, a devious smile on his handsome face.

"I'll be in it with you, but first ..." He flicked his tongue over my clit, his gaze never leaving mine. "I need to watch you touch yourself."

His slightly stubbled chin scraped against the inside of my thigh as he licked and sucked my sensitive flesh. "Okay," I panted. At that point, I probably would have agreed to anything.

"Kane, that feels so good." I slammed my eyes closed, losing myself for a moment.

To my disappointment, he rose. "Have a seat and spread your legs."

I sat, then Kane placed a leg over each arm of the chair. He strolled over to a cabinet, opened a drawer, and produced a black velvet bag. Opening it, he approached again. "I bought this for you the other day." He gave me the vibrator.

I took it from him and watched as he removed a small remote and turned on the camera before he sat down in front of me. "Turn it on," he ordered. "Show me how you fuck yourself when I'm not with you."

Fumbling for the button, I pushed it and the toy hummed to life. I ran it over myself, coating it with my desire as his attention fixated on every move I made. His lips parted as I eased it inside, gasping as it filled me. Desire surged through my bloodstream, and the lust in Kane's eyes intensified.

"Faster." The gravel in his voice sent shivers over me.

My moans echoed through the room as my back arched off the chair. "Kane," I said breathlessly, nearing the edge of an orgasm.

Seconds away from complete bliss, he rose and removed the toy from me. "Have I given you permission to come?"

My lip jutted out in a slight pout. "You know that women can come more than once, right?"

The corner of his lip twitched. "Are you talking back to me?" He circled the chair with his hands folded in front of him.

"What if I am?"

A mischievous glint sparked to life in his brown-eyed gaze. He gripped my arm and pulled me from the seat to my feet. "You will be dealt with." Kane reached down and tugged my dress over my head, leaving me naked. His attention traveled over my body, his erection evident in his jeans.

He led me to the barrel, then bent me over and secured my hands to the front. Kane nudged my legs apart with his foot, then fastened them as well.

"Now I have the perfect view of that sweet cunt. But first, I have something for you."

I glanced over my shoulder to see what he was doing, but he had turned away from me, blocking me from seeing. He briefly disappeared, then gripped my hair, forcing my head back. A soft piece of leather slipped around my neck.

"What is it?" I asked.

Kane walked to where I could see him, then held up a mirror.

My eyes widened in surprise at the black choker with a red scorpion near the little circle. "A collar?"

He stroked my hair. "Just a reminder that you belong to me." Kane undid his jeans and freed his thick, long dick.

I licked my lips, eager to please him. It was funny how I considered myself a strong, independent female, but with Kane, in the sex department, I wanted him to dominate me.

He wrapped his fingers around his shaft, his hand moving up and down.

Growing wetter by the minute, I continued to watch him. His full lips parted, and his irises darkened. My core pulsed with longing, but I refused to beg for him to be inside me.

"Open." He stepped closer, then shoved himself into my mouth, nearly choking me.

Tears welled in my eyes as he thrust. Kane grabbed my hair, staring down at me as he controlled my every move.

"I love seeing you serve me, Brie. Catering to my every need. Such a good girl, but you talked back, and you have to reap the consequences of not obeying me." His lips parted and he groaned as his come hit the back of my throat.

I greedily swallowed, more turned on than I had ever been in my entire life.

When he finished, he pulled out. I desperately wanted to rub my aching jaw but couldn't move my hands.

Kane knelt before me, then ran his thumb along the corner of my mouth.

He leaned over, his breath fanning across my cheek. "So beautiful with my come on your lips. Did you like watching me jack off? Did it turn you on?"

I whimpered. "Yeah."

"Do you want me to fuck you hard? Shove my cock in you until you're begging to come?"

Breathless at the idea of him taking me over the barrel, I nodded.

"I bet your pussy juices are running down your legs." He stood, then walked away.

I heard the drawer open again, then he returned and ran his hand along the inside of my thigh.

"You're so fucking wet—all for me. My pretty little slut, willing and waiting to be fucked."

Jesus, this is hot.

He parted my ass cheek, then I felt the tip of something ease into my asshole.

I gasped, the pleasure rippling through me.

His chuckle filled the room. "Your butt plug has a scorpion on the end. I'm claiming every inch of your body." Kane ran his fingers over my slit and massaged my bundle of nerves, nearly driving me over the edge.

I yelped as he bit the back of my thigh. "I want to eat your pussy until you come so many times, you're begging me to stop."

"Yes. Oh, God, please."

"Are you ready for me to fuck that cunt and tight little ass?"

"It's all yours."

"Yes, it is."

His footsteps rang through the area, then I caught sight of him from the corner of my eye. What was he doing?

Without a word, Kane opened the door and left.

"Kane? Kane! Don't leave me here!" Surely, he would be right back.

I glanced at the wall clock under the camera, the light blinking green.

I shifted, attempting to get comfortable, but it was no use. Thinking about everything he'd said, my core clenched. He'd gotten me all hot and bothered, then left me hanging. I suspected it was my punishment for talking back. *Dammit.* Maybe my smart mouth hadn't been worth it. I could have had at least two orgasms by now.

The minutes ticked by until I wondered if Kane had forgotten about me. What if another society member came in? My nerves kicked up at the thought that someone else might join me again, and this time, I wouldn't be able to fight or defend myself. I would be at someone's mercy, touched against my will. Tears welled in my eyes, then anger overshadowed the panic. If he thought this was funny, he was in for a big surprise.

After nearly an hour passed, the door swung open, and a masked figure dressed in a black cloak entered ... then another, and another, and another. Nine guys circled me, except for one. That one stood in front of me.

A prickle of fear rippled over my naked body. *What the actual fuck?*

I searched frantically for the red scorpion that would tell me it was Kane, and I nearly cried with relief when I spotted it. But the deadly insect wasn't near his collar. It was a small, fake tattoo on the back of his hand. I glared at him, but he didn't respond. Since I couldn't see his face, I had no idea if he was smiling or pissed. Worse than that, I was sprawled, naked, in front of several members of the society.

"As you know, one of our own tried to touch what was mine. He will be dealt with," Kane said, his voice disguised by his skull mask.

"Per the rules, to mark a female, the society watches as we fuck her." Kane pulled back the hood of his cloak, then dropped it on the floor, revealing his black shirt and slacks. I quickly spotted the scorpion near his collar. Maybe I should have been pissed that I was on display for everyone to watch, but the minute I realized Kane was the one that would touch me, I was okay. I was aware that everything was confidential here. If the identities got out, it would be hell for the guys.

Kane walked behind me, then I felt his fingers between my legs. He massaged my clit, and I sank my teeth into my bottom lip. I glanced at the others standing around me and moaned with pleasure. Who knew I would love an audience? Kane spread me apart, then the sound of a zipper filled the room. He slammed inside me so suddenly, I arched my back and cried out in shock. Kane leaned over and bit my shoulder, fucking me, driving into me hard, over and over with his powerful thrusts.

My core clenched around his shaft as he pinched my clit. I was mentally begging him to let me come, but I knew he wouldn't give me permission. He gripped my hips, digging his fingers into my flesh while grunts of dominance clung to the air.

I whimpered as a familiar, delicious sensation swirled in the pit of my stomach. I wasn't sure if I could stop it even if I wanted to. There was something incredibly hot about the guys watching while Kane marked me.

"Come for me," he demanded.

I writhed against him, greedy for my orgasm. My breath caught in my throat as a soul-obliterating climax ripped through me, leaving me limp and satisfied.

Still trembling with my release, Kane quickened his pace, pushing into me several more times before a low, guttural moan escaped him, and his body shuddered.

I bit my lip, knowing that he was faking. Once everyone was gone, I would finish him off.

As quietly as the cloaked figures had entered, they left.

Kane removed the butt plug before he uncuffed my hands, and I shook my arms, tingles prickling my limbs as I tried to straighten.

Without a word, Kane located a blanket from the dresser, then helped me stand. I propped myself against the barrel, not trusting my legs to carry me. Kane wrapped the soft, plush material around my body, completely covering me. I snuggled into it, not realizing how cold I was. Kane crouched, then scooped me into his powerful arms. He carried me out of the room, down the hall, then through another door. The automatic lights turned on, and I suspected it was his office from the desk, table, and couch.

Kane kicked at the chair, then sat in it, still holding me.

"Can I take off your mask?"

"Yes."

I reached up and carefully removed it, then kissed his cheek.

Kane stared into my eyes, then his lips crashed against mine. "No one will ever mess with you again." He pulled me closer to him, my face pressed against his chest as I listened to the steady beat of his heart.

Chapter Thirty-Eight

Kane

I hated myself. I hated that I'd trusted a member of the society, and he'd tried to fuck my girlfriend. I paced the floor in my living room, replaying the events of the previous evening over and over. My hands clenched, recalling how I had punched the bastard until his face was unrecognizable right before I locked him in one of the empty society rooms. Brie was totally fine with role-play, but I hadn't planned that shit, and his dick wasn't mine. No one touched her. I barked out a laugh, finally understanding why Jagger was hotheaded. I wasn't cool with him for a long time because I was the same and refused to admit it.

After I marked her in front of the rest of the society, the team took Jimmy to the river and performed a society baptism, which included nearly drowning him multiple times while threatening his life. Even though Brie had indicated she was open to being watched while someone fucked her, it had been a spur-of-the-moment decision. Not that I would have told her, but after Jimmy pulled his shit, I had to make sure no one else crossed that line with me. Ever.

My phone buzzed in the back pocket of my jeans, and I reached for it, seeing Quinn's message.

He's alive but dealt with.

Does he understand if he says one word …

He does. I might have helped him along with that.

I chuckled. Quinn was brutal when someone fucked with his friends on or off the field.

Excellent. Thanks, man.

Little grey dots danced on the screen while I waited for his reply.

Not a thing. We're brothers.

I tossed my phone on the couch, relieved by the update. At first, I'd been concerned that Jimmy would open his big mouth and turn against the society, but now that I'd heard from Quinn, I felt much better.

My cell buzzed again, and I scooped it up, smiling at the image that popped up on my screen—Brie … naked.

I miss you.

I glanced at the clock.

On my way, beautiful. I just need to grab my duffel bag.

Brie responded with heart emojis.

She had no idea that she was the brightest part of my life and that I would do anything for her. I whistled as I ran up the stairs to my bedroom and tossed clean clothes into my bag. I had toiletries at her place already, so I didn't have to worry about packing those all the time. Hopefully, she would feel comfortable spending the night here soon.

Twenty minutes later, I rang her doorbell, eager to kiss and hold her.

The door cracked open, then her beautiful blue eyes peeked around the corner. She ushered me inside before she locked up behind me.

"I was about to ask if you were still naked and hiding from the neighborhood, but I can see you're in yoga pants and a hoodie."

"I'm so glad to see you." She pushed up on her tiptoes, wrapping her arms around my neck.

I tossed my bag onto her couch and pulled her against me.

"You're the best part of my day, babe." I leaned down, kissing her gently.

"Mm, you, too. I'm glad you're staying tonight. I was wondering if you might help me with something. I talked to Alida about it, and she thought it was a good idea."

I gave her a cautious look. "Is this going to give you nightmares? You've been doing really well." I brushed strands of her blonde hair from her cheek.

"I think it's because I finally found out where I'm from. That had been tearing me up for the last several years. And ..." She glanced away before looking at me again. "I've done some research on cults."

"Do you have questions? Each one is different."

"It seems like they brainwash their followers. Did they do that to us, Kane?"

I kissed her forehead, hating that I was her only gateway to the past. The only reason I talked about it was to help her. I swore I would never look back the day I left the compound, but it hadn't happened like that. The abuse had caught up with me ... in a hole underground.

"Can I show you?" Brie's blue eyes filled with eagerness. She took my hand and led the way.

I walked down the hallway, a growing sense of trepidation nagging at me. Whatever it was, it was important to Brie, and she was what mattered. Her healing. When she healed, a part of me did, too.

"Sit." She pointed to the bed.

"Bossy much?" I laughed, climbing onto her mattress and propping myself up with pillows. Brie opened a drawer, then joined me with a metal lock box in her hand. She stared at it, then glanced at me.

"Mom gave me this. I've never looked inside of it before. She said when I was ready, it would be there. The only thing she would tell me was that it wouldn't make sense until I had my memories back. But, in a way, I do ... with you. So, I was hoping we could open it together, and you could help me understand what we were looking at."

"Are you ready?" I hated second-guessing her, but I had to make sure before we skipped through the fields of terror straight to hell.

"Yeah." A brave smile eased into place.

"Let's do it." I hoped I didn't regret my decision later.

The click of the box opening filled the room, and my pulse spiked while I waited to see what she was looking at.

Carefully, she lifted the contents out before she pushed away the container and sat next to me.

"Jesus," I whispered as I focused on an image of a younger Brie with bruises and cuts all over her face and arms.

Brie flipped the photo over. "It has the date on the back, then a note saying I was at Memorial Hospital. I look like hell."

"Do you remember any of that, babe?" I placed my palm on her knee, hoping to show my support.

She shook her head. "No." She glanced at me. "Mom and Dad said that I was banged up, but ... I don't understand. Did I get the bruises before I left you that night?"

Brie was right, that didn't match her running through the woods the evening she escaped. Even if she tripped a few times or ran into a thick tree limb, the marks on her didn't add up.

I held out my hand to study the picture, assessing the damage. "Do you know if you had bruises on your legs?"

"No, I can ask Mom and Dad, though."

I squinted, narrowing in on her thigh. A dark mark peered out from beneath her hospital gown. The world blurred, and my stomach churned. Had Brie been found and raped before her parents had discovered her on the side of the road? There was no way I would share my suspicions. Maybe her mom and dad could talk to her.

"Okay." I gave it back to her. "What else do you have?"

"Another picture." She paused, then, "Holy shit!" She turned the photo toward me. "Kane, he looks like Jagger Whitlock!"

I took it from her, shocked. "I'd forgotten about Lyle."

"Who?" Brie leaned over, looking again.

"Lyle. He was a year older than I was." A messy lump of emotion clogged my throat. "We were good friends and practiced football after our chores."

"What happened to him?"

"He died when the FBI stormed the compound. Lyle was terrified and ran in the wrong direction. He got caught in the line of fire when they took out one of the elders."

Brie fell silent, focusing on Lyle. "The first time I met Jagger, I couldn't figure out why he seemed so familiar. It was like I could feel a pull to him, but I wasn't attracted to him. It was weird as hell."

"That makes sense. Even though Jagger and Lyle aren't related, they look a lot alike. Jagger's hair is darker, and his eyes are bluer than Lyle's were, but similar build and expressions."

Brie tucked Lyle's photo back into the box. "You can have that picture if you want. I'm sorry you lost him." She leaned over and pressed her mouth to mine.

"I'll let you hang on to it for now, if that's okay. We weren't allowed many personal belongings, but sometimes, the elders would take pictures and give them to us. My guess is that you grabbed yours and took them the night we ran."

"I could see myself doing that." Brie revealed the following image, her mouth rounded in surprise. "Kane?"

My mouth curled up. "At least there's something good in this box."

"You looked so different then." Her attention darted from the image to me, then back to the photo.

"Yeah, my hair is shorter and darker. Plus, I'm not a scrawny little kid anymore. But you've changed, too."

Brie frowned, then studied the girl next to me.

"We couldn't touch. It's why we're standing a foot apart. That's

Donna, Kimberly, and Joe with us." I pointed to each person as I named them. "It was one of the holidays we celebrated."

"Christmas?" Brie asked.

"No. We didn't celebrate like other people do. It was most likely one of the annual rituals, but I don't recall for sure."

Brie placed the picture into the box, then turned to me. "Were you ever happy there?"

I massaged the back of my neck, searching for the right words. "Unless your memories return on their own, you'll never understand how dark and twisted the cult was. What we lived through ... we shouldn't be sane. But we're strong, and we've fought to piece our lives back together." I took her hand in min. "You and football were the two things that saved me, Brie. Even when I thought you'd left me behind, I thought about you every day."

Brie focused on her peach comforter. "I want to remember you." Her voice barely hovered above a whisper.

I placed my fingers beneath her chin and tilted it up. "You don't need to remember me then, baby. You have me now."

Brie grabbed my wrist, fighting against the tears building in her eyes. Bringing her mouth to mine, I poured all my feelings into that kiss. Nothing and no one meant more to me than Brie, and I promised myself that I wouldn't ever let her go again.

I released her. "I should stay focused on the contents of the box, but you're making it difficult." I smiled.

"What box?" She giggled and kissed me again. Brie straightened, then revealed the next item.

I stared at it as my stomach twisted in painful knots, and a sharp wave of pain impaled me.

Chapter Thirty-Nine

Kane

"Kane? What is it?" Brie's eyes filled with concern. "Do you know the men in the picture?"

Hatred crawled over my skin, leaving goose bumps in its wake. I thought I'd seen the last of them and told myself they were burning in hell to help myself cope, but here they were.

I cleared my throat, struggling to control the onslaught of dark memories slicing me open again. "Those are the elders," I finally managed to say.

"Like the leaders, right?"

I nodded, unable to tear my gaze away from the men. I shot to my feet and pressed my forehead and fists against the wall, whispering football plays beneath my breath. As hard as I'd tried to keep my shit together, I lost it in front of Brie. The one thing I promised myself I wouldn't do. It would only scare her about her past. My job was to protect and help her heal, not rip her apart.

"Kane, I'm going to touch you."

Brie slipped her arms around my waist and pressed against me, the heat of her body comforting me. We stood in silence, not moving for what felt like an eternity. Finally, I placed my hand on top of hers, then I turned to her.

Cupping her face, I tilted her head and kissed her. All I could feel was the thud of my heart against my ribs as I lost myself in that moment, driving away all the darkness. Brie was the only thing that mattered. Not the past. Not the memories. Just her.

I pressed my forehead against hers.

"We can put the box away." She hugged me and rested her cheek against my chest.

I smoothed her hair. "I think I need a break before we go any further, babe."

"We can take it a little at a time, ya know? I can't imagine what it's like for you."

I sucked in a deep breath, grateful for the break. "Why don't we get out of here?"

She looked up at me and smiled. "Where are we going?"

"Let me make a phone call. Why don't you get ready. Do whatever you normally do when you're in public."

She laughed, then pulled away. "What are you up to, Kane Cooper?"

God, she's beautiful. "Guess you'll have to find out." I gave her a cocky grin before I stepped out of the room and made my call.

Brie turned in the passenger's seat, glowering at me. "What do you mean you haven't ever done this before?" She folded her arms over her chest, pushing up her breasts.

"You can't bribe me with your gorgeous tits, babe. I won't say another word." I flipped on my signal and turned onto a back road. We weren't that far from the school, but the city wasn't big.

"Far, Far Too Long" by Alexander Nate played through the

stereo while my girlfriend pouted. I didn't miss her fingers tapping to the beat, though.

I slowed, then pulled onto a long driveway that wound up a hill.

"Holy shit." She leaned forward. "It's beautiful."

"The colonial house was built in the early nineteen hundreds. It's one of the tucked-away historical homes in Oregon. Everything has been restored, but the columns and other architectural features are original." I parked the car in front of the four-car garage and turned off the engine. Freshly trimmed shrubs lined the walkway, and the bright green set off the grey shutters around the windows.

Brie's face lit up, sending my pulse thundering into overdrive. That's what I needed, to see her happy. I hopped out, hurried to her side, and opened the passenger's door. Holding out my hand, I waited for her to grab her purse, then she placed her palm in mine.

"So, you know this property pretty well. I mean, we have permission to be here, right?" She stopped in her tracks, covering her mouth, then pointing above us. "Oh my God. I love the balcony. Is it off the master bedroom?"

"It is."

She spun on her heel, her childlike excitement contagious. "Are we able to see it?"

"I arranged a tour of the house."

She bounced on the balls of her feet, then threw her arms around my neck. "Thank you. This is perfect."

I laughed, then laced my fingers through hers. Approaching the manor, I rapped my knuckles on the mahogany door, and it swung open. A beautiful woman greeted us with a wide smile. Her hand fluttered over her heart as her eyes landed on Brie.

Brie's mouth gaped, then she looked at me, confusion etched in her features.

"Mrs. Cooper?"

"Welcome, Brie. It's so nice to see you again. Please, come in." Mom glanced at mine and Brie's joined fingers, then winked at me as we entered.

"This is your home?" Brie asked me.

"Well, it's my parents'." I rubbed her back, her expression registering that I'd brought her to my family's place. Since she'd already met Mom, and they'd hit it off, I thought it would make Brie feel more comfortable.

"Kane called and asked if you two could join us for dinner."

"Oh, that sounds wonderful." Brie smiled. "I wanted to thank you again for your help with the alarm system. I haven't had any more problems." Brie squeezed my hand, hard.

"I'm so relieved. I was ready to pack you up and move you in with us." Mom smoothed her emerald-green blouse, her blue eyes filling with a protectiveness for Brie.

Even though I was close to my parents, I hadn't talked to them about how I knew my girlfriend. Not yet.

"Kane said you would love to see the house?" Mom's heels clicked against the marble floors as she led us into the foyer. "Honey, why don't you let Dad know you're here, and I'll show Brie around."

"Thanks, Mom." I leaned over and kissed her cheek. "You're the best," I whispered in her ear.

Mom smiled, then she placed her palm on Brie's arm. "Why don't we start on the second floor?"

"Thank you. I noticed the balcony, and it's stunning." Brie chatted with Mom as they made their way up the stairs.

I shoved my hands into my pockets, watching them act like they'd known each other for years. Flickers of my possible future flashed through my mind.

"Someone's got it bad." Dad chuckled as he strolled out of the living room.

"Hey, thanks for making time for us. We needed a break from studying." I hugged Dad.

"Brie Langston, huh? She's from a really good family. And from what I hear, she's settling in well with new friends."

My brows knitted together. "Why would you keep an eye on her? That's kind of weird, isn't it?"

Dad patted my shoulder, and we walked toward the back of the house. "Your mother had me check on her a few times. Seems as though she's pretty invested in Brie, especially after the break-in."

"Mom loves the strays." Hell, she would probably disown me if she knew I was behind the break-in.

"Lucky for you, huh?" Dad's laugh echoed through the foyer. "Is it serious, son?"

I hadn't ever been embarrassed around my dad, but he'd caught me off guard.

"Yeah." I gave him a sheepish grin. "It's why I wanted to bring her over, but there are some things you should know."

Dad halted at his office. "Then let's have a seat, and you can fill me in."

I strolled in, remembering all the conversations about football, girls, grades, and my future we'd had in this room.

Dad shut the door, then walked around his oak executive desk, settling into his leather chair while I sank into the one in front of him. His laptop was closed, a stack of papers sitting on top of it.

"Are you reviewing a team?" I nodded to the pile.

"I am. You boys have some stiff competition over the next few weeks. It's time to bring your A game. But we're not going to talk about ball when you have a young lady here."

"I think she would join that conversation, actually. She seems to understand the game pretty well." I placed one ankle on the opposite knee and rubbed my jaw. I'd prepared for this chat in in my head a million times, but I had no idea how it would play out.

"You and Mom have given me so much. I want you to know I appreciate and love both of you."

Dad shifted in his chair. "You're our son. We would move heaven and earth for you. But, Kane, you've also worked your ass off to rebuild your life. We're both proud of you."

"Thanks. I honestly thought I'd left the cult in my rearview mirror, then ..."

Dad's gaze narrowed, but he remained silent.

I sucked in a breath. "Brie's real name is Lyndsay Jennings. She was the girl that I helped escape the cult."

He blinked excessively, staring at me in shock.

"She has amnesia, so she doesn't remember those years. Her parents found her on the side of the road, unconscious."

"Holy shit." Dad leaned back, the chair squeaking beneath his weight. He rubbed his face with his large hand. "You're positive it's her?"

"A thousand percent. She's older but still looks the same."

Dad inhaled, his eyes wide as he took a moment. "Son, are you all right? That's a lot for you to handle."

"Yeah, she's asking questions, and I'm able to share some things, but I'm trying to be careful. She's been working with a psychiatrist for the last few years, Alida. I've talked to her with Brie once. I will again if needed."

"Son, I'm not sure this is a good idea. You were approached by the NFL; you have your entire life ahead. If you dive back into the emotional trenches, it could really mess with your head."

The hair on my arms bristled. I wasn't expecting Dad's reaction.

"I'm aware. I've thought about it, but there's a lot you don't know about those years. I was the one that helped Brie escape, but she was also my girlfriend. We were in love. The plan was to run and build a new life together. The plan got fucked up, and I sacrificed myself in order for her to leave. Brie was supposed to bring the cops so they could raid the compound and free everyone." I stared at my feet, the pain still stabbing me in the chest. "It didn't happen because she got hurt, and her amnesia kicked in."

Dad massaged the back of his neck as his lips pursed. "What I'm hearing from you is that you've been in love with this girl most of your life?"

"Yeah. And now she's back, and she doesn't have any memories, but she wants to be with me, too. We're together, working through shit with a therapist." I held my dad's gaze, refusing to back down. As much as I respected him, nothing would change what Brie and I had.

His forehead creased, his telltale sign that he was thinking. "Does your mother know?"

I shook my head. "Not yet. I wanted to talk to you first. I think Mom will want to take Brie under her wing, make sure she has what she needs."

Dad's low chuckle filled the room. "Okay. You've said what you needed to. It's clear that your mind is made up, so how can I help? I realize you're grown, but you'll never stop being my son. I can't speak for your mom, but you and Brie have my full support."

Staring at the floor, I wiped the moisture that had pooled in my eyes. How had I gotten so lucky with Mom and Dad? Right then, I promised myself that I would make them proud.

"Just get to know her and give her a chance. She's smart, beautiful, and has a big heart. Dad, she's a fighter. We'll get through this."

Dad nodded. "I've seen firsthand that, when you set your mind to do something, nothing stops you. I trust that when you need us, you'll let me know."

"I promise."

Chapter Forty

Brie

"Thank you for the tour of your incredible home," I said to Mrs. Cooper as we returned to the foyer.

"You're welcome to visit anytime. Why don't we find the men?"

The door swung open, and a cute strawberry-blonde-haired girl strolled in. She frowned, her brown eyes assessing me. "Who are you?"

"Alexandria, that is no way to speak to our guest."

"Sorry," Alexandria muttered, flipping her hair behind her shoulder. "I'm Alexandria, Kane's sister."

I tried to disguise my surprise but failed miserably.

Alexandria's gaze narrowed. "He didn't tell you about me, did he?"

"Well, we haven't talked much about family yet. I know your mom because I'm renting my house from your parents." I placed my hand next to my mouth and leaned closer to her. "Kane hasn't even met my parents yet. Try not to be upset with him."

Alexandria's brows shot up. "Oh, you're his *girlfriend?* Kane has a girlfriend? He's never, ever brought a girl here for us to meet before."

I was pretty sure my heart melted right out of my chest and created a puddle at my feet. Kane had said he hadn't been in any serious relationships since leaving the cult, but I hadn't realized that he hadn't introduced any girls to his parents.

Mrs. Cooper slipped her arm around my shoulders. "Alexandria, do you have homework to finish before dinner?"

Alexandria's expression fell. "Yeah. I'll get it done."

"Thank you." Mrs. Cooper gave her a warning look, and I fought to suppress my giggle.

Once Alexandria was out of earshot, I asked, "How old is she?"

"Thirteen going on thirty. That girl has more attitude than any other child I've met in my life." Mrs. Cooper laughed. "Honestly, she's smart, funny, and is a great kid. She's just a teenager."

"She seems full of sass."

"Both of our kids are. I'm guessing that the men are in Taye's office. Let's check."

I followed her down a hall toward the back of the house, then she knocked on the door before she opened it.

I strolled in after her, my gaze on Kane.

He stood and offered me his chair. "Um, Brie, meet my dad."

I finally looked at the man behind the desk, and my eyes nearly popped out of my head.

"Coach?" My attention bounced between the three of them. "Coach is your dad? I had no idea."

Coach stood, smiling warmly. "We don't make a habit of announcing the relationship since people would assume Kane gets special favors. But welcome. It's nice to officially meet you. My wife and son are big fans of yours."

Heat crawled up my neck and cheeks. "I'm a fan of them as well."

I glanced at Mrs. Cooper, who was beaming with pride at both of her men.

Over the next several hours, I spent time with Kane and his

family, hearing how he had adjusted to his new life and focused on football. Although Coach never said anything, I suspected Kane had filled him in on our past together. With his occasional serious, sideways glances in my direction, it seemed that he was concerned about Kane's career with me around again. I wasn't sure if it was me or because I brought up Kane's past. Either way, I would prove him wrong and support Kane every step of the way.

"Are you ready?" Kane asked, taking my hand.

"Yup." I patted the overnight bag I'd packed when we stopped by my place after dinner with his family.

Kane strolled into his home, and I followed him in. "Did you get an alarm system?" I laughed. "I think I'll look at your windows and doors. Ya know, make sure everything is locked."

Kane wrapped his arm around my waist and pulled me against his muscular body. "You can check anything you need to. I'm just glad you're here." He placed a sweet kiss on my mouth.

"Me, too, but I'm nervous since your bedroom is upstairs, and I didn't bring my handcuff." After Kane had shared details of his past and how it affected him, I was less self-conscious about the restraint, but it still bothered me.

"I'll hold you all night long. You haven't had any night terrors when I've stayed at your place, so I think you'll be fine. Just remember you're safe."

"I know." Dread wrapped around my chest and squeezed tight. I was grateful that Kane had confidence in me. I couldn't say the same since I wasn't able to control the nightmares.

Kane led the way and showed me the upstairs. The evening I'd broken in, I'd seen the main floor but not the second one.

"How are you feeling about the game Saturday? Your dad seems concerned that I'm in your life and bringing all the baggage of our past with me." I set my bag on the desk in Kane's room. His king-size bed was centered against the far wall beneath the windows. I stared at them, my heart jumping into my throat.

"Brie?"

My gaze shifted to the dark wood floors as I wondered if I would be safe at his place. "I don't trust myself, Kane. The window is so close to the bed, and ..."

"Babe, I seriously think you'll be okay. I would like you to try to sleep without your cuff, but if you're going to be worried and stay up all night, that's not going to work either." Kane walked over to his closet and opened the door. He removed a box from the top shelf and dug around for a minute. "Here. This is your backup. I picked it up a few days ago." He handed me a wrist cuff and chain similar to the one attached to my bedframe.

I sighed, relief overtaking me as I sank onto the edge of his mattress. "Thank you." I chewed at the imaginary hangnail on my thumb.

Kane set the cuff on the nightstand. "I never want to put you in a situation that's not okay with you, babe. So, if you want to try to sleep without the restraint, I'm going to be next to you all night. I'll take care of you. If you aren't ready, then I'll help secure it. There's no pressure, Brie."

I glanced at him, butterflies fluttering in my belly. Kane had proven over and over again that he would do anything to show up for me. I loved that about him. I loved the man standing in front of me. *Holy shit.* For the first time in my life, I was head over heels in love. That scared me even more than sleeping without the cuff.

"I want to try it without the ball and chain." I mustered up the most confident smile I could manage.

"Okay. I'll get it ready, though, in case you wake up and want to secure it to your wrist."

He walked over to my side of the room, then knelt. "It was a big night, huh? I mean, with my family." Kane took my hand and kissed my palm, sending tingles through me.

"Yeah. There were a few surprises for sure. Your sister and the fact that Coach is your dad. I understand why you keep that one quiet. But you're amazing on the field, and even if it was public knowledge, no one could discredit you due to your talent. I just wonder why I didn't put it together earlier." I ran my hand over his dark hair, the soft strands tickling my palm.

"There are thirty families with the last name Cooper here and in the surrounding area. Dad and I try to keep things strictly as coach and player on the field. I guess it's been easy to separate the two. I mean, he's my dad but not."

"He is, though, Kane. It's obvious that they adore you. Did you know your bio father?"

"No. From what I understand, my mother showed up at the compound already pregnant with me. She wanted a new life without him."

"Do you ever wonder?" I wrapped my arms around his neck.

"Not really. It seems that family has nothing to do with blood relations. I'm happy with the one I have."

"Exactly. And soon, you'll meet mine and learn that we both ended up with amazing parents." I leaned down and kissed him. "Thank you for sharing that part of your life with me."

"I figured you should see the good stuff in my life since we talk a lot about the fucked-up shit." Sadness flickered through his expression.

Kane rose and gently laid me back on the mattress, settling between my parted thighs. I wrapped my legs around his waist, lifting my hips against his erection.

"I love you, Brie." Kane's eyes met mine.

I lost myself in his soft gaze. Nothing else in the world mattered except for us. "I love you, too."

Kane kissed me, and my mouth melted into his, moaning as his tongue slipped between my parted lips. He slid his hand beneath my sweater, cupping my breast and stroking my nipple through the lace fabric.

"Your top and bra are in my way." He gave me a panty-dropping smile as he climbed off me, then we both ditched our clothes.

To my surprise, Kane rolled on a condom. He usually waited until I gave him a blow job.

He joined me on the bed again, then sucked my taut bud, plumping my breast with the other hand. I relaxed into his gentle touch. He trailed kisses down my stomach and to the inside of my thigh, nipping at my skin before he swiped his tongue over my slit.

"I could eat you all day." His voice was husky, lighting me on fire and sending currents of electricity surging through me.

His tongue licked me, then fucked me, spearing so deep he hit my clit with his teeth and his nose buried into my flesh. My back arched off the bed as I threaded my fingers in his hair.

"Kane, oh, God. Baby." I propped up on my elbows, watching as he worshiped my pussy. He placed one of my legs over his shoulder, allowing him even better access. All I knew was that I couldn't hold on much longer, but I didn't want him to stop. I rocked my hips, grinding against his mouth, on the edge of losing control. My head fell back, and my eyes slammed closed. I trembled with sheer pleasure, and time stopped as my body convulsed with a mind-blowing orgasm. I gasped, digging my nails into the back of his neck as I came undone.

Kane moved up, positioning his hips between mine and gazing at me with hunger in his eyes. He lined up his shaft at my entrance, then eased in slowly, torturing me.

He kissed the corner of my mouth, then said, "I love you, Brie."

I moaned softly, arching against him as I rocked my pelvis to his. "I love you more." At that moment, I realized that my heart was just as invested as my body while he made love to me.

Kane grabbed my side, angling his hips and moving deeper inside me. My hands traveled over the dips and valleys of his strong shoulders and back, and I dug my nails into his ass cheeks, pulling him to me.

I was panting as he thrust faster, hitting a spot that made me cry out with my orgasm.

I writhed against him, demanding more.

Pleasure contorted his face, and a deep, guttural sound escaped him while his entire body tensed. Trembling, he poured himself into me.

Shocked, Kane blinked at me several times, then his mouth crashed down on mine, taking and giving as though I were the oxygen that kept him alive.

He broke the kiss, his smile brighter than a Christmas tree.

"You came." I traced his jawline, enjoying everything about this beautiful man.

He nodded. "That hasn't happened since ... since you left the compound. I guess you were what I needed all along."

As hard as I tried, my emotions ran over me like a bulldozer, and tears streamed down my cheeks. "I'm home, baby. I'm finally where I belong, and being with you is the only thing that matters."

He cupped the side of my face in his warm palm. "I hope you're okay with the pro ball life because you're going with me. No way in hell am I ever leaving you again."

I gaped at him. "Really?"

"I can't be my best self without you by my side. It will mean moving. You'll travel and probably finish your last year of college online, but you'll have the other wives and girlfriends around, too. It will be a different life, but I want you with me, Brie."

I didn't have to think about it. We'd come this far to find each other again, and deep in my heart, I knew I wanted him and no one else. Plus, we had another year together before he was possibly drafted.

"Meeting new people, traveling, being with you ... it sounds wonderful."

Kane's body relaxed even more. "I'm so relieved to hear you say that."

All I could do was smile at him, reveling in our moment together. For the first time, my life seemed absolutely perfect.

Chapter Forty-One

Kane

As Coach strolled in, I sat on the locker room bench with the other team members.

"Great practice, guys, but don't get cocky. Yes, we're undefeated and over halfway through the season. Which means that every game over the next few weeks will determine if you play for the championship."

We all roared, claiming victory and stomping our shoes on the concrete floor.

Coach laughed, then quieted us down. "Stay focused. Don't get too sure of yourself; that's when the mistakes happen, and shit goes south. Keep those grades up and stay out of trouble. We've not clenched the title yet."

"Yes, sir, Coach!" we all said in unison.

"Have a hell of a day." Coach gave us a small wave before he left and headed to his office.

"Hey, man, you've not been around the society much," Quinn said, sitting next to me. "Everything all right?"

"Yeah, just been busy with other stuff. I assume everything is fine, or you would have told me."

"It's all good. After the shit Jimmy pulled, no one wants to cross you or step out of line."

I stood, then closed my locker door. "Good, let's keep it that way."

Quinn rubbed his shoulder, a quizzical expression on his face. "So, you and Brie Langston, huh? I mean, the whole world saw you kiss her at the game a few weeks ago. I'm guessing that's who is keeping you busy and away from the society." He shot me a playful smirk.

"Pretty much." I grabbed my backpack off the bench, then hauled it over my shoulder. "It's different but good. We've worked out a lot of shit."

"Definitely looks like it. Well, if you think this is like 'the one'"—Quinn added air quotes—"then you might want to start thinking about who you're going to pass the mantle to at the society. You've got the place running pretty damn well since you dealt with Jimmy. Maybe you could continue to lead but have Brie in the rooms with you. I mean, we lost Calloway last year. If we change leadership again, that's gonna suck."

"I get it, but we will all eventually graduate, so shit will change anyway. I've got one year left, and if Brie agrees to what you're suggesting, then I'll consider it."

"Calloway could have done that, but I think Teagan wasn't on board. He was pussy-whipped." Quinn shook his head, bewildered.

I chuckled. "You'll understand when you find the one, man. In the meantime, keep an eye on things, and let me know if there are any concerns."

"Anything you need, boss." The corner of his mouth kicked up.

I walked to Coach's office, chewing on what Quinn had mentioned. I'd been so wrapped up in reconnecting with Brie that the society hadn't even crossed my mind. He was right, though. I needed to figure out what to do. I rapped my knuckles on Coach's door, then poked my head in. "Busy?"

"Come on in." He waved me forward.

I closed the door behind me, then sank into the chair in front of his desk.

"What can I do for you, son?"

"Just wanted to say hi. See how Mom and Alexandria were after dinner last week." I stretched my legs out, my jeans rustling with the movement.

"I think it went well. How did Brie do with learning who I am?"

I grinned. "She was definitely surprised, but she had nothing but good things to say about you and Mom. She seemed to like Alexandria, too."

Dad laced his fingers behind his head, his dark-eyed gaze assessing me. "You're doing well on the field, Kane. It seems that you're doing even better now. Keep up the good work."

Even though I didn't necessarily need Dad's approval, I wanted it. When he mentioned that I might lose focus and fuck up my career because of Brie, I decided to prove him wrong. "Thanks, I appreciate that. Brie is fully supportive of my goals."

"Good."

"In fact ..." I stared at my feet for a moment, a silly grin slipping into place. "She's agreed to go with me if I get drafted and play for the NFL."

Dad nodded, tapping his fingers on his desk. "You still have time to figure out the relationship in case anything changes."

Irritation flickered inside me. "I realize that, to you, it's sudden, but Brie and I have a history. I've loved that girl since we were kids. Nothing will change that, so maybe get used to the idea that she's in my life for good this time."

Dad held up his hands, palms facing me. "I didn't mean to imply that things would go south. I'm just trying to process what you've shared with me, and I can't help but be concerned. As a parent, I have that right."

My lips pursed together. "I know, but maybe start looking at all this differently. I've had this anger driving me my entire life, then after the FBI busted the compound, it was all I had left. Now, yeah, we're dealing with some bad memories, but I feel like a void has closed inside me now that she's back."

Dad steepled his fingers together, staring at me. "I felt that way with your mother."

"You did?"

"Yeah. We fit, ya know? It wasn't hard to love her, and I knew, beyond a shadow of a doubt, she was it for me."

"Exactly. That's how it is with us, too. I've loved Brie for a long time. If she hadn't lost her memories, I think we would have stayed together. I mean, who knows, but she's here now, and that's all that matters."

"Okay, then. I'll stop questioning things between the two of you. Plus, I'm pretty sure your mother would not be happy with me if she knew I was concerned. She has really taken to Brie. It's become her mission to make sure Brie knows she has a family here as well as in Tennessee. She mentioned reaching out to Brie's parents, but I told her not to yet. She needed to ask Brie if she was comfortable with that. Plus, what if she hasn't told them she's in a relationship yet?"

"Brie hasn't told them, so I would say that's a no on contacting them. She's had a lot on her plate with school and trying to remember enough of her past for it to make sense. I've helped some. Honestly, I hope like hell that she never remembers. It's too fucked up, and I don't want her to live through it again."

A knock at the door halted our conversation, and I stood.

"Talk to you later, Coach." I answered and nodded at the defensive line coach, Matt, as I left the office.

Even though it was only a little after five in the evening, it was dark. A light rain began to fall as I exited the building and headed to the parking lot. The cold temperature didn't bother me much since I was used to being on the field, but the wind cut through my sweatshirt and chilled me to the fucking bone.

I reached my Jag, climbed in, and tossed my backpack onto the passenger's seat. Pushing the button to start the engine, I then flipped the heat on high. Brie was probably freezing her sweet little ass off. Luckily, we could warm up in my bed later.

My cell rang, and I fumbled around in my bag for it. I didn't get many calls unless they were from Mom or Dad, and I'd just left Dad. All my friends texted me if they needed something. The society had a different untraceable messenger app that Sterling had created and burner phones.

I stared at the screen, not recognizing the number. Answering, I held the phone up to my ear.

"Hello?"

"Is this Kane Cooper?"

"It is. How can I help you?" I didn't recognize the woman's voice.

"This is Linda Opus ..."

That name seemed familiar, then it hit me. I listened as she continued speaking, then my heart stuttered, and I stopped breathing for a moment.

"Are you sure?" My voice cracked, heavy with emotion, as I struggled to keep my shit together.

Once Linda confirmed why she'd called, I closed my eyes and dragged in deep gulps of air. No fucking way was this happening.

Chapter Forty-Two

Kane

After my hands stopped shaking, I messaged Brie that I would meet her at her place. Nausea swam up my throat, my stomach churned, and I swallowed my fear. Nothing much scared me anymore, but Linda had shaken me to the core of my being.

I revved the engine, trying to calm down enough to drive. Turning on the headlights, I shifted into drive and pushed the accelerator only in time to slam on the brake.

"Fucking hell." Marc stood in front of my car in a black hoodie like the stupid little bitch he was. I did not have time for his bullshit. Why he kept meeting me on school property was beyond me. If he were smarter, he'd follow me to the grocery store, then approach me.

I threw the door open and jumped out, fury driving me as I stomped toward him, the wind blowing the rain into my face. I rubbed my jaw as I closed the gap between us. "What do you want?"

"I wanted you to know that I'm not leaving, Kane. You and your asshole friends can't force me to leave." He held up a hand. "I have an attorney, and I'm suing you for every fucking penny you have. Your potential NFL career is about to be over before it even starts." He sneered at me.

Disbelief sucked me under, then I came to my senses. "Let's get real, Marc. You want Brie. The only reason you're interested in suing me is to get her back."

"However it works out." He gave me a half shrug.

I clenched my teeth so hard I thought I would break a goddamn molar. "What do you want in order not to sue me?" I hated negotiating with him when I had bigger problems to deal with.

"A half a million, and you walk away from Brie."

I nearly choked on my laughter.

"What's so funny, asshole?"

I held my hands up in surrender. "I'm sorry. You caught me off guard. If I give you what you want, you have to sign a waiver, stating that you'll never come after me or my family again. Deal?"

Marc's nostrils flared, then he seemed to relax. "I get Brie?"

Sure, douchebag, because you forget she has a mind of her own. The quickest way to resolve this problem was to tell him what he wanted to hear, even though I didn't believe a word that was about to come out of my mouth. "You can have her. She's pretty fucked up, just like you said. I have to focus on my future."

"She's a mess, but she's *my* mess to manage." He tipped his chin up as though he were an all-powerful being.

"How do I reach out when I have the money and contract together?"

Marc rattled off his phone number, and I punched it into my cell. "I'll need an address for the agreement, too."

The lights from my car illuminated his face, and I resisted the urge to put the little shit in the hospital again.

Marc provided the information I needed, then I shoved my cell into my back pocket.

"You have forty-eight hours. No more, or I'm coming after you."

"Marc, be reasonable. It takes a bit to gather that kind of money.

Plus, if you sue me, Brie will never respect you again. Much less want to fuck you. Play this right, or you'll lose the girl."

He slapped me on the shoulder, nodding. "Forty-eight hours." We shared a pointed look before he walked away.

"Motherfucker," I muttered, then headed back to my car. Slamming the gear into drive, I peeled out of the parking lot, my tires spitting gravel behind me.

In record time, I pulled up to Brie's house. The indoor lights filtered through the thin front-window curtains, and I could see her walking around. That shit wouldn't cut it. I would pay for blackout curtains myself, but no one got to see my girl inside her home.

Scrubbing my cheeks with my hands, I attempted to clear my mind. In minutes, my entire world had imploded, and I had to figure out what to do first.

I locked my car before I jogged up the sidewalk and rang the bell. Brie must have been waiting for me because the door quickly opened.

"Hey." She smiled, and, for a moment, I was all right again.

"Hey, babe." I closed and locked up behind me, then pulled her in for a hug. "I've missed you today."

She snuggled into me, her cheek resting against my chest. "Me too."

I kissed her head, then released her. "Babe, we need to do something."

"Oh, that sounds promising." She grabbed the front of my hoodie, bunching it between her fingers.

"I wish, but this isn't what you're thinking. I need to see the rest of the contents in the box, Brie." My tone was low and serious.

Her features twisted in confusion. "Is something wrong?"

I rubbed her arms. "Please, can we see what else is in the box?"

"Of course." Her brows lowered, her forehead pinching together.

I followed her to her bedroom and waited while she joined me on the edge of the mattress with the metal box. She flipped it open, and I spotted the newspaper clipping still on top of the other items. She lifted the contents, then handed it to me.

Dread bundled inside me, and I felt sick as I read the article. I set it on her lap, then sorted through the rest. My attention landed on a little silver chain with a hand-carved moon. I looked at her, my blood pounding so hard in my ears that I couldn't think straight for a minute.

"Do you recognize this?" I held it up for her.

"No."

I swallowed, preparing myself to tell her the dark, ugly truth. "Your father made it for you. He had someone inscribe it on the back."

"What does it say?" She leaned closer as I flipped it over, running my fingers across the smooth wood. "*Lyndsay, you'll forever be under his eye.*" My stomach clenched so hard I thought I would puke on her floor.

"Kane? What does that mean?"

"Nothing good." I reached for the newspaper article. "Remember I mentioned the men in this picture were elders in the cult?"

"Yeah." Her voice was soft, vulnerable.

"That guy is Barry." I pointed to the bald man on the left. "That's Sam, Wagner, Mike, Rigs, and Mitch." My finger hovered over the guy in the middle. Something similar to fear scraped its ugly nails down my spine.

Chapter Forty-Three

Kane

"Brie, Wagner is your biological father. He's the leader of the cult."

Brie's gasp filled the room, her hand flying over her mouth. "That can't be right, Kane. Are you sure?"

"Babe, I would never fuck with you about something like that. Wagner is responsible for everything that happened to us. He made the law and enforced it, as well as abused and brainwashed us."

The color drained from Brie's face. She grabbed my forearm, squeezing hard. "You said *is*."

My head hung down, and a sharp ache pierced my chest. I opened and closed my mouth a few times before I finally found the right words. "Brie, a lady named Linda contacted me after football practice. She's reaching out to all the victims of the cult that are still alive that she could locate and letting them know that Wagner will be released from prison tomorrow."

Her eyes bore into mine, and heavy silence descended over us. So many emotions registered in Brie's expression that I couldn't pinpoint her feelings about the news.

Afraid I wouldn't be able to tell her the rest, I continued before I lost my nerve. "The wooden moon and the inscription ... it means no matter where you are, he will always be watching you."

Brie shivered with the ominous promise from her father. "I-I don't understand, Kane. What do you mean?"

I took her hand in mine. "When Wagner was arrested, I was outside by that time. They threw him on the ground and pinned him down. He spewed threats as the FBI cleaned out the compound, but the one thing he promised above all else was that when he was free ..." *Shit.* Warm, prickly horror clawed its way up my chest, and I was suddenly lightheaded. "That he would find you and resurrect the Light of David again."

Brie began to tremble uncontrollably, tears filling her eyes. "I'm not safe anymore? He's coming for me?" Panic threaded through her voice.

I shook my head. "Fuck no. No way, babe. I won't ever let that happen. I'm older, stronger, and smarter than I was when we were in the cult."

"How can you make that promise? Things went wrong last time. What if they do again?"

I drew her against me, holding her. "Brie, you've changed your name and moved across the country. The cult was in the mountains of Montana. That's where your parents found you that night. You lived in Tennessee for a while, but you're here with a new identity. I think someone would have reached out to you by now."

"Is that enough?" Her voice trembled with her words.

"I think so. It will give us a head start to see what we need to do to keep you safe from the bastard."

She sniffled, then stared at me. "You, too, Kane. You're all over the press with your college football success. What if you're not safe either?"

I rubbed her back. The phone call and shit with Marc had

happened so fast, I hadn't had time to think through the news about Wagner yet, but she was right. If nothing else, he would use me to get to her. He was a sick and evil bastard and would stop at nothing to get what he wanted.

"Pack your bag with whatever you need. For now, you're staying with me. I'm not leaving you alone. I need to call Mom and Dad. We'll go by their place before we go to mine."

Brie rose, her nose and cheeks red from her tears. I fucking hated this. I was sick and tired of my past dictating my life. Worse, it had come for us right when I thought we would be okay. Anger ripped through me, clouding my vision. I'd lost Brie once, and I refused to lose her now. I would do anything to ensure it didn't happen and that Wagner never touched her again.

"Let me call Mom and Dad, then I'll help you pack." I kissed her forehead before I headed to the living room.

I fished my phone out of my back pocket and pulled up Dad's number in my favorites. Fear seeped into my bones, weighing me down.

"Hey, son. I'm just leaving campus, so if you hear static, it's this crazy wind."

"Can you hear me?" I tried not to yell at him, but I could barely make out what he was saying.

"Hang on. Let me get to the car."

Rustling filled the line, and I held the phone away from my ear.

"Shit, sorry about that. What's up?"

"Are you and Mom home tonight?" I shoved my hand through my hair, my nerves raw and on edge.

"Yeah. Your mom should already be there. Alexandria has basketball practice, but she's catching a ride with a friend. Would you and Brie like to join us for dinner?"

"That sounds good. I need to talk to you guys about something. It's serious and has to do with our past. We're in danger. Wagner, Brie's biological father, is about to be released from prison."

The sound of Dad starting the car filtered through the phone.

"I'll let your mom know as soon as I get home. Meet us there, son. I'll see you soon." Dad disconnected the call. One thing I could say about my parents was that, if shit was going down, they dropped everything and showed up for me. This time, they were showing up for Brie, too. I just wished the circumstances were different.

"Hi, sweetheart." Mom hugged Brie the moment we stepped into my parents' house.

"Hi, Mrs. Cooper."

"Brie, call me Amelia. I insist," Mom said before she turned and embraced me.

"Hi, Mom. Thanks for having us."

"Your father filled me in. Let's head to the living room where we can talk comfortably." Mom took my hand and patted it. "Kids, it's going to work out. I'm not sure how, but it will."

Brie nodded, then wrapped her arms around herself while we followed Mom.

Dad stood staring out of the windows and turned as he heard us join him. "Hey, kids."

"Hi, Coach," Brie said before she settled in on the cream-colored leather couch.

I sat beside her while Mom sat across from us in the matching loveseat. Dad continued to pace in front of the fireplace, wearing a hole in the brown Persian rug that covered a large section of the dark hardwood floors.

"Brie, have you reached out to your parents about any of this?" Mom asked.

Brie wrung her hands in her lap. "No. I don't want to worry them."

Mom's kind gaze landed on my girlfriend. "Hon, they need to know. Parents want to protect their grown children, too. Why don't you call them? I'm happy to chat with your mom and let her know what we're doing to keep everyone safe. She can reach out to me every day if she needs to."

Brie worried her lower lip in her teeth, then collected her phone from her purse. "Where can I make the call?"

"Feel free to use the formal dining room. You'll have privacy there," Mom said.

Brie stood, and I squeezed her hand, showing her my support before she left. Not even a minute later, Brie joined us again. "No one answered the landline or their cells. Mom and Dad must be outside or on a walk. They love to be outdoors during the fall." She settled in next to me.

Dad cleared his throat. "I made some calls on my way home, so we'll have a few additional people joining us shortly."

"Who?" I asked, slipping my arm around Brie.

"Pierce and Sutton Westbrook. They own a security company based in Spokane and have another location in Portland. I caught them while they were in Portland on business. Also, Pierce has worked with the FBI on several cases. They come highly recommended by a longtime friend of mine, Franklin Harrington, who is close with the Westbrooks. He was with them when I called. You might have heard of his son and daughter-in-law, Hendrix and Gemma Harrington."

"Oh, wow!" Brie's excitement filled the room. "They're the lead singers for August Clover. I love their music."

"That's them. Franklin is a well-known attorney. I'm not sure how much he's practicing now, but he'll be joining us as well. He can help us figure out what to do and if we have any legal recourse."

I drummed my fingers on my thigh, deep in thought. "Are we hiring security?"

Dad's lips thinned. "I don't know yet, but I'm open to the idea if it keeps both of you safe."

Brie chewed on her thumbnail, and her knee bounced with her

anxiety. The doorbell rang, startling her. I wasn't sure how to comfort her when I was barely holding my shit together.

Voices traveled through the foyer as Mom and Dad's housekeeper answered the door and walked the guests to the living room.

Brie and I stood, waiting to introduce ourselves.

"Franklin, it's great to see you." Dad approached him and shook his hand.

"Always a pleasure. That football team of yours is looking really good for the championship this year." Franklin flashed Dad a wide smile, then smoothed his blue button-down shirt and turned to Mom. "Hi, Amelia. It's nice to see you again."

"Franklin, thank you for joining us. This is our son, Kane, and his girlfriend, Brie."

"Kane, I've heard a lot about you from your father," Franklin said.

I smiled, chuckling. "I hope it was all good." I shook his hand.

"Always. He's your biggest fan." Franklin's warm smile settled my nerves a bit.

"Hi, Mr. Harrington," Brie said.

"Please, call me Franklin."

I glanced behind Franklin and spotted a tall, broad-shouldered guy with an attractive blonde woman next to him. I suspected they were the Westbrooks.

"You must be Pierce and Sutton," Dad said. "Welcome."

"Thank you. It's nice to meet all of you," Pierce said. "This is my wife, Sutton."

After the introductions were made, we all settled in.

"Brie, I understand that your father will be released from prison tomorrow," Franklin started.

"Yeah. I didn't get a call, but Kane did. I'm not sure why the woman didn't call me too." Brie glanced at me.

"I don't think she knows who or where you are, which is to our advantage. I was easier to track. I've been in the same place since the FBI raided the compound. Also, they kept in touch with the social worker that helped me find Mom and Dad." I squeezed her hand.

"Is there a possibility your father has lost track of you as well?" Pierce asked.

Sutton remained quiet but was scribbling notes in a notebook.

"Most likely. I mean, I don't know. After I left the cult, I ended up with amnesia. I don't remember anything. Kane does, though," Brie explained.

Pierce turned his attention to me. "Kane, what can you tell us?"

I gently rubbed the back of Brie's hand, stroking it with the pad of my thumb and hoping to keep her calm.

"Wagner is the head of the cult that Brie and I were in. We were born into it. I helped her escape when she was fourteen, but whatever happened to her ... it caused amnesia. The plan was for her to get out and bring help. It didn't happen that way, though. A few months after Brie escaped, the FBI raided the place and made arrests. Apparently, they had someone on the inside, and it was only a matter of time before they dismantled the organization. I'm not sure why Wagner is only serving five years, but he's being released tomorrow." A heavy weight settled over my shoulders, threatening to smother me. "He'll look for Brie and possibly me, too."

Franklin crossed his legs and smoothed his black slacks. His blue eyes flickered with concern, but I suspected his mind was sifting through ideas of how to help us.

"Does Wagner have any idea that you're in Oregon, Kane? You're all over the media, so unless you changed your physical appearance, he probably knows." Pierce's brown-eyed gaze narrowed.

"I look a lot different than I did at fifteen, but yeah, it's possible. I had some reconstructive surgery after I was beaten." Panic ripped the air from my lungs. "If he does, I'm afraid that he'll find Brie, and I'll have helped him."

"Son, you can't go there. Let's give Franklin and the Westbrooks time to figure this out." Dad's tone was firm with a hint of gentleness.

We continued to talk over the next hour, and I provided as much detail as I could. Brie had grown quiet, listening and absorbing the severity of the situation.

"I'll make some calls first thing in the morning and see if I can learn why Wagner is being released after five years and what he was charged with originally. Legally, I'm not sure what we can do, but I'll look for any opportunity to put him back in prison," Franklin said.

Sutton tucked her hair behind her ear, then continued to take notes.

"Kane, you're high profile with your career, so I'd like to see if you're open to bodyguards for you and Brie." Pierce leaned forward, clasping his hands together.

I shook my head as though it might clear the fog from my overwhelmed brain. "I'm all about protecting Brie since she's my main priority, but if the NFL catches wind of this ..."

"It could cause problems," Dad interjected. "As in teams not signing him."

"That won't be a problem," Sutton finally piped in. "Our guys blend in very well. No one has to know that you have eyes on you at all times."

"That could work, right?" Brie asked me, hope filling her face.

"Yeah. I think so." I stretched my legs out in front of me.

"I'll look at the schedule, but where are you staying tonight?" Sutton asked.

"At a friend's place. It has an excellent alarm system, and I would feel safer if Brie and I stayed there."

Brie nodded, but I wasn't sure if she realized I was talking about staying at the society's house. There were bedrooms on the main floor, or we could sleep downstairs in my office. Each door lock required a thumbprint, and Wagner sure as fuck wasn't on the list of approved people.

"Okay. As long as you can stay in a safe place. We should know more in a few days. Franklin will look into the legal side, and I'll call my FBI contact to see what else we can learn. Even though Wagner is being released tomorrow, it doesn't mean the FBI won't have eyes on him. It happens." Pierce rose from his seat, and Sutton followed.

"We're going to head out so we can start making calls. Sutton will reach out later with the names of your bodyguards. There will be one for each of you," Pierce added.

Franklin stood, then we exchanged phone numbers before saying our goodbyes. All Brie and I could do now was wait, and it fucking sucked. Even though I'd tried to soothe Brie's fears, I realized we were sitting ducks.

Chapter Forty-Four

Brie

"I didn't think that the society was in a house." I wandered into the kitchen, spotting the beer cans and alcohol bottles that littered the granite counters.

"Sorry, I wasn't expecting company other than the members." Kane grabbed a black trash bag beneath the counter and started to clean up. I wondered if it helped his anxiety to keep busy. It certainly did mine.

"Let me help. I need something to do." I began flipping open the top cabinets, searching for where the bottles belonged.

"How are you feeling about the conversation with Franklin and the Westbrooks?" Kane didn't look at me but continued to clean.

"I'm good with the security if it's low profile. We don't even know if Wagner is looking for us, and I don't want the situation to screw up your career." Finally locating where the liquor was stored, I cleared the counter. "Are there any Clorox wipes?"

"Under the sink."

Once I located them, I sanitized the hell out of every surface in the kitchen and living room. I was a bit terrified to think about what state the bathroom might be in since men occupied the place on a regular basis.

"Hey, listen. You're probably going to see the guys if we stay here very long." Kane ran his fingers through his hair, ruffling the dark strands.

"Okay." It took me a moment to realize why he brought it up. "I won't tell anyone who is in the society. I promise. I think I might have a few ideas anyway."

"Oh?" Kane folded his arms over his chest, his biceps bulging through his black, long-sleeved T-shirt.

"Well, it would make sense if they were your closest friends on the football team." I eyed him, watching his expression fall. "I won't say a word, babe. If I did, it would hurt you, too, and I wouldn't do that."

Kane dropped his arms and joined me on the other side of the kitchen. He brushed the hair off my cheek. "You're not my concern, babe. I don't want the guys to stress about being ratted out. Some of them know you're friends with Teagan. She knows who some of them are as well. Teagan and the old leader of the society hooked up last year."

I shoved at his muscled chest. "No fucking way. She's never said a word, Kane. Not even a clue. I had no idea."

Kane chuckled, and it warmed my heart. It had been an intense evening, so a lighter conversation was nice.

"You can talk to her about the society or me, but not anyone else." He placed a kiss on my forehead. "It's not me you need to convince, though. I trust you, but the guys might be a little apprehensive. I'll talk to them and give them a choice to use the downstairs entrance and not hang here for a bit."

"Okay, whatever you feel is best." I opened the refrigerator. "Do you have something to eat? I'm starving."

Kane laughed. "Junk is about it." He snatched a bag of chips from the top of the fridge and handed the Doritos to me.

At this point, I was okay with anything to eat since I was stressed out.

Kane's phone rang, and he removed it from his back pocket.

"This is Kane."

I stood rooted in place, hoping it was good news, like Wagner had been gunned down and was dead.

"Okay. Yeah, I'll email our schedules to you along with the address of where we're staying. Thanks, Sutton."

Kane disconnected the call. "Sutton is ready to send bodyguards over, which means that I would have to share the location of the society." He rubbed the back of his neck as tension hung in the air.

"Kane, we don't need to stay here. I have an alarm system, remember? We can stay at my place. Plus, it's in a neighborhood, and from what your mom said, there is one super nosy lady that reports all the gossip in the area. She'll be perfect to keep an eye on the house along with the bodyguards. And the guys won't resent me for screwing with their groove. They have a good thing going here."

"You're right. It was just the safest spot I could think of when we were talking through all the shit. I'll email Sutton your address. We can swing by my place, and I'll grab some clothes."

Brie took my hand. "Maybe you need to leave some at my place, so you don't have to pack every time. Your family knows we're together, and even if they saw your jacket or belongings at my house, it's not a big deal."

Kane leaned down and kissed me. "I would love that. Let's get out of here before one of the guys shows up."

I placed my hand on his chest. "At least you got a clean kitchen out of the deal." I smiled, ready to leave and snuggle up to Kane on my couch.

A few hours later, we arrived back at my place. We'd made a quick trip to the grocery store, then I helped Kane pack. It was the closest

I'd ever come to living with a guy, and I was ready to have him with me full time. I just wasn't sure how he felt about it yet.

Sutton had messaged that we had two bodyguards, Vaughn and Zayne. They had flown in from Spokane and were already in Oregon. It was apparently only a forty-five-minute flight on Pierce's plane. My family had money, but not that kind of money. A private plane sounded like a hell of a lot of fun.

Later, Sutton and Pierce met us at my house and introduced Vaughn and Zayne. I swear they'd walked off the cover of a magazine. They were as handsome as Pierce was. What was more interesting was Vaughn's eyes—one blue and one brown. I bet the ladies tripped over themselves when they saw him. Once Kane and I met everyone, they left, and we settled in for the evening.

"Are you feeling better now that the bodyguards are here?" Kane asked.

"Yeah. I know there's an alarm system, and you're here, too, but just so we're clear ... we're not hiding here. We have classes, games, and friends. Pierce and Sutton said for us to stick to our normal routines." I strolled over to the kitchen, and Kane followed. "I thought I'd cook something to eat."

"Sounds good. What can I help with?" He leaned against the counter, watching me remove the plastic wrap over the pepperoni pizza we'd picked up.

I set the temperature and timer, then popped the food into the oven. "I was thinking." I straightened, grimacing. "I haven't told my parents about you or the cult. I realize I need to introduce you and let them know we're together, but there's all the icky shit I have to explain as well, and they're going to want me to move back to Tennessee. I won't go back, and they'll be stressed and worried. I can't put them through more hell. Not after everything they've done for me." I swore Kane could hear the rapid rhythm of my heart slamming against my ribs. The mere idea of telling my parents sent my anxiety through the roof.

"I think now that we have security, it will help, but ..." A crease dented the smooth skin between his eyebrows. "Are you positive that, if your parents insist that you move back home, you won't go?" Uncertainty danced across his features.

I closed the gap between us and slid my arms around his waist, peering up at him. "No. I won't go anywhere without you, Kane. Fate has brought us together again, and our souls reinforce the strength in each other."

Kane grabbed my chin, tilting my face so I had to look at him. "I love you, baby. You're the one bright light in all of this darkness. With that said, if moving back to Tennessee will protect you and keep you safe, I'll go with you. I don't want you to worry about talking to your family. We'll figure this out together."

"Okay. I'll see what day this week they're available for a video call." I pressed my lips to Kane's, grateful that he was willing to do what was necessary to protect me—protect us. But I would do the same for him. Kane had sacrificed enough for me, and I refused to let him do it again.

Chapter Forty-Five

Brie

"Are you ready?" I asked Kane while I opened my laptop.

"Yeah. Are you?" Kane placed his warm palm on my thigh beneath the kitchen table, giving it a gentle squeeze.

I logged on to the video call, and seconds later, Mom and Dad came into view. My heart squeezed at the sight of them. I'd missed them more than I'd realized.

"Hi!" I beamed at them. "How are you?"

"Hi, honey. It's so nice to see your beautiful face." Mom's eyes glistened with moisture, and she dabbed at them with her finger. Dad wrapped his arm around her, smiling at me.

"I miss you guys so much." I smiled, willing myself not to start crying along with her. We had a ton of ground to cover. "I have a lot to fill you in on, but first, this is Kane." I motioned to him.

"Hi, Mr. and Mrs. Langston. It's nice to meet you."

Good god, this man melted me into a hormonal puddle with his manners. Reeling in my overactive thoughts, I chided myself for having a sexual fantasy about my boyfriend and forced myself to focus on my parents.

"Kane is our quarterback and has already been approached by the NFL." I was pretty sure Dad would be impressed. Who wouldn't be?

"Wait, you're Kane Cooper?"

Kane flashed them a confident smile. "I am."

Dad's eyes lit up when he realized who I was dating.

"I'm watching every one of your games that's on here. You've got one hell of a throw."

"I owe that to my dad." Kane shifted in his chair and placed his arm on the back of mine, rubbing my shoulder.

Mom watched Kane's every move. Knowing her, she was taking in what I wasn't saying—that we loved each other.

"Are you coming home for Christmas? I know it's still a few weeks away from Thanksgiving, but I'll need to buy a ticket for you." Eagerness danced in Mom's expression.

I glanced at Kane, wondering if he would want to visit Tennessee with me. "Let me get back to you on that." I might want Kane to go with me, but after my family learned how I knew him, I wasn't sure if they would welcome him or slam the door in his face. A ball of anxiety lodged in my throat.

We continued with the small talk for a few more minutes, then it was time to drop the bomb on them.

"So, Kane and I actually knew each other before attending Whitmore." I wondered if they would put it together.

"Oh? From where?" Dad asked. "Kane, have you attended school in Tennessee?"

"No, sir. My family is from Oregon." Kane's shoulders tensed with his confession.

Mom frowned. "Then how do you know each other?"

I cleared my throat, sitting on my hands so no one would see how hard I was shaking. "Well, Kane is from my past. He knows that I have amnesia and might never regain my memories, but he's filled in some gaps for me while we've reconnected."

The air in the room crackled with tension. "I also opened the box. We've seen the newspaper article and the pictures."

Dad's brows furrowed, and Mom covered her mouth with her palm. I wanted to give them a moment to absorb what I'd shared before I continued.

Mom's other hand fidgeted in her lap. "We weren't sure about the newspaper article, but for some reason, I clipped it. It was just one of those unexplained nudges, and the timing of when we found you and the fact that we were in Montana where the Light of David was located ... we wondered. Then there were the items we found on you. It seemed like it was a strong possibility."

"You were correct. Kane and I are from the Light of David." I gulped, swallowing my fear as images danced along the edges of my mind. "Kane can answer some questions for you. I've had a few flashbacks, but nothing that has triggered a lot of memories."

Kane rubbed my arm. "Honestly, I hope she never remembers. It was a very dark time for both of us."

My boyfriend continued to fill them in on the night he helped me escape and how we were connected. He explained that he'd fallen in love with me when we were young and was shocked to learn that I was attending Whitmore. Mom and Dad asked a few questions but seemed to respect that we didn't want to dive into the gory details.

I stared at the folded newspaper article peeking out beneath my computer. My fingers balled into fists in my lap. I'd brought it to show Mom and Dad again. The idea that Wagner was free slapped me in the face, and tears prickled my hazy stare.

"Do you recognize the men in the newspaper?" I held up the clipping, nausea bubbling in my belly.

"We don't recognize who they are, but I remember seeing them in the article. Something was seriously off, but I couldn't pinpoint it at the time. Your mother and I were more concerned about the young lady that we'd found on the side of the road."

I sucked in a deep breath. "These are the elders of the cult. This guy here ... his name is Wagner, and he's just been released from prison." My chin trembled as I forced myself to speak the following words. "He's my biological father."

I watched helplessly as shock then fear registered on their faces.

"Where is he now?" Dad asked, his voice shaking. Not much rattled my dad, but that was before he knew I was the product of a cult and had an insane sperm donor.

"Sir, all we know is that he was released from prison in Nebraska. I received a call to let me know. Brie didn't get one, so I'm guessing no one realizes who she is, including Wagner. However, I immediately spoke with my parents, and they've hired full-time security. We've met the men who will discreetly follow us and keep us safe."

"Mom, Dad, you have to keep this quiet. It could jeopardize Kane's football career."

Dad's gaze flashed with anger. "I don't give a shit about a career if that psycho is looking for my daughter."

"Rodger," Mom said, attempting to calm him.

"Kane, please thank your parents for us. I would like to contact them to pay for half of the security services."

I had forgotten that Mom had already met Amelia when she'd rented the house and picked up the keys the day we moved in.

"Mom, you already know Kane's mom. Amelia and her husband own the rental. Those are Kane's parents."

My mom had impeccable posture, but her shoulders sagged with relief. "I really enjoyed talking with her. That makes me feel better. I'll contact her later today."

"She's been really good to me, Mom and Dad. I've had dinner a few times at their place and spent some time with her."

"Mom *loves* Brie is more like it," Kane added, winking at me. "Mom and Dad want Brie to feel as though she has family here while she's away from you guys. I don't think there's anything my parents wouldn't do for her."

I stared at my lap, overwhelmed with a sense of belonging, something I hadn't ever experienced outside of my own parents.

"They seem to have proved that with hiring security so quickly. I'll thank them and discuss details about payment. Brie, you should come home. We can keep you safer here." Mom's expression turned grim.

There it was. At least I'd anticipated it. "I'm not moving back to Tennessee. I'm staying here. I have a life with Kane, and I have friends. I love Oregon and Whitmore, and I refuse to let Wagner scare me off."

Dad grimaced. "You've always been a strong-willed girl, but I suspect it's kept you alive. I'm not fond of your choice, but we'll support it ... for now. If that son of a bitch shows up, though, you're on the first plane here, young lady."

I nodded, not trusting myself to respond. I wouldn't agree or disagree at this point because I had no idea what life would look like down the road.

"I'll stay in touch better and send you Kane's phone number as well. I don't want you guys to worry, but I needed to let you know what was happening."

A few minutes later, I logged off the call and slumped against the table, releasing a tired sigh. "Holy shit. That wasn't fun." I turned to Kane, who looked as relieved as I was that it was over.

Kane rubbed his temples and sighed. "At least I've met them, and our mothers like each other. That's a plus. I'm sure your parents will have questions, too, so be prepared."

I gave a half shrug. "I don't think I'm the one who needs to be prepared. I don't have many memories from back then." I worried my bottom lip with my teeth. "Honestly, I'm not sure it's important to remember. I think my brain is protecting me from the abuse, and since you've explained where we came from, it's enough. I think I'm finally at peace with it."

Kane pulled me in for a kiss. "You know I'll answer any questions you have, but I hope you never regain your memories. It's safer that way."

Chapter Forty-Six

Kane

The week had passed painfully slowly, with only a few texts from Sutton that they were in touch with the FBI concerning Wagner. The bastard hadn't shown up at Whitmore, but every fucking second of the day, I looked over my shoulder and held my breath. The one good thing? I was with Brie every night, holding her while she slept.

"Kane!" Coach called after me as the team jogged to the locker rooms.

I slowed, waiting for him.

"Hey, son," he said quietly. "I wanted to see how you and Brie are doing with everything going on. Honestly, your game is spot on, so I can't really tell if it's messing with your head like it is mine."

I swung my helmet in my hand, glancing at Dad. "I won't lie. It's hard. I'm paranoid as hell. One thing I've appreciated is how discrete Vaughn and Zayne are. I rarely see them, so I doubt anyone not looking for them would even realize who they are. It helps not having to worry about the news getting out."

Dad patted my back. "Pierce and Sutton were very understanding of us trying to keep this out of the press."

"Do you think the NFL would pass on me if they found out about Wagner and the cult?" Even though I asked the question, I wasn't sure I wanted to hear the answer.

"It's a possibility, Kane. If they think you're a danger to the rest of the players, then yeah, I think they would have to make a tough call."

"Guess I'll ensure that they don't find out and pay to have security forever." I clasped my helmet tighter, talking myself off the ledge. Brie was the most important thing in to me, but football was a close second. They had both saved my life and kept me sane, and I couldn't handle it if I lost everything again.

I glanced over at my beautiful girlfriend, curled up at the other end of the couch, studying. She looked sexy as hell in my grey hoodie that hung off her petite frame. When she got home from classes and cheer practice, she changed into sweats and found a blanket to curl up under.

We'd somehow worked out a good study routine and kept our grades up despite our stress. With the extra time together, I'd fallen even more in love with Brie's strong spirit and drive to move forward.

My phone rang, pulling my attention away from her. Reaching for my cell on the coffee table, I checked the screen before answering.

"It's the Westbrooks," I said to Brie before I answered.

"Hey. Hopefully, you have good news." I paused. "Sure, she's right here. Hang on." I muted the call. "Babe, they want to talk to both of us."

She closed her psychology book and set it on the floor. "Okay." Brie scooted closer to me, then I unmuted the phone and placed the call on speaker.

"We're here," I said.

"Hi, Brie," Sutton said. "How are you holding up?"

"I'm all right. I'm hoping you have some good news." Brie stuffed her hands into the pockets of the sweatshirt, shivering.

I pulled her closer and set the phone on my knee.

"Pierce has some information, so I'll let him talk."

"Hey, guys," Pierce said. "I'll jump right in. Brie, the reason Wagner was released was because when he was arrested, some of the charges didn't stick because no one testified against him. One of the big ones that didn't hold up was kidnapping across state lines."

Brie frowned. "He kidnapped kids?"

I swallowed hard, not realizing that the elders had snatched children, but it didn't surprise me.

"Brie, do you know who your biological mother is? Franklin explained that you have amnesia, but I wanted to double-check," Pierce asked.

"No. I didn't even know about Wagner until Kane told me."

I glanced at Brie. "I think I can help. Her mother was in the cult with us."

"Wait. I think I had a flashback of her." Brie's gaze clouded with fear. "She was at the compound and had light brown hair in a bun."

"Yeah, Bernadette," I said.

A pause filled the line. "From what we've learned, Brie, she wasn't your biological mom," Sutton said softly. "You were one of the children that were kidnapped when you were little. Maybe two years old."

Every nerve ending inside me stood on high alert. I looked at Brie, wondering how she was taking this new information.

"Is she alive?" Brie brought her fisted hand to her mouth.

"We're not sure who she is, but we're working on it," Sutton explained.

"The FBI has been on this case for a while, even with Wagner in prison, but a DNA sample will speed up the process, if you're open to it," Pierce said.

"How does the FBI know all of this?" I asked, trying to fit the pieces together.

"I can't provide a lot more information, but a few other people have come forward once they learned that Wagner was released. One of them took care of Brie when Wagner brought her to the compound. They also mentioned that when Wagner would get drunk, he would brag about all the stolen children," he shared. "And Brie, there's a bigger reason that I'm calling other than DNA. My contact would like to have you set up a meeting with Wagner."

"What the actual fuck?" I shot off the couch, sending my cell clattering to the floor.

Brie snatched it up. "Pierce? Sutton? Are you there? Kane dropped the phone."

"We're here. I know that was a big ask," Sutton admitted. "I think my reaction was similar to Kane's."

"No. This is not up for debate. She's not meeting the bastard," I stated, leaving no room for question ... or so I thought.

Brie's expression turned stoic. "What good will it do if I meet Wagner?"

My jaw clenched as I shook my head. This was not what I was expecting.

"You would be surrounded by the FBI and our men, Brie. No way would you go in alone. Wagner would have no idea that anyone else was there. If you can get him to admit that he kidnapped kids and transported them across state lines, including you, then depending on which state the children were from, the penalty could be up to twenty years per offense."

Brie slammed her eyes closed. "You mean he would go away for life."

"Yes. And with the other people that have come forward, it's looking really good to put him behind bars again since he was never tried on those crimes."

"Shit." I massaged the back of my neck, my muscles so knotted with tension it was giving me a headache. "Brie." I shook my head. "We can leave and start a life all over again. We'll change our names, but don't do this, baby."

Tears slipped down her cheeks, and she angrily brushed them away. "I need some time to think about all of this. There's no way I can give you an answer right now. I'll do a DNA test, though. I'm not sure when, but at some point, I would like to know if my real mom is around."

"Of course. I will say that time is of the essence. Could you let us know by this weekend?" Pierce asked.

"I won't have an answer before Kane's game Saturday. We both need to be as clearheaded as possible so he can stay focused on the field."

"Sounds fair."

"Thanks for calling," I muttered, not meaning a fucking word I'd said.

"Let us know if you need anything," Sutton chimed in before everyone said goodbye, and I disconnected the call.

I stared down at Brie, my blood boiling with anger mixed with sheer terror. "No. We're not even entertaining this."

Brie stood and hugged me, clinging to me as she cried.

"Oh, baby. I love you so much, but I can't allow you to be bait for a deranged lunatic. It sounds as if maybe there are other people that can do it."

Brie sniffled, then looked up at me. "I love you, Kane. Honestly, I'm not going to decide anything until after your game on Saturday."

As I held her in my arms, I realized the agony that had taken up residence in my soul would never go away.

Chapter Forty-Seven

Brie

I smoothed the sheets and comforter on my bed, then my attention fixated on the chain and wrist cuff. Kane had already left for classes, which gave me some time alone. It was Friday, which meant I had a day and a half before I reached out to the Westbrooks with an answer. I sat on the edge of the mattress, the fucking chain taunting me. If I didn't help catch Wagner, wasn't I still chained to my past? I would have to constantly look over my shoulder, wondering if he would come after Kane and me. What if I could gain some information from Wagner that reunited families, including mine?

I'd spent the last several days agonizing over what to do. Kane was a hundred percent against the idea, and I didn't blame him. If it were him contemplating meeting with Wagner, I would throw a good old-fashioned hissy fit, the Southern girl way. I didn't consider myself Southern, but I'd been around plenty of girls back home who manipulated their guys and always got what they wanted. I thought it was pretty low, but I could see the reason for it in this situation.

I groaned, then hopped up. Gathering my backpack and purse, I made sure the windows and slider were locked before I left. From the corner of my eye, I spotted Vaughn walking a dog I hadn't ever seen. His baseball hat was pulled low over his forehead as the dog took a shit on my lawn. At least Vaughn had a doggie bag with him. I stifled a giggle. Picking up crap wouldn't be my choice of job, but at least he was sneaky about looking out for me. Zayne had stuck with Kane, which had helped calm my overactive nerves.

My cell buzzed as soon as I climbed into my Lexus and started the engine. I shivered, rubbing my frozen hands together while I read Gabby's message that had popped up on the screen of my car.

Meet you in class. Don't be late because you're stirring your coffee with Kane's cock.

Grateful for her humor, a fit of giggles snuck up on me. It had been a shit week, and it felt good to laugh.

Pulling out of the driveway, I realized I already had my answer concerning Wagner. I was in way over my head, but that was a problem for another day. Tension slithered down my spine, my muscles rigid with anxiety. I pushed away the dark thoughts, reminding myself to stay focused on classes and the game tomorrow. Kane needed all the support I could provide him.

Chapter Forty-Eight

Brie

"Y"ou don't have to do this, babe. You can still back out."
Kane knelt next to me in my living room, and I cupped
his cheeks in my hands.

"If I have the ability to stop this once and for all, then I owe it to
you for saving my life, to myself, and to all the moms out there that
lost a child." I kissed Kane, pouring my heart and soul into him.

"Remember everything we discussed and stay focused on the end
result. It will make your day with him easier."

Kane had spent the last two weeks prepping me for questions
that Wagner might ask, how he would treat me, and what was
expected of me as the daughter behind the Light of David. More than
once, I'd needed to take a break since memories were bombarding me,
little pieces at a time. It wasn't as much as what I saw as how it felt—
disgusting, slimy, evil. I had desperately wanted to talk to Gabby
about the situation, but it would only put her in danger. I'd forced
myself to only speak to her about everyday life, classes, and my relationship with Kane.

"I love you, Brie. Please be careful." Kane pressed his forehead against mine.

The doorbell rang, breaking up our moment.

Once the FBI found out how to contact Wagner, they provided me with the information, and I reached out to him. As hard as I tried, I was a fucking mess, and I was struggling to stay focused on my classes. If it weren't for Kane, I wouldn't have managed. He was constantly there, supporting me even when we weren't talking.

It had taken a few more days before I could arrange a meeting with Wagner. The FBI had provided me with a phone specifically for that purpose, and they monitored all my conversations with him. It was only a few, but I hated Wagner for what he'd done to Kane. Tomorrow was Thanksgiving, and I hoped like hell we would have something to be grateful for. At least we would spend the day with Kane's family, which made my heart a little lighter.

Kane rose, checked who was at the door, then opened it. Pierce and another man strolled in, filling the space with their commanding presence.

"Hi." I gave them a small wave as I joined them in the living room. I assumed the guy with him was his FBI contact. It was a good thing he wasn't going in with Wagner; he looked like a cop, and Wagner would spot him from a mile away.

"Brie, this is Brian," Pierce introduced us. "He's with the FBI and will be in your ear the entire time." Brian's brown hair was thinning, and he appeared to be in his late forties, with dark bags under his eyes.

"Thank you." I mustered up a smile, even though there was nothing to smile about. I was about to meet a monster and pretend I wanted to help him rebuild the cult. I was tight with nerves, steeling myself for what would happen in a few hours.

"Let's head out. It's going to be a long day," Pierce said, standing near the door. "It will take an hour to fly to Montana, then another hour to drive to the meeting spot. Do you have any questions, Brie? The FBI and my men will be hidden, but we'll all be there."

"Including me," Kane said, slipping his arm around my waist.

"I'm ready," I managed to say without my voice quivering.

Even though I tried to prepare, the next several hours seemed like weeks as each agonizing second slowly ticked by.

My attention darted around the shadows of the large trees, but I didn't see Wagner. We'd agreed to meet in a private area of a national park. I told him I needed privacy for us to feel comfortable talking. At first, I didn't think he would buy it, but he did.

Tucking my hair behind my ear, I reminded myself to allow the fake diamond earrings to show. Sutton had created the listening devices, and the FBI would hear every word between us, but it would help if I kept my hair out of the way.

A tall man stepped out from behind a tree and walked toward the picnic table in the middle of the overgrown area. It was probably a beautiful spot to chill and have lunch during summer, but winter was right around the corner, and someone hadn't taken care of the grass in a while.

My heart rate spiked, and I struggled to catch my breath. Cautiously, I approached the man I recognized from the newspaper article. Undiluted fear and the darkest rage exploded inside of me.

"Wagner?" I asked, plastering on a fake smile.

"Lyndsay?" he asked, raking his blue eyes up and down my body as though I were on display to purchase. Hell, to him, I probably was.

A malicious grin slipped over his face. "You're absolutely beautiful. Come give your old man a hug."

Swallowing the bile that had swam up to my throat, I forced myself to touch him. I might not remember the son of a bitch, but he had a slimy, disgusting feeling about him.

Pretending the best I could, I threw my arms around him. "Dad." I stared into the trees behind him, reminding myself that the FBI and Pierce's guys were hidden, surrounding us.

Wagner rubbed my back, then squeezed my ass, pulling me against him. *Don't barf. Please, don't barf. If this fails, you'll have to see him again.*

I pulled away, pretending that what had just happened was normal. According to Kane, the elders could touch someone any way they wanted.

He was several inches taller than I was, with sandy blonde hair, thin yet muscular. But his eyes ... As our gazes connected, I realized we had the same shape and color of eyes, cheekbones, and forehead. There wasn't any disputing that he was my father. "For being in prison the last five years, you look great. You must have worked out a lot." Brian had encouraged me to feed his ego. Men like Wagner were cruel narcissists, but if I played to that, it would help solidify that I wanted to be in his life again.

I walked to the picnic bench, watched where he sat, then settled across from him.

"How are you, kiddo? It's been years since I've seen you." He rubbed his clean-shaven chin, his attention landing on my breasts. I hadn't thought about him looking at me like he wanted to ... An uncontrollable shiver slithered down my spine. He disgusted me, and I hated that I shared his DNA. I shoved the thought out of my head, realizing that if I wanted this to succeed, I would have to deal with my feelings later. It wasn't about me anyway. This was for Kane and every child that had been ripped away from their families.

Clinging to my anger, I answered. "I'm in college in New York, studying law, actually." I smiled at him as I fed him phony information.

"Wow. I always knew you were smart, but law, huh?" His gaze thoughtfully narrowed. "Good for you. You'll be an incredible asset to the Light of David. Not to mention, you have the perfect body to reproduce and grow the family." He offered me a sickeningly sweet smile, and I fought the urge to punch the motherfucker in his face and run.

"Honestly, since you're my dad, I feel like I can share this with you. There's a lot that I don't remember from our time together. Hopefully, you'll be patient with me as you teach me the ways again. I want nothing more than to stand by your side and resurrect what you worked hard to build."

Wagner reached over the table and took my hand in his. "I've recruited new elders that I want to introduce you to. Do you remember the introductory ritual?"

"I was young, so I don't remember which ritual was for what. As I said, I've not had a mentor from the Light of David with me for years. You'll have to reteach me. I hope that's okay."

Wagner released my hand. "Why are you really here, Lyndsay? That boy Jacob helped you escape, then I haven't heard a word from you at all. It sounds suspicious to me."

Feigning shock, I managed to tear up. Brian had coached me on how to respond to Wagner's questions. He was smart and wouldn't fall for my bullshit story immediately. It would take some serious acting on my part.

I brushed away the tear that had slipped down my cheek. "It was awful. I was a stupid teen, scared of the virginal ritual, and I ran. Once I saw what was beyond the compound, it was too late. If I'd tried to come back, you wouldn't have let me. After the arrests, I had to lay low and stay off the radar, preparing myself for the time that we could rebuild everything that was destroyed ... together. Father and daughter. I've had a taste of the free world, and it's not for me. Please, forgive me for sinning against you and the elders." I wrung my fingers together on top of the table. Every move and every word out of my mouth was to convince him that I was on his side. It had to work.

"I always knew you were special, Lyndsay. Let's do this. I'll introduce you to the elders, then we'll schedule the introductory ritual."

My heart knocked against my chest like it was attempting to run away without me. "That sounds perfect." I paused. "I'm so glad you're free."

Wagner's chuckle echoed through the small clearing. "You and me both. However, I did learn what I want to do differently in our religion."

"I'm excited to hear more about the changes. I was thinking about how we could grow faster, though." My forehead scrunched, and I leaned on the table. "We need children. We need to teach them right from wrong and how to serve while they're still young. That we are the light, and the world is the darkness. How can we do that, Dad? How can we spread the truth quicker?"

A vicious grin slipped into place. "We take them."

Pretending to ponder the idea, I straightened. "Isn't that risky? You just got out of prison. It's my job to protect you now." I was beginning to think I'd missed my calling. Maybe I should consider becoming a professional bullshitter if this played out well.

Wagner's brow rose slightly. "I love your dedication, and hopefully, it will continue."

"Of course, it will. I've been waiting for this day way too long. Do you know how powerful we will be together?"

He seemed to like that idea because his lips kicked up in a smile. "I like the way you think, but I'm not surprised. After all, you are my daughter. I knew the minute your mother left you in your playpen one spring day, that she wasn't worthy to raise you in the way of the light."

"What do you mean? I thought that Bernadette was my mother?"

Wagner threw his head back and laughed. "Your mother was nothing but a dumb two-bit whore with no damn sense. I fucked her once, then she reached out to let me know she was pregnant. Most men would run from that situation, but I saw opportunity written all over it. I was barely beginning to form the Light of David, and I knew in my gut that you were supposed to be with me and not her. The minute she left you to go into the house for who knows what, I had someone snatch you right out of your playpen. The rest is history."

I stared at him for a minute. "Did you take others? I mean is this how you think we should grow our religion again?"

"Darlin', they've never brought me up on kidnapping charges, so yeah, it will work. Especially if you're the bait. We'll reel the little kids right in with a beautiful young lady, and no one will see it coming. I'll plant you in the neighborhood, have you get to know a family, then bam." He clapped his hands together, and I jumped. "That's how it will play out. It's the perfect plan. We'll move you around to make sure the cops can't track you."

My stomach clenched with the idea. "I like kids. I'm sure I could pull it off."

"Excellent." Wagner stood. "I gotta go, baby girl. I'll call when I have the ritual set up."

"I'm excited," I said, standing.

"Give me a hug. It sure is good to see you."

I rounded the table, smiling as though he was the father of the year. Wrapping my arms around his neck, I braced myself for his hands to roam. Instead, he spun me around and slid his arm around my waist as the other pulled out a gun from the waist of his jeans.

"Did you honestly think that I would fall for your lies? Not once have you reached out while I was in prison."

The metal of the barrel pressed against my temple. "It's not what you think. I was afraid if I told you the truth, you would reject me. I'm desperate to be in your good graces again." My body trembled against his, and for the first time in years, I prayed I would survive.

"Talk fast, beautiful. Time's running out."

I gulped, hoping this was the right move. "I had amnesia. Something happened when I left the compound, but I don't know what. It wiped my memories, and just recently, a few are coming back. I received a phone call that you were being released soon, so I knew it was my chance to reconnect and make things right." Tears streamed down my cheeks, and I sniffled.

"Good thing you're coming with me now."

"What? Dad, that won't work, and the FBI will come after you again. I have school. If I go missing, they're going to immediately think it was you. We'll screw up everything before it has a chance to succeed."

"They'll never find you, Lyndsay. I hope you said goodbye to your friends." His evil chuckle sent shivers down my spine.

He released me, then moved the gun behind me. "Walk and don't pull any shit with me."

I did as he asked, terrified that there was no way out and I was headed back to the pits of hell.

Chapter Forty-Nine

Kane

"You have to do something!" I yelled in the van parked a few miles from the meeting spot. Brian had allowed me to stay with him and Pierce and listen to the conversation with Brie and Wagner, but I wasn't allowed anywhere near Wagner. I understood why now. If I were close, I would deal with Wagner myself.

"Kane, calm down. We're trained to handle these situations and do it all the time. Brie just trapped Wagner into confessing about the kidnappings. We don't want to lose her either," Brian explained.

"I've lost her once. Don't make me lose her again." My hands trembled, and I turned tó Pierce.

"Sit, Kane. We've got this. If you can't manage your emotions, you have to leave. One of my men will escort you to a hotel an hour away. Your choice." Pierce's tone was calm and confident.

My chest constricted as I stared at him. One thing I knew was that I wasn't leaving as long as Wagner was near Brie. Now he wanted to take Brie with him. No. Fucking. Way.

"Ready?" Pierce said into his earpiece. "As soon as it's clear."

I held my breath, waiting to see if Wagner would walk away with my girlfriend, or if she would walk away alive.

Pop. The sound registered over the speaker, and I shot out of my chair, horror registering on my face. "Was that a gunshot? Who got hit?" I was so rattled I struggled to breathe.

"Wagner's down, sir," a man's voice responded.

I nearly crumpled to the floor with the news, then it registered in my brain that they hadn't mentioned Brie.

"Is Brie—is she?" I stammered.

"The young lady is in our custody. She's unharmed," another man responded.

I knelt, my shoulders shaking with my silent cries. *Jesus.* I'd almost lost her for good.

Picking myself up, I pulled myself together. "When can I see her?"

"We're on the way," the man replied.

Without asking, I slid the van door open and hopped out. I felt as though I were suffocating.

A few minutes later, a car drove up, and Brie jumped out and ran to me. She threw her arms around my neck, and I lifted her, her legs automatically locking around my waist.

"I thought I'd lost you," I cried into her hair.

Her cries wracked her body. "Me, too. I was so scared. Then ... then he just dropped to the ground. When I turned, there was a bullet hole in his forehead. It whizzed right over me."

"You're safe now, baby. It's over. Wagner's gone. No way would they let him kidnap you again."

I held Brie until her tears calmed, then gently set her feet down. "You were fucking amazing." Tucking her hair behind her ear, I leaned down and kissed her. "I think you should consider acting."

"Excellent work, Brie," Pierce said, joining us. "I'm sorry one of my men had to take him out while he was holding you, but we didn't have a choice. We were ready to go with a sniper, then the FBI gave the order. I'm grateful that you were able to get him to confess, and we have what we need to go after the other elders that are still in prison. We'll bait them, and I think they'll confess when they're told that Wagner rolled over on them. His death will remain quiet until the FBI has the other confessions."

"Thank you. I hope the bastards get the chair and rot in hell for stealing little kids." She folded her arms over her chest, anger and fear flashing in her gaze.

There was the fire that I loved.

Brian approached us, his attention landing on Brie. "If you ever want a job working undercover for the FBI, Pierce has my number."

Hell. Fucking. No.

Brie released a nervous giggle. "If Kane is offered a spot with the NFL, I'll be busy traveling with him during his football season, but I'll let you know if I change my mind."

I slipped my arm around her waist, pulling her closer.

"Thank you for taking care of him. And coaching me. I was scared to death." She rubbed her arms, shivering.

"Of course. Let's get Brie debriefed, then home," Pierce said, patting me on the back. "I suspect you two are ready to call it a day."

"Pierce?" Brie asked.

He turned his attention to her.

"Is this what you and Sutton do? I mean, I understand that you provide security, but you work with the FBI and take down the bad guys like today?"

Pierce's brown eyes grew thoughtful. "Pretty much." He offered her a kind smile.

I had a feeling there was a lot more behind his answer.

It was nearly ten in the evening when Brie and I arrived at her place. We both had called our parents, updating them about Wagner. They had no idea Brie had agreed to work with the FBI, so it was a lot to explain. Even though I understood their frustration that we hadn't shared beforehand, Brie and I had realized it would be better to wait. We were stressed enough without adding our parents to the mix.

"I've never been so happy to see this little house as I am right now." She punched in the code for the alarm, then slipped off her tennis shoes. "Check the fridge. I had one of Gabby's friends pick up some drinks to have on hand."

I locked the door behind us, then removed my shoes.

"How are you doing?" I asked, walking into the kitchen and grabbing a beer and cider from her refrigerator. Giving her the drink, I sat on the loveseat. After talking about Wagner, the information the FBI had gathered, and the fact that Wagner was dead, I wasn't sure I had much more to say, but I needed to see how Brie was doing. There was no way we would process this overnight.

"Numb." She popped the tab on her can, then took a sip. Curling up in the corner of the couch, she turned to me. "Thank you for trusting me to do this."

"Let's make one thing clear. Under no circumstances will you work for the FBI or Pierce and Sutton." I arched a brow at her.

"I think I need to remind you that you can pull that with me in the bedroom but not anywhere else." She smirked at me.

"If I weren't so drained from today, I would turn you over my knee and spank you."

She rolled her eyes. "Promises, promises." Brie giggled, then ran her thumb up and down the cider can. "That's not what I want to do, so please don't worry about it. The time I spent undercover with Wagner was enough to last me a long, long time."

Brie set her drink on the floor, then crawled over the couch to my side. She straddled me and cupped my face. "I love you, Kane. There's no way I could have gone through what I did if you hadn't prepped me. Wagner ..." Her shoulders slumped. "He was really sick. I don't remember the introductory ritual, but it didn't sound like it was a good thing."

I wrapped my hands around her slender waist and looked at her.

"You would have been raped by each elder while everyone watched. Their reasoning was to make sure you were impregnated by one of the elders," Kane snarled. "They're sick, twisted bastards who should be raped and thrown into a hole until they died a slow, painful death."

Brie grew quiet. "Do you think the new elders will come after me? Are we going to live our entire lives looking over our shoulders? You're going to be on television, Kane."

I drew her in for a hug, and she rested her head against my shoulder. I'd asked myself that question a million times since Wagner had been released from prison. Would my career lead them straight to Brie?

"Baby, I don't have the answer to that, but I've been thinking a lot about our future. What's best for you and me as individuals and as a couple. I think we will have to wait and see what happens over the next year. We've been through enough, and I don't think it's wise to make any more decisions. Let's settle in, finish college, and we can prepare for the rest of our lives one day at a time."

Brie raised her head. "Okay."

"But there's one change I would like to make." I slid my hands under her butt, squeezing her.

"What's that?" She kissed the tip of my nose.

"I want you to move in with me."

Brie stared at me as if I'd told her I had a vagina. "Are you sure? Kane, my night terrors ... and I'm in therapy. I'm still a mess. And what if I never recover my memories, but what if I do?"

I pressed my mouth to hers, silencing her fears. "Do you love me, Brie?" Our eyes connected, and I gently ran my knuckles down her soft cheek.

"More than you'll ever know."

"Then move in with me. We'll work through it together. If you remember, fine. If you don't, fine. There will be times you'll have the entire place to yourself to have your sessions and space to think. Have your friends over, Brie. Live your life. Just do it at my house instead of here."

A smile crept over her face. "When you put it that way, how can I say no?"

My chest warmed with her answer. I pressed my mouth to hers her, losing myself in her touch, thankful she was with me instead of with Wagner. I hoped he was rotting in hell as I kissed his daughter.

Chapter Fifty

Brie

Even though I was elated that I was moving in with Kane, I was nervous as hell to tell his parents during Thanksgiving, but they were excited about the news. Plus, they could rent the place out again, so it was a win all the way around. Gabby congratulated me and insisted on helping me move and unpack. I would definitely take her up on the offer. Shitty tasks were always better with your best friend.

I helped Amelia in the kitchen that sported black granite counter-tops and state-of-the-art stainless-steel appliances. The white tile floor offset the dark colors beautifully. Kane and Coach watched the football game, which gave me more time to get to know Kane's mom. To my surprise, Alexandria joined the guys, yelling at the game as much as they did.

"Kane is the happiest we've seen him since he came to live with us." Amelia's smile was warm.

"Me, too. I was worried that my amnesia would interfere, but he's attended my therapy sessions several times. Alida has helped us both."

Amelia pulled the turkey out of the oven, then placed it on the stovetop. "I'm glad you're both talking to a professional. Although you both have support, there's only so much we can do. We're not trained to help you process the trauma."

"Alida likes him, and it's easier when I see her on my own to talk about Kane since she knows him." I lifted my nose, sniffing the air, my mouth watering. "I'm starving. I can't wait to taste all of the amazing food."

"There will be plenty of leftovers to send you and Kane home with." Amelia wiped her hands on her white-and-red-checked apron.

I rubbed my belly, grinning.

"I promised after we ate that I would call Mom and Dad. As much as I love being here, I miss them terribly." A wave of guilt washed over me for staying in Oregon instead of flying to Tennessee.

"Of course, you do, hon. The first few holidays are the hardest. It will get better, and we're not a replacement for your family, simply an extension." Amelia opened the drawer, grabbed a few oven mitts, then tossed them on the granite countertop before briefly hugging me. "I always hoped that Kane would find someone to call him on his shit but would also love and support him. He needs that balance. You're perfect for him, Brie. Coach and I couldn't be happier for the both of you."

"I love him." My cheeks flamed red with my confession. I wasn't used to discussing my private life with my boyfriend's parents.

Amelia laughed as she turned her attention to the pies. "Do you want to get the mixer out of the drawer near the refrigerator?" She pointed me in the right direction.

Over the next half hour, I helped Amelia with the rest of the food, then set the table.

"Why don't you tell the men and Alexandria to wash their hands. I'll grab a few bottles of wine and sparkling cider, then we can eat." She untied her apron and folded it, placing it on the island.

"Okay." I hurried to the living room to let everyone know when the doorbell rang.

"I'll get it," Coach said. "I thought Jon and Trisha were going to call before they dropped by, but we have plenty of food."

I strolled to Kane, then pushed up on my tiptoes, planting a kiss on his mouth. "This is our first Thanksgiving together."

Kane cupped my chin. "Our first together since being out of the cult. As I said, their holidays are different, but we spent twelve years in the same dining hall."

I hesitated, hearing voices in the foyer. "At least Wagner is dead, so hopefully—"

"Hi, honey."

I spun on my heel, not believing what I was hearing. "Mom? Dad? Oh my gosh! What are you doing here?" I rushed over, hugging them both.

"Hi, sugar," Dad said, embracing me.

I caught Amelia out of the corner of my eye, smiling widely.

I knelt and pulled my little brother in for a hug. "And you! Oh my gosh, you've grown so much, Conner."

"We missed you, so we decided to join you here," Mom explained. "With some help from Amelia, we were able to surprise you so we could spend the day together."

"Thank you all so much. This is amazing." I glanced over my shoulder at Kane, who looked as happy as I felt. "You all remember Kane."

Kane walked over to us. "It's good to see you again, but in person and not video this time. How was the trip?"

Conner groaned. "Long. But the plane was so cool." His eyes widened with excitement.

"Hey, who's here?" Alexandria asked, making her way down the stairs to the foyer.

"My family." After introductions, Coach hung up everyone's coats, then we settled in around the table.

"The food looks wonderful. I'll help you clean up later," Mom said to Amelia. "It will give us a chance to chat."

"I would love that. I'm so glad you made it on time, too," Amelia said, patting Mom on the shoulder.

The next several hours consisted of stories about holidays, funny moments, and gossip from back home. The guys chatted football while Alexandria and Conner became fast friends.

My heart was so full I thought it might burst from my chest. Every person I loved was at the table with me. I leaned over, resting my head on Kane's shoulder, realizing that none of this was possible without him.

"I love seeing you this happy," he softly said against my hair.

Our gazes connected, and I nodded. "It's all because of you."

"You've got it all wrong, baby. It's all because of you."

Chapter Fifty-One

Kane

I was happily surprised that Brie's parents had arrived. Since we had only met once on a Zoom call, I was eager to spend time with them.

"Hey, I'm going to hang out with Conner and Alexandria in the game room. Is that okay?" Brie's blue eyes filled with so much excitement I would have given her the moon if she'd asked.

"Of course. I'll stay and talk to your parents, get to know them better."

Brie, Conner, and Alexandria excused themselves from the table, then raced out and up the stairs. Laughter filled the home, breathing new life into the holiday.

I leaned back in the chair, my attention sweeping over Rodger, Carolyn, and my parents. Silence filled the room as everyone stared at me, and my jaw clenched. I pulled in a deep breath, trying to steady my galloping heart and collect my next words, but I wasn't sure there was any other way to articulate it.

"Is Conner mine?" I asked, my throat tight with nerves.

Carolyn and Rodger looked at each other for a moment.

"As soon as we met you over the video call, and Brie explained how you two knew each other, we wondered, too," Carolyn shared.

"He looks just like you," Mom said, her voice hushed.

"We definitely can't deny that." Dad wiped his mouth and tossed the navy linen napkin on his empty plate.

My brain scrambled for the details, then I said, "We were young, and birth control wasn't allowed in the cult. Brie and I had been together a handful of times before I helped her escape. The timeline adds up." I scrubbed my face with my palms, trying to wrap my mind around the strong possibility that I was a father at the age of twenty. As a lightbulb went off in my head, my brows shot up to my hairline. "Brie introduced him as her brother. She doesn't know?" I jumped out of my chair, pacing the length of the table. "Holy crap."

"When we found her and took her to the hospital, she was badly bruised on the inside of her thigh. She agreed to a rape kit, but Brie had absolutely zero understanding of what that even meant. I stayed with her and held her hand the entire time. Unfortunately, all they could confirm was that yes, someone had raped her, but she wouldn't talk. Brie looked at us, terrified and trembling."

Tears clouded my vision. The Langstons confirmed the suspicion I had when Brie shared the contents of the box.

"When the results came back from the rape kit, the doctors confirmed that she was pregnant. The police and the Department of Human Services agreed that we could take her home and care for her while they searched for her family. They suspected that Brie learned she was pregnant, then ran away. As you already know, her parents weren't ever located until Wagner was released from prison. May he rot in hell," Rodger said. "My apologies, I shouldn't have said that in front of everyone."

Dad barked out a laugh. "You mean the evil, sorry son of a bitch?"

Rodger nodded. "That."

As much as I appreciated Dad momentarily putting everyone at ease, I tried to breathe past the agony but couldn't. It hammered me into the ground, stealing every ounce of strength. Hadn't Brie been through enough? Why had the past continued to throw us curveballs when we were both finally happy?

Rain pattered softly against the dining room windowpanes, and the drops slid down the glass like tears. Even Mother Nature was grieving with me.

"Right before Wagner died, he admitted to stealing Brie from her mom. Does anyone have a clue who her mom is?"

"No, but she might want to do a genealogy test to see if she can find some of her blood relatives. We've never discussed it with her, though. There was just always something more important, like helping her with the night terrors," Carolyn explained.

"That makes sense, but I'm struggling with something. Wouldn't Brie have remembered having a baby?" Frustrated and confused, I gripped the back of the chair.

"Her amnesia blocked out everything, including the c-section. When she was diagnosed, we felt it would be better to tell her Conner was her little brother. He was already family and so was she. After working with a therapist, we all agreed that it was the best way not to traumatize her even more, and at the same time, care for our grandson. In our mind, they were ours."

"We feel the same about Kane," Mom added, taking Dad's hand.

I rubbed my eyes, thinking about what to do next. "What do I need to do to find out one way or the other?"

"Are you open to a paternity test?" Rodger asked.

"Of course. And honestly, he looks exactly like me when I was younger, so I think it's just a formality." I massaged the back of my neck in an attempt to soothe the tight muscles. "Once we know for sure, then we can decide the next steps, I guess. I have no idea how I'm going to keep this from Brie until we have more information. She's smart; she'll sense something is wrong."

"I'm happy to pay for an expedited test," Dad said. "It's been hell to figure out what's best in this situation, and even though we've worked with a therapist over the years and took their suggestions, I still wonder every day if we made the right decision." He blew out a tired sigh. "The sooner we have results, the sooner we can decide what to do. Is it best for Conner to continue to think Brie is his sister? If he's Kane's, where will he live? Amelia and I would want to be in his life on a regular basis, so how would that work with us across the country?"

"Honey." Mom patted Dad's hand. "I think you're verbalizing everyone's thoughts, but let's take one step at a time. First, we need to collect Conner's DNA in a way that won't raise suspicions. If Brie suspects a connection, she hasn't said anything."

"Probably because she just witnessed her biological father being shot right before he attempted to kidnap her," I said, bowing my head with the weight of the world on my shoulders.

Everyone at the table gasped in horror. "She didn't tell us that," Carolyn stated.

"She didn't want to worry anyone, and it's over. I'm not sure talking about it will help her process. However, her nightmares have been better since I'm around at night. Brie is moving in with me, by the way. I'm not sure she told you that either, but we told my parents earlier." After I shared that with Rodger and Carolyn, I realized that it hadn't been my place, but it was too late now. Hopefully, Brie wouldn't be pissed at me.

"She's so happy, I would never kick up a fuss as long as she's safe. It's clear she loves you, Kane. We're thrilled that you two found each other again." Carolyn sighed and leaned back in her seat. "And we came prepared. I have some strands of Conner's hair I collected this morning from his comb. It's in a baggie in my purse."

"I'll make an excuse to run some errands tomorrow and drop by the office for the test." I suspected that Brie could use a few minutes to herself.

"We can help keep her occupied while you do that. We would love some time alone with her, too," Carolyn said.

"That's perfect. It will work out well then." I glanced at Dad.

Even though this was more important, we had a game Saturday. If we won, we were on our way to the playoffs.

My thoughts spun out, relieved that I would probably have a good-paying job after graduation. If Conner were mine, I would need a good income to support him. Only time would tell if he was mine and how it would all play out.

Chapter Fifty-Two

Brie

I stomped my foot on the floor of my bedroom, gaining my boyfriend's attention. "Kane Cooper, I refuse to pack another box until you tell me what's wrong. You've been mopey and moody ever since my family arrived. Do you not like them?"

Confusion flickered across his expression. He closed the distance between us, kissing me with such tenderness a rush of warmth flooded my body.

"I really love your family, babe. Please don't think it's them."

Relieved, I slid my arms around his waist and rested my head on his chest. The steady rhythm of his heart lulled me into a sense of security.

"Then what's wrong?"

"I've got a lot on my mind. Since we won another game, the pressure is on to deliver the championship. Plus ..." He skated his palm up the length of my neck as his gaze intensified. "I need to make a decision about the society. Now that you're in my life, do I continue as its leader or pass that along to someone else?"

I pulled away from him, my eyes narrowing. "What do you mean *continue?*" I folded my arms over my chest, attempting to control the bubble of anger that had burst inside me.

Kane grinned. "If I stay, you and I can use any room we want."

That grabbed my attention. "Isn't being in the society also having access to all the girls?"

"It is, but I'm not interested in that, babe. Only you. I promise. In fact, any time I'm there, I'll bring you with me if that helps. I can meet with the guys, make sure things are running well, then use the rooms with you." Kane shoved a hand into his pocket, giving me a sheepish look. "Besides, I own the house the society is in."

My mouth hit the floor. "What? You own that place? Like the mortgage is in your name kind of own?"

"There's no mortgage. I bought it outright, then remodeled it."

Completely caught off guard, I shook my head, trying to clear it. "Are there any other big secrets you'd like to share with me before I move in with you?"

Silence filled the gap between us as I realized there was something else. Kane sat on the edge of the bed. "I was going to tell you after I handled it."

"Handled what?" I tossed my hands in the air, exasperated and getting madder by the second.

"Marc, your ex is threatening to sue me if I don't walk away from you and pay him half a million dollars. I had a forty-eight-hour deadline, but I've managed to put him off for a bit."

"Oh, my God. Kane, why didn't you tell me before? Surely, we can take care of that idiot. Now that he can't blackmail me anymore, I'm not afraid of him."

Kane rubbed his palms together. "Maybe if you tell him there's no chance of the two of you ever being an item, then he'll drop it."

"Of course, I'll talk to him. What about the money?"

"I've already talked to an attorney. It would be Marc's word against mine since Jagger told the cops it was self-defense and he saw it all. Legally, Marc's full of shit. My lawyer said this crap happens when someone is high profile."

"So, you're not paying him, and this nonsense wouldn't hold up in court?" I had to make sure I was clear about what was transpiring.

"Yeah, but it took me some time to hear from my attorney because he was on vacation, and I didn't want to talk to anyone else. Now it's just a matter of making sure Marc leaves for good."

I huffed. "Even though you should have told me about Marc, I was dealing with Wagner, so I understand why you waited."

"And the society?"

I joined Kane on the edge of the bed. "Can I help you run it? As long as everyone knows that you're mine, then I think it would be fun to use the rooms, vet the girls, and maybe even come up with new ideas."

Kane swept his thumb along my lower lip. "That was not what I expected you to say. Like at all." He flashed me a grin. "Let me talk to the guys, but I like the idea of you as my queen."

"Me, too." I crawled onto his lap and straddled him. "I think packing can wait for a little bit." I rocked my hips against his growing erection. "Is there anything else you need to tell me?"

A flicker of an unrecognizable emotion danced across his face. "Not at the moment." He leaned forward and kissed me as his hands slipped beneath my sweatshirt and up my back. I melted into him, ready to feel him inside of me.

Chapter Fifty-Three

Brie

The wind whipped my hair into my face as I hurried across the soggy, green lawn to the library. Marc had agreed to meet me there. Kane had insisted on a public meeting if I wouldn't let him stick around. I loved Kane for being protective, but in order to have a candid conversation with Marc, I didn't need my jealous boyfriend lurking nearby.

Feeling empowered, I hurried up the steps, clutching my coat closed. For some dumb reason, I hadn't zipped it, and the wind was blowing the rain sideways, soaking me.

I flung the door open to the building, then wiped my feet on the mat. The squeak of my shoes filled the hall as I walked across the tile floor to the library's entrance.

The familiar scent of books greeted me with open arms, and I paused, appreciating the moment.

I quickly spotted Marc at a table in the corner, and I hurried to him.

"Hi," I said, pulling out a chair across from him and sitting down, ready to get this over with.

His eyes lit up. "Thanks for calling."

"Sure. I wanted to chat with you." I set my purse on the seat next to me. "Kane talked to me."

Marc's expression faltered, then he caught himself. "Did he send you to try to talk me out of suing him?"

I offered him a smile. "No. It was my idea to meet with you. Marc, we have history together, and I understand that you miss me, but this isn't the way to my heart. Not even close. Neither was blackmail. There are things I liked about you, at least until you showed up here acting as though you owned me. I'm a human being with feelings, not a possession."

Marc's nostrils flared. "It's him, isn't it? He's poisoned you against me."

Are you fucking kidding me? What happened to accountability?

"Marc, you did that all by yourself. Blackmailing me to make you popular and to fuck you pretty much turned me against you. You showing up here was just the final straw. No one gets rough with me. Not anymore. I'm not that scared girl you used to know."

"If you don't come back to me, I'll tell the world about your night terrors and how fucked up you are in the head."

I unwillingly flinched. Marc hit my soft spot, and he knew it. "Go for it. And I'll share all over TikTok, Instagram, Twitter, and every social media platform I can use and tell all the ladies how small your dick is." I held up my pinky. "Pretty sure you won't have dates or sex for a long time."

I refrained from laughing as Marc's face turned beet red. "Here's how this is going to play out. You're leaving today. If I find out you've opened your mouth or are still on campus, it won't end well for you." I stood, glowering at him. "I have an entire football team at my disposal, and once I tell them you're trying to hurt Kane and me, they'll fucking bury you alive. If you ask me, that's a shitty way to die." I smirked at him. "At least you wouldn't be able to talk anymore, though."

I grabbed my purse and slipped the strap over my shoulder. "Goodbye, Marc." Waltzing out of the library, I nearly jumped with joy. I had finally stood up to Marc on my own, and it felt amazing to take control of my life. Giggling, I ran out of the building and into the rain.

"I'm free!" I bolted down the sidewalk with my arms spread as people stared at me like I'd lost my mind. I had. For the first time in my life, I couldn't care less what people thought of me. If Marc wanted to push the limits, I was ready for him, and so was the society. Kane had already spoken to them about handling Marc. I spun around, the rain soaking my skin as I raised my face to the sky.

"What are you doing?" Kane yelled at me from the other side of the lawn. He ran toward me, the water splashing up from the ground with each step.

"Celebrating!" I giggled as he caught up and wiped the raindrops from my cheeks. "It felt so good to stand up to Marc on my own, Kane. Thank you for trusting me."

Kane flashed me a boyish grin. "I'm proud of you, babe. Do you think he'll leave?"

I shrugged. "No clue, but I held my ground, and that's what I'm happy about. However, I might have mentioned the football team was waiting to bury him alive."

A laugh bellowed from Kane's chest. "I love you, babe." Kane's mouth crashed over mine as the rain continued to fall. His kiss stole the air from my lungs and made my knees weak.

"I love *you*, Kane Cooper."

"Let's go home."

I took his hand as we ran, laughing like two little kids.

"That's the last shower we'll take here together," I said to Kane as I handed him a plush cream bath towel. I dried my hair the best I could before I walked into my bedroom, the cold air chilling me again.

"You mean the last time I'll make love to you in *that* shower." He strolled out of the bathroom with the towel slung low on his hips.

"True, but I'm okay with that. I'm excited to officially move into your place tomorrow." I glanced at my phone. "It's almost time to video chat with my family."

Concern ghosted over Kane's features.

"What is it?" After standing up to Marc, I wasn't sure anything could get me down.

Kane tugged on his long-sleeve Whitmore University T-shirt, then stepped into his jeans. I dressed in a warm sweater and skinny jeans. Realizing I wouldn't have time to dry my hair, I walked to the bathroom to get my brush.

"Brie, there's something we need to talk about before we chat with your mom and dad."

"You sound really serious, Kane. What's wrong?"

He ran a hand over his damp hair, his gaze landing on the floor, then traveling back to me.

"While you were meeting with Marc earlier, I got a phone call I've been waiting for."

My stomach plummeted to my toes. "Is everything okay?"

"Yeah, everything is fine, babe. But ..." He sighed, then sat on the bed. "At Thanksgiving, when I saw Conner, it made me think."

"He's a doll, isn't he? And such a good kid. Mom and Dad have done an amazing job with him."

"They have." Kane stood and gently grabbed my shoulders. "I didn't know until today when the phone call came through, but, Brie ... your parents aren't Conner's mom and dad."

"Kane, what are you talking about?" Anxiety pulled and tugged at my insides, and for a fleeting second, I was pissed that Kane was trying to tear my family apart. "You're not making any sense."

"I took a paternity test, and the Langstons provided Conner's

DNA, while I gathered some of your hair from the pillow you sleep on. Brie, you and I are Conner's parents."

I gulped, confusion clouding my thoughts. "What? The test proved *we're* his parents?" I shoved my hands through my hair, frantically trying to understand what was happening. "Why didn't anyone tell me?"

"To protect you and Conner. Rodger and Carolyn said that you were pregnant when they found you unconscious on the side of the road. At some point, you probably hit your head, plus with the trauma of the cult and the pregnancy, you blocked it all out. Conner was delivered by c-section. Your scar is faint, but I saw it when we were in bed together. I didn't think anything about it. It was the tattoo I focused on."

I raised my sweater, exposing my lower abdomen. "No, that happened ..." I hesitated. "Mom and Dad told me I had a deep gash when they found me. It needed stitches, so they kept me in the hospital for a week and a half." Fear, grief, and anxiety were a few of the emotions that overshadowed my words. I diverted my eyes from Kane.

"You were in the hospital twice. The first time when they found you, then when you delivered Conner. Babe, they said you were so fragile that they were afraid it would send you spiraling into a deep depression. Rodger and Carolyn hoped your memories would return, not so much about the cult, but for Conner's sake." Kane rubbed my arms as he waited for me to say something.

Fear seized me as I realized Conner had been living a lie, too. "How is Conner going to feel when he finds out everyone hid this from him? They lied to both of us." My pitch rose with my questions.

"I don't know, babe. I'm not sure what the next step is. I had to confirm that I was his father first."

I searched his face, frowning. "I never paid attention before, but he looks like you. He has the same brown eyes and shape of the brows."

"And your cheekbones and beautiful mouth."

"Holy shit." I sank onto the mattress, staring at the floor. "We're parents, Kane." Tears streamed down my cheeks while I desperately tried to remember being pregnant and having Conner, but I couldn't grasp onto a memory anywhere.

"Brie, I know a lot will change, but I'm thrilled to have Conner. He's the good part of both of us. He's a smart, good kid from what I've seen. Even if Rodger and Carolyn had told you the truth, you might have blocked it out. Conner needed stability and care that you weren't able to give him yet. We can now."

"Poor baby is going to be so confused when he finds out. I don't even know how to tell him. He's been with Mom and Dad since he was born. Shit, I can't even make sense of this, how is a five-year-old supposed to?" I hiccupped.

Kane pulled me against him, stroking my back as I cried into his clean shirt.

"We'll figure it out. I think Alida will be able to help, too. Our parents know, so they'll help us make the right decision about the next steps."

"Coach and Amelia know?" I wiped the moisture from my cheeks and sat up.

"They suspected as soon as your family arrived on Thanksgiving. We all did," he gently explained.

"How did I miss it, then?" I clenched my fists, furious with myself.

"My guess is that your amnesia had something to do with it. Part of the time, you knew that I was familiar, and I was, but you spent the last five years with a little guy that looks a lot like me. I've been with you all this time, baby, just as a mini-me."

What he said made sense, but it didn't stop the burning sensation in my chest. Conner was mine and Kane's. Holy shit, I had a son. I wasn't sure how to process the news until my racing pulse slowed, my thoughts quieted, and acceptance trumped the crazy and overwhelming feelings.

"It's time to talk to your family." Kane kissed my forehead and cupped my face. "No matter what happens, babe, I love you, and I want to be in Conner's life. He's our son, and out of all the hell we lived through, he was made out of love."

I grabbed his hand, his words grounding me. "I love you, too. I'm just terrified I'll be a horrible mother."

Kane's smile was sweet and filled with love. "Brie, that's not even possible. You clearly have a great relationship with him. Rodger and Carolyn said you've helped raise him. Stayed up at night when he was teething, fed him, changed his diaper, and played with him. Somewhere in your heart, I think you realized Conner was ours."

I knew Kane was right, but it didn't mean I wasn't scared shitless about what our future looked like. Then I reminded myself it wasn't just ours. It was Conner's, too, and that little boy deserved nothing but the best. He'd been the light in my dark world and taught me what real, unconditional love was all about until I reconnected with Kane. Now I would do anything to protect my guys from whatever the world might throw at them. But I knew we were stronger together ... as a family.

Before I was able to process the news further, a FaceTime call rang on my phone. I glanced at Kane. "It's Mom and Dad." I tapped the icon to answer, and their faces filled my screen.

"Hey." I nervously tucked my hair behind my ear. I had no idea how this conversation would play out. "Kane just told me everything about Conner."

"Oh, honey, I'm so sorry it all came out like this. I'm so sorry if we hurt you," Mom said, tears streaming down her cheeks.

"I'm not mad. You and Dad had to make the best decisions you could in a crappy situation."

"It weighed on us heavily, Brie. We were terrified that when you learned the truth it would tear us all apart." Dad ran a hand through his hair, clearly upset.

I shook my head. "No, you and Mom are the reason that I was able to be with Conner. You kept us together in a loving, safe home. I only hope I can continue to do the same with my son."

Kane reached for my arm and gave it a gentle squeeze.

"You and Kane will be amazing parents, honey. You already are a wonderful mother to Conner," Mom explained.

Overwhelmed with gratitude, tears welled in my eyes. "How are we going to do this? How are we going to help Conner with the truth? Mom, Dad, I can't do this without you. There has to be a better way than living halfway across the country from each other."

"First, we all need to have a Zoom call and talk to Conner, but I think it will help him if we have a plan in place," Dad suggested.

"I agree," Kane said.

"I'm sorry, baby. I should have included you in the call." Slightly embarrassed that I'd been so self-absorbed, I adjusted my phone so my parents could see Kane as well.

Over the next hour, we discussed how and when we would tell Conner the truth and what the plan looked like. It would be a transition for all of us, but we were ready.

<h1 style="text-align:center">Chapter Fifty-Four</h1>

Brie Six Months Later

"Why didn't you hire movers, Mom?" I grabbed a box from the U-Haul, sweating my ass off. It was late May, and the heat had hit a record high of ninety degrees.

"Because you and Kane have half the football and cheer team here to help. Why would I take a great learning opportunity from them?" She laughed, then hurried down the ramp. "Not to mention, Kane's family is helping, too. At least it's not over a hundred degrees here like it is in Tennessee."

We walked together to the front door of Mom and Dad's new house. "It's different from back home, but I'm so happy you're close again, and that Conner is here. It's been hard without him the last several months."

"Me, too, honey. Your father and I adore Kane, and he's so good with Conner. We simply wanted to be nearby to help with our grandson while you two finish school and Kane prepares for his last year of playing ball. Plus, we've been a huge part of his life since he was born. It would be too hard on all of us not to be able to see him every day. A gradual shift will be best for him, and this will make it happen."

"Giddy up, Dad!" I turned around, laughing as Kane ran across the front yard with Conner on his shoulders, giggling. My heart warmed at watching the two men I loved most in the world.

"I don't think I could do this without you and Dad." I set the box down on the new living room floor.

"Conner has a new set of grandparents and his dad now. You're surrounded by people who love you." Mom patted my cheek, and I pulled her in for a hug. Sometimes, nothing made me feel better other than realizing my mom was there for me.

Over the last several months, Kane and I had discussed looking for my biological mom, but it had been too much to take on while acclimating to our new role as parents. After some additional sessions with Alida, Kane and I decided to talk to Conner with our families. In some ways, Conner was too young to fully understand what we had shared with him, but he seemed to adjust quickly with the help of an amazing therapist that specialized in working with blended families. When I'd shared with Alida how well Conner was adapting, she said she suspected it was because I'd been in his life the entire time. She also advised us to be prepared for a lot of questions and for the families to consider how we would answer them. To me, it had been simple. We would tell him the truth.

Kane led the team to the playoffs, then won the championship. Nothing was set in stone, but the NFL had reached out to him multiple times, and we hoped like hell he would be drafted, then offered a contract after he graduated.

My meeting with Wagner paid off in spades. It was enough new information to press charges and keep the additional elders behind bars for years. Some of them would most likely die before they were ever released. I can't say that I felt bad for them. The fuckers deserved to rot in hell ... slowly.

After the sentencing, one of the elders, Randy, admitted that he'd followed me the night I escaped the compound, then beat and raped me. He assumed that I would die in the freezing temperatures, but he'd underestimated me.

I guess my subconscious had shown me bits and pieces of the hell I'd lived through in my dreams and flashbacks. In a way, I was grateful I couldn't remember most of what had happened.

Thankfully, the cult wasn't the only bullshit I'd put behind me. Since the day I had a chat with Marc, I hadn't heard a word from him. I wasn't sure if he had returned to Tennessee or not. Honestly, as long as he was gone, I didn't give a shit.

To my surprise, Kane walked away from the society, leaving it in other capable hands. He said it was part of his past, and all he wanted to focus on was his future with me, Conner, and his career. I was pretty sure I fell even more in love with him that day.

After discussing it, we decided to keep the house and allow the society to continue using it. I was all for the idea. He hadn't told the members yet, but I suspected they would be relieved that they didn't have to move again.

"Watch your head, bud." Kane crouched down as he entered the home, Conner still on his shoulders. "I have the best workout buddy ever." Kane grinned at me, his smile lighting up his handsome face.

"Are you excited to spend time with all of us this summer?" I asked.

"Yeah!" Conner yelled, his voice echoing through the foyer.

"It's a good thing we have plenty of space. We'll get your play-room and bedroom set up for you," Mom said.

Kane knelt, and I lifted Conner off his shoulders. "Why don't you see if Grandpa needs any help?" I ruffled his hair, which had grown darker over the summer.

"Let's explore while the guys help unload the truck." I held out my hand to Kane.

"How are you doing?" he asked as we walked up the stairs.

"Good. I think the arrangement will be great for Conner. Plus, we'll have time to study. At least we have the summer to spend with him before classes start. I think spending some nights and days with both sets of grandparents and us will help him realize that the only thing that changed was our names. We're all in his life."

I slowed as we reached the end of the hall. The six-thousand-square-foot home would allow plenty of space for Conner when he was here part of the time. Mom would enjoy decorating their new place too. She and Amelia already had plans to shop for new items. It had been a relief to watch everyone get along so well, but we all had one little guy we loved with all our hearts bringing us together.

"His new birth certificate will be in soon. I'm kind of excited to see my name as his father."

We strolled into a large room filled with windows. "Me, too."

Kane stood behind me, pulling my back to his front. "Never in a million years would I have thought I'd be standing here with you in my arms. Everything I ever hoped for has finally fallen into place."

I turned and placed my palms on his shoulders. "Me, too. It's crazy how much can change in a year." Laying my forehead against his chest, I took a breath, then peered up at the man who had healed my soul. "I still worry about remembering the past and what that will do to me—to us."

Kane stroked my cheek with his thumb. "Brie, we've tackled a lot together. If your memories return, we'll get through that, too. The most important thing is that you and Conner are next to me."

The floor creaked, and I peeked around Kane. Quinn, Sterling, Jagger, Anderson, Teagan, Everlee, Gabby, Leighton, and our families filed into the room. Conner held Alexandria's hand as she smiled down at him. She quickly took the aunt role seriously and doted on Conner as if he had always been a part of the family, and I loved her for that.

Kane took my hand, then knelt in front of me.

"What's happening?" I asked him in a hushed tone.

"Brie, the first time I laid eyes on you, we were younger than Conner. Over the years, we became best friends, then fell in love. Not a day has gone by that you weren't on my mind and in my heart.

This time, I won't let you go. Fate brought us together, or maybe it was our love for each other that remained strong. Through all the pain and chaos, we found each other again. I love you more than I'll ever be able to articulate. The only thing that would make me happier is to call you, my wife. Marry me, Brie."

Conner raced forward, his big brown eyes wide. "Here, Daddy."

"Thanks, bud." Kane released my hand, then opened a little black box Conner handed him. The large pear-shaped diamond caught the light, sparkling.

My gaze traveled from the ring to Kane's face, my soul so full of emotion that I was having difficulty talking. Everyone grew silent as they stared at me, waiting for my answer.

"Yes. A million times yes, Kane. I would love to be your wife."

The room erupted in cheers as everyone clapped. Kane slipped the white-gold ring on my finger, then stood.

"I love you, baby." He tucked my hair behind my ear, then laid a searing kiss on me in front of all our friends and family. "Everything that is good in me is because of you."

"I love you, too, Kane. Thank you for never giving up on me." I couldn't wait to take his last name and begin the next chapter of our lives together. Kane had saved my life, then he saved my heart. Tears streamed down my cheeks as I realized that my past had broken me but had also given me the greatest gift of all. Love that lasted a lifetime.

If you love Kane you're sure to love and hate Quinn! _Toxic Obsession_ is FREE in Kindle Unlimited. Click here to binge read today.

Don't miss the bonus scene with all of our fave bad boys. Click here to access it.

Before You Go ... Download Your FREE Book

Don't for get to sign up for J.A. OWENBY'S NEWSLETTER and download your FREE book, Love & Sins. Stay up to date concerning exclusive bonus scenes, updates on upcoming releases, and more. https://authorjaowenby.com/newsletter/

One wrong decision
shattered my soul.
LOVE
& Sins
A Love & Ruin Prequel
International Bestselling Author
J.A. OWENBY

Also by J.A. Owenby

In the Shadows Series

In the Shadows, a Dark, Stalker Standalone

The Whitmore Elite Series, Dark, Football

Forbidden, a prequel

Illicit Obsession, a standalone novel

Ruthless Obsession, a standalone novel

Sinful Obsession, a standalone novel

Toxic Obsession, a standalone novel

The Beautifully Damaged Series

Beautifully Damaged

Beautifully Broken

Beautifully Shattered

The Love & Ruin Series

Love & Ruin

Love & Deception

Love & Redemption

Love & Consequences, a standalone novel

Love & Corruption, a standalone novel

Love & Revelations, a novella

Love & Seduction, a standalone novel

Love & Vengeance, part one of a duet

Love & Retaliation, part two of a duet

J.A. OWENBY

Copyright © 2023 by J.A. Owenby

This book is a work of fiction. Names, characters, places, and incidents either are products of the author's imagination or are used fictitiously. Any resemblance to actual persons, living or dead, business establishments, events, or locales is entirely coincidental.

Edited by: PNWSandy Edits from KRS Author Services

First Edition ISBN: 978-1-949414-87-5

A Note From the Author

Dear Readers,

If you have experienced sexual assault or physical abuse, there is free, confidential help. Please visit:
Website: https://www.rainn.org/
Phone: 800-656-4673

This book may contain sensitive material for some readers. River and Holden's story is considered a dark romance with language, sex, and violence.

About the Author

International bestselling author J.A. Owenby grew up in a small backwoods town in Arkansas where she learned how to swear like a sailor and spot water moccasins skimming across the lake.

She finally ditched the south and headed to Oregon. The first winter there, she was literally blown away a few times by ninety mile an hour winds and storms that rolled in off the ocean.

Eventually, she longed for quiet and headed up to snowier pastures. She now resides in Washington state with her hot nerdy husband and three purebred Siberian cats who insist on using her computer as their napping spot. She spends her days coming up with ways to torture characters in a way that either makes you want to throw your book down a flight of stairs or sob hysterically into a pillow.

J.A. Owenby writes new adult and romantic thriller novels. Her books ooze with emotion, angst, and twists that will leave you breathless. Having battled her own demons, she's not afraid to tackle the secrets women are forced to hide. After all, the road to love is paved in the dark.

Her friends describe her as delightfully twisted. She loves fan mail and wine. Please send her all the wine.

You can follow the progress of her upcoming novel on Facebook at Author J.A. Owenby and on Twitter @jaowenby.

Sign up for J.A. Owenby's Newsletter:

https://authorjaowenby.com/newsletter/

Like J.A. Owenby's Facebook page:

https://www.facebook.com/profile.php?id=100064095791999

J.A. Owenby's One Page At A Time reader group:

https://www.facebook.com/groups/JAOwenby